The Jakarta Pandemic

A novel by
Steven Konkoly

Dedication

To my wife...for her constant encouragement and support. I would still be about "halfway" done without her.

To my children...for ensuring a balance between work, writing and family. Mostly in their favor.

To all of the men and women who have served in our Armed Forces. Your sacrifices will never be forgotten.

Arrival

Chapter One

Friday, November 2, 2012

Alex is jarred awake by a loud pulsing vibration. He squints in the darkness, and labors to turn his head toward the source of the persistent buzzing sound. *Shit, my iPhone.* The phone's display illuminates a half empty glass of water on the nightstand. Alex watches, still helpless as the phone moves closer to the edge of the nightstand with each vibration. He starts to break through the murk of a broken sleep cycle, and reaches for the phone to check the caller ID. *Dr. Wright.* A jolt of adrenaline shoots through his body, and Alex starts to head out of the bedroom to the hallway.

"Alex Fletcher," he answers in a whisper.

"Oh Alex...Sorry. I thought I'd get your voicemail."

"No problem Dr. Wright. I usually don't keep my phone on the nightstand. Just happened to end up there tonight," says Alex, closing the door to the master bedroom.

"I'm glad you're awake Alex. I'm fairly confident we've seen our first cases of the mystery flu tonight. Cases started rolling into the ER's early this evening."

"You said ER's. More than one?" Alex asks.

"Yes. Three cases at Maine Med. Two came from Westbrook and one from Falmouth. And one case at Mercy, patient walked over from somewhere in the west end. I also have a confirmed case at Maine General in Augusta, and possible cases at Eastern Maine Med up in Bangor."

"Confirmed as what?" says Alex.

"Confirmed as nothing I've ever seen before. That's why I think we're dealing with this new virus out of Hong Kong," says Dr. Wright.

"That's more than six cases. How did this pop up here first and not Boston? It doesn't make a lot of sense," says Alex.

"Boston has been hit with several dozen cases, possibly more," he says.

"What do you mean? I didn't see anything on the news, or on any of the websites. We've been keeping an eye on this."

"I don't know what to tell you, but I know for a fact that Boston has been slammed. A friend of mine at Mass General called to tell me to

4

get ready. He said that area hospitals in Boston saw dozens of cases trickle in overnight Wednesday, with more showing up as the day progressed. Several dozen more by the time I talked to him."

"Why didn't the media catch this yet?" says Alex.

"Well, between you and me, and I don't have to remind you that this entire conversation never happened."

"Of course. Absolutely Dr. Wright," Alex says instantly.

"We have been instructed by the state health department to report all cases directly to them so they can coordinate resources and notify federal health agencies. I assume that direction filtered down from DHS. They also asked us not to notify the media, in order to avoid a panic. I can understand part of that logic, but if you ask me, I think they're trying to keep this under wraps because they're not prepared. Unfortunately, this is the only direction we've received so far from the state or feds. Or maybe that's a good thing for now. Aside from rushing us more useless avian flu detection kits, nothing else has been done. Alex I have to let you go. I have a long night ahead of me."

"Sorry to hold you up. Thank you for the call Dr. Wright, I ah…really appreciate the heads up, seriously," says Alex.

"My pleasure. It's really the least I could do to thank you for making a trip over on such short notice, especially considering the fact that the state's anti-viral stockpiles are likely to fall under federal control very shortly if the flu spirals out of control. Your samples will really come in handy."

"Could you use some more? We've been instructed to keep our distribution of Terraflu to a minimum, but I have no problem hooking you guys up. Really," replies Alex.

"I'll take whatever you can give me at this point. I have a really bad feeling about this one."

"What time works for you tomorrow? My schedule is pretty clear so I can make a trip over any time," says Alex.

"How about 12:45? Hopefully I'll be back from the hospital at that point. My first patient is at one. We could take care of it then," says Dr. Wright.

"Sounds good. Good luck tonight," says Alex, and the phone call is disconnected.

He heads back into the bedroom, and looks over at Kate, who is soundly asleep. He walks over to her and kisses her on the forehead. She barely moves. *We really need to get a dog.*

He leaves the bedroom and walks to his home office. He activates his computer, and checks the Boston Globe and Boston Herald. *Still nothing. I know where to find it.*

He checks the International Scientific Pandemic Awareness Collaborative website. He navigates to their pandemic activity map to check for any updates. The map has changed dramatically, and is now completely interactive, linked to Google Earth.

Color coded symbols represent reported flu locations, and when you pass the mouse over one of the new icons, basic information appears in a text box, which can be further expanded for more detailed information. *Someone's been busy.* Light blue symbols represent cases of interest. Yellow stands for confirmed isolated cases of H16N1 or a light outbreak. Orange signifies a confirmed small scale outbreak, and red indicates a medium sized outbreak. Violet warns of a large scale outbreak.

He zooms in on North America. *Cases in Canada, Mexico, Central America...wait, wait, look at this, Los Angeles, San Diego and San Francisco.* He looks at the East Coast, and see's no colored icons. Alex adjusts the map to focus on southern California. He places the cursor over the yellow Los Angeles icon.

"Los Angeles. Population 4,089,245. Isolated outbreaks. 190+ cases reported. Uncontained. Isolated outbreaks among ethnic Asian populations."

In a separate desktop window, Alex navigates to the Los Angeles Times homepage. He looks for the California/Local section. *Here we go.* He finds an article titled "Hong Kong Flu hits Asian community."

"Cedars Sinai confirms at least a dozen cases of Hong Kong Flu. Mainly confined to Asian community. UCLA Medical Center confirms several cases. Mainly Asian community. East LA Doctor's hospital sees its first cases late in the evening on October 31. Community leaders decry nearly one day delay in reporting cases to the public. Employee at Cedars Sinai contacts Los Angeles Times with information about suspected flu cases. Cases were being kept isolated from other patients, and under a tight information seal. Times reporters launched an immediate investigation into all area hospitals, uncovering several dozen more cases." *Looks like a cover up.*

Alex puts cursor over the yellow San Francisco icon.

"San Francisco. Population 853,758. Isolated outbreaks. 100+ cases reported. Uncontained. Isolated outbreaks among ethnic Asian populations."

He then moves the cursor south to San Diego and places it over the yellow icon.

"San Diego. Population 1,501,397. Isolated outbreaks. 120+ cases reported. Uncontained. Isolated outbreaks among ethnic Asian and Mexican populations."

He changes the view to China, and sees that dozens of southern coastal cities are shaded either orange or red. Hong Kong and the surrounding areas are shaded violet. Alex passes the mouse over one of these areas.

"Greater Guangzhou city. Population 12,100,000. Massive outbreak. 8,000+ reported cases. Uncontained. Containment efforts focused on Guangdong Province." *8,000 plus cases in one city? I thought there were only 26,000 altogether in China yesterday?*

Alex passes the mouse over a few more cities in the area around Hong Kong, and sees similar text fields. Alex quickly adds up the other numbers, and calculates roughly 77,000 reported cases in southern China. *Very rough numbers.*

Alex zooms out of China, and settles on a world view. Colored dots appear to sweep outward in a concentric wave from Southeast Asia. A solid perimeter of blue dots extends from Japan, through South Korea and Vladivostok, then reaches across northern China and connects with Pakistan and India. India is covered in blue dots and yellow dots. Orange icons appear centered over several major cities within India. Oddly, Java Island contains no dots. Alex places the cursor over Java.

"Java Island. Population 150,000,000. No reports." *Something's up over there.*

Beyond Asia's ring, blue colored dots litter every continent, concentrated on nearly every major city. Alex wishes he hadn't seen the map. He feels his stomach churn, as wave of anxiety blankets him. Still, he walks back to the bedroom and lies down next to Kate. He feels secure lying here with her. He closes his eyes and starts breathing deeply, in an attempt to relax and induce sleep. Alex doesn't meet with success for another hour.

Chapter Two

Friday, November 2, 2012

Alex Fletcher's body shudders and his eyes flash open. He searches the bright room to confirm that he still lies in bed with his wife, Kate, in their Scarborough, Maine home. His heart pounds through his shallow breath. He touches his forehead with the back of his right hand, and wipes the sweat on his gray T-shirt, leaving a dark stain near the neck. *Jesus. I don't ever want to see that bridge again.*

He turns his head to look at his wife. Her face is turned away, and she has the covers pulled up over her neck. All he can see is her jet black hair. *Thank god she didn't wake up. I don't need her starting on the VA counseling again.* Alex has dodged a phone call to the Togus Veteran's hospital for the better part of nine years.

He sits up in bed slowly, careful not to wake Kate. The sky to the east is clear, and the room glows with pre-dawn light. Alex slides out of bed, walks over to Kate's side, and kisses her on the forehead. Her head stirs lightly, and then settles back into the pillow. Her mouth forms a nearly imperceptible smile. She looks peaceful buried under the covers, and Alex watches her for a few more moments, trapped by her tranquility. Kate sleeps soundly every night. Alex's heart thumps rapidly, as he walks quietly to the master bathroom.

Several minutes later, Alex sits down to check for any updates to the flu situation, and navigates to his internet homepage. He scans the national and international headline summary section of the homepage, and starts to shake his head slowly. "China acknowledges deadly disease within border." "China imposed quarantine to keep deadly disease out." "Unknown disease spreads through China." "China admits WHO teams to outbreak areas." "Deadly disease outbreak in China." *No surprises here. Only took them two days to acknowledge what the rest of the world already knew.* Alex clicks on the first headline.

By Sarah Whitmore (Associated Press Writer)
From Associated Press

November 2, 2012 5:46 AM EDT

BEIJING - Chinese health ministry officials released an explanation for the two day long travel restrictions imposed by the Chinese government. Officials acknowledged the appearance of widespread cases of a still unknown disease, mainly confined to the southern and southeast coastal industrial regions. Chinese health officials confirm that the cases are not H5N1, or any known variant of the deadly 2008 Avian Flu. They have confirmed that the disease is a pneumonic flu-like illness, and that deaths have occurred in a relatively short period of time. No details regarding the number of cases was released.

WHO and CDC teams will be admitted to the affected areas to access the situation, identify the pathogen, and implement strategies to contain the disease. Chinese officials highlighted their belief that the disease originated outside of China, suggesting that the coastal outbreak pattern supports the idea that the disease epicenter is not located in China. They stressed the importance of allocating more resources to investigating similar cases or leads within the region, outside of China.

Chinese officials explained that the quarantine was designed to prevent further importation of infected travelers. They assured the international community that the Chinese government stands committed to fully embrace any assistance offered by the international community to resolve the current crisis.

"We imposed strict quarantine and travel restriction measures immediately, while our scientific teams investigated the outbreaks, and our disease response teams formulated a strategy," Ministry Health spokesperson, Li Huang said.

"Ministry discussions quickly addressed our responsibilities as a prominent member of the international community, and the Chinese government decided that full cooperation and information sharing would be the most responsible course of action. History has taught us many valuable lessons, and as a great nation, we have translated these lessons into effective action," Foreign Affairs Ministry co-chairman, Xho Chieng said.

WHO resources' first priority will be to isolated outbreak areas and ensure implementation of an effective pandemic response plan within China.

CDC teams have been tasked with identifying the disease strain, its behavior, and the characteristics of the illness it causes. This information will help shape response efforts.

Both the Chinese government and the WHO have pledged to publish information as it becomes available to them.

Alex quickly reviews two more of the posted articles, and finds them to contain the same information, which raises an immediate red flag for Alex. Since China's Health Ministry has facilities on par with the CDC, if the Chinese haven't identified the virus, the world could be dealing with a novel flu strain. Vaccine research and development would start from scratch. *Not good.* Alex stands up from the chair and thinks about heading to the master bathroom for a quick shower before Kate claims the space for the rest of the morning. *If she hasn't already staked her claim.*

■

Alex exits the kids' bathroom dressed and freshly showered, having lost his bid for the master bathroom. He quietly descends the hardwood stairs, and eases into the kitchen unnoticed. The smell of coffee overtakes him as he surveys the area. A small sauce pot simmers on the stainless steel gas range, cooking what Alex really hopes is something other than Kate's lumpy oatmeal. A red toaster just to the left of the stove promises to deliver a more suitable breakfast alternative. A glass of orange juice, two open bread loaves and several containers sit in disarray on the black granite kitchen island. Kate moves quickly between the island, refrigerator and stove.

Kate is dressed in a knee length Navy blue skirt, and a pressed French blue shirt. Her Navy blue suit coat sits folded over the back of one of the black high-back stools at the kitchen island. Her hair, arranged in a tight pony tail, starkly contrasts her deep blue eyes and fair complexion. Compared to Kate, Alex looks like he just returned from a Caribbean vacation, owing to a mix of Sicilian and Irish genes. His black hair is not as pure as Kate's, but his eyes share the same deep blue color. The toaster pops.

"Toasts ready!" Kate says, as she turns around and sees Alex.

"Oh. Hey. Good workout?"

"Not bad. Quick one. I Didn't get up in time for a run…up a little late last night. I got a call on my cell from one of my infectious disease doctors," he says.

"What time?" she says, and eyes him warily.

"Just past midnight. He thinks the mystery flu has already hit Portland," he says, putting both hands on the island.

"What makes him so sure? We haven't seen anything on the internet, or the news," she says.

"I think we might be a day behind the west coast. After I talked to him, I saw some articles published out of LA referencing possible cases, and the ISPAC website lists LA and San Francisco as having several dozen confirmed cases of the new flu. Dr. Wright also said that the cases didn't resemble anything he's seen before. I think he tried to run some lab tests, and came up empty," says Alex.

"Did he say that?" she presses.

"No, but he definitely said the cases didn't resemble anything he's seen before. I don't think he was talking about symptoms."

He hears some mumbling from the great room, and glances toward the sound of the voice. He sees that the family room LCD TV is fully operational, set to the Military Channel. Their twelve year old son, Ryan, scurries into the kitchen to collect his breakfast. He is already dressed for school, in faded blue jeans and a red long sleeved rugby shirt. He shares the same hair color as his father, but little else. He was born with emerald green eyes, and his mother's fair skin.

"What's up Mr. Man?" Alex says.

"Not much dad. Hey, are you picking me up today after cross-country?"

"Yep. 4:45 right?"

"Sure, but around back. So I don't have to walk around to the school pickup circle."

"I certainly wouldn't want to add another 100 yards to your workout."

"None of the parents pick their kids up at the circle Dad."

"You are as right as your mother."

"You're in a slightly antagonistic mood this morning," Kate adds.

"Yeah, I feel like pushing it today," replied Alex.

He smiles at Kate and raises his eyebrows. Ryan continues past his dad and pulls a plate out of the cherry cabinet over the coffee maker. He begins to assemble toast with butter and raspberry jam.

"Did you see what's going on in the Orient?" says Alex.

"Nice. Could you find a few more politically incorrect terms to slip into your conversations? Don't listen to your dad Ryan," she says, and turns back to the range.

Ryan looks up at his mother back, and then shifts his glance to his dad. Alex raises his shoulder and mouths the word "I don't know."

Ryan returns to the family room and the volume from the great room TV increases.

"Mom, can you get my juice for me?" Ryan yells over the noise.

"Can you grab that for his royal highness?" says Kate.

"Surely my royal queen," he replies and delivers the glass to his son.

"Hey, should I teach Ryan the Chinese national anthem?" says Alex.

"You could probably skip it and we'd all be fine," says Kate.

"I don't have it all memorized yet, but here it goes…"

"Please, really you don't…"

"Me Chinese. Me play joke. Me go pee pee in your Coke," he sings. "How's that for politically correct?" says Alex.

"Excellent…I hear the State Department has some openings in the Far East. So what's happening in China?" she says.

"They finally admitted to a full scale outbreak of a mystery virus in the south, and they also claim to have imposed the travel ban because they were confident the disease didn't originate in China. They were trying to keep it out."

"How does that make any sense? So they tried to keep the virus from entering their own country, but did nothing to keep it from spreading outside of China?"

"Well they did manage to keep the secret from spreading outside of China. I read an Associated Press article, and one of the Chinese officials sounded proud of their efforts. Like they did a much better job handling the issue this time."

He lowers his voice.

"It's un-fucking-believable really. Like in 2003, when they put their first astronaut into orbit. Who gives a shit? It took them forty years to finally steal enough information about our rocket program to put a human in space. Congratulations. And now? Well, now they only sit on information critical to mankind's survival for two days, instead of weeks. I don't think we can ever trust them. I have a bad feeling about this one," he says.

"Whatever it is, we'll be ready," Kate answers.

"Hey, I'm gonna eat and run. Emily's in the shower, so she should make the bus. I promised the folks at the Mercy ER that I would stock them up with TerraFlu, so I want to hit them early. I guarantee that Biosphere is going to ask us to stop signing over samples," he says, and pulls out a coffee mug.

"Is that a big deal? Aside from making your day easier than it already is."

"Very funny. Our samples are scarce already, but eliminating them in the face of a pandemic crisis will not be perceived as a cool move by Biosphere."

"Can't the doctors just write a prescription for the pharmacy?"

"Sure, and at this time of year, the pharmacies should be well stocked with anti-virals, but the availability of my samples speaks louder than you think. Most of the offices are looking for any reason to stop seeing reps, and they barely tolerate us as it is. It'll get ugly quick if Biosphere restricts samples," he says.

"They won't buy off on the 'greater good of the community' speech? Stockpiling drugs for the national pandemic response?"

"Would you?"

"Probably not," she admits.

"Especially when they know for a fact that they won't see any of it when the shit hits the fan. Health and Human Services will swoop down and grab it all for selected treatment centers," he says.

"Sucks to be you today," she says.

"Let's hope not," Alex says as he walks over to fix some breakfast.

"Seven o'clock. Turn on the Today Show," Kate says.

Alex finds the remote and turns on the kitchen TV, just in time to see Matt Lauer appear on the screen.

"Someone better say something about the fact that the Chinese sat on this for two days," Alex says.

"Good morning, on Friday, November 2nd. The news dominating the thoughts of all Americans today comes to us from Southeast Asia, where the evidence of a growing pandemic virus is mounting. Earlier this morning, Chinese government officials verified that an unidentified flu strain has caused several major outbreaks in the southern coastal regions of China. They have also confirmed that the cases are not caused by a strain or variant of the H5N1 Avian Flu. This announcement sparked uproar in the scientific community, where fear of a new pandemic is rising.

"Turn it up honey. I can't hear over that frigging Military Channel," says Kate

Alex raises his voice, "Ryan, can you turn that down? We're trying to listen to something important about the world over here."

Kate responds first, "Are you seriously going to get into it with him again, just turn up the volume, please, we'll miss the whole segment by the time you two figure it out."

Alex shakes his head and raises the volume so he can hear Matt Lauer clearly.

"Thomas McGreggor from the Department of Health and Human Services joins us this morning to shed some light on these developments. Mr. McGreggor, welcome."

"Thank you Matt."

"Could you describe the Department of Health and Human Services' role in preparing and responding to a possible pandemic?"

"Gladly Matt. The department has many roles, all critical to our nation's robust capability to deal with a pandemic. Our encompassing goal is to implement the national strategy to prevent or slow a pandemic's entry into the United States, and to limit the domestic spread of the disease."

"Tom, that sounds like a momentous task. How is it possible for one department of the government to implement and monitor such a broad objective? Frankly, some experts just don't think it's possible for a single department to accomplish these goals, and they question whether your department has the reach and authority to enforce the national plan."

"Well, you're right when you state that we can't possibly do this alone. It would not be possible for us to oversee implementation of every aspect of the national plan, or enforce it, as you say.

DHS directs each state, county, city and organization to create their own strategies and procedures, aligned with the goals of the national pandemic response strategy."

"You're talking about the three hundred and eighty one page national plan?" Matt asks.

"Yes. Our department empowers local governments to build partnerships with health care facilities and community business leaders, and encourages them to develop an effective communications infrastructure for the timely dissemination of information."

"We've heard from several experts, who all agree that the national plan is solid, but argue that very few of the recommendations in the plan have been implemented. The statistics are sobering. Some experts cite a compliance rate of less than ten percent with the plan's recommendations. It appears that most states, cities and towns don't seem to be able to find the money to implement your recommendations, and little money is flowing down from Washington. Critics also suggest that most of the money that the Congress and Senate is willing to allocate to pandemic response, is heading overseas to fund the WHO."

"Certainly these critics like to point fingers at Washington whenever they can, but several reviews and accounting estimates conducted by our department indicate that implementation of these strategies cost very little in terms of money. Are they time intensive, requiring the cooperation and effort of numerous local organizations and governments? Absolutely. A pandemic is a complex emergency, requiring an effective and coordinated response on many levels. Preparation for a pandemic is similar in scope. The bulk of the costs occur once the pandemic strikes, and when this occurs, each state will receive disaster level funding to ensure continuity of pandemic response operations."

Matt shifts in his seat.

"I don't know if I agree. Let me read directly from the DHS manual. 'Ideally, states develop a multilayered strategy that delineates responsibilities at all levels of society to ensure the viability of government functions and services, such as energy, financial, transportation, telecommunications, firefighting and public safety. This strategy will assist businesses and utilities with continuity of operations, collaborating with the healthcare sector on issues like stockpiles, available beds, isolation and quarantine plans, surge capacity, personnel protection, communications links and pharmaceutical supply and distribution. It will coordinate offsite treatment and triage locations, medical stations, and implement a mass fatality plan.'"

Tom, this sounds like an expensive proposition. My parents' hometown can barely scrape together enough money to repair minor damage to its roads. Where will towns and cities get the money to implement these preparations?"

"Well first, I don't agree with the statistics that claim only six percent of the national plan is implemented. We've seen amazing progress throughout the nation, without reliance on more federal money. An appropriate level of funding is available at all levels, for implementation of the plan. However, this is not the first time we've heard this criticism, and as a department, we are working hard to increase the funding of these grants. Our goal is to develop and implement a comprehensive national pandemic response strategy, and if more money is required, then we'll take the case to Capitol Hill."

"I hope you're right, because the situation in China has health officials concerned that the world might be on the verge of another pandemic."

"Matt, the United States is in good hands. Since 2008, our nation's pandemic response capability has been vastly improved. From vaccination production and research capability, to anti-viral stockpiling. We learned a lot from the Avian Flu, and applied those lessons to the national plan in place today."

"So given the events unfolding in Asia, what is DHS's primary concern at the moment, and what part of the national plan is being implemented?"

"We are working in close coordination with the CDC and WHO to receive real time information regarding all aspects of the crisis. Our number one priority will be to prevent this disease from entering and spreading in the United States. Currently there is no indication that the disease has spread to the United States, though we have activated passive foreign traveler detection protocols. Customs officials have been alerted to identify and track any foreign travelers that appear ill."

Alex talks to the screen, "Is this for real? It's already here. How could he not know that? Full of shit."

Kate silences him with a hand signal, so she can hear the rest of the segment.

"Will these travelers be detained?" says Matt.

"Not under passive protocols. Active protocols require a massive personnel increase, as you can imagine, and will be implemented when it is certain that a pandemic grade illness is headed to our borders."

"Has DHS considered the possibility that the disease has already entered the U.S. in considerable numbers? For nearly three days, travelers have left China for the U.S. and hundreds of other locations abroad, and the ISPAC website indicates that it may have already hit the west coast."

"We've definitely considered this, and fortunately, the number of passengers traveling to the U.S from China within a three day period is small. We are tracking all of these passengers and taking steps to ensure that if any of them are sick with this disease, they will be identified immediately. We feel confident that the disease is limited to China right now. China's own detection and response capability is first rate, and we have been assured by the Chinese that only essential travelers departed China during the time in question, and that these passengers were screened prior to leaving the country.

Even if their screening didn't catch all of them, we can count on the efforts of our own customs officials, and the efforts of our neighboring countries. Right now, we are taking the appropriate steps given the information available. And thanks to the Chinese government, the information is flowing much more efficiently than in 2008.

As for the ISPAC website. None of their figures are official CDC or WHO statistics. If the flu arrives in the U.S., we'll know first."

"You've gotta be shitting me," says Alex.

Kate stifles a laugh.

"Thank you Tom."

"My pleasure Matt."

"After the break, we'll turn our attention to Hurricane Terrence."

Alex turns the TV off.

"That guy didn't sound very convincing," Kate says.

"If this guy represents the government's attitude toward the situation, then we're screwed."

"Looks like your day is most assuredly going to suck," Kate says, wearing an overly fake sympathetic face.

"Yeah, I really need to get rolling here."

Chapter Three

Friday, November 2, 2012

Alex parks his car in front of Mercy Hospital on State Street. Before eight, he always finds a convenient spot within easy walking distance. After that, he'll likely end up parking near the Reiche School, and be forced to walk a few blocks in his suit, drawing stares from the seemingly inexhaustible flow of rough looking pedestrians that orbit the hospital. He dials Mike Gallagher, his Portland colleague and only good friend at Biosphere.

"Hey Alex, what's up?" Mike says.

"I got a call from Dr. Wright last night. Late. He was either in his office or at Maine Med. He said that several suspected cases of the mystery flu rolled in last night. Three of them at Maine Med, one at Mercy and a few cases scattered up north. He said that one of the cases is a guy from Falmouth. The others are from Westbrook and Portland," says Alex.

"Jesus. Already? Fucking Falmouth?" Mike says.

"Yeah, but what's worse, is that he also said the hospitals down in Boston started seeing cases late Wednesday night. A friend of his at Mass General called him Thursday morning, and told him the cases started trickling in on Wednesday night, and have continued ever since. I scoured the Boston papers on the internet, but didn't see shit about it," says Alex.

"They probably want to be one hundred percent before they start running stories about the flu," says Mike.

"I don't know. Dr. Wright also said that they were told by the state to sit on the information for now. Only report to the state. He was told the state would disseminate the information to the feds."

"What did he mean by 'sit on it?'" asks Mike.

"He said they were told to keep the media out of it until further notice. To avoid a bum rush of the system I guess," answers Alex.

"First case in Falmouth of all places. I need to get Colleen and the kids out of the school," he says.

"I definitely think you should keep your kids out of the schools at a minimum, and your wife needs to get out of the classroom, at least for a couple of days until they can figure out what's going on with this thing. Can you convince her to take a few days off?" says Alex.

"I don't know. I think I can convince her to let the kids stay home, but she just started teaching at the high school last year. Fucking near impossible to get a job at the high school level in Falmouth. She's afraid to do anything to piss them off."

"I can imagine. Just make sure she plays it smart. Give her one of those stupid patient education handouts about washing hands, and send her to school with a case of Biosphere hand sanitizer bottles," Alex adds.

"Yeah, because we all know a little hand sanitizer will stop the flu in its tracks," says Mike.

"Better than nothing," says Alex.

"I don't know. I need to give her a call man. I'll ring you later," says Mike.

"Good luck," Alex says, and disconnects the call.

■

Alex sips a hot cappuccino and admires the trees that flank Route One just north of Falmouth's commercial center. After supplying the Mercy emergency room with at least ten times the amount of Terraflu drug samples he was currently authorized to distribute, he charged a Starbucks coffee to Biosphere Pharmaceuticals and decided to take a scenic drive north toward Yarmouth. It was a little late for peak leaf peeping, but he wasn't disappointed. Dense marvels of orange, red and brown, still served as the foreground for today's stark blue sky.

As he leaves Falmouth, he wonders how many people in town know about the mystery flu case that had been in their midst. He didn't see any mention of it on the internet or the in the papers. *Probably not very many. They're keeping this really quiet for now.*

During his visit to the ER, nobody mentioned the flu case that Dr. Wright said had passed through their doors the night before, and he didn't see any unusual signs of activity inside the ER. Not wanting to compromise his source of information, Alex resisted every urge to push for information. The only thing out of order was a single police officer stationed at the ER entrance, chatting with hospital security. Alex has been through these doors over a hundred times, and this is the first time he has ever seen an officer posted at the hospital.

Alex enters Yarmouth, and starts to pass through the business district. A few minutes later, he sees a modern, two story medical office complex come into view on his left. He activates the left turn signal, and cruises over the yellow median into the Yarmouth Medical Building's parking lot.

Alex parks near the door, and walks around to the back of his company car, a hybrid Subaru Forrester, to open the hatchback. He pulls a black nylon sales bag from the rear cargo area and slings the padded carry strap over his shoulder. The strap pulls down on his Navy blue suit coat, exposing most of the white dress shirt on his right shoulder, so he adjusts the bag and his jacket. Alex stands behind his car for a moment, and enjoys the warm breeze blowing across the parking lot. The winters in Maine are long enough for Alex to fully appreciate the gift of a seventy degree day in early November. He takes a deep breath, and starts for the entrance.

"This should be interesting," Alex whispers to himself. *Especially since they have no clue it's already here.*

Alex opens the door to the office, and notices that the waiting room is more crowded than usual. *Shit.* He is immediately greeted by Pamela, the practice's crass and extremely loud receptionist.

"Alex, where the hell have you been? The doctors were talking about you this morning. I was about to give you a call to see if you had any TerraFlu samples. A bunch of patients called in for samples or to get prescriptions filled in case the Chinese try to get us all sick again. I told them that if they were worried about the Chinese getting us sick, they should quit shopping at Walmart. Did you see they recalled those cheap summer plates they sold at Wal-Mart and everywhere else? Some kind of toxic chemical in the paint. What a surprise, right? Anyway, you could probably get back to see Dr. Kline today."

Alex glances at the patients waiting in the waiting room and sees that almost every pair of eyes is focused on him. A distinguished looking man with graying hair, dressed in khaki pants and a blue dress shirt turns to his similarly smartly dressed wife and starts to whisper, never taking his eyes off Alex.

In an overly civil tone, Alex says "and good morning to you Pam. Can I head back right away?"

"Sure, just don't loiter too long. She should be finishing up with a patient in a few minutes, so you should be able to grab her to sign for your stuff," she says, never looking up from her paperwork.

"Thanks Pam," he says, and the door buzzes as Pamela remotely unlocks the door with a hidden button Alex has yet to locate.

He opens the door and walks down the hall to the small room where the practice keeps drug samples, drug vouchers and basic medical supplies. As he moves deeper into the building, he sees Donna typing at a computer terminal in the centralized triage area. She looks up from the screen with a grimace and nods her head in the direction of the drug room, giving her tacit consent to his presence, and his intention to head deeper into the building. Since the practice's conversion to Electronic Medical Records (EMR) a year ago, Donna rarely seems to leave the triage computer station. As the practice's only triage nurse, she spends most of the day answering patient calls, and asking questions to determine how rapidly the patient needs to be seen by one of their five healthcare providers.

Alex smiles, raises his right hand, and calls out to her, "How goes the fight Donna?"

"Shitty. I hope you're leaving some TerraFlu samples. I've gotten at least twenty calls this morning about the flu…in addition to all of the usual fun"

She stabs harshly at the keyboard, "Come on dammit!"

"I'm going to leave as much as I can. Does anyone think they are sick with the killer flu yet?"

"Oh yes, one woman swears she has it. Must be seen immediately. She's in with Kline right now. She's fine. Nothing but a cold. A lot of panicky people out there, especially with that China thing."

"Yeah, what do think about it?"

Donna's phone rings, and she puts a finger up in the air to stop Alex's questioning.

She presses a button on her desk phone, which activates her headset, "Yarmouth Family Practice Associates, Donna speaking. Is this a medical emergency?"

She listens, pauses, and asks, "Can you spell your last name for me?"

She starts typing, and Alex renders a mock military salute. Donna nods her head, rolls her eyes and continues talking with the patient on the phone. Alex smiles and proceeds down the hallway to the sample closet. He opens the door and turns on the light. The drug samples are held in orderly plastic bins, installed from floor to ceiling opposite the door, and arranged by disease state. He knows that TerraFlu is kept on the left side, toward the floor. He sees that the bin is empty, as expected. He sets his bag down, unzips it, and removes TerraFlu samples from the bag.

The TerraFlu samples are packed into small, green and blue logo covered cardboard packages. Each package houses a plastic stock bottle, containing only two pills, which equates to half of a full course of therapy. TerraFlu is taken once daily for four days. Alex starts to stack the samples in the plastic bin labeled TerraFlu, when he hears a door open in the hallway outside of the closet, followed by a conversation.

"Look, let's keep a close eye on the congestion and coughing, and if it doesn't start to clear up in a few days, we'll take another look at you. Alright? You certainly don't have the flu, and you certainly don't have anything that came from China. They haven't detected any strange illnesses or bugs yet, and when they do, we'll have plenty of time before it makes it to the states."

"Thanks Dr. Kline, I appreciate you seeing me so quickly, and don't forget to set aside some of that TerraFlu for me."

"Don't worry Helen. We're sure to get some samples in the next few days. Make sure to check out with Cindy on your way out."

Alex steps over to the door, and pokes his head out, still holding a package of Terraflu. He sees Dr. Kline entering data on her EMR tablet, and waits a few seconds, mainly to ensure that Helen is no longer within earshot.

"Hi Dr. Kline, do you have a minute? I brought some TerraFlu samples to help you weather the media storm," he says, and shows her the Terraflu package.

"Just in time. Thanks for coming so quickly Alex. I really don't have a lot of time to talk. The Today Show killed my morning, and probably the rest of the week. Every cough and sniffle is the next pandemic."

"Yeah, I don't think anyone trusts the Chinese anymore, and it'll only get worse given the media's talent for scaring the hell out of everyone. At least you have a potent anti-viral in your arsenal," says Alex, holding the sample up in front of Dr. Kline.

"I have to admit that I have been thinking more about Tamiflu lately, especially since it worked so well against the Avian Flu. Any news on TerraFlu's efficacy against pandemic flu strains?"

"Actually, since the medical and scientific community can't really predict the next pandemic strain, neither Tamiflu nor TerraFlu is considered to be effective against a novel pandemic strain. However, TerraFlu works well against the seasonal flu, better than Tamiflu. I have a few studies that can demonstrate its superiority beyond a shadow of a doubt." *Company provided catch phrase, which nobody buys.*

"Yeah, but if a pandemic hits, and I have to choose something first line, I'm going with Tamiflu. At least until TerraFlu is proven effective against whatever strain hits us," she says with an overly apologetic look.

"Fair enough, but they'll still have to prove that Tamiflu works against it too. Pandemic flu aside though, would it be fair to say that TerraFlu is still your first line choice for seasonal flu?"

"Absolutely. Alex, I have to run. Please leave as much as you can for us. I don't anticipate a pandemic any time soon, just the regular seasonal variety, and I'd hate to resort to using Tamiflu if no samples are available."

Alex chuckles, well accustomed to this word game.

"No problem Dr. Kline. Thanks for taking the time to talk with me. Good luck today. Oh, I almost forgot, I need you to sign for the samples."

He holds out his computer tablet, and she signs the designated spot on the screen with the attached stylus.

"Thanks," Dr. Kline says in a distracted voice, as she starts to study her own electronic tablet, which contains her next patient's information.

As Alex re-enters the drug closet, he hears her knock on a patient room door and open it. Alex continues stocking the TerraFlu bin.

Alex can appreciate her concern regarding TerraFlu's efficacy against a pandemic flu. Like Tamiflu, TerraFlu is considered effective against all known influenza strains, however, TerraFlu has never been field tested against a pandemic flu. In late 2009, post launch laboratory data showed TerraFlu to be just as effective as Tamiflu against the 2008 H5N1 pandemic strain. Unfortunately, the scientific evidence gathered during this study did not prove strong enough to convince the Food and Drug Administration to give Biosphere's drug an official indication to treat pandemic grade flu strains. As a result, Tamiflu remained the public's first choice against future pandemics. Luckily for Biosphere Pharmaceuticals, TerraFlu demonstrated significant superiority in treating the seasonal flu, which accounts for the vast majority of sales in the anti-viral drug class.

Regardless of the FDA's decision, Alex is confident that Terraflu will work fine against any pandemic flu, however, he doesn't plan to take any chances with his family's safety. Over the past few years, Alex has taken more than enough Tamiflu samples from his customers' drug closets to treat his own family, in addition to stockpiling the same amount of TerraFlu.

Alex finishes putting the rest of the TerraFlu samples into the plastic bin, closes his bag, and walks out of the closet. Alex continues to walk out of the office, passing Donna, who is still buried in telephone calls. He walks past her work station and nods in her direction, but receives no sign of a reply. He is not in the mood for any further interaction with Pamela, so he opens the door to the waiting room, and ducks behind a patient standing at the receptionist window. He avoids eye contact with patients in the overcrowded waiting room, and heads straight for the exit door.   He walks briskly out of the office into the rare warm November air.

He glances at his watch. *10:15. Not bad for a morning's work.* Alex could make a few more sales call in Yarmouth, before grabbing an early lunch, but he's not feeling particularly motivated to work today. He puts away his sales bag, and climbs into the company car. He sits there for a moment, and thinks about his next move, when he suddenly grabs his iPhone, and dials his company voice mail. He forgot to check it this morning when he got started, and would not be surprised to find a few **messages from corporate headquarters regarding the crisis in China, and its impact on Biosphere. In the wake of recent events, Alex anticipates** some very distinct guidance regarding customer interactions.

Alex dials his voicemail account, and finds a new message. *Conference call at 11:00. I guess I have time for one more office visit.* He places his iPhone on the front passenger seat and starts the car.

Chapter Four

Friday, November 2, 2012

Alex sits in the parking lot outside of Yarmouth Internal Medicine, a few blocks away from Yarmouth Family Practice Associates, and presses the speed dial button with his usual teleconference number. He looks at the clock on the car. 10:59. *Just made it.* He waits for the prompt, and then enters his district conference code. Satisfied that he is connected to the right conference number, he presses a button on his dashboard, and the call is transferred to his car's speakers. The car resonates with a painfully uplifting muzac version of a Pearl Jam song, which Alex instantly decides is a form of sacrilege. *I can't decide if I would rather listen to this for thirty minutes or Ted.*

At 11:03 the dreadful music is interrupted by the voice of Ted Winters.

"Good morning team. How is everyone today?"

Most members of the team talk over each other as they attempt to be the first one to answer Ted's question. *Same thing every time. Why do people still try to answer?*

"By now most of you have probably guessed why we are having a teleconference. Today is an exciting day for Biosphere Pharmaceuticals, and an even more exciting day to be selling Terraflu. The events unfolding in Asia provide an unprecedented opportunity for Biosphere Pharmaceuticals to position itself as a leader within the world healthcare community." *Is he reading from a script? I'm going to hang up the phone before I slam my head into the steering wheel.*

"First, I want to thank everyone for their efforts yesterday. The Biosphere Medical Inquiry System was overloaded yesterday with calls asking for more information about TerraFlu's expected pandemic effectiveness." *Is this a surprise?*

"We attribute this spike to your efforts in the field. Getting in front of the doctors, and putting TerraFlu at the forefront of their thoughts." *Of course it must have been us. Why would a rapidly spreading flu virus cause a spike in interest?*

"On that same note, Biosphere is actively engaged with the World Health Organization and the Centers for Disease Control to test TerraFlu in patients diagnosed with the new flu that is spreading throughout Asia." *And the U.S.*

"Since neither Tamiflu nor TerraFlu is proven effective against this new virus, Biosphere sees a great opportunity establish TerraFlu as a first line choice. If negotiations proceed smoothly, TerraFlu could be tested immediately. So, if any of your customers ask you about this, you can mention that Biosphere is actively partnered with the WHO and CDC, with the goal of assessing TerraFlu's efficacy against this flu. Any further inquiries need to be directed to our one eight hundred medical inquiry line. Any questions about this?" *Please, no questions.*

"Ted, this is Dave down in Portsmouth." *There's only one Dave on the team.*

"What's on your mind Dave?" Ted responds.

"Can we give them an estimated timeline for when TerraFlu will be tested?"

"Good question Dave. Right now Biosphere is still negotiating the start of the tests. If approved, I assume the tests will start immediately." *No, no Ted. That's just going to confuse him more!*

"So the tests are going to start immediately?" asks Dave

"Not exactly, but if they start…"

"Dave, it's Alex. What I understood from Ted was that no decision had been reached, but the company is working on getting WHO and CDC approval. When and if they get approval, the testing will probably start pretty quickly. But this could still be days away. Does that sound right Ted?"

"Yes. I couldn't have said it better myself. Thank you Alex." *Anything to move this torture along.*

"So, the next agenda item addresses samples. Effective immediately, you are to cease all sampling activity, and return all samples to your storage lockers. Either today or tomorrow, you will receive a shipment of discount vouchers, to distribute to the offices in place of samples."

Alex hears several voices at once, all protesting the new policy.

"Hold on, one at a time. Cheryl, I heard your voice first."

"Ted. Yesterday was hard enough having to limit samples. Now we can't give any out at all? The offices are going to eat us alive. I won't be allowed in the door once they hear about this new policy. They're going to need a couple thousand more operators for that toll free line."

"Alright. Let's calm down. First, I understand the concerns. This was not an easy decision for the company to make, but Biosphere is actively negotiating a partnership with DHS. Samples are a key component of these negotiations. All of our manufacturing facilities have started to increase the production of TerraFlu, so we can keep the pharmacies stocked, and also provide a strategic stockpile of TerraFlu to the government if needed. What you need to tell your customers, is that Biosphere is now part of the national pandemic response plan, and that all of the nation's TerraFlu samples are being reserved for national pandemic efforts."

"Is that true Ted? Are we really part of the plan, or is this still a big maybe? These people aren't stupid, and they're already highly suspicious of our industry. What do I say if they directly ask if Biosphere's strategy is an official part of the national response plan?" says Mike Gallagher.

"As far as management is concerned, Biosphere is part of the plan. That's it. We are part of the plan. If they want more information, they can call the toll free number."

"At what point is Biosphere going to discontinue supplying the pharmacies?" asks Alex.

"Why would we do that?" replies Ted.

"Well, if the company is hell bent on establishing this partnership with DHS, and the existing drug stockpile is a major negotiating factor, why wouldn't Biosphere just give it all over to the government?"

"That doesn't make any sense Alex. How would our customers prescribe TerraFlu? I don't think the company would want to cut off its main income source. That's business 101," he says softly chuckling. *This guy is either really stupid, or is just swimming in a tub of the company Kool-Aid.*

"That would normally be the case, but if they could get the government to buy all of the existing stock, and all further production stock, at sky high government prices, why would they bother sending it to the pharmacies? They could even lower the price, but negotiate TerraFlu as the primary government provided anti-viral during the pandemic. They could lock in all future government stockpile purchases. Nothing like guaranteed government subsidized income. Shit, if they did that, they wouldn't even need any of us anymore."

Alex can hear everyone muttering on the line. *Sorry Ted.*

"That's exactly where you're wrong Alex, because, the next agenda item involves future plans for the field force. The company wouldn't be planning for your future, if there wasn't one."

"Well, they don't have Uncle Sam's money yet," Alex adds.

He can hear some laughter on the line. *Ted has got to be about to explode.*

"Look, that's just a paranoid theory, OK? I don't want to waste any more time discussing this, and I certainly don't expect you to waste any time discussing theories like this with your customers. Anyway, back to the agenda. Can we reel it in here for a moment? Everyone OK?"

The chatter on the line tapers away.

"Alright, so in the event that H16N1 arrives in the United States, Biosphere plans to redeploy the field sales force to areas reporting the highest number of initial cases, most likely large metro areas. Our likely redeployment area will be the Boston area, and surrounding major cities. It could be as far away as Hartford, or as close as Portland. The company wants to saturate these areas with sales representatives in order to capture market share from Tamiflu, and establish TerraFlu as doctors' first choice to fight the pandemic. Biosphere will simultaneously launch a massive direct-to-consumer campaign via TV and radio."

There is complete silence on the line.

"Any questions about this strategy?" he asks. *I really can't believe this, but I can't say it's a surprise.*

"Ted, does this mean that we could be sent away to augment another group, in an initial outbreak area?" says Alex. *Not me.*

"Actually, you would not be augmenting another group. You would be fully integrated into that group. But yes, that's the concept."

"For how long?" asks Cheryl.

"That hasn't been determined yet. This is preliminary, and we don't have all of the details yet."

"Where would we stay? Would we bring our families?" asks Amy.

"I wouldn't bring them closer to the infection," interjects Alex.

"I'm not sure. There's some talk about reserving blocks of hotel rooms for reassigned representative, but nothing about families," says Ted. *Of course, why would a family concern Biosphere, or Ted.*

"This is just an idea right now, but it has gained a lot of traction, and I wanted to give you all the heads up. It makes sense in more ways than one, and will provide us with an incredible opportunity to make a real impact during the pandemic. This strategy could be credited with playing a major role in stopping the spread of the flu in the U.S. We can all reap the rewards of this strategy." *He's pissing the Kool-Aid all over us now.*

"If there are no more questions, I'll let you get back into the field. First stop today should be your storage lockers. Drop off all of your samples. You should have those vouchers by tomorrow. Good luck."

Alex ends the call. *Unbelievable.* He has no intention of joining the Biosphere rapid deployment force, and is essentially finished with Biosphere. He stares out at a particularly brilliant orange red tree on the edge of the Yarmouth Internal Medicine's parking lot. *I know exactly what needs to be done.* Alex starts his car and heads to the nearest turnpike on-ramp.

Chapter Five

Friday, November 2, 2012

Alex pulls into the parking garage at Maine Coast Internal Medicine's (MCIM) flagship medical office building. The state of the art eight story building houses nearly a hundred medical providers from several of MCIM's previously scattered office sites. He parks as close to the main entrance as possible, and grabs his computer tablet. An insuppressible grin forms as he strides toward the elevator lobby.

Alex arrives on the 5th floor, and approaches Dr. Wright's receptionist. A sign above and behind her displays over a dozen physician names. All of them are internists, and more than half of them specialize in infectious disease. MCIM provides infectious disease specialists to most of the hospitals in southern Maine, and Alex can only imagine how busy they might be today.

"Hey Jodi. How are you doing today?" he says.

"Not bad you know. It's Friday. Got an appointment with Dr. Wright I see?" she says.

Alex knows Jodi from one of MCIM's old sites in Portland. When all of the practices merged, the receptionists were scattered to work with different groups in the new building. Jodi is one of very few receptionists at MCIM that Alex recognizes from his first year as a pharmaceutical representative nearly eight years ago.

"Let me ring his office. I know he's around, I saw him roll in about fifteen minutes ago. Crazy day around here."

"I bet," says Alex. *And I suspect you don't know the half of it.*

She dials the phone and speaks into her headset.

"Dr. Wright, Alex Fletcher is here to see you."

She listens.

"Alright, I'll send him back."

"You can go on back, he's in his office."

"Thanks Jodi. Take care."

Alex turns to the right, and walks toward an automatic door, which slides open as he approaches. Alex enjoys walking back to Dr. Wright's office, especially since most of Dr. Wright's colleagues refuse to meet with him, or utilize his samples. Alex catches their glares, and is occasionally accosted on one of these sanctioned trips through territory normally forbidden to pharmaceutical representatives.

In most cases, Alex figures their disdain to be a smokescreen, subconsciously created to draw their own attention away from the fact that their profession's existence is inexorably and inseparably dependent on the pharmaceutical industry. Alex knocks on Dr. Wright's door, which is already open.

"Come in Alex, and shut the door behind you if you would. I have a reputation to uphold around here," he says.

"I think that reputation is already in question," Alex replies, shutting the door.

Dr. Wright stands up and walks around the desk to shake Alex's hand. He is tall and thin with dense black hair and thick eyebrows. A dark complexion suggest a Mediterranean ancestry.

"Damaged beyond repair. Sorry to be curt Alex, but I'm jammed with patients this afternoon, and I have to hit Maine Med again later. I only have a minute or two."

"No problem Dr. Wright, I won't take up much of your time. I just wanted to thank you again for giving me a heads up last night," he says.

"Okay…" says Dr. Wright, shuffling some papers on his desk and eyeing Alex suspiciously.

"Biosphere told us to stop sampling Terraflu effective immediately. They're holding all drug stock in reserve for some partnership with DHS. Pretty screwed up, if you ask me," Alex says.

"You have to be shitting me Alex. Really? DHS? They couldn't pick a worse partner. Those samples will never see effective use. Are you telling me I can't get any more samples?" he says, clearly angry.

"We'll get to that in a second. What's worse is I think they're going to stop shipping to the pharmacies. They're hell bent on mismanaging this crisis at every level. There's even serious talk about deploying reps like the National Guard, to promote TerraFlu in hot spots hit hard by the flu. I could get relocated to Hartford to spread the good word."

"This is really tragic Alex. I'm sorry things at your company have taken such a sad detour. You're not going to be part of that deployment nonsense, are you?" he asks.

"No. I have no intention of ever returning that call if it comes. Which brings me to my first and only agenda item."

"I didn't realize there you were a man of agendas," Dr. Wright says, raising his eyebrows.

"There's always an agenda," he says holding out his computer tablet. Dr. Wright takes the tablet from Alex.

"Since I don't anticipate working for Biosphere much longer, I don't see any reason to assist them in making matter worse out there. So, if you will sign my tablet, I will give you all of my samples."

Dr. Wright sits back down in his seat, clearly stunned.

"You're not breaking the law by doing this, are you?"

"No, not at all. I'm just going to make some people very, very unhappy."

"Thank you very much Alex. Seriously, this means a lot to me, and will mean a lot to the other grumpy asses working with me, when the time comes. I still think the drug samples are an invaluable resource," he says.

Dr. Wright signs the tablet and hands it back to Alex.

"Seriously, this is great Alex."

"My pleasure. If you can keep this on the down low for a while, I'd really appreciate it. I don't want Biosphere to figure this out until I'm ready to deal with them. And don't say anything about the Biosphere strategy to anyone. That could probably get me in more trouble than the samples. Confidentiality agreement stuff."

"Not a problem Alex. Actually, I don't think I'm going to keep the samples here just yet. Too tempting for staff and other docs. Samples have a tendency to disappear around here, despite their perceived unpopularity. No, I'll pull my Land Rover around to your car, and pile them in there for now. You fit all of it in your car?" he asks, surprised.

"I put all of the seats down, and it's jammed full. It may not be as much as you think, but I just got a shipment a week or so ago, so it's more than I usually have in my storage unit."

"Whatever you have, I will gladly take off your hands. Where are you parked?"

"Second level, pretty close to the elevators."

"Beautiful, I'll be there in a few minutes."

Alex picks up the computer tablet, and checks Dr. Wright's signature. He has just signed for Alex's entire allotment. He decides not to close out the transaction until he disables the wireless card. If he presses "complete" right now, the transaction will probably set off some kind of alarm at their data collection center. Alex is sure that any transactions of TerraFlu samples will be flagged for immediate review. *Last thing I need right now is Ted going apeshit.*

Alex opens the "Intel Pro Wireless Manager" and disables the wireless card. He then clicks on the "Complete Transaction" icon. The transaction will be instantly transmitted when he enables the wireless card. *Sometime next week probably.*

"See you in a few," Alex says and moves to open the door. He looks back and see's Dr. Wright taking off his white coat, and pulling his car keys out of his desk.

"Hey Alex. Before you open the door."

Alex takes a few steps back toward Dr. Wright's desk and leans in.

"If I were you, I'd make a few trips to the store and stock up on necessities. I heard from a very well-placed source that they are close to making an announcement about the classification of the mystery flu. If this turns out to be a truly novel flu strain, we are headed for a disaster of epic proportions. Remember the talk I gave at your regional sales meeting down in Stamford? Think about the worst case scenario I described, and make it worse. Much worse," says Dr. Wright in a hushed tone.

"Jesus," says Alex.

Dr. Wrights just nods his head and grimaces. Alex leaves his office and walks back down toward the automatic door. Giddiness overtakes Dr. Wright's foreboding aura, and Alex starts to grin again. *I can't believe I just did that.*

Alex waits impatiently in front of the elevator, and starts to think about the lecture Dr. Wright gave to over two hundred sales representatives and managers, in a jam packed ballroom at the Stamford Hilton. Dr. Wright spoke for close to an hour and a half about flu strain mutations, characteristics of history's deadliest flu's, flu transmission variables, and nearly every other scientific aspect of the influenza virus. His talk was received with a standing ovation.

He remembers the talk vividly, because it preceded his own harrowing lecture about the potential impact of pandemic flu on society. Thirty minutes of power point doomsday predictions, each slide edited and approved by Biosphere's northeast regional manager, who wanted to drive home the importance and urgency of the sales force's vigor in promoting Terraflu's laboratory efficacy against pandemic grade viruses. Biosphere launched Terraflu with several FDA sanctioned clinical trials demonstrating its superiority against seasonal flu strains, but it was still viewed as unproven against pandemic grade viruses.

Due to a seemingly unending series of FDA hurdles, Biosphere's new anti-viral drug, Terraflu, missed the full onslaught of the 2008-2009 Avian Flu pandemic. Still unapproved for distribution, Biosphere executives watched helplessly as Roche Pharmaceuticals' mainstay anti-viral drug, Tamiflu, solidified its position as the preferred anti-viral treatment during the Avian Flu crisis, and dominated the market.

Consumer confidence in a pharmaceutical product had never been higher. When Terraflu was finally approved by the FDA early in the summer of 2009, news of the Avian Flu had waned from most Americans' list of daily concerns.

Alex had recently completed his six month probationary period with Biosphere, when his manager, Ted Stanton, eagerly volunteered his district to provide the lecture. When nobody from Alex's district team volunteered to stand in front of the entire northeast regional sales team, Alex reluctantly agreed to spare Ted the agony of assigning the lecture to one of the team's less enthusiastic and capable members. The decision to give the lecture changed Alex's life.

First, it solidified his opinion of Ted as a micromanaging, egocentric, compassionless ass kisser. He had his suspicions from the very beginning, but Ted had never done anything overt to threaten Alex's autonomy, or sour their relationship. At least not before Alex volunteered to give what appeared to be the most important lecture of Ted's career. Sure, he'd witnessed some despicable leadership behavior, but in Alex's mind, he couldn't hold this against Ted. Ted's leadership came mainly from books. He was hired by Biosphere right out of college to sell vaccines, and quickly rose to the rank of district manager, where he appeared to be stuck for the past three years.

Despite the relative calm they enjoyed, there was an underlying current of tension, barely palpable, but strong enough for Alex to sense. Ted was uneasy in Alex's presence. In part it was probably due to the fact that Ted wasn't given a choice when it came to Alex's assignment to the district. Biosphere was expanding its sales force for the upcoming launch of Terraflu, and rumor has it that Ted received a call one week before the job had been officially publicized. The call, supposedly placed from the vice president level at headquarters, informed him that his district would be joined by a decorated war veteran and seasoned pharmaceutical sales rep. Ted Stanton was more than displeased with forced assignment, and his attempt to torpedo the decision was apparently a big part of why his fast tracked career had skidded to a halt.

This explained Ted's initial discomfort, but Alex is pretty sure that most of the distress stems from the massive gulf between their age and experiences. In 2003, while Alex was commanding Marines under the constant threat of enemy machine gun and artillery fire in Iraq, Ted was busy dodging keg stands and tequila shooters in his fraternity house at UCONN. Alex never really talked about his experiences in the Marine Corps with anyone at Biosphere, even after martinis and liberal amounts of wine at team building dinners. He spent most of these fancy dinners graciously listening to his colleagues boast of their exploits, personal and professional, as they continued to fuel their delusions of grandeur from the same bottles of wine that Alex had selected as a reward for being subjected to their nonsense.

Alex had included copies of his military decorations with his original resume submission to the Vice President of Sales. Biosphere was a small company in the grand scheme of pharmaceutical companies, and Alex suspected that copies of his decorations, or rumors of them, had found their way to Ted. Whatever the cause, Ted had kept his distance from Alex, which was exactly how Alex liked it. Until the big lecture in Stamford brought them a little too close for comfort.

No fewer than thirteen videotaped practice lectures later, two of which were full dress rehearsals in a rented conference hall similar to the one in Stamford, Alex was ready to kill Ted with his bare hands. The mere mention of his name or the buzz of his iPhone caused Alex to clench his fists. Alex had seriously miscalculated the situation when he volunteered to give the lecture. He didn't factor in the possibility that this lecture was a key part of Ted's of career redemption, and the oversight cost him dearly. Hourly emails and texting. Daily phone calls. Constant revision and supervision of his proposed slide deck. Alex was convinced that Ted had quit doing everything except for micromanage this thirty minute lecture.

He even got Michelle Harke, their regional manager, in on his act. Apparently, several bigwigs from headquarters would be there to listen to Dr. Wright's talk, and the possibility existed that they might stick around for Alex's talk. A few weeks out from the lecture, all of his slides started to filter through Michelle's desk, and before Alex knew it, he had two sets of revisions to process, each set often contradicting the other. He seriously considered sending a letter bomb to each of them. Despite the nonsense, Alex's talk was hailed as a success by both Michelle and Ted, though it paled in comparison to Dr. Wright's talk, which would have been a hard act to follow by any speaker. Alex smiled and shook their hands after the talk, cringing inside as they patted him on the shoulder, and silently promising himself that he would never volunteer for anything at Biosphere again. Fortunately, the experience wasn't a total loss for Alex.

The most important result of the regional lecture stemmed from his research. Alex combed the internet for a variety of sources, and found a broad continuum of opinions, speculations and predictions about the future of pandemics. Most articles and international disease control agencies agreed that the 2008-2009 Avian Flu served as the best model of a worst case scenario. Despite over twenty million deaths worldwide, casualties in the United States, Europe and most other modernized nations were minimal. Close to twenty thousand deaths in the United States were attributed to the Avian Flu, which was still far below the forty to fifty thousand deaths annually attributed to the regular seasonal flu. The overall impact on society was minimal.

However, the deeper he dug into the topic, the more he started to believe that most of these articles and reports were a little too optimistic. When he stumbled upon the International Scientific Pandemic Awareness Collaborative (ISPAC) website, he found all of the decidedly less optimistic opinions and research condensed into one convenient location. ISPAC had been privately founded on the heels of the Avian Flu pandemic, to counter the prevailing optimism, and spur the international community to strengthen pandemic response planning and resource allocation.

Alex spent countless hours studying document after document, until he was convinced that Avian Flu was just the tip of the iceberg in terms of pandemic potential. Alex had a hard time condensing all of the available information and research into a thirty minute talk, but when he was finished, and the final revision had been approved by his regional manager, Alex's slide presentation could have fueled the next blockbuster Hollywood disaster movie. Alex shakes himself free of the reverie as the elevator door opens. *We might end up needing that stockpile after all.*

Chapter Six

Friday, November 2, 2012

Alex walks out of Hannaford's with his second shopping cart. He made two separate trips into the store, the first one to buy non-perishable items, which nearly overflowed from the cart, and the second to buy perishable, refrigerator stocked items. He felt pretty strange going in for the second time, but managed to stand in a checkout line far enough away from the first one to avoid any uncomfortable glances. Alex wasn't sure why he even cared.

The store was about as crowded as he would expect for a Friday afternoon, which despite the looming threat, didn't really surprise him. Alex knows the public will wait too long, and one electrifying news report will send everyone into the stores at once, effectively crippling the food supply system. Most of the grocery stores, just like the big retail stores, have become so efficient, that they carry little additional stock on hand to meet even the slightest additional demand.

He scans the parking lot, noting mostly empty spaces. *This store is one bad news report away from mayhem.* Alex decides to call his family and friends to urge them to hit the stores now. He loads the groceries into his already packed car, and starts to drive home.

■

Alex turns his company car left from Harrison Road onto the Durham Road loop. Ryan sits in the rear passenger side seat, just barely visible to Alex in the center rear view mirror, staring out of his window. After the turn, they pass four houses, two on each side of the street, and then the road splits. He turns the car right at the split and heads toward their home. If he continued past his house, and kept driving, he would end up back at the split. Durham Road is a loop, and has only one access point, the turn he just took from Harrison Road.

The subdivision contains thirty four houses, located on both sides of the street, and evenly spaced on half acre lots around the loop. Since both Durham Road, and the streets surrounding it were built on recently converted farmland, most of the trees throughout the neighborhood are still smaller than the houses. Compared to most of the older, established neighborhoods nearby, the trees on Durham Road still look like saplings.

As he passes more houses on the way home, he starts to see some of his neighbors. The first neighbor he sees is Todd Perry, in front of a red colonial with gray doors. Todd is adjusting a sprinkler head in the front yard, when he notices Alex's car, and looks up to wave. Alex waves back through the side passenger window.

Alex glances to the left as he passes a gray colonial with dark blue doors, and a three car garage. Thick evergreen bushes crowd the sides of the walkway leading to the front door, standing guard over wide raised beds filled with yellow and orange fall flowers. He waves at Julia Rhodes, who is watering a flower bed close to her mudroom entrance. She looks up as he passes, returning his wave.

Alex pushes the garage door opener as he passes the Walkers' house at on the right. He looks at their house, a yellow contemporary colonial with green doors, and does not see any signs of activity. The Walkers usually start to spill home at around five thirty. First, Ed arrives with at least two of their children. Then at about six, Samantha pulls in with whichever kid had a late practice.

As Alex pulls in the driveway, the right side garage bay door finishes opening, and Alex pulls his car into the garage.

"Make sure you have all of your junk," says Alex.

"Got it," Ryan replies, and opens his door.

Alex closes his door and carefully slides behind his wife's Toyota Forerunner, trying not to dirty his suit. *She never pulls in far enough.* As he opens the screen door, and walks into the mudroom, he can smell dinner. *Garlic, onions, ginger. Pprobably a stir-fry.*

He hangs up his suit jacket in the mudroom closet, and takes of his shoes, kicking them into the open floor space of the closet.

"Hey honey, smells great!"

"Yeah, I thought a stir-fry with was in order for tonight," she says.

Alex crosses the kitchen and gives her a kiss, holding her for a few seconds. He looks around.

"Are you making rice for the stir fry?" says Alex.

"Yep, already in the pressure cooker. Don't you have anything better to do other than hawk me?"

"Probably not."

He hears Ryan enter the mudroom and kick his shoes off his feet. One of the shoes bangs against the closet door.

"Take it easy on the house in there," Alex yells.

"Sorry dad," Ryan says and flashes by them on his way upstairs.

"Hey, no hug for your mom?" says Kate.

"Sorry mom," Ryan says and returns to the kitchen to begrudgingly hug Kate.

"Dinner will be ready in a few minutes. Tell Emily to wash her hands and start making her way downstairs. You too. Love you," she says.

"Love you too mom. I'll be right down," he says and scoots upstairs.

"Anything good happen?" he says, nodding at the TV.

"The UN declared an emergency session. They're considering a travel and commerce ban against China. Chinese officials plan to release more information about whatever is going on over there," she says.

"When?" he says.

"Some time tomorrow."

"Hey look at that. They've officially named it the China Crisis. How original. They should call it the China corn-holing," he says.

"Jesus. Come on. I'm trying to cook over here," she says, shaking her head.

"How about the great Chinese bend over of 2012? Is that less graphic?" he says.

"Really. That's enough," she insists.

"I'm gonna change," he says, and starts to head toward the stairs.

"Grab the kids on the way down. I'm pretty much done here," she says.

"You got it," he says and starts to disappear up the stairs.

Alex closes the bedroom door behind him as he starts to pull off his tie. He turns on the flat screen TV, which takes a few seconds to display a picture.

"CDC officials have confirmed the flu strain as an H16 variant. Little is known about the new strain at this point, and many serious questions remain unanswered. So far, neither the CDC nor WHO has responded to demands for information. CNN news correspondent David Gervasey reports from ISPAC headquarters in Atlanta, Georgia. David?"

"Denise, roughly fifteen minutes ago, we were fortunate to get a brief interview with one of their senior spokespersons, Dr. Allison Devreaux."

The screen changes to the previously recorded interview with Dr. Devreaux.

"Dr., what can you tell us about the virus that we don't already know?"

"The virus has been classified as a new subtype. H16," she answers in a French accent. "The strain is classified as H16N1."

"This subtype has never been seen before in humans or animals, so it is truly a novel strain. Right now, our own scientists are trying to match its genetic characteristics with previously seen subtype strains. In this way, we can make some rough predictions regarding its behavior.

We know that the virus is highly contagious, and its acquisition by a host leads to typical flu like symptoms, including high fever, marked weakness and pulmonary distress. In essence, it behaves like a highly pathogenic disease. We know this from our investigation of an ever increasing number of cluster outbreaks throughout the far Pacific Rim, and we are extremely confident that the strain found by ISPAC investigative teams outside of China, is the same as the strain causing the outbreak inside of China."

"When do you anticipate further information to be available from your field teams?"

"We receive constant reports, and engage in discussions with these teams around the clock. When new information is verified, we will post this information on our website. You can also subscribe to our Pandemic News Alert service, and receive automatic email updates as new information is posted. We are striving to pass all relevant information on to the public, so that they can make the most informed decisions to prepare for a potential pandemic virus."

"Does this look like a pandemic on scale with the 2008 Avian Flu?"

"Frankly, not enough information exists for us to draw any conclusions. The virus is highly contagious, certainly. At this time, we just don't know anything regarding Clinical Attack Rates, Case Fatality Rates, infection and symptom timelines…all of the key parameters that allow us to project its spread and impact on the world's population.

However, based on its efficient capacity for human to human transmission, I feel confident projecting that this virus will rapidly reach all corners of the globe. Let us hope that this virus in not as deadly as the Avian Flu. Thank you David."

The screen cuts back to a live broadcast from ISPAC headquarters in Atlanta. David Gervasey stands in front of the modern ten story glass and steel structure.

"You heard it here first Denise. We're going to remain in place to get the latest information as it becomes available."

"Thank you David. As you can see, live ISPAC website information is located at the bottom of our screen, and we will be broadcasting any new ISPAC website updates as they are posted. Stay with us, we'll be back in a moment."

Alex stares at the screen for a few more seconds, and then returns to his closet to change into jeans and a gray long sleeve fleece pullover. He heads back toward the stairs, and stares down the hall at his office door. *I need to get the kids down to dinner, or I'll have more to worry about than viruses. I need to check one more thing first.*

He enters the office, and types "Hong Kong International Airport" into Google. The search engine's first link is the airports official website. He scans the page and clicks on "flight information," then "departures." The screen fills with the days scheduled departing flights.

Jesus. If this virus is deadlier than the Avian Flu, we're in trouble. By noon, on any given day, over a hundred flights depart HKIA for every major city in world, and by midnight that same day, flights originating from HKIA land in major hubs on every continent. From there, these passengers embark on journeys to every conceivable corner of the planet. Within sixteen to eighteen hours of leaving Hong Kong, an infected passenger could be sharing a pint of Guinness with friends in a Dublin Pub, sipping tea with family in the suburbs of Damascus, or meeting a friend for Italian food in Boston's North End. *And this thing has been brewing in China for more than three days. This thing is everywhere.* Alex minimizes the web browser, and gets up to call the kids to dinner.

■

The Fletchers eat dinner sitting at a large rectangular pine table located between the kitchen and family room. The eating area is separated from the family room by two half walls, with a wide opening centered between them, anchored by sculpted wood columns extending from the top of the half walls to the ceiling. Alex serves butternut squash soup to everyone, and Kate starts the evening interrogation.

"So, anything huge going on in class for anyone? Emily?" says Kate.

Emily replies, "Not much, we're still learning some Spanish. I have homework again."

"Yeah, you're going to have a lot more than the one spelling test you had last year. Try like homework every night, and more tests. I have like two hours a night now," Ryan says,

"Well I think we're going to have about the same as you, I heard from Lauren that her friend in Mr. Leahy's class already has over an hour of work to do every night," says Emily.

"I doubt it. I never had that much work in third grade. Third grade is like Kindergarten compared to Middle School."

"OK crazies, Ryan wins the award for most oppressed by homework. Anything other than that going on this week?" says Alex.

Both children shake their heads slowly.

"Really there's not much," says Ryan.

"Of course not," says Alex.

"I think I might join cross-country like Ryan. Lauren is running in it," says Emily.

"You already have soccer practice three times a week," says Kate.

Kate looks at Ryan and asks, "Don't they run their meets on Thursday?"

"Yeah, but the meets are optional, and they're done by four-thirty. They only run like a mile or maybe less. She could probably do it."

Emily's face brightens.

"If she wasn't so slow."

Ryan emits a terribly annoying laugh, and Emily reaches over the table to hit him. Kate grabs her arm, and points her finger at Ryan.

"That's enough! Both of you. No hitting, and you, cut it out," Kate says.

Alex shakes his head, half smiling, and then turns to Ryan.

"Really, quit agitating your sister. It's starting to become a very annoying habit," he says and returns to Emily.

"Anyway, sweetie, I don't think you should double up on practices in the same day. Soccer comes first, and you make as many running practices as you can. Sound good?"

He turns his head back to Ryan and raises his eyebrows, sending a clear warning to his son.

"As long as she makes a couple practices, they don't care. It's a really laid back program," Ryan answers.

"Thank you Ryan. There you go sweetie. Go ahead and sign up. We'll go out and get you some running shoes," Kate says.

"Thanks mom," says Emily.

Alex realizes that he is the only one at the table eating and talking.

"Alright, let's get some food down, or you won't have enough energy to walk to the school bus, let alone run any races."

Both kids start eating their soup, and Alex can tell by their initial response that they like the soup.

"Honey, the soup is awesome."

"Thanks. Whole Foods was stocked with different squashes, so I picked up a bunch," she says.

Alex nods his head, and finishes his soup. Kate is only half way through her bowl, when Alex gets up, walks to the kitchen island, and grabs their dinner plates. He puts them in an open space on the table, and sits down to wait for everyone to finish their soup. He gives Kate a nod, and she starts their planned conversation.

"Ryan, did you guys talk about the situation in China at school?"

"A little bit."

"What did you talk about?"

"Well, Mr. Brett asked us if we had seen it on the news, or on the internet this morning. I heard some of it when you guys had the kitchen TV on, and I saw and article on CNNkids.com at school."

"Cool. What did you think?"

Alex starts to load Emily's plate with rice, stir-fry and tofu. She protests the amount with her hands, trying to wave off the second heap as Alex hovers the wooden spoon over her plate. Alex acknowledges her silent refusal and moves the spoonful to his own plate.

"I don't know. Everyone seems pretty mad at China. Aren't they doing the same thing they did in 2008? Keeping everyone in the dark."

Kate answers, "Well, nobody really knows what's going on over there. At least this time, the world knows something is brewing. What did Mr. Brett say?"

"Not much. He really just wanted to get some discussion going. We spent some time talking about the 2008 pandemic, and looking at some facts about China."

Alex says, "Nice. Did any of your teachers talk to you guys about pandemic flu, in general, or anything like that?"

Kate finishes her soup while they talk. Emily is busy emptying her plate, clearly happy not to be the focus of attention.

"Yep, we talked about it in science. How the flu spreads. How scientists classify strains of flu. Past pandemics. It was pretty cool. Pretty scary too. Dad, do you think we could have another pandemic? Ms. Ullman said that major pandemics usually don't happen so close together, and that's why the Swine Flu pandemic never really took off."

Alex answers, "Sounds like you guys really learn some advanced shiiii….stuff in that class. Sorry."

Emily laughs, "Daddy, your starting to talk like Mommy."

"Thanks a lot Emily," says Kate.

"Another impartial witness to Barnacle Bill's mouth," says Alex

Kate shakes her head, clearly wanting to give him the middle finger as she taps her index finger on the top of her water glass.

"Anyway, historically speaking, your teacher would be right. However, there are a lot of experts out there that think it can happen at any time if the conditions are right. So, to answer your question, I don't think anyone can really predict these things," says Alex,

Alex looks at Kate, and rubs his chin. Kate picks up on his cue.

"You guys really don't have to worry about it. You know that right? We've made some preparations at the house over the past few years that will get us through any major crisis. Pandemic, major storm, whatever it might be."

Both kids nod their heads. They appear to have anticipated this talk.

"You mean all of that stuff locked up in the basement?" says Emily.

"Yeah, that's part of it. We have plenty of food, water and supplies stored down there. We also have our own power supply. The sun. And we can keep the house warm with the wood burning stove," Kate answers.

"Can't we heat the house with the furnace if we have solar power?" says Ryan

Alex laughs, "This kid's too smart. Yes, we could, but the furnace eats up a lot of power. During the summer, when the sun is strongest, we could get away with it. But who needs to use the furnace in the summer right? Other than to heat up water. Winter is a different story, because the sun is so much weaker. Even on a beautiful day, the batteries will charge slower than a crappy day in the summer. We'd really have to watch the charge level," Alex says.

Kate brings the conversation back on track.

"What I want you two to understand, is that we are prepared for anything really scary like that, and that you don't have to worry about it. Other people need to be worried, because most other people won't be prepared at all. They may actually not even believe it's happening until it's too late for them."

"How will we know if it is happening?" says Emily.

In a calm tone, Alex says, "Your mom and I know what to look for. Trust us, we'll know. The hard part will be convincing others to listen and prepare."

"Right, and if something like this happens, we need to be ready to stay in our house for a very long time, without coming into contact with anyone. Even friends and family. Unless they prepared like us," Kate says.

"Like last year? That really sucked. Please don't take us out of school for no reason again," says Ryan.

"We didn't take you out for no reason. Swine Flu had the potential to be worse than the Avian Flu, and the Avian Flu killed close to fifty thousand people in the U.S. in 2008. We weren't ready for it at all, and it really scared the ah…you know what out of us. Fill in the blank honey?" says Alex.

"Ha ha," Kate says through a fake smile.

"But nothing happened, and it was embarrassing. Plus, it took me forever to catch up? Remember some of the teachers didn't want to let me make up some of my tests?"

"That won't happen again." says Kate.

"What does a pandemic do to you?" says Emily.

"Sweetie, the pandemic flu makes you really, really sick. Worse than you've ever been before. That's why you get a flu shot every year."

"To keep from getting the pandemic flu?" says Emily.

"No, you get the shot for the regular flu, which can make you pretty sick too. The pandemic flu is worse though," says Kate.

"Don't worry about it sweetie. No one in this family will get sick. I promise. Just finish your dinner and start your homework. Then we can have some dessert," says Alex.

Emily digs into her stir fry, as Ryan finishes his plate. Alex sees that Emily still looks worried.

"More stir fry sweetie?" says Kate

"No thanks Mom, I had more than enough. Everything's great. Especially the soup," replies Ryan.

Chapter Seven

Friday, November 2, 2012

Kate and Alex sit on a dark brown leather sectional couch in the great room. Two recessed lights over the mantel cast indirect light over the entire family room. The flat screen TV shows NBC news anchor Kerrie Connor framed next to Dr. David Ocampo, Director of the ISPAC's Live Trend Analysis Division. Information displayed at the bottom of the split screen indicates that Dr. Ocampo is broadcasting live from ISPAC headquarters in Atlanta, Georgia.

"Dr. Ocampo, thank you again for your time. Good luck to both you and your organization."

"Thank you for the opportunity to educate the public, and if I may, your viewers can always obtain the most updated information pandemic information on our website, www.ispac.org."

"Thank you again Dr. Ocampo. When we come back, we'll hear about the massive preparations underway on the Florida peninsula in preparation for the anticipated landfall of Hurricane Terrence."

Kate pauses the recording, and looks at Alex, slowly nodding her head.

"Rewind to the part about the WHO underestimating the flu's potential," says Alex.

Kate scrolls back a few times to find the right segment.

"That's it. Right there," says Alex.

"Dr. Ocampo, WHO representatives have repeatedly criticized this premise, labeling your organization's research in this area of study as flawed. They say that your casualty projections are excessive, and that your assessment of the impact on essential services is exaggerated. Dr. Pierre Neville, head of the WHO's pandemic impact study group, is quoted saying that the 'ISPAC's predictions are alarmist science fiction.' How do you respond to the WHO's stance toward the ISPAC's projections?"

"The problem with their criticism of our projections is that the WHO leans way too heavily on the experiences of the 2008 pandemic. They insist that 2008 is the perfect model for all future pandemics. On the contrary, we believe that the 2008 pandemic flu strain was a relatively weak pandemic strain, especially compared to the 1918 Spanish Flu, which killed millions. In 2008 the world's healthcare system and essential services infrastructure was barely challenged."

"How so?" presses Kerrie.

"During the Avian Flu pandemic, hospital based care remained available to a majority of sick patients, at least in most modernized and developing countries. This drastically improved outcomes, and contributed decisively to the low overall case fatality rate. Although the situation in many developing nations approached, and in some cases crossed the tipping point, most modernized nations' system were never truly challenged by the 2008 pandemic. This outcome would be different in the face of a deadlier and more infectious virus. The tipping point for inpatient healthcare availability, in both modernized and developing nations, would be reached quickly, and the result would be catastrophic."

"Even for the United States?" she says.

"Everywhere. In any given area, we calculate that all available inpatient services such as hospital beds, ventilators, and medical staff would be occupied within two to three weeks of a pandemic reaching that area. In the U.S. alone, based on 1918 pandemic flu patterns, every existing hospital beds would be occupied within a few weeks . Once inpatient capacity is filled, patients would be given a set of home-based care instructions and turned away.

"Turned away? Where would they be sent?"

"Home."

"Really? That doesn't sound like a great option."

"It isn't. The predicted survival rates for hospital based care versus home based care differ greatly. Eighty to eighty-five percent versus ten to fifteen percent for a medium risk patient. If you're a high risk patient with secondary complication like heart disease or diabetes, you're as good as dead," he states morosely.

Kerrie looks stunned by his last statement.

"Kerrie, this isn't science fiction. It's a commonsense based statistical prediction. A complicated one that accounts for hundreds of factors, and balances trends from several pandemic models. Not just one, like the WHO model."

Kate stops the recording.

"That's sure to cause a stir within the WHO," she says.

"At the White House too. They're all in each others' pockets. He basically put it all on the table. Tomorrow should be interesting," Alex says.

"How can anyone really ignore or dismiss what he said? You have to stop and at least think about it," she says.

"Don't worry. First of all, nobody wants to believe it could be a real problem. Most of these people don't give a shit about any potential crisis."

Alex raises his hands, gesturing toward the neighborhood.

"If it's not happening to them right now, they don't care. Oil prices are lower than a few months ago? Great. Forget about the fact that the price threshold rises every year. Why do anything? Got a little scared during the 2008 pandemic? Sure, but what's the chance that it will happen again so soon? Not likely according to the government. And last year's Swine Flu pandemic turned out to be a joke. So why should anyone worry? The local news hasn't even picked up on the possible cases right here in Maine. Who knows what it'll take for people to take it seriously. Which reminds me, I should check out our stockpile. I haven't been down there in a long time, and it couldn't hurt to see what we have on hand. Just in case."

"Sounds good. You measure the Frito supply while I check on the kids, and start moving them along to bed."

Kate gets up from the couch, and walks behind it toward the doorway leading from the front of the family room to the staircase in the foyer. Alex places the empty glass on the coffee table, and holds his hand over his head for Kate's hand. She grasps his hand over the back of the couch and gives her hand a kiss.

"Good luck. Make sure Ryan finished his homework. He was drawing earlier."

"Love you."

"Love you too. I'll be in the bunker if you need me."

Alex picks up his glass and walks into the kitchen. He glances at the clock on the DVR. 8:12. He places the glass on the kitchen island and grabs a yellow legal pad and a pen from the kitchen desk. He turns toward the basement door and opens it. The stairwell leading down is dark, barely illuminated by the soft lights under the kitchen cabinets. He turns on the lights to the basement, and descends the unfinished stairs.

Facing him on the way down, a storage shelf stands against the concrete wall directly across from the stairway. The shelf contains larger kitchen items that don't fit in the kitchen or pantry. Alex scans the shelf and sees a cobalt blue Mixmaster, an espresso maker, a blender, several trays, dozens of large wooden or stainless steel bowls, and several large plastic serving trays.

He reaches the basement floor, and turns the corner into a large, well lit, unfinished area that encompasses two thirds of the total available basement space. This area is filled with lawn furniture, several bicycles, two kayaks, a dehumidifier, an old sofa, assorted luggage, and a working refrigerator. The front wall of basement, adjacent to the stairway, is occupied by stacks of fifty gallon plastic storage bins that hold everything from summer clothing to painting supplies. Everything without a place in the upper floors of the house ends up stored in one of these bins.

Alex walks along the staircase wall toward another door located toward the back of the basement, just past the spare refrigerator. As he walks to the door, he glances to his right, at the seasonal storage area, which gives him a general feeling of disarray. Every year, he intends to better organize this area, but as the weather turns colder, he finds himself hauling everything through the bulkhead door at the last minute, and jamming it in, wherever it will fit.

He approaches the door, which sits in a wall that runs from the back of the staircase to the back wall of the basement. He takes his key chain out of his jeans, and finds the key to the door. He opens the deadbolt lock with one of the keys, and then the doorknob lock with another. He pushes the door in a few feet and reaches his right hand into the pitch black room to find the light switch along the wall. He flips the light on and walks several feet into the back room of his basement. The three overhead light bulbs, spaced evenly from front to back, expose an unfinished basement area that stands in direct contrast to the room he just left

This room is immaculate and well organized. Floor to ceiling storage shelves stand flush against most of the outer concrete walls. In the back southeast corner of the house, almost directly across from the door, stand two 275 gallon fuel oil tanks for the furnace. The furnace itself is located about fifteen feet to the left of the tanks, along the southeast side wall of the basement, in a slightly recessed area. An oversized water heater sits a few feet to the left of the furnace. In the middle part of the room, sits a large rectangular cream colored plastic box, standing three and a half feet tall, four feet deep, and six feet wide.

The box is a PowerCube Generator and Storage (G/S) 900 module, configured to store the electricity generated by their south facing rooftop solar panels. He can tell by the full bank of green LED lights, that the system is fully charged and operational, free of any detected faults. One PowerCube can provide 6000 Watts of continuous power output, for as long as the batteries hold a charge.

Alex looks back over his right shoulder at a five foot tall black metallic safe next to the door. The safe is three feet wide, and has two built-in locks, one toward the top, and one at the bottom. The locks are opened by the same key, which hangs on a small nail, hidden nearby in the basement rafters. The black steel rectangular box is a gun locker. The weapons inside are cleaned, oiled, and ready for action. The locker also holds ammunition.

Alex turns his head back toward the center of the room. *Where to start? Fuel tanks.* He walks nearly straight ahead to the two fuel tanks, and checks their fill gauges. One tank is completely full, and the other tank is two thirds full. *Pretty good levels for the beginning of November.* They filled the tanks at the beginning of May, and only used one third of a tank to heat water for nearly six months. Three years ago, they installed a second tank in response to skyrocketing oil prices. Alex writes in his notebook. *Call Dead River Oil to fill tank.*

He turns around, and decides to start at the wall adjacent to the door. The metal storage shelves starting here, and extending to the front concrete wall of the basement, contain spring water in two gallon containers. Each four level shelving unit holds thirty of these containers, all on the lowest three shelves. The containers are stacked five in a row, two rows high on each shelf. There are eight shelving units along this wall, all together holding nearly five hundred gallons of water.

All of the containers are marked with their date of purchase. Each week, at least one of the oldest containers is removed, and placed in the kitchen for consumption. During the weekly grocery run, this container is replaced, ensuring that the water supply stored in the basement is slowly turned over throughout the course of the year, preventing the inevitable decay of the plastic containers.

The system employed to rotate water through the shelves is also applied to most other stockpiled items. They regularly rotate food, water, medical supplies, batteries and other shorter shelf-life items into their daily lives, and replace them on a weekly or at least a monthly basis.

The Fletchers started their stockpile by first purchasing all of the shelving units, which cost a small fortune, and then slowly filling them with essentials. They didn't buy everything at once, but instead purchased a few items in each essential category, once or twice a week, until the shelves were filled. It took them less than a year to fill the shelves with enough food and supplies to survive at least a year.

Alex quickly walks down the row and checks for any obvious leaks pooled on the floor. The only thing that catches his attention is the date marked on the front of newest container, 2/12/11, and the thick layer of dust covering the rest of them. The systematic rotation of their stockpile ceased after the 2010 Swine Flu scare, which fizzled just as quickly as it arrived.

At the end of the water row, he faces the first of eight shelving units placed along the front basement wall of the house. The first shelving unit contains health and medical supplies. The top shelf is fully stocked with over-the-counter medication, like Motrin, Tylenol, Sudafed, and antihistamines. Alex grabs a few to check their expiration dates. His random spot check finds nothing ready to expire.

Prescription drug samples occupy the shelf below. Alex surreptitiously acquired all of the prescription drugs from physician offices throughout his sales territory. Their stockpile contains over forty courses of antiviral therapy split between TerraFlu and Tamiflu. He has also sent the equivalent of one course of therapy to each close member of their family. If a pandemic strikes, he plans to reserve two courses of Terraflu and one course of Tamiflu, for each member of his own family. This plan leaves twenty eight courses for neighbors and friends.

The bottom two shelves contain first aid supplies and vitamin supplements. Most of the space is dedicated to first aid, filled with gloves, masks, assorted size and shaped bandages, compresses, triangular bandages, medical tape, scissors, antiseptic solution, antibiotic ointment, gauze, eyewash, thermometer, hand sanitizer, several first aid manuals, instant cold packs, and alcohol wipes.

Two makeshift portable first aid kits sit on the floor in front of the unit. Alex bought these military style butt packs and attached two aluminum D-rings to their straps, so that they could be hooked onto anything. Each kit is filled with the basics for treating wounds and minor illness. One of the kits is marked with medical tape and contains a basic surgery kit. Alex spies several bottles of children's and adult vitamins tucked away among medical supplies.

Satisfied with the medical supplies, Alex glances at his watch. 8:34. *Already twenty minutes down here? Jesus.* The remaining seven shelving units along this wall contain food items. Alex sees dozens of large airtight plastic canisters filled with brown rice, barley, other grains, flour, oats, and different types of beans. Each canister holds close to twenty pounds of dry food. He passes medium sized airtight bins filled with sugar, nuts, seeds, tea, dried mushrooms, dried peas, and other dried vegetables that could be used for soup.

Two of the shelving units are packed with canned goods. Everything from diced tomatoes to artichoke hearts, in large cans, can be found on these shelves. The bottom two shelves of these units are filled with nonperishable soymilk containers. Alex checks the dates on a few of these containers and sees that they are good until 2013. Beyond canned goods and airtight canisters, the shelves contain numerous boxes of dry cereal, crackers, and snack bars. Coffee, condiments, salt, spices, hot cocoa mix, flavored drink powder, and boxes of vegetable bouillon fill in the gaps.

Overall, their food supply was more than adequate to last a year, possibly longer. Most meals would consist mainly of a grain and bean, with at least one can of vegetables a day. They had plenty of seasonings to keep the meals interesting.

The first shelf past the far northern corner of the basement holds several dozen bottles of wine, and several cases of canned beer. Some of the cases have been there over two years, and Alex wonders if they're skunked. A few twelve packs of bottled beer sit in front of the shelving unit, on the floor. He writes 'Beer and wine run' in his notebook. *Priorities.*

The shelving unit immediately next to this one is jammed full with boxes of trash bags, paper cups, paper plates, plastic silverware, paper towels and napkins. Three large economy sized packs of toilet paper are stacked in front of this unit. One of the packs is ripped open and half empty. He writes in the notepad. Buy more toilet paper. *Another critical item. Nobody wants to start wiping their ass on the back of printer paper or cardboard. .* This reminds him to make another note. Go to Home Depot and buy four large plastic buckets and lots of trash bags. *Makeshift crappers if the water goes out.*

The last shelving unit on this wall, immediately to the left of the hot water tank, holds fifteen small green Coleman propane cans, four rechargeable/battery operated walkie-talkie's, assorted lighters, thirty unscented pillar candles, one hand-crank powered weather/emergency radio, a Uniden handheld scanner, and at least fifty packages of batteries. Staring at the batteries, Alex calculates that the batteries alone are probably worth more than five hundred dollars. *That's pretty much it.*

He turns his attention to the circuit breaker located to the right of the oil tanks. An electrical transfer switch is located adjacent to the circuit breaker, which is either set 'To Grid' or 'To House.' When set 'To Grid,' electricity flows from the photovoltaic panels to the batteries, until the batteries are fully charged. At this point, the electricity is diverted through the power box to the electrical grid, where it is bought by Central Maine Power, and discounted from the Fletchers' electric bill. In the 'To House' setting, the batteries are charged by the solar panels, and their electrical flow is connected to circuits in the house. Under normal circumstances, this switch is set to 'To Grid.' Alex confirms that both switches are in the proper position.

Alex turns toward the door, intent upon leaving. He writes one more note. 'Get checklist for other stuff.' He'll need to review their pre-printed pandemic checklist, which addresses other issues like their investments, filling up their cars, and buying extra gas in case they needed to relocate somewhere further than one tank would take them. They developed this checklist over the past few years, combining recommendations found in various online sources. He makes another note. 'Fill up empty gas containers. Fill up cars.' He has several empty gas containers in the garage, enough to hold about twenty gallons of gasoline all together. As he approaches the door, he looks at his watch. *Almost nine. It's like a time machine down here.* He glances at the gun locker and hesitates for a moment.

"Fuck it."

He stands on his toes and reaches up into the rafters of the ceiling. He finds the key and unlocks the gun metallic door. The locker holds four weapons, ammunition for each weapon, gun cleaning supplies and a few accessories. A rifle and a shotgun lean against the small rack extending from the bottom of the locker to a shelf near the top. Two pistols and their magazines sit on the shelf, along with four boxes of pistol ammunition. The rifle magazines and ammunition lie at the bottom of the locker between the rifle and shotgun. A small shelf on the locker door holds a few dozen loose shotgun shells. The top shelf also holds a scope for the rifle.

Alex grabs the rifle and removes it from the locker. Out of military habit, he grasps the slide handle and pulls it back, opening the rifle's breech. He tilts the weapon and holds it slightly forward and up, pointing the barrel toward the closest light in the room. At this angle, he looks through the ejection port into breech end of the rifle barrel. He can see light through the barrel, which indicates that the weapon is clear, and not loaded. The entire process took less than one second

"Clear." He whispers.

Satisfied that the weapon is safe, Alex can handle the Colt AR-15A3 Carbine more casually. This weapon is his favorite, most closely resembling the M-4 rifle he carried for years as a Marine officer. He racks the slide a few more times, squeezing the trigger to confirm ease of action. He then racks the slide again, and aims at the far end of the basement, sighting in on a can of tomatoes. Holding still, he lines up the front and rear sight of the rifle on the can, and steadily pulls the trigger. Click. The sight is still set on the can. *A perfect trigger pull.* Alex puts the rifle back in the locker, and grabs the shotgun.

The Mossberg 590 Combat Shotgun is huge in Alex's grip. Alex slides the pump action all the way back, opening the breech. He examines the barrel. *Clear.* He then racks it forward, releases the safety and aims it at the far wall of the basement. Click. He pumps the shotgun a few more times, aiming and pulling the trigger.

He places the shotgun back on the rack, and removes one of the pistols. He points the sleek, black .45 caliber Heckler and Koch USP semi-automatic pistol at the floor and pulls the slide back with his left hand. He visually inspects the weapon's chamber. *Clear.* He then turns around, and aims at a box of Cheese-Its across the basement. Click. He replaces it and grabs the second pistol.

He clears the Sig Sauer 9mm pistol, and sights in on the same cracker box. Click. *Perfect action.* Alex bought this pistol for Kate, before he left for Iraq in 2003. While stationed at Camp Pendleton, they lived off base in Carlsbad, California. He always worried about a home invasion, especially when he was out of town.

He knew she couldn't effectively use the .45. It was too large and clunky for her small hands, so he bought a pistol she could easily handle. The pistol fell far short of Kate's idea of the perfect farewell gift, given that she was being left on her own to juggle work, a three year old son, and a midterm pregnancy. All while her husband invaded Iraq. Less than perfect actually. The pistol sat high on a shelf in their bedroom closet, untouched for over six months, until Alex returned.

"You still have that one?" Kate asks.

Alex takes a quick breath, clearly startled.

"Uh huh. This one is yours. You're just lucky I didn't give it to you for your birthday."

"Oh really! I missed out. Is that what all of the Captain's wives and girlfriends got?"

"Some of them perhaps."

Kate seductively raises her eyebrows.

"I've been waiting for you upstairs. All that talk earlier about the Hulk, I was hoping you might show me what happens when you get angry."

She briefly caresses his left shoulder and suddenly withdraws her hand.

"That is, if you're done stroking your guns down here."

Alex put the pistol back in the locker.

"Oh, I'm done with them. They were just a little warm up. You know how weapons turn me on."

"Lock up, kiss the kids goodnight, and meet me upstairs. Don't take too long, or I'm going to bed."

"Aye, Aye skipper."

Kate smacks Alex's rear and smiles as she heads upstairs. Alex locks the gun locker and replaces the key.

Chapter Eight

Saturday, November 3, 2012

Alex's calf muscles burn as he pushes through the last hill on Harrison Road, and turns right onto Durham Road. He slows his pace after the turn, and starts walking with his hands clasped together over his head. Alex prefers not to run in morning, but he woke up at five feeling very anxious, and knew that he wouldn't be able to fall back asleep. Not wanting to stare at a computer screen again, he decided to run over to the Hewitt Park to do some outdoor calisthenics. He left the park with the intention of an easy jog back home, but the temperate, humid morning was perfect for a run.

As he slows, the Quinns' garage door starts to open. Alex moves over to the sidewalk on the left side of the road, and stops to let George pull out of the driveway. Rear assist camera systems are standard equipment on most cars, but it's early and the sun hasn't peaked through the deep orange clouds on the low horizon. Alex isn't taking any chances. A Honda Odyssey pulls out of the garage bay. *Not George.* He watches the car back down the driveway and stop even with him at the sidewalk. Sarah Quinn opens the car window.

"Nice run?" she says.

Sarah and her husband are competitive runners well beyond Alex's league. Alex answers, his breathing labored from four faster than anticipated miles of running.

"Yeah. Not bad actually. I felt like I was grinding away all of my remaining knee cartilage for the first ten minutes or so, but I felt pretty strong after that. No run for you guys this morning?"

"Maybe later. I'm heading over to Hannafords. Didn't you read the paper?" she says.

"No. I left the house pretty early. What did it say?"

"The new flu is everywhere. They think there might be upwards of around a hundred cases in Maine. Most of them in Portland. New York City's been hit the hardest on the east coast. Boston's been hit. Hartford. They've known since Thursday night that it's been in the greater Portland area, and nobody said shit. A reporter at The Herald broke the story. It's even worse on the west coast."

"I saw something yesterday morning about the west coast. LA and San Francisco," he says.

"Yeah, they tried to keep it under wraps there, but one of the papers cracked it wide open. Why would the government want to keep this a secret? God damned idiots. They never learn," she says.

"Probably trying to keep panic to a minimum," he says.

"Well they screwed that one. This expert from one of the disease control agencies said that everyone should have at least two weeks of food and essentials on hand. Maybe more. He said that the virus is spreading faster than expected, and that they predict major disruptions to the food supply…and all kinds of other stuff. Saw it on CNN. I think his name was Ocampo. Anyway, we figured the stores would be mobbed. What about you guys? George is going to head over to Lowe's when I get back. You two should head over together and take our pick-up."

"We're actually set right now with food and supplies. Thanks though. You should get as much non-perishable food as possible. Water too. Is your oven propane or electric?"

"Electric," she replies.

She looks slightly annoyed at his brush off and sudden lecture.

"Then George should get as much propane as possible. Small green cans like the kind you use for camping, and a couple of the big ones like for your gas grill. If we lose power, you'll lose your stove. You guys have a camping stove, right?"

"Yeah, and we probably have a bunch of those green propane canisters too."

"Get more. Hey, if George has any questions about stuff to buy, have him give me a call. I sort of did a project on this topic for my company. You should get going. Could you give us a call at the house to let us know what it's like at Hannafords?"

"Sure, I'll give you a ring," she says.

The driver window rises as she pulls the car out of the driveway. She waves as the car accelerates toward Harrison Road. Alex continues walking and turns left at the split in Durham Road, taking the long way around the loop. Alex moves into the street to avoid being soaked by the Burtons' sprinklers. He can't imagine why anyone would still run their sprinkler system this late in the fall. He continues walking on the side of the street and approaches the Murrays' house, which is a standard looking colonial, gray with dark blue doors, and two dormers protruding from the front roofline. Like the Fletchers, the Murrays have a finished walk-up third floor. As Alex walks by the Murrays' house, Greg opens the mudroom door and calls out to Alex. Alex walks up their driveway to meet him and they shake hands.

"Sorry to ambush you like that."

"No worries man. I've certainly seen worse, but nothing like those plaid pajama bottoms. Jesus, I hope nobody sees us out here. I'm a little worried about my reputation," Alex says, staring at his orange, purple, green and brown plaid trousers.

"Thanks jackass. Carolyn got me these for Christmas last year, and I can't exactly throw them away. She gets a little sensitive about presents."

"A long time ago, I told Kate to leave the clothes shopping to me. She used to buy me the same stuff," he says nodding at his pants.

"Want to hear a conspiracy theory?" says Alex.

"You always have a new one brewing," says Greg.

"This one's old. Anyway, I suspect that the wives buy stuff like this to keep the other ladies at bay. Except there's a fatal flaw in their plan," he says.

"Sexy is sexy?" Greg says, and raises both arms to flex his bicep muscles.

"Well, that is true, but their plan backfires when they all buy crap like this at the same time, and we all look equally crappy. Then it all comes down to sexy, where you and I have a considerable advantage. Unfortunately for you, I think Carolyn's trying harder than the other wives."

"I'll let her know your theory. I'm sure Kate would love it too," Greg says.

"Yeah, please don't. Just because she doesn't buy my clothes, doesn't mean she can't control what I wear. She's already told me that I can't leave the house without a collared shirt. I guess when you turn forty; you're no longer allowed to wear t-shirts or a sweatshirt in public. She always pulls out the latest J. Crew catalogue, which appears out of nowhere, and points to the fifty year old, impossibly handsome, gray-haired father of three young children, who is raking leaves in khaki pants and an impeccably clean oxford shirt. Tucked in of course, with a nice belt. And…god forbid, a sweater vest."

"Yeah, sounds familiar. It is futile to resist."

"Pretty much, until I say 'wow, his wife looks almost fifteen years younger than he does.' I usually get clocked over the head with the magazine."

"Living on the edge my friend," Greg says.

"Hey, I have to keep her sharp. So, what dares brings you outside in those pants?"

"Not much, I just wanted to see if you guys already went shopping. Did you see the paper?"

"Not yet, but I heard about it from Sarah Quinn. She's on her way right now," says Alex.

"We saw the evening news, and I thought about what you said the other day, so we both made trips last night to Hannafords. Thanks for the heads up? Sounded a little crazy until last night. Then the news this morning. This thing is all over the country," says Greg.

"Yeah, I meant to call you again last night. I'm glad you got out. We finished the last of our runs yesterday. You might want to consider braving the madness, and hitting the stores again," he says.

"We might. We did it with the kids last night, but I don't think it would be such a good idea if the place is mobbed. I couldn't believe it wasn't more crowded last night. I definitely need to hit Cabela's and Home Depot."

"Me too. Even with all of the shit we have, I still never feel like it's enough. If this thing goes code red, you guys are welcome to ride it out at our house. We have the solar power, the wood burning stove, and plenty of food. Everything we might need, and plenty of it."

"Thanks Alex, but if it gets that bad, I'm pretty sure we're gonna drive to my parents' house outside of Albany. My parents' house is pretty isolated, so we figured we'd hang out there until everything cools off."

"The offer still stands if anything changes," says Alex

"Thanks man, seriously. God knows we'd probably be better off at your house, but we should be fine at my parents. They stick to themselves and still have a functional sixties era nuke shelter in their backyard. They're stocked to the gills over there. I don't think my dad ever bought off on the end of the cold war."

"Sounds like it should be perfect. When do you think you'll make the trip?" says Alex.

"Good question. Carrie's not sure how she can take off from the pharmacy, especially if a lot of people start getting sick. They'll be swamped and probably have to double up on pharmacists."

"She should consider getting out of that pharmacy as soon as possible. Every sick person in the town is going to walk up to that counter. Seriously, that's one of the last places you want her to be. Maybe she could take a few days off to spend at her grandma's bedside," says Alex

A sly smile spreads across Greg's face.

"Not a bad idea. I don't feel comfortable with her at the pharmacy either. Patient zero in Scarborough is guaranteed to fill a script there."

"Yeah, and judging by the apparent spread of confirmed cases, that may be a possibility sooner than you think."

Alex glances at his watch.

"I'm gonna head home so I can get a quick shower before the Today Show."

"Sure thing Alex. I'll catch you later today."

■

Alex leans against the footboard of their sleigh bed, facing the television.

"You're blocking my view," says Kate, propped up by a few pillows.

Alex slides over to the far left side of the footboard as Weekend Today starts.

"Good morning, I'm Amy Robach, with Lester Holt. Welcome to Weekend Today, Saturday, November 3rd, 2012. Overnight, there have been several major developments related to the brewing pandemic, both domestic and abroad. First, yesterday evening, world health officials announced that the flu-like disease spreading like wildfire throughout China, and now starting to hit the rest of the world, is a new H16 subtype. H16N1. Previously, only fifteen influenza subtypes had been discovered in either humans or animals. So far, very little is known about the characteristics of the H16 subtype, aside from reports that the virus is highly contagious among humans.

As a result of these early observations, the World Health Organization increased the pandemic warning level to phase four, officially recognizing that the new virus demonstrates efficient human-to-human transfer. Experts predict that the World Health Organization will soon upgrade the pandemic warning level again, in response to the flu's rapid worldwide spread. So far in our own country, several hundred laboratory confirmed cases of H16N1 have been reported, striking nearly every major city, with New York City and Los Angeles being the hardest hit.

This morning we will hear from the ISPAC's Dr. David Ocampo, who appeared on our network last night, and from Dr. Hans Gustavson, director of the World Health Organization's Infectious Disease department. Both have agreed to appear together and share their most current thoughts regarding the crisis.

In a possibly related story, the Indonesian government just announced a strict travel and communications ban, barring all foreign journalists. Since 2010, strict religious control of media content has cast a thick shadow over Indonesia, and this latest move has launched some speculation regarding a possible major flu outbreak within Indonesian borders."

The camera shifts to Lester Holt.

"Thank you Amy. We are very fortunate to have two highly esteemed world health officials with us this morning, to discuss recent developments. Dr. David Ocampo, from the International Scientific Pandemic Awareness Collaborative, is joining us from his situation room at the headquarters in Atlanta, Georgia; and Dr. Hans Gustafson, a senior director within the World Health Organization, is joining us from his operations center at the United Nations, right here in New York. Gentlemen, thank you both for appearing on our show."

"My pleasure Lester," says Dr. Gustafson.

"Pleased to be here," replies Dr Ocampo.

"First off, the past day or so has brought the fear of a deadly pandemic back into the public spotlight. A novel influenza virus is now confirmed, and the virus is spreading. What is your reaction to the events of the last day and should we be concerned? Dr Gustafson?"

Dr. Gustafson is dressed in a dark gray suit, white shirt and yellow tie. He is fair skinned, with blue eyes and soft, rounded features. His hair is a very light shade of brown. He speaks with a light Dutch accent.

"Thank you Lester. Of course the unfolding events are of great concern to everyone around the globe. However, I must stress that the full capabilities of the WHO, CDC, and other major national health agencies have combined in a synergistic effort to respond and contain this new virus. We are applying all of the lessons learned from 2008, and the WHO's pandemic response capability today, is ten-fold what it was in 2008. The world's pandemic response system is working as it should, and given the information in my possession at this time, I am confident that the situation will remain under control in Asia."

"Dr. Ocampo?" says Lester Holt.

"Well, I wish I shared Dr. Gustafson's optimism this morning, but it appears that we did not wake up on the same planet."

"How so Dr. Ocampo?" asks Lester.

The screen shifts momentarily from Dr. Ocampo to Dr. Gustafson, as the camera registers a look of disgust on Dr. Gustafson's face. The new look stands in stark contrast to his congenial comments moments ago. The screen focuses on Dr. Ocampo.

"I'm not sure where to start. I agree that a massive international response has been initiated, on a scale larger than 2008, however, almost all of those resources are committed to China. It's too late to contain this in China. Up until yesterday, ISPAC field teams were the only teams investigating widespread reports of pulmonary illness outside of China, and these reports are multiplying at an alarming rate. Only one team has failed to report so far, and disturbingly enough, that team gained access to Jakarta more than twenty four hours ago."

"What is holding up their report?" says Lester.

"Actually, we've had no communication with this team since it entered, and have petitioned the United Nations to demand that Indonesia allows this team to report to us. Something is definitely amiss in Indonesia. As a matter of fact, without getting too far ahead of a soon to be released ISPAC update, we are entertaining the very likelihood that Jakarta is the epicenter of the H16 virus."

Dr. Gustafson interrupts.

"Excuse me, but that conclusion is simply not supported by what we currently know. China has by far the largest number of H16N1 cases seen anywhere. We're just not seeing it in similarly large numbers anywhere else in the world. This is why we have allocated the vast majority of our resources to China. To contain the outbreak at its source. This is basic pandemic response procedure, in which the WHO is well versed."

"I'm not casting doubt on the competency of your scientists' work, but based on simulated disease propagation patterns formulated by my department, in which we are also very well versed; Hong Kong International Airport was clearly the primary virus propagation hub. Plenty of international flights depart from dozens of mainland Chinese airports, but the initial cases all started along routes from Hong Kong. In several sites we've identified patients who can be traced back to Jakarta, and in most of these cases, based on progression of disease, we are confident that they were sick when they left Jakarta.

China has a very cozy economic relationship with Indonesia, and is one of very few countries whose citizens enjoy unhampered travel within Indonesia. Maybe because of this relationship, China took on a higher proportion of sick Indonesians than the rest of the Asiatic region," says Dr. Ocampo.

"Once again, we have not seen any data to support your theory," Dr Gustafson insists.

"Regardless of the epicenter, it's clear that the virus is out and spreading. Would you agree with that at least?" he says with a frustrated, brief laugh, and looks to Lester for a reaction.

"I don't think this is an occasion for humor," Dr Gustafson replies.

"You can dodge the question all you'd like, but I have thousands of confirmed cases of a novel, highly contagious, highly pathogenic, pandemic grade flu virus, all over the world. All outside of China. Containment at the epicenter is no longer a viable pandemic response strategy. Mitigation certainly, but not containment."

"If this information has been passed to the WHO, then I assure you that we will process that data, and if appropriate, adjust pandemic the current response strategy. Until then, it would be irresponsible to react to every rumor and theory."

Dr. Ocampo shakes his head and looks down. He looks up a second later, and his face displays true disappointment.

"Dumping all of the world's pandemic response resources in China is a dangerous gamble. Honestly Dr. Gustafson, even if the WHO wanted to reallocate its resources, how could it possibly expect to withdraw from Chinese soil. I think your organization is stuck there, and I hope someone at the WHO wakes up to this predicament before it's too late."

Dr. Gustafson remains composed, but his normally pale face clearly shows the red glow of a mottled rage.

"Gentlemen, let's take a break. We'll be back with Dr. Ocampo and Dr. Gustafson in a moment," says Lester.

Kate mutes the television and Alex runs to the bathroom. When he returns, Kate is sitting on the side of the bed, stretching her arms skyward. She stands up and stretches downward into a forward bend.

"Should we keep the kids home from school at this point forward?" Kate says and rises back up.

"Probably not a bad idea. Turn the volume back on," he says and points at the screen.

"Welcome back to the show. Unfortunately, Dr. Gustafson had to cut the interview short to handle an emergent development; however, in the brief segment before the commercial break, it became clear that two clearly opposing viewpoints exist regarding the current pandemic threat. Where does your organization plan to go from here?"

"Lester, I hope I didn't run Dr. Gustafson out of town, so to say. He is a very brilliant doctor and scientist, but I gather the sense that his true opinions are being held hostage by the overwhelming and overreaching bureaucracy of the WHO. Where do we go from here?

Well, our organization is tiny compared to the WHO, and is mostly an investigative body.

Our main objective is to learn as much as possible about this new virus. We know it's highly contagious. We know it's highly pathogenic, meaning that if you are exposed to it, you are very likely to get sick from it. I'd like to know what happens when the virus takes root in a patient. A behavioral map so to say.

How long does a patient remain asymptomatic with no detectable symptoms? How long after infection does it take for the patient to start spreading the virus? How many hours, or days does a patient shed the virus, while showing no symptoms? This is especially critical, since this is when a patient is most likely to spread the flu.

Then, we want to know about the symptoms, especially the progression of symptoms. Is there an immediate risk of death like that seen in the 1918 Spanish Flu? How long until pulmonary complications arise? Everything. The more we know, the more we can predict and help direct national and international strategy."

"How far away are you from establishing this behavioral timeline?"

"Lester, I believe a rough timeline will be available shortly, possibly in the upcoming press release later this morning. Sorry if I sound like I'm dodging your question. Everything related to H16N1's behavior is very preliminary."

"Dr. Ocampo, before you get back to work in Atlanta, do you have any recommendations for our viewers? Something they can do right now to help prepare and protect their families from the possibility of a deadly pandemic."

"Sure Lester. Individual families can log onto our website and obtain pandemic preparedness checklists, or call our toll free number and this list will be read to the caller by an automated system. The best way to safeguard your family is to execute as many items on those checklists as possible, starting from the top of the checklists. The more important items and tasks are listed first."

"Can you give our viewers more specific advice?"

"Sure, just remember that the lists are detailed, but if you start at the top, you'll hit the most important items. As for specific advice, in a nutshell I would recommend that you buy as much non-perishable food and water as possible and avoid contact with others. That's the quick version Matt. Once again, I urge everyone to visit our website or call our toll free number, which I am being told right now, is displayed at the bottom of your screen."

"Thank you very much Dr. Ocampo. Best of luck to you and your teams. Especially the missing team in Indonesia."

"The pleasure is all mine."

"And now to Karen Hill for our international news update."

Kate turns the TV off.

"NBC seems to love Dr. Ocampo," says Kate.

"Looks like they're the only ones that love him. He just schooled that WHO idiot live on millions of TV sets nationwide. That was great," says Alex.

"That was definitely not a good showing for the WHO. What do you think about the Indonesia link that Ocampo brought up?" she says.

"Who knows. Ever since that place went hardcore Muslim, nobody really knows what's going on there," he says.

Their home phone rings. Alex walks over to the cordless phone charger on Kate's nightstand, and removes the phone. He looks at the caller ID. "Maine call." *I bet that's Sarah calling from Hannafords.* He answers the call.

"Alex Fletcher."

"Hey Alex, it's Sarah. Hannafords is mobbed. I wouldn't even bother trying to head over here. It'll be empty in a few hours. Really unbelievable. It was a madhouse. When I left, every single cart was gone, and at least a dozen people rushed me while I was loading groceries into the minivan. It was scary. I've never seen anything like it.

They have two police cruiser parked in front of the store with their lights flashing. I think it's the only thing keeping situation from falling apart. They need more. Anyway, I just wanted to call and let you know. I wouldn't bother right now. There was a line of cars extending at least a mile down Route One. It's a total mess."

"Thanks for calling Sarah. Are you sure you're alright? You sound a bit rattled."

Alex meets Kate's glance. Kate's raised eyebrows and flat smirk say "So what." Alex covers the phone with his hand.

"Just trying to be nice. It sounds pretty fucked up over at there. Cops and everything," he whispers.

He raises his finger to keep Kate from responding.

"No, I'm fine. I've just never seen people acting that way before. It was fine when I arrived, but the store filled up within minutes. Crazy."

"Alright Sarah, let us know if you and George need help with anything. OK?"

"Sure, thanks Alex. Say hi to Kate for me."

"Will do. Later."

Alex disconnects the call.

"She said every cart was being used, and that a mob of people followed her out of the store to get her cart."

"Jesus," she says.

"I can't wait to see what it's like out there. I have to admit, this is kinda exciting. You got gas right?"

"Yesterday," she says.

"Good. I'm going to start moving the wood into the garage today, and make a few trips out to buy some essentials."

"Like Xbox games and HDVD's?"

"I think those count as essential," he replies.

"Do we have any cash?" she asks.

"Not yet. We have $16,000 in our money market. I can take that out any time I want. I can also borrow against our 401k and get a money wire into our checking account. If nothing happens, I'll redeposit the money in our Fidelity account. Call it a reallocation of investments. The market hasn't done shit for us this year anyway."

"That'll be weird having big money like that stashed around the house," Kate says.

"Mafia weird. Big money rolls stuffed in our pockets weird," Alex jokes.

"Yeah, but with nothing to spend it on."

"How about a boat?" says Alex.

"Nice try," she says, and starts to walk toward the bathroom.

Chapter Nine

Saturday, November 3, 2012

Alex approaches Hannaford's from the direction of the Maine Mall. The back of his Subaru is filled with "essential" items from Home Depot and Best Buy. Alex left the Maine Mall slightly disappointed, since neither store was mobbed like Alex had predicted, or secretly hoped. He was less than a minute away from finding out why.

As Alex approaches a point about one mile down the road from the Hannaford's Plaza, traffic starts to slow. The oncoming lane is devoid of traffic, so Alex pulls over a few feet into the lane to get a better view down the road. He sees a police cruiser with flashing lights near the only turnoff before Hannafords, at Copley Road. *This is for Hannafords? Fuck.*

"That's where everyone is?" he whispers.

Alex got the idea to check out the Hannafords parking lot on the way back, but he had just planned to scan the lot and continue to Route One. Now, Alex wonders if he can even get through to Route One on this road. *Maybe they have a bypass lane set up.*

The traffic comes to a halt a few hundred yards from the police cruiser. *Come on, I really don't need this right now.* Alex laughs out loud at this thought, because he really doesn't have anywhere to be at the moment, and he could have chosen from several other routes taking him far clear of this Hannafords.

"I did this to myself," he mumbles.

After several minutes of mindlessly tapping the steering wheel, Alex decides that he doesn't need to sit in traffic any longer, especially since he's not part of the Hannafords rush. The police cruiser sits at the Copley Road intersection, which can be used as a detour to Route One, and Alex is sure he can talk his way through to the turnoff. Alex pulls his car out into the oncoming lane, and starts to slowly roll toward the cruiser at the intersection. He now sees that the cruiser is not actually blocking the intersection, and that its occupant is standing at the far end of the intersection talking with the driver of a gray sedan. The police officer detects Alex's car and immediately turns in his direction. *I hope this guy's not too pissed off today.*

As Alex continues to move past the cars to his right, a black Suburban lurches out from the line of cars to block his path. *Jesus!* Caught off guard, he jams his foot down on the brake, bringing his own vehicle to an immediate stop about five feet from the enormous truck. His iPhone flies off the front passenger seat to the floor of the car, and he feels the contents of the cargo area shift and hit the back of his seat. The Suburban is positioned at a forty five degree angle to his car, blocking most of the oncoming lane. The front driver window opens, and Alex opens his own to apologize and explain what he's doing.

A young woman with blond hair, possibly in her early thirties, leans her head out of the window and screams at him.

"Where the fuck do you think you're going? Get back in line and wait like everyone else. Who the fuck do you think you are?"

Alex hears a similar sentiment from a few of the other cars to his right. A scowling man, in a small black sedan right next to him, is waving emphatically and yelling. Alex has no intention of lowering his passenger window to hear the tirade.

Alex addresses the woman in the suburban with a loud authoritative voice.

"I'm not going to Hannafords. I'm turning left at Copley. Nice mouth."

"I don't give a shit where you think you're going. You won't have any luck getting in from that direction either. I've been dealing with this for nearly two hours, so back the fuck off."

She pulls her head into the car momentarily to yell into the tinted darkness behind her.

"I told you all to shut up. We'll get there when we get there."

Mom of the year. Alex feels his adrenaline start to surge, and he wants to escalate the argument. *Calm down. Nothing to gain from it.*

She puts her head back out as the police officer appears in front of her truck. Alex can hear him tell her to roll up her window and get back to the other side of the road. He walks up to Alex's window.

"I'm really sorry officer, I just wanted to get to the intersection so I could take a detour and get home. I'm sorry I caused a little stir."

"Not a problem. There's been a run on the Hannaford's. Started around seven this morning, and got worse. Wait until that lady moves her truck, and continue to the intersection. Make sure you take a left. There's no way to get through to Route One anyway, and I can tell you for a fact that nobody will let you through the line to try it. It's getting ugly out here. Hannaford's ran dry within a couple of hours, but there's a rumor that they're dispatching some more trucks today. That's what everyone's waiting for. Wishful thinking if you ask me."

"Thanks Officer…Patrick," he says glancing at the officer's name badge. "Good luck today. Looks like you might need it."

"You said it. It's going to be a long one. All shifts are working. You better get moving. Semper Fi."

"Yeah, Semper Fi," Alex replies, having forgotten about the U.S. Marine Corps stick affixed to his rear left passenger window. *No wonder he didn't reach in a throttle me for being stupid.* Alex moves past the black Suburban, and slowly approaches the intersection. A few more cars angrily honk at him, until he turns left. He gives Officer Patrick a "thumbs up" as he completes the turn. *Pretty soon, you're going to need more than luck. More like riot gear.*

■

Alex rinses his plate in the sink and gingerly sets it down on top of a small pile of precariously balanced dishes in the sink basin.

"Feel free to put that in the dishwasher," says Kate from an unseen location in the great room.

"The kids didn't," he says.

"Do I even need to dignify that with a response?" she says.

"Oz has spoken," he says, and opens the dishwasher, which is jam packed with clean dishes.

"Son of a…"

"Oh, is the dishwasher clean?" she says, and Alex detects an antagonistic tone in her voice.

"One of these days Alice. One of these days," he mumbles.

"What was that? I couldn't hear you," she says.

"I was just commenting on what a delightful surprise it is to discover the dishwasher full, and ready to be emptied. A dream come true."

"This particular dream comes true for me so often, I decided it would be selfish of me not to share it with you today," she says.

"Thank you so very much for your consideration. Anyway, I'll take care of it after I talk to my parents," he says, and sits down at the kitchen island.

"You must really not want to empty the dishwasher."

"Funny," he says, and picks up the cordless.

"Not in here please. I'd like to unwind without you pacing around the house all stressed out."

"Not a problem. Hey, can you call Sam on your cell and make sure that the kids don't stray over to the McDaniels'? Matt and Jamie work in the schools, and I would just feel better if we kept a little separation from them. For now at least," he says.

"Can't you call?" she says.

"I don't like making calls like that. You're better at these touchy situations," he says, and starts to slink away toward the stairs.

"Better at the dirty work, you mean," she says, and he hears her get up from the couch.

"I'll take a walk over to the Walkers'. I could use some sun. Have fun on your call," she says.

"Oh, I'm sure it will be a blast. Thanks hon," he says, and vanishes up the stairs.

He settles into his office chair, and dials his parents' home number. His mother answers.

"Hey mom, what are you guys up to?"

"Well, your dad just got back from the grocery store. Lucky he got there earlier in the morning. He said there was a line of cars stretching back something like two miles when he drove home. One of your dad's golf buddies was over near the Dunkin Donuts and saw the mob start to form at Albertsons. Thankfully, he called your dad."

"Same thing is happening here. I just drove by a line that was nearly a mile long."

"This is insane Alex. I still don't see why everyone is so riled up right now. We watched the news last night, and they said that the flu was unlikely to get past immigration authorities in great enough numbers to drive a crisis."

"Please tell me you didn't hear this on FOX news?"

"Fox news is fine. This was a senior official from DHS, not some unemployed expert from one of the other networks. This came right from the source."

"Alright, well I'm glad you guys got to the store. You should get more food if you can. Where's dad now?"

"He ran out to Home Depot. He just called and said that it was mobbed, but not as bad as Albertsons."

"Mom, you guys should consider coming out here if things get really bad. Regardless of what you hear on FOX, I don't think the government will be able to contain this on any level. The head of Maine Medical Center's infectious disease department agrees."

"Yeah, but the DHS guy last night said that they are keeping tabs on everyone that comes into the country, even if they don't show symptoms," she replies.

"Do you really believe they can pull that off? What about the hundreds of people they come in contact with within the first few hours of arrival? Are they going to investigate all of them too? This isn't just coming at us from Asia anymore. It's global. Any passenger, on any plane from anywhere in the world could be infected."

"Well, there's only so much that can be done, and at a certain point, you just have to deal with it." *Throw the towel in mom.*

"I agree, that's why you two need to take a trip to see your grandkids. If the situation out there deteriorates, you'll be in the best place to weather the storm. You still have the TerraFlu that I sent, right?"

"Oh yes, it's still in the upstairs bathroom closet. We don't need to take that yet, do we?" *I think I've been over this ten times with them.*

"No, not yet mom. If you experience flu-like symptoms, then you should start taking it. Fever, headache, exhaustion, congestion. I'm going to send you an email with a self-assessment guide. You won't remember all of this."

"Sounds good. How are the kids doing?" *She's not even listening.*

"You really should ask them yourself, like within the next few days," he says, and then relents.

"They're doing great. Ryan is having an amazing cross country season. He can almost outpace me on runs, and he's probably the fastest sixth or seventh grader on the team. And Emily is in the middle of the fall soccer season, and she wants to start running like Ryan. Between the two of them, we're being pulled in every direction."

"What does Kate think about all this flu stuff." *What?*

"Does she think you're overreacting too? She's been the voice of reason in the family since you got back from Iraq. I still think the war made you a little paranoid. Sorry to say it, but it's true."

"Thanks for the psych eval mom, I'll pass it along to the doctors. And for the record, she's more worried than I am," says Alex.

"Well, she probably doesn't want to upset you." *What does that mean?*

"Really mom, you guys should consider coming out. Make it your annual trip. If nothing happens in the next few weeks or so, you can go home having enjoyed the kids, and one of the best times of the year to visit Maine. The leaves are turning, and the weather's been great. Lodging is free, and we can take a couple of trips up north to check out the colors."

"I'll talk to your dad about it again. If things get really bad, we'll seriously think about it. I don't think your brother will consider it though."

"Who said he was invited? Just kidding Mom. Hey don't let him make the decision for you. He chose to work nearly two hours away in Denver, and Karla isn't exactly helpless." *Well, she's close to helpless*

"Things are hectic for them. They're both extremely busy with their jobs and the kids are busy with sports and school activities."

"What do you think we have going on over here?" says Alex.

"If you guys were closer, we'd help you too."

"I think **Danny** is a little too focused on a big salary, and way too dependent on your support. I can think of other terms for it, but I promised Kate I wouldn't bitch about it with you guys. Anyway, I can feel my blood pressure skyrocketing. Bottom line, they can deal with their own kids for a couple weeks without your help."

"We'll see how things go. I'm willing to bet this whole thing will clear up in a few weeks, just like the Swine Flu. A trip sounds nice, but…"

"I know. Danny and Karla need more time to figure out how to take care of their own kids. Sorry. I promised I wouldn't. Anyway, just don't wait too long mom. I think the situation has the potential to deteriorate very quickly. Think about it and let me know. You guys are always welcome out here, and so are my brother and his family. Love you guys."

"Love you too Alex. Give Kate and the kids a hug for me."

"Will do mom," he replies and disconnects the call. *They aren't taking any of this seriously.*

■

Alex sweats profusely. In just under one hour, he has hauled roughly one third of their firewood into the garage. Two cords of firewood were dumped on their driveway in late August, and with the reluctant help of his son, he finished stacking the wood along the outside back wall of the garage by the middle of September. *Sometimes I wish I was a hard core procrastinator.*

He grabs another oversized stack of wood, and starts the grueling trek around the side of the garage. As soon as he clears the rear corner of the garage, he sees Charles Thornton walking over from his house across the street. Alex picks up the pace, hoping to disappear into the garage bay before he arrives.

Alex has made a practice of tactfully avoiding Charlie Thornton as much as possible. He has painfully learned that any conversation lasting more than three minutes with Charlie, will inevitably shift to the politics of hunting, and the liberal conspiracy to deny his children the right to enjoy a tradition on which this nation was founded.

Alex approaches the front corner of the garage, and looks up at Charlie, who is clearly headed over to talk to him. *Unavoidable. God damn it.* Alex enters the garage bay, and places the wood on a neat stack along the outside wall of the garage, furthest away from the mudroom door. *Two cords are going to jam this garage shut.*

Charles is half way up the driveway as Alex emerges from the garage.

"Hey Charles. Not tromping around the woods today?" Alex says, wiping his forehead.

"Shit, I wish. Linda's still at the office, trying to unscrew the temp situation at National Semi. Three of them walked off the job yesterday. Unannounced. I still have no idea why, but if we don't get some replacements in there by Monday, we could lose our contract with them. We have at least thirty floating around there.

Anyway, we heard about the crowds at the stores, so I took off to try and get some grocery shopping done. I started over at Sam's Club. Forget it. I couldn't get close to the place. Same story at Hannafords and Shaws. Did you manage to get to any of these stores today? Linda and I have been so busy at the office that we never made our weekly shopping run. Our house is empty. Looks like we're eating out tonight." *Like every night. I don't think Linda cooks much.*

"Yeah, you and the rest of the town. I couldn't get near Hannafords this morning. Drove by around eleven, and the line was over a mile long just to get into the parking lot. That's just in one direction. We have enough stuff on hand for now," Alex says uncomfortably.

"I heard they closed all of the Hannafords stores in the area. Picked clean by ten. I'm worried about getting my dad's meds. They should at least keep the pharmacy open at Hannafords. All I need are some refills."

"You should ask Greg Murray about that. His wife might be able to hook you up. She's a pharmacist over at the Scarborough Hannafords," says Alex. *Sorry Greg.*

"That's right. Do you know if they're home?"

"Carolyn might be home right now if the store is closed," says Alex.

"I'll have to check. So why are you stacking your wood inside the garage. Don't you normally keep it out back?" he asks. *What dragged you all the way over here Charlie?*

"Well, ever since we put in the wood burning stove, we make a lot more trips to get wood. Kate hates going outside to grab the wood, so I figured if it was inside the garage, she'd keep the fire going, and quit turning up the thermostat." *Outright lie.*

"You gonna move it all inside?" he says.

"I don't think so. We won't go through two cords this winter. Barely burned through one last year. But who knows what the boss will want," says Alex.

"Wives. Give them whatever they want right? Well, I gotta get back to the house and figure out dinner. Probably need a reservation to get in somewhere tonight. Hey, if I can't get into a restaurant, you might hear the thunder of one of my rifles. I've seen fresh signs of deer in the woods back by the park." *A little more than three minutes this time.*

"No worries here. I've been on the receiving end of blasts that could make your ears bleed." *Or tear your limbs off.*

"I bet. You ever do any sniping? That's the ultimate hunting in my book." *Is he serious?*

"No, but we routinely had snipers assigned to our battalion. They didn't seem to enjoy their job much."

"Hell, I'd give anything to trade places with them for a few hours."

"I don't know. Nothing out there shoots back," Alex says and glances toward the trees north of the neighborhood.

They both look at each other for a second, and Alex feels like he's being sized up.

"Yeah, maybe not. Anyway, have a good night Alex. I'll catch you later," he says, and starts walking back down the driveway.

"You too Charlie," replies Alex.

He returns to the wood stacked behind the garage. *Definitely gonna keep an eye on Private Pyle over there.*

■

Alex steps out onto the mudroom stoop and looks around for Kate. He doesn't see her in the front yard, so he heads down the driveway. He spots her four houses down, petting a chocolate lab in the Coopers' driveway. Alex approaches Kate and leans down to pet the Coopers' dog Max, who starts to wiggle and squirm his way over to Alex, stopping short to roll over onto his back. Kate stands upright as Alex rubs Max's chest.

"Very good boy. Yes you are. Any sign of Paul and Nancy?" he says without looking up at Kate.

Kate leans in a rubs Max's neck.

"No. I thought I saw their car drive by our house on the way out...maybe an hour ago?" she says.

Alex stands up and takes in the trees. His eyes strain in the direction of the Thorntons', without turning his head.

"Let's get rolling before we attract some unwanted attention," he says, and nods toward Charlie's house.

Kate looks over at the Thorntons' house.

"Jesus Christ. Don't look!" he whispers forcefully.

"What are you in third grade? None of their cars are out. They never park in the garage," she says.

"I'd just like to get off the block unmolested," he says, and the start to walk briskly toward the other side of the Durham Road loop.

They continue to walk through the loop, passing the Murrays' and the Bishops' houses to their right. Alex catches some movement in his peripheral vision from the Santoses' yard, on the other side of the street, but nobody calls out to them. They pass by the Cohens' house, also on the left, and see that both of their cars are fully packed. One of the cars has a top carrier, which is open and halfway stuffed with duffel bags. They both pick up the pace to get by the Cohens' house.

"They don't have any immediate family down here right?" Kate asks.

"I was just thinking the same thing. I think Margaret's parents are retired and live up near Bar Harbor," he says, still thinking about it.

"Yes, that's right. Her parents own a huge place on the water up there. They spend a few weeks each summer up there, and most of the weekends," she says.

"Looks like they're taking off," he says.

They continue walking toward Harrison Road, where they plan to turn right and connect with Everett Lane. Everett Lane runs parallel to their neighborhood, and connects with several other streets behind their subdivision. This is one of their favorite walks, which takes them a few miles through surrounding neighborhoods, and eventually connects with Hewitt Park. Several foot trails extend for miles through the land trust preserve surrounding the park, but Alex and Kate usually turn around once they reach the park.

As they approach Harrison Road, a black Toyota Sienna mini-van careens onto Durham Road, barely making the turn ahead of a red sedan on Harrison Road. The mini-van's tires squeal.

"What the fuck," Alex exclaims, pushing Kate slightly off the sidewalk onto the Quinns' lawn, and putting himself between the van and his wife. Alex quickly recognizes the Perry's van as it approaches, still moving way too fast for a neighborhood road. He sees Todd behind the wheel of the van as it closes the distance. *I really hope he keeps going. No luck.* The van slows as it pulls parallel to the Fletchers. The window is already down.

"Can you believe this shit?" Todd yells at them.

"What's going on Todd? Is everything alright?" Kate asks, almost sounding overly concerned.

"No. I've been all over Portland and it's the same story. I guess you have to get up at fucking five in the morning to get groceries now," he says, barely below the level of screaming.

"Yeah, I think from this point on, you might be right," says Alex.

"What am I supposed to do, camp out with my entire family? Four kids in a minivan, just so we can fill up a cart full of groceries. They have to figure something else out. Not everyone can afford to sit around Hannaford's all day," he replies, his tone calming down slightly.

"Todd, why don't you have Susan give me a call. We can watch your kids for a few hours in the morning, and you can both head over really early. Take separate cars, get in line separately, then you can play a little catch up and get two loads of groceries. Don't go together. They won't let you grab two carts if they see you're together," says Kate.

"They, who the fuck are they? Some punk ass kid at Hannafords?" he says loudly.

"No. The police. Nancy Cooper saw the cops break up a couple trying to load two carts into one car," Kate says.

"Jesus. It's a fucking police state already. Hey, sorry to bite your heads off. I'm just a little frustrated by all of this nonsense. I appreciate the offer to watch the kids. We may take you up on it. I'm gonna have Sue call her parents, maybe they can drive down from Augusta tonight and help us out. Thanks. I've been so pissed off, I can barely think straight," he says calmly.

"Just keep us in mind Todd. We've got nothing planned for tomorrow, so it's really no big deal for one of us to head over and keep the kids company, or you can pack them up in their pajamas and herd them over to our house. I'll feed them pancakes," offers Alex.

"Thanks guys. I'll run it by Susan," he says.

"We might be out tonight for dinner, so leave a message and we'll call you when we get back," says Alex.

"Thanks again guys. I'll give you a call later," he says.

"See ya Todd," says Kate.

Todd accelerates the van to a reasonable speed and makes a controlled turn toward his house. Alex and Kate start walking again.

"Loose cannon alert," she says. "Susan told me he had a short temper."

"Confirmed. Are you really gonna get up at the ass crack of dawn to watch their kids?"

"Oh I'm not getting up. You are?"

"That's what I thought," he says.

They turn on Harrison Road and walk holding hands toward Everett Lane. A chilly breeze sifts through the towering maple and oak trees along Harrison Road, sending a cascade of dried yellow, red and brown leaves to the ground.

■

The Fletchers' Subaru crosses the Casco Bay Bridge, headed away from Portland. Traffic is surprisingly light, and Alex takes a moment to look left, across the oncoming lanes, He stares out into the Casco Bay. Lights sprinkled across Peak's Island are barely visible, giving the island a sparsely populated feel. Indeed, at this time of the year, the island holds fewer than a thousand residents, and the number decreases every week as seasonal home owners retreat to the mainland for the harsh winter.

As their car continues, the view of Peaks Island is washed out by the blazing deck lights of a massive petroleum carrier docked at the oil terminal on the northern tip of South Portland's industrial waterfront.

Alex feels bloated from dinner. He could have stopped with a nice salad after the appetizers, but the allure of seared ahi tuna was too much to resist. Kate made a similarly delicious but regrettable decision, choosing the citrus glazed salmon. Both of them ride in silence across the bridge. As they crest the bridge and start to descend, they see two police cars at the first intersection. The cruisers' roof lights flash a light blue warning to the approaching cars.

As they draw closer, Alex gains a clear picture of the situation at the bottom of the bridge. The police cruisers are positioned to barricade the two lanes of forward traffic, leaving just enough room for vehicles to drift into the far right turn lane. A police officer stands adjacent to the far right cruiser, motioning traffic toward the turn with a red illuminated wand. As their car approaches the police officer, Alex slows the car to a stop and lowers his window.

"Evening officer. What's going on down there?"

The officer leans down with a serious expression, takes a look around the car, and then settles his eyes on Alex. His glare softens, erasing any trace of anxiety from the encounter.

"Nothing to be worried about. We have about three to four hundred cars jammed into the Shaw's and Hannaford's lots, waiting for tomorrow. Lots of people roaming the lots, eating at McDonalds, ordering Dominos. A regular zoo down there. We tried to move them out of there, but it became pretty apparent that nobody planned to go anywhere. Not much we can do right? We're just trying to keep any more cars from jamming into those areas. We're gonna be up all night walking those lots."

"Well, if it's any consolation, I hope you have a relatively uneventful evening," says Alex.

"Thanks, though I'm not very optimistic at this point," the officer says, and tips his hat toward Alex.

Alex raises the window and slowly turns onto Broadway Avenue. He turns left at the next stop light and heads toward Scarborough.

"That's a little creepy," he says.

"Do you think people are really going to sleep in their cars all night?" Kate asks.

"I guess, though I can't imagine what it'll be like in that parking lot at about 2:30 in the morning. It won't take much to turn one of those parking lots into a mob, or a free-for-all. Especially when the Hannaford trucks start rolling in. I think the police will have their hands full."

"What's happening dad?" Ryan asks in a groggy tone.

"I thought you guys were asleep," Alex responds.

"Emily's out," answers Ryan.

"The police officer said that the parking lots at Shaws and Hannafords were full of cars waiting for the stores to reopen in the morning. People have been waiting all day to get food, and they probably ran out at some point today. The police are directing everyone away from the area."

"Why are they all trying to get more food? Don't they have enough by now?" he asks.

"A lot of people are a little worried about the flu pandemic causing a long term food shortage, so they rushed to stock up on groceries, all at once, and the stores weren't prepared for that many customers at one time. Most of the stores ran out of food items early in the day and had to close, which makes people even more nervous."

"Where do the stores get their food?" he asks.

"Large distribution centers somewhere around here I guess. The centers pack up those large Hannafords semi's and send them out every day," she says.

"Yeah," says Ryan says, and Alex senses that he is fading away.

Far down the road, they see the flashing blue lights of a police car approaching them from the opposite direction. Alex instinctively slows the car, even though their car's speed was already within the speed limit. The police car approaches them, and speeds by, heading in the direction of the shopping complex.

"Was that a Scarborough cop?" Kate asks.

"I don't know. The car was going too fast. They all look the same," responds Alex.

"Why would it be the Scarborough police? We aren't in Scarborough yet," says Ryan.

"Good point, though if it was a Scarborough cop, then it might indicate a real problem back at Mill Creek. I think that's why your mom asked," says Alex.

Kate looks at him uneasily and nods in agreement. For the remaining ten minutes of the trip home, they ride in silence.

Chapter Ten

Sunday, November 4, 2012

Alex sits alone in his office, surfing through several bookmarked websites. Sweat drips off his face, and he wipes it onto his T-shirt with a sweep of his left arm. The gesture does little since his entire gray T-shirt is drenched with sweat. He opens the office windows and walks to the bathroom to grab a towel.

Alex woke up at seven for a light run, but once again found the weather irresistible. As promised by local meteorologists, warm, humid air from Hurricane Terrence continues to pour into New England, bringing unseasonably warm temperatures. Alex checked their thermometer and found that it was already sixty two degrees in the shade on their deck. Stepping outside, moist, salty air filled his lungs, and he felt like their neighborhood had been transported to Florida. One hour later, he returned to their neighborhood, with the complete understanding that he would pay for it later. He hadn't run more than forty minutes in several months. Adding twenty minutes nearly killed him.

He skims several stories. "China cuts off all contact between international community and WHO teams…no communications with any of their team in China for nearly fourteen hours…action possibly taken in response to WHO request for teams to redeploy from China…China responds to growing coalition of nations acting outside of U.N. authority…will respond militarily to defend sovereignty. Last known figures from China…total cases 820,000…total deaths estimated 39,000…Case Fatality Rate 21%...ARDS account for over half of known deaths."

Alex jumps over to the ISPAC Pandemic Map, which he keeps minimized for quick access. The map of China shows expanded red and violet areas, growing inward from the coast all the way east to Fuzhou. Shanghai and Qingdao, two major coastal cities, sit in areas shaded red. The greater Beijing area is colored orange, with a several small red dots indicating medium cluster outbreaks within the area. Alex places the cursor over the China icon.

"China. Population 1,350,678,400. Massive outbreak. 820,000 reported cases. Concentrated WHO effort to contain outbreak unsuccessful. WHO teams status unknown due to communications blackout imposed by Chinese government. Uncontained."

Alex goes back to the news articles.

"Indonesia to allow full WHO and U.N. support…submits formal apology to U.N. for treatment of inspection teams…pleads for immediate assistance…deaths estimated at 73,000…over 2 million cases of Jakarta Flu." *How did they figure that out?*

"More cases of Jakarta Flu appearing in major European cities…London confirms several hundred cases…" *Now it's the Jakarta Flu.*

Alex opens another windows web browser and types the words Jakarta, survey team and ISPAC into Google. He opens the first listed link. "U.S. Special Forces rescue ISPAC survey team." *That might explain some things.*

By Jered Gillian (Associated Press Writer)
From Associated Press

November 3, 2012 7:32 PM EDT

JAVA SEA – Aboard USS MESA VERDE LPD-19. U.S. Navy public affairs officers released scant details about a "high risk rescue operation," conducted in the pre-dawn hours within sight of the Jakarta skyline. Navy officials confirmed the safe recovery of the five member survey team sent nearly four days ago to investigate reports of a disease outbreak in Jakarta. ISPAC officials lost all contact with the team upon arrival at the Soekarno-Hatta International Airport in Jakarta.

Around 2 AM local time, a U.S. destroyer transiting through the area, picked up a distress signal indicating that the inspection team was aboard a civilian vessel headed to open water. Navy officials say that an immediate rescue mission was launched from USS MESA VERDE, involving both Navy and Marine Corps special operations assets.

"The joint Navy and Marine Corps team planned and executed a flawless rescue operation, under considerable time constraints, while facing numerous unknown variables," reported LCDR Terrence Hill.

ISPAC epidemiologists suspect the possibility that Indonesia may be the epicenter of the recent H16N1 pandemic outbreak. Information carried by this team may shed important light on that theory.

Navy officials declined to comment whether the Amphibious Task Force's primary mission in the area involved recovery of the missing ISPAC team.

He returns to the minimized browser to scan some domestic articles.

"Current food shortages are being addressed by administration officials, as the nation is plagued by inadequacies in the food supply chain. City and State legislators are pleading with the administration to allow emergency funds to be released so that local governments can augment local law enforcement to deal with the crisis. Dozens of injuries and deaths nationwide have been attributed to the food shortages. Funds would also be used to help local food distributors take the drastic steps needed to boost the supply system, and get distribution back on track…"

"Department of Health and Human Services officials are on the lookout for suspected Jakarta Flu cases in the U.S., and urge anyone with flu like symptoms to report to the nearest hospital for testing. So far, DHS implemented border protocols appear effective, though many organizations, including the CDC, ISPAC and dozens of legislators, have accused DHS of not doing enough…"

Alex switches to the Pandemic Map again, and pans over to Europe. He sees several dozen major European cities with Yellow icons, and hundreds of light blue icons spread throughout Europe. He notices the same trend continuing throughout western Asia, Russia, the Middle East and Africa. Mostly yellow icons, for light or isolated clusters, though Lebanon contains an orange icon. Alex passes the cursor over the icon.

"Beirut. Population 2,432,580. Small cluster outbreak. 580 cases. Haret Hreik neighborhood outbreak epicenter. Uncontained."

Alex moves the cursor further south over Israel. He notices a few light blue icons throughout Israel in coastal cities. Haifa, Tel Aviv and Gaza City.

"Israel. Population 7,745,930. Suspected/Isolated cases. 12 cases. Israeli government closed borders to all foreign travelers. Strict quarantine and border protocol procedures in effect. Contained."

Alex goes back to the other open webpage, and calls up the Google page. He then types in "Israel and Jakarta Flu." What he sees does not surprise him.

"Israel's parliament unanimously supported the immediate closure of Israel's borders, in response to the developing Jakarta Flu threat. Only Israeli citizens or Jewish descendants will be admitted, pending quarantine and anti-viral treatment." "In a controversial move, Israel's parliament did not include the West Bank as part of the internal Israeli quarantine zone. Parliamentary leaders cited the extreme difficulty with controlling entry into the West Bank, and other security concerns, as their primary reasons for the decision. The entire Israeli military has been mobilized and placed on high alert, tasked with enforcing the quarantine on all borders. Reserve military units have been activated to assist with domestic quarantine efforts." *Tough bastards.*

"That's it for me," Alex announces, as he rises from the chair to check on the rest of his family.

He really didn't need to check on Ryan. He'd be shocked to find him awake. He never expects to see him before 10 AM on weekends anymore. Emily is a different story. She usually gets up at the same time on weekends as she does during the week. Sometimes earlier. Alex peeks into both of their rooms to confirm that they are still asleep. Ryan is buried in his covers, his dark hair barely poking out of the top of the blankets. He pushes open Emily's door, and walks a few feet into her room, then peeks around the corner at her. She has tossed all of her covers off, but still looks solidly asleep. Both rooms are dark, with the shades pulled tight.

Alex walks down the hallway to the master suite, and peers around the corner. Like Ryan, Kate is buried in covers, her long black hair spilling out from the top of the blankets onto her pillow. He can hear her breathing deeply. Unlike the kids' rooms, their room is bathed in light. Kate likes to rise naturally with the sun, or at least she claims to like it. Alex can't remember the last time she woke up within three hours of dawn, especially during the summer months, when the sun starts rising at four-thirty. *Looks like I have the house to myself.* Alex backtracks to the master bathroom and starts the shower.

■

As Alex pours pancake batter onto a non-stick frying pan, he hears someone walking down the stairs. He can immediately tell that it's Kate by the creak of the stairs.

"Good morning my love. You're right on time." he says without turning around.

She takes the final step down onto the hardwood floor in front of the stairs and responds.

"How did you know it wasn't Ryan?" she inquires.

Alex senses a trap.

"I can just tell," he says, not taking the bait.

"Alright…just as long as you're not implying anything about my weight," she says.

"Nope. Everyone has their own unique signature coming down the stairs. Ryan sounds like he is stumbling down after being shot. Emily takes three years to descend. I fly down the stairs, and you glide gracefully with a purpose," he says, smugly.

"Don't push it," she says, moving directly for the coffee maker.

"Pancakes. Yummy. And the coffee is made. You're my hero. How many times a week can we have pancakes?" she asks.

He flips the pancakes over and steps away from the stove to give her a hug and a kiss.

"Do you mean if we go into quarantine, or in general? Because in general, I could eat them every morning, but in quarantine, we're probably looking at no more than once a week," he says, still holding her.

"Maybe one of us should stand in line at the store and just buy pancake ingredients," she says, and he can't tell if she's serious or joking.

He lets go of her, and returns to the stove to take the pancakes off the pan. He puts them under tin foil on a large plate to the left of the stove, on the granite counter.

"Actually, after today, I think we're done visiting public spaces, or interacting with other people. Did you check the ISPAC map?" he says while pouring another batch of pancakes onto the frying pan. The oil around the edges of the pancakes sizzles when the batter hits the pan.

"No, I just came straight down when I smelled the pancakes," she says.

"They've named it the Jakarta Flu, so I guess they're fairly certain that the epicenter is in Jakarta. The Navy rescued the missing ISPAC team from Indonesian waters. Based on the flu casualty predictions I saw in one of the articles, I can understand why they Mullahs didn't want them snooping around. The estimate I saw was two million cases."

"Are you kidding me?" says Kate.

"No. That's why I think today is our last day out and about. The numbers are rising very rapidly here and abroad. It's already out of control."

"Hey, I'm good with starting our quarantine right now," she says, taking a coffee mug down from the cabinet.

"I think we should let them hang out with their friends today, and call it good. That way we can start the quarantine on a better note. Emily has a play date set up with Jessica, and I think Ryan is planning to invite Connor and Daniel over today. That should be fine."

"I don't know, what if Jessica's uncle visited them last night, after shopping at the Shaw's in Falmouth, right behind the wife of the guy, or the sister of the guy who's in the hospital…"

"I understand what you're saying," he says calmly, "but I feel confident we'll be fine letting her go over there. She can wash her hands a lot. It'll be fine. Let both of them enjoy the day. It's beautiful out," he says, pointing out of the windows over the kitchen sink.

"Alright. I'll talk to Elaine and make sure they wash their hands a lot. Maybe she'll cancel the play date," she suggests.

"Maybe, but don't count on it. Even if she does, Emily will find another. At least Jessica's parents seem pretty responsible," he says.

"Yeah, I guess. Are some of the pancakes ready? I don't feel like waiting another hour for the kids."

"Almost. If you set the table, I'll pour a few more."

"Deal. Hey, did you see any cars in front of the Perry's this morning," she asks, having just spotted the Sunday paper.

"No, I checked on my way out for a run at about seven, then again an hour later. I walked out about ten minutes ago, pretending to check the mailbox, and still nothing."

"What the hell are they thinking?"

"I don't know, maybe they all went out shopping together," he suggests weakly.

"With four kids? I doubt it," she says.

"Loose cannon alert?" he says.

"More like idiot alert," she responds.

Quarantine

Chapter Eleven

Monday, November 5, 2012

Alex finishes the last four pull-ups of his pyramid exercise routine, and stares out at the sunrise through the northeastern window of their finished attic. The low horizon sky holds a scattered pattern of wispy clouds that reflect a deep burnt orange color from the still hidden sun. A deep blue and violet sky towers over the clouds, still holding on to the brightest stars in the eastern sky.

Alex stretches for about five minute, and heads downstairs to see if Kate is back from her morning walk. He detects no activity in the bathroom, which is usually her first stop after returning.

He walks back down the main hallway of the second floor and heads toward their office to check some of the internet news sites before cleaning up. He stares out of the double window and sees Kate slowly walking down the street. She stops in front of the Carters' house, and walks up the driveway to pet their chocolate lab Kelso. Kelso enjoys the full range of the half acre lot, cut off from the rest of world by an electric fence.

Occasionally, Kelso manages to escape his electric prison, and inevitably winds up in the Fletchers' backyard, smothered in milk bones and other treats. *I'm pretty sure we are his first and only stop during an escape.* Sometimes, the kids just let him in the house to hang out. Alex is convinced that Kate and the kids might steal a dog if they don't get one soon. *We'll get another when everyone is truly ready.* Just over a year ago, the Fletchers' lost their yellow lab to a tragic accident at a local dog park. Alex stares out at a patch of grass across the street.

When his mind drifts back into his office, he notices Kate standing in their front yard, waving up to him. She looks frustrated. Alex wonders how long he she has been trying to get his attention. *Drifted out again.* He shifts his stance and meets her eyes, returning the wave. She still stares at him strangely. He opens the window and feels the warm air envelope him. *Another beautiful day.*

"Hey honey. Nice out huh?" he yells through the screen.

"Very nice. Another gift before the winter buries us. What were you staring at up there?" she says.

"Nothing, just thinking about something," he says.

"You must have been thinking really hard, you've been staring out of the window for over five minutes," she says.

"Nothing much. I'm just tired," he says. *She won't buy that one.*

"Alright," she says. *Definitely didn't buy it. I'll get a PTSD lecture within the next twenty four hours. Guaranteed.*

Kate starts walking toward the mudroom and Alex keeps watching her. He loved her more than anything. Seeing her shattered and in tears at the dog park was the worst moment in his life. Alex realizes that he is squeezing the window sill, both of his forearm muscles flexed. He eases his grip as Kate drifts from his view.

Alex turns around, and walks across the office to the closet. He opens the door, and pulls open the top drawer of a file cabinet. He locates a brown hanging file marked "Checklists," and removes the folder inside. The folder holds a few different checklists, specifically created for different emergencies or contingencies. He thumbs through them, seeing one for "Nor'Easter" and another for "Coastal Flooding." He finally finds the "Pandemic" checklist.

Alex takes two copies out of the folder, and replaces the folder in the cabinet. He walks back to the desk and sits down. Before glancing at the checklist, he shakes the computer mouse, to jar his computer out of standby mode. The flat screen monitor jumps to life, and displays a family picture taken on a beach in Mexico. He takes a close look at the list.

-Call Dead River to fill up oil tanks and propane. *Need to do this anyway.*

-Fill up cars. *We'll keep them filled.*

-Fill up all fuel canisters. *Next time at gas station.*

-Inspect solar power system. *Done*

-Inspect stockpile and fill in any gaps. *Done*

-Test walkie-talkies. *I'm sure they're fine.*

-Test generator. *I'm sure it works.*

-Withdraw all cash from checking and savings accounts. *Let's not get crazy.*

-Borrow from 401K to get maximum amount of cash. *Overkill.*

-Trade non-retirement investments for gold backed funds or bonds. *Paranoia.*

-Contact schools. *Next week.*

He jots a few notes onto the checklist and gets up to take a shower. He hears Kate fumbling around in the kitchen on his way past the stairs.

■

Alex wanders down the stairs to find Kate pouring coffee into a dark blue mug. She looks up at him and smiles. He can hear the Today show on in the kitchen.

"Good workout?" she asks.

"Not bad at all. I actually went for a run earlier too. It's still pretty warm out. Hey, I have to hide in my office again for a teleconference at eight. This one should be really interesting," he says.

Alex walks up to her and kisses her.

"Have you transmitted the nuclear bomb to Ted yet?" she asks with a devilish smile.

"Not yet. I was thinking about hooking my computer back up on Tuesday. I may just do it today and get it over with. He's going to flip out. Anything good on the Today Show?" he asks, looking up at the TV screen. *Christ, another missing kid in the D.C. area?*

"Not really. Still no word from the Chinese, our carriers are converging on the region, and Asia is crawling with the flu."

"Yeah, I checked. The numbers have skyrocketed, and Europe is exploding too. It's gonna be the same here in about a week," he says, and grabs a tall glass from the cabinet above the coffeemaker.

"That's what they said. Not about the U.S. though. DHS is holding a press conference at nine," she says.

"They didn't mention cases in the U.S?" he asks.

"Oh no, they definitely highlighted over a thousand cases nationwide. Confirmed."

"That sounds conservative. The ISPAC estimates the number of cases in the U.S. could hit 20,000 by the end of the week, based on all of their variables and that kind of shit," he says, waving his right hand above his head.

"Twenty thousand. Did they give their estimate for the Jakarta Flu's basic reproductive number?" she asks, opening the refrigerator.

"Yeah, initially they set it around four, but they took pains to mention that this number fluctuates hourly in their projections, and that it may turn out to be higher," he says.

"Infectious about seven to ten..." her voice trails off.

Kate turns around from the open refrigerator, and her eyes look upward. *Calculating.* She responds to mathematical or statistical challenges like a deep programmed Cold War mole, suddenly activated by a trigger phrase, and trapped in a computational trance until she is released by the answer. Within a few seconds, she breaks the spell and looks at Alex.

"Based on four as an average, the U.S. will hit roughly a million cases around November twentieth. If the case fatality rate is similar to what they are seeing in China, we could be looking at close to two hundred thousand deaths."

"Three weeks from now," he says dryly. "Hey, did Ryan roll down? I thought I heard him rummaging around down here earlier."

"Yeah, he was down here pouring some cereal. He forgot about no school. He made a beeline back up to his room when I reminded him," she says, nodding at the half filled cereal bowl.

"I don't think we'll get much resistance from him right now. Emily on the other hand...I don't know," he says.

"She can be pretty tough to deal with," she says.

Alex smirks, "I wonder where she gets that?"

"That's why you love me so much," she counters, bending over to pull the toaster out of a drawer in the island.

"Among other things," he says, and grabs her from behind, pressing his body against hers.

"You bad boy. Why do you always sex me up in the kitchen?" she says, standing up and nervously looking over at the stairs.

"Probably because you bend over a lot in the kitchen. I can't help it."

"Yeah, well you better make sure the kids don't see you. I don't feel like explaining it to either of them, especially Ryan."

"No kidding," he agrees.

"So, what's the plan for today?" she asks.

"Some breakfast, teleconference, then I was thinking maybe we could all take a bike ride to the beach. Get everyone out of the house," he says.

"Sounds nice," she adds.

"We should make the best of the weather. Some Canadian air is coming our way toward the end of the week, and another storm. The party's over."

"I would suggest we go out for lunch, but I guess that wouldn't be a great idea. Right?" she asks.

"I was thinking the same thing, but I don't know. There could be a couple hundred cases in the Greater Portland area, maybe more, but that's just a tiny fraction of what's brewing out there. We can leave the house as long as we can pretty strictly control our exposure. No busy places. When the number of cases really picks up, I don't think we should go anywhere, for any reason," he says.

"How many cases is that?" she asks.

"I don't know, but I think we'd be fine riding our bikes down to Higgins beach and grabbing a bite to eat at the Beachside Café. If it's still open."

"It usually closes a few weeks into November," she says.

"Then it looks like we'll be taking a family bike ride to Higgins beach," he says, and pulls down a box of cereal.

■

Alex sits in his office checking his personal email. A Bluetooth earpiece rests in his right ear, blaring intolerably optimistic music, as he waits for the rest of his sales district to join the teleconference. He hears a double beep, which indicate that someone has joined. He thinks he hears Dave from Portsmouth mumble something.

"Is that you Dave? It's Alex."

"Yours truly," Dave replies. *I wonder if he's still working.* Dave has a reputation as being slightly less industrious than the rest, and certainly more cynical.

"Hi Alex. How are things up in Portland?" *Sounds like Karen.*

"Pretty crazy. How about Concord?" he guesses.

"Same thing. All the stores are jammed. I finally got through Hannaford's yesterday."

"Any flu cases?" he presses.

"Something like a hundred cases since Saturday. I tried to get in to see some of the infectious disease people at Concord Hospital earlier this morning, but they're not letting in drug reps." *I'm sitting here in sweat pants and a T-shirt, and she's already out there trying to get herself exposed to the Jakarta Flu.*

"You probably don't want to be anywhere near an E.R., or any hospital for that matter. It's not worth it," says Alex.

"That's a no shitter," says Dave.

"What do you mean?" Karen asks blandly. *Is she kidding?*

"Hey guys, it's Cheryl. Who's on?"

Two representatives cover each of the five geographic sales areas. Portsmouth-Southern New Hampshire, Concord-Northern New Hampshire, Portland-Southern Maine, Augusta-Central Maine and Bangor-Northern Maine. Everyone answers except for Ted. Alex hears another double beep. *Here's the man of the hour.*

"Good morning everyone. Let's make sure everyone is here," says Ted.

Ted conducts a roll call. A few of Alex's colleagues sound excited to be on the teleconference. Alex purposely sedates his acknowledgment.

"Thank you for joining me on such short notice. I have some good news and some bad news." *I have a feeling Ted's bad news is good news for me.*

"Since I always like to end on a positive note, let's start with the bad, though I hate to call it bad. More disappointing than anything else." *This guy is a real treat.*

"The disappointing news is that Biosphere will not enter into an official direct partnership with DHS." *What a shame.*

Alex hears grumbling on the line. He also swears he heard a muffled cheer.

"I know, I know…not exactly what I was hoping for either, but from what I understand, DHS wanted more control over Biosphere's operations than our executives were comfortable with, so the negotiations are currently stalled. I am told that this may not be the end of a possible deal, especially given the rapidly deteriorating situation around the country. There is still hope."

Dave interjects a comment, "Ted, I saw a blurb on CNN about Roche enhancing their deal with DHS."

"Yes, but even without an official deal, Biosphere is taking steps to secure their role," says Ted with a hint of pride. *More like force their role.*

"Biosphere agreed to relinquish 80% of its current sample inventory to DHS, for regional utilization. I don't have any specifics, but I assume that those samples will be added to the nation's anti-viral stockpiles, which will be controlled by the government. I don't know when that will happen or how, but be ready for the call. The remaining twenty percent will be retained by representatives for the good news." *I have a bad feeling about this one.*

"I am excited to announce that effective immediately, our district will augment the Boston District's efforts in northern Massachusetts," he says.

The phone is dead silent. *Not a lot of excitement about this one.*

"Ted, this is Steph. When is this going happening?"

Stephanie Brennan lives north of Concord with her husband Tom and three young children. Alex figures she'll be on the fence about complying with this initiative, but will eventually cave in to Ted's pressure. She'll be more concerned about losing her job and a comfortable income. Alex knows they barely scraped together enough money for a down payment on a house they purchased a few years ago, immediately after her husband was hired as a middle school science teacher in Concord. Alex couldn't imagine any way they could afford to stay in their house on Tom's income alone.

"Good question Stephanie," Ted says. *Like she's a third grader.*

"All of the assignments are made, and hotel arrangements are set, so we'd like put all of you in place tomorrow."

The phone erupts with protest, and Alex removes the Bluetooth earpiece. *Too early for this.* He activates the speaker phone feature of his iPhone. Ted is trying to calm the group.

"Alright, Alright. One at a time. I haven't even given you the details. I realize this is short notice, but let's face it, the pandemic is spreading quickly, and our corporate strategists agree that a huge opportunity exists if we execute this plan quickly," he says.

"What exactly is the opportunity?" asks Alex.

"Uh…well the opportunity is to educate front line providers regarding the Jakarta Flu. You'll all receive new educational pieces to use in the field when you meet with your new coordinating manager down in Massachusetts. So…the first part of the opportunity is to assist healthcare providers with making decisions that can help contain the pandemic. And…and the samples you'll have in your car will let them treat patients with symptoms right in their offices, improving containment efforts." *That wasn't part of his script. Sorry Ted.*

"This sounds like a PR scam," interrupts Dave.

"Dave, you beat me to it," adds Alex dryly. "I don't see how this could possible help the situation. The Jakarta Flu is about to jump like wildfire across the country. Injecting a few sales representatives into the situation…I don't see how that will accomplish anything, aside from provide Biosphere with a nice press release."

"I don't know Alex, if we get out there as quickly as possible with the samples and these new informational pieces, we might be the one factor that turns the tide. It's worth a try at least," says Karen with a cheerleader voice. *She has no idea what we're all up against.*

Karen Caldwell has little to lose, beside her life. Recently graduated from the University of New Hampshire, she rents an apartment with roommates in downtown Portsmouth, and tirelessly commits all of her time to a career at Biosphere Pharmaceuticals.

"You can take my spot Karen," says Alex.

"Look, nobody is taking anyone's place. All of the assignments have been submitted to the regional office, so there won't be any changes," says Ted forcefully. *I'm not saying another word.*

"I will email you all of the details. Hotels, coordinating manager contact information, all of it as soon as the teleconference is finished."

"Ted, this is Mike. Why wouldn't the Portland reps stay put? You know, to help contain any outbreaks in the more populated areas of Maine? Someone has to be left behind." *Wishful thinking.*

"We will be keeping two reps in Maine for that purpose," Ted answers.

"What are our assigned areas?" asks Jack Hathway. *You ain't stayin up in Bangor, that's for sure.*

"Well, I was going to send that in the email, but I don't see any reason not to give you the basics," says Ted, sounding torn. *I'm sure that HR directed them to fire this bomb via email. I'll be dropping a bomb of my own as soon as this conference finishes.*

"Let me start by saying that the regional manager wanted to minimize the geographical distance that the reps were displaced, to keep you as close to your families as possible." *Bullshit.*

"So...Jack and Brian, you'll relocate to Portland and cover all of Maine. The good news for you is that you'll still be working under me. The rest of you will have new temporary managers."

"Are you fucking kidding me?" says Mike.

"Take it easy Mike, if you think..."

"Take it easy? You're basing the northern Maine reps in Portland and moving the Portland reps down to Massachusetts? How does that make any sense?" he nearly yells.

"What I was about to say, is that if you think about it, you'll actually be closer to your family than the northern Maine guys. The regional manager wanted to make this as fair as possible for everyone," he says with conviction.

"So, where will the rest of us be fairly and justly relocated by Biosphere?" asks Dave.

Ted reads the rest of the assignments, each one invoking a minor protest, except from Karen in Portsmouth and Melissa in Concord. Alex remains silent and Dave adds a few more sarcastic comments. Mike injects a few well timed obscenities, keeping Alex's attention loosely riveted to the call. Ted ends the conference abruptly, reminding the group to check their email for the details. He never suggests that they take rest of the day off to prepare for an immediate and indefinite relocation. Alex knows that he truly doesn't care.

Alex's iPhone rings. *Mike.*

"Hey there dissident," says Alex.

"Yeah, fuck you too. Why were you so quiet?" he quips.

"You know, I felt like laying into Ted, but it suddenly hit me. Who cares? I have no intention of driving down to Lawrence tonight to check into the asshole inn. I gave all of my samples away last Friday. I'm pretty much done with Biosphere. What about you? You're not heading down to Mass, are you?"

"I don't know. If I don't show up, all hell will break loose. I'm just not sure what to do," says Mike.

Alex spins in his chair and looks over at the Thorntons' house. He sees Charlie Thornton back out of his driveway and head toward the other side of the Durham Road loop.

"Well, what was your plan for leaving town if you needed to? I mean, how were you going to explain it to Ted?" Alex asks.

"You know, I thought we'd all just be doing the same thing we've always been doing. Calling on offices, and driving around. I figured that if this thing got really bad, I could just call Ted up and tell him I have the flu. I never anticipated being reassigned down to Boston this quickly. This twist jacked up the whole plan. I might head down to Lawrence for a few days and just pretend that I'm working, then call in sick and drive back. I won't ever have to set foot in a doctor's office," says Mike.

"I don't know Mike. They know we're pissed about this. Especially you. I wouldn't be surprised if you showed up and they stuck you with a district manager for a few days. You'd be calling on offices from sunrise to sunset…maybe longer."

"Fuck me," says Mike.

"I think you should tell Ted that your wife is sick and that you need to stay in the area to take care of your kids. Maybe he'll…"

"Hey, sorry to cut you off, but that's him buzzing through," he says, exasperated.

"Just stay calm, and tell him that your wife has severe diarrhea with vomiting, and that you probably won't be able to leave town until it clears up in a day or two. That should buy you some time to work on another excuse," says Alex.

"Alright, I gotta go…"

"Diarrhea and vomiting…get descriptive, he'll leave you alone," Alex says slightly laughing.

"Got it," Mike says and disconnects the call. *I hope he's got it.*

Alex decides that this is a good time to give Ted's heart a workout. He flips opens the screen to the electronic tablet sitting on the right corner of the office desk, and turns the screen so he can see it from his seat.

The desktop activates and he opens the "Wireless Pro" icon, and selects "Wireless Device." He moves the cursor to highlight "Wireless On," and pauses for several moments, staring at the screen. He looks outside at the clear sky, keeping his thumb on the "left click" internal mouse button.

"Adios Biosphere," he says and presses his thumb down.

Alex checks the screen and sees that the wireless icon in the lower right corner of the screen is pulsing green. He wonders how long it will take for Ted to call. He estimates by the end of the day. *Maybe sooner.*

Alex stands up and heads downstairs to the kitchen. On his way, he sees that the kids' doors are still closed. He glances at his watch. 8:21. Kate sits at the kitchen island, sipping coffee and reading the paper, while occasionally glancing up at the TV. Alex picks up the mug he forgot to bring up to the office and walks over to the coffee maker, refreshing his half-filled mug with steaming hot coffee.

Without looking up from the paper, Kate asks, "So, did it live up to your expectations?"

"And far exceeded them. I have to drive down to Lawrence, Mass tonight, so I can report to my new temporary manager," he says emotionlessly.

Kate immediately turns to him, "Really?"

She looks like she might believe him.

"That's what the company wants," he says matter-of-factly.

"But you're not…" she says, oddly doubtful.

"No, I'm not going anywhere," he says.

"I didn't think so," she says, "but for a second, you sounded serious."

"Not a chance. Hey, are you sure you should be reading that paper?" he asks.

Kate casts a puzzled glance that reads "and why wouldn't I read the paper?" She suddenly realizes why Alex asked the question.

"Shit, I never gave it a thought. One kid wrapping all of the papers could infect half the block, or the entire subdivision," she says and holds the section of paper she was reading, up by the corner, between her thumb and first finger, like it was rotten. She starts to get up and head over to the trash.

"I don't think it matters now, but that's the kind of thing we need to watch. Nothing should come into the house, even the mail. Most of what we get in the mail is garbage anyway," he says.

"What about the bills?" she asks.

"Well, we could…" he pauses, stuck in thought. "I don't know. I guess as long as we wash our hands, and just keep it in one place it shouldn't be a big deal."

"The flu can only survive a few days on the paper anyway, right? We can sort through it weekly, with gloves even. Looks for any bills, and throw all the junk in box in the garage. We'll need the paper for kindling at some point."

"Sounds like a plan," she says.

"Anything good on CNN?" he asks.

"Nothing new, except for the new Flu Watch Center. All of the news channels have a version of it. Twenty four hour flu updates. Situation Rooms, Pandemic Watch Centers, and The Pandemic Truth Zone," she says.

Alex raises his eyebrows.

"Fox News," she says with a grin.

"Up to the minute pandemic information for the whole family" he says in an overly serious voice.

"Any sign of the kids?" she says.

"I peeked in to check on them. Ryan is buried in his covers. No sign of life. Emily's covers were pulled back, so she could roll down at any time. Did you call your office?" he asks.

"Yep. I told them I had diarrhea and a fever, and that I'd work on my files from home. Your diarrhea angle really works," she says.

"Yeah, something about the possibility of shitting in your pants or blowing out the office crapper really cuts down on the questions. Nobody wants to be around someone with diarrhea, and they certainly don't want to catch the diarrhea bug. That's why you have to throw the fever in there. The fever adds the element of contagiousness to the equation. No questions asked," he says proudly.

"I'll have to take over the home office and work the rest of the morning. Maybe we can take a ride to the beach with the kids after lunch," she suggests.

"If they wake up by lunch," he says.

Alex hears his iPhone ring and realizes he left it in the office. He gets up from his stool at the kitchen island and starts toward the staircase.

"That might be Mike. He threw a fit during the teleconference. Really out of character for him. He's usually a cool customer, even during the worst of Ted's ideas."

"Have fun," she says.

"As always," he replies.

On the way up the stairs, he feels a sudden burst of adrenaline. *It could be Ted.*

Chapter Twelve

Monday, November 5, 2012

Sunlight pours into the great from several oversized windows facing the backyard and the northeastern side of the house. Kate and Alex lounge on the couch, watching the DHS press conference. Assistant Deputy Director Paul Harding is already fielding questions from the press.

"Suzanne Wilkins, CNN. According to the National Pandemic Plan, your department is tasked with assessing the surge capacity of medical and emergency response systems. What is DHS's assessment based on worldwide Jakarta Flu trends?"

"Currently, our assessment is positive. Based on worldwide trends and our nation's pandemic response capability, we anticipate sufficient surge capacity to handle the pandemic.

A few major factors affect this assessment. First, the U.S. is a nation with a modernized healthcare system, second to none in the world. I know that a few countries have already hit their surge capacity, but those models will not apply here. We have an incredible healthcare system, and the Strategic National Stockpile gives us the ability to enhance this system if necessary.

Secondly, not every single person that is infected requires hospital care. The vast majority can be treated at home, especially when given anti-virals to reduce the severity of symptoms. At this time, we do not anticipate the Jakarta Flu overwhelming the healthcare system. With that being said, we are closely watching all aspects of the pandemic, and will take the immediate and necessary steps if, and I emphasize if, that assessment changes. Thank you."

A woman in the second row speaks up immediately after John's comment.

"You mentioned the anti-viral stockpile again as a key strategy for keeping the pandemic under control. The nation's stockpile program is close to thirty two million doses short of the projected 2012 goal to have enough doses for 25% of the population. Is this shortage figured into that assessment?"

Another reporter sitting behind her, fires a follow up questions before the assistant Deputy Director can react.

"And what about reports of resistance to Tamiflu? Or that the Jakarta Flu may require higher doses due to higher virulence?"

Paul takes control of the situation.

"Ladies and gentlemen, one question at a time please. First, the department's assessments take into account the state level shortfall. As of last month, the Strategic National Stockpile contained nearly 39 million doses of Tamiflu, which is only a few million doses short of our goal. Unfortunately, stockpiling at the state level fell well short of our expectations. Our department directed that 32 million doses be purchased at the state level, and currently, state stockpiles only account for about 7 to 8 million doses."

The room to starts to stir, as reporters started whispering.

"However, DHS has reached an agreement with Roche pharmaceuticals that will bridge this gap. Roche has agreed to divert their entire current inventory to the Strategic National Stockpile, and for an indefinite period, production of their anti-viral Tamiflu will be dedicated solely to pandemic response efforts."

"I didn't hear anything about Biosphere?" says Kate.

Before Alex can comment, his iPhone rings. He checks the caller ID and freezes, staring at the display. *Ted.*

"Are you gonna answer that, or…"

She stops when she sees the look of anguish on his face.

"Ted?" she says. Alex nods his head, wincing.

"Can you take the call in the study? I'd like to watch the rest of this," she says in an overly unsympathetic tone, trying to force a little black humor into the situation.

"Great. Some wife I have," he says, barely smiling.

He gets up from the couch, and lets the call go to voicemail.

"I'll check his message, then call him back. I might need a drink for this one," he says, as he leaves the great room.

Kate calls him back, "Honey."

Alex pokes his head around the corner.

"Good luck. I know this won't be an easy call. Just stay calm, and let the cards fall where they fall. Let him do most of the talking. You already know your position. You really don't need to explain anything to him. If he gets out of hand, tell him to call you back when he is feeling better."

"Thanks hon. That sounds like a better approach than the one I was formulating," he says and starts to walk toward the study.

As he crosses into the mudroom, his phone beeps twice, indicating that a message is waiting on his voicemail. Alex steps back into the kitchen to get a cup of coffee. He doesn't expect the call to last very long, but feels comforted by the thought of a strong, hot cup of coffee. He refreshes his mug and opens the refrigerator to pull out some creamer.

"Quit stalling," a voice calls out from the great room.

"I'm working on it," he replies, laughing to himself. *She's right. I really don't want to hear Ted's message.*

Alex finishes fixing his coffee and heads into the study, a small room adjacent to the mudroom. One wall is filled with floor to ceiling built-in maple bookshelves. A tall dark round table with a brushed silver lamp sits between two dark brown leather club chairs, along the wall with a double window. Crown molding wraps around the ceiling, tying into the bookshelves, and a cherry antique desk sits against the wall shared with the mudroom. A tall fern variety sits in the corner southeastern corner.

Alex and Kate turned the room into a study after living in the house for two years. They intended the room to serve as an escape from the noise generated by two highly spirited children. They envisioned sitting together in leather chairs, sipping port wine, and delving into novels, while the children played on their own or watched TV in the family room. Still a pleasing room to both of them, they abandoned the idea of long escapes soon after completion, instead, substituting brief moments of shelter behind the study's closed door, before one of the children inevitably discovered their location. Now, the room mostly serves as an oversized and excessively comfortable phone booth, conferring a moderate degree of privacy.

He closes the door and opens the white plantation shudders covering a double window. The room is bathed in direct sunlight, mostly falling on the floor to ceiling bookcases. He sits in the leather chair opposite the wall of books, keeping the sun out of his eyes. He dials his voicemail and listens.

Not good. Ted's message was short, simple and sounded serious. "Alex, please call me immediately."

He auto-dials Ted's number and waits. Ted picks up on the second ring.

"Ted Stanton," he answers.

"Hey Ted, it's Alex. I got your message," he says. *Stick to the basics. Don't offer information.*

"Yes, I had a question that I figured you could resolve. After the teleconference, I logged in to the manager's database, to take a quick look at inventories. To gauge how much each of you should pack up for the trip down to Massachusetts. Anyway, I was cycling through each of you, and I saw that your inventory was empty. Something must be wrong with the system again. I just wanted to touch base with you to confirm that this was a mistake, before I call headquarters and start to raise hell with administration. I don't want the system to create the false impression that we rolled down to Mass without... you know, the maximum ammo load out."

Alex calculates his options. Lying to Ted would get him off the hook, at least until tomorrow morning, when Ted finds out that he didn't show up in Lawrence. It's also likely that he'll receive an alert message from the samples management division today, exposing the lie. Alex is convinced that all sample transactions will be flagged due to the moratorium placed on giving TerraFlu samples to physicians. Mostly, he didn't relish the idea of lying, under any circumstance. *Here goes the high road.*

"Actually Ted, the database is correct. I gave my entire sample allotment to the head of the infectious disease department at Maine Medical Center. Dr. Wright, from Maine Coast Internal Medicine." *Kaboom.*

"That's a...ah, that's a good one Alex," he replies.

Alex detects a mix of hope and doubt in Ted's voice, leaning heavily toward doubt.

"Seriously Ted, he asked me for samples last Friday, and I couldn't refuse him. His department is best positioned to distribute those samples for optimal use against the Jakarta Flu in the greater Portland area, and probably most of Maine. His argument was convincing, given..."

"More convincing than a direct order from the company to halt all, and I repeat, all sample transactions? Are you goddamn kidding me? Do you know what you've done?" he screams into the phone. *Stay calm. Listen to Kate.*

"Yes, it was much more convincing. Morally, a better thing to do with the samples," says Alex.

"Morals? This isn't about morals. This is about failing to follow direct company guidance. My guidance, you...you have no idea how this is going to look. You know what, you know what...I wash my hands of this. You've been a pain in the ass from the beginning god damn it. Since day one, you've made this job hard for me. And I never wanted to hire you in the first place. I'm reporting this immediately to the regional manager. We'll see how much longer you're around. I don't think you realize how important these samples are to the company and to the ongoing negotiations with the government regarding a partnership..."

"You know, I just watched the DHS teleconference, and they announced a sweeping relationship with Roche Pharmaceuticals. I don't think the government really cares about a relationship with Biosphere, and frankly, neither do I. Is there anything else Ted? I don't plan to be on this call much longer," replies Alex, starting to feel his face flush. *Back it down.*

"Be prepared to answer to the regional manager, human resources, everyone, for this. I'm making a few calls, and then I'm heading to Portland to confirm that your storage locker is empty. I'll expect you to meet me there to open the locker."

"I won't be available for that Ted. You're authorized to access my storage locker. You know that, or at least you should. It's on the rental agreement for the storage facility. I plan to be available by phone, and that's about it. I don't want to take any chances with the flu out there you know. You live a little too close to Boston for my comfort."

"You will show up when and where I tell you to show up, or I'll report that too," he asserts. *He's starting to lose it.*

"That sounds good Ted. I'll talk to you later," Alex says, and starts to move the phone away from his ear. He hears Ted talking loudly, and puts the phone back to his ear.

"Sorry, I missed that." *Don't want to appear rude.*

"I said that you better not fail to show up tomorrow morning in Lawrence," he barks.

"Or you'll report me? Sounds good Ted," he says, and disconnects the call.

He deactivates the ring tone, and switches the phone to vibrate. He knows that Ted will probably place several more calls to Alex, in attempt to get the last word. He always insists on the last word, at meetings, teleconferences, phone calls, and holiday parties. Alex figures that Ted feels an entitlement to it as their manager, or that he read about it in one of the dozens of business leadership guru books he sickeningly cites on a regular basis. Alex can see the chapter in his mind. "Effective leadership tactic number forty-five. Getting the last word. He laughs out loud at the thought, and takes a drink of coffee.

Buzzzzzz. *Here he goes.* Alex slouches in the chair and holds the phone up to eye level. *Yep.* Ted S. For a moment, Alex is tempted to answer the phone. He stands up, tucks the phone into the front pocket of his jeans and heads back out into the kitchen. Kate is pouring a fresh cup of coffee.

"How did it go?" she asks.

"Not great, but not bad. He started to flip out, so I cut the call short."

"I'm sure he appreciated that."

Alex's phone starts to vibrate again. He pulls it out of his pocket, checks the display and places it on the granite island.

"Yeah. That's call number two since I hung up. Did I miss anything good?" he says.

"Ah, not really. Well, there was one interesting question about their point of entry strategy. Someone asked why they put so much stock into point of entry screening, when the WHO has for years declared this strategy ineffective, as well as several other organizations."

"Like the ISPAC. I've heard Dr. Ocampo say it was a waste of resources three times in the past week alone," he says.

"So what do you think will happen with your job now?" she asks, shifting the subject.

"Well, I figure they'll fire me, especially when I don't show up down in Massachusetts tomorrow, but who knows."

"That's asinine. Shifting all of you down there," she says.

"I know, believe me. The only thing I don't know is how long it'll take to get rid of me. I bet it'll be pretty quick."

"Well, I'm glad we have some money saved up for this. I feel bad for the people who can't quit their jobs," she says.

Alex's iPhone buzzes again, dancing on the granite surface. Alex leans over the phone to check the display. He shakes his head as he looks at Kate.

"Again?" she asks.

"You know it. He'll keep at this for a while. He hasn't left a message yet, which tells me he really doesn't have anything constructive to say."

Chapter Thirteen

Monday, November 5, 2012

Alex sits in his office chair, staring out of the window at the neighborhood. The sun is low on the horizon, slowly creeping into Alex's view from the left, preparing for its rapid plunge below the western skyline. The day is still bright and warm, carrying a comfortable southwesterly breeze into the office through two open, screened windows. Alex savors the pleasant draft, knowing that a similar breeze might not push through the house again until mid-May. Several neighbors have returned from work, their cars sitting in their driveways, or inside open garages.

He sees Jamie McDaniels's white Volvo Cross-Country station wagon pull into the driveway across the street. She stops the car short of the left bay door, which starts to open as her two girls, Amanda and Katherine, pour out of the right rear door of the wagon. Jamie usually picks them up from after-school care and arrives home about an hour earlier than her husband Matt.

Alex continues to watch, as Jamie opens her door and stands up out of the car to shout something at her girls. She is dressed smartly in a white blouse, with pointed white collars that extend over a dark blue vest. Her dark brown hair is set at shoulder length. Alex can imagine that she would not be difficult on the boys' eyes in her French class at Falmouth high school.

Her husband will arrive around five thirty, after a series of school administrative meetings. Matt McDaniel is the newly hired principal for the ailing Portland High School. Because of their close contact with the schools, especially Falmouth, Alex and Kate consider the McDaniels' household to be at high risk. They plan to watch the McDaniel household very closely.

Alex hears his wife yelling up the stairs.

"Your phone is buzzing again. 860 area code. Why don't you just turn it off if you're not going to answer it? It's starting to drive me nuts down here."

Alex walks to the top of the stairs. Ryan's door is shut and the door to the kids' bathroom is open. Alex breathes in the warm shampoo scented air funneling out of the bathroom. He walks down the stairs.

"I'll just put it in my office. I want to keep tabs on who's calling. 860 is Hartford I think. Shit, that could be the regional office."

He turns the corner and sees Kate holding his iPhone up to her ear, apparently talking on the phone.

"No, I believe what he was trying to say is go fuck yourself…Yes…Yes, I understand your position, but his hasn't changed"

Alex is momentarily stunned, standing at the end of the banister.

"Please tell me you're kidding," he pleads, and she starts to laugh. She stops laughing and displays her trademarked devilish smile.

"You know I would never do anything like that," she says.

"Uh, I wouldn't put it past you. Let's just leave it at that," he replies, snatching the phone from his wife. He gives her a long kiss on the lips.

"Where's Emily?" he asks.

"She's out on the picnic table with some books," she says.

Alex takes a few steps away from the stairs, and glances out into the backyard. Dressed in brown pants and a light blue hooded sweatshirt, Emily sits at the picnic table with a book open.

"Hey hon, if one of our kids is going to be out of the house, one of us should be with them. At least really close by. I don't think it's a problem right now, and please don't think I'm picking on you for any reason. I just think they need to get used to the idea of a more restrictive environment, and I'd feel more comfortable if we directly managed their contact outside of the house," he says, cringing.

"Well, I wouldn't exactly say that being confined to the yard is not restrictive. I told her she had to stay in the yard, and I explained to her that if any of her friends came over, she needed to come tell me, so I could handle the situation. I think these are adequate rules."

"I wasn't implying that her being out there alone is wrong, I'm just saying that when the schools close, every kid on the block is going to be home, with nothing to do, and many of them with parents that still don't fully grasp what is happening. We'll need to be all over our kids."

"I was keeping a close eye on her from the kitchen, but you're right," she says, looking out at Emily.

"Let's see who called from 860," he says and dials his voicemail.

As he listens to his voice mail, Ryan walks into the kitchen to get a glass of water. Alex nods at Ryan, paying attention to the message. Ryan and Kate sit down together at the dinner table, and start talking. Alex catches Kate's glance and shakes he his head. He starts to walk to the study.

"Regional manager," he calls out across the kitchen, disappearing into the mudroom.

Alex takes his favorite seat in study, facing the bookshelves, and sits back deeply in the leather chair. He takes in the rich smell of new leather furniture, and closes his eyes for a few moments, centering himself for the call to Michelle Harke. He redials the number and reaches Michelle's secretary, Anna.

"Hi Anna, this is Alex Fletcher up in Portland, Maine. I just received a call from Michelle indicating that she wanted me to call her immediately," he says.

"Oh, hi Alex. Yes, she just let me know. Let me put you through to her," says Anna. Anna's tone didn't betray any knowledge of the issue at hand.

"Hey Alex, thank you for calling me back so quickly," she says.

Alex can read nothing from her tone. Michelle has always been difficult to read. On the surface, she projects a warm, semi-casual approach to her job, but her word choice betrays a business only hardwiring that Alex never trusted.

"No problem at all Michelle," he responds. *Say as little as possible.*

"Ted told me that you depleted your sample inventory on Friday, which baffles me considering the amount of direction sent to representatives regarding the disposition of field samples. I know that all of the district managers communicated the no-sampling policy to their reps, and I know that headquarters reinforced and explained the policy via email. I didn't think there could be any confusion about the policy, but clearly there might have been a miscommunication. Can you help me with this one?" *Buddy O' pal.*

"I'm not sure I'm going to make this any easier for you, or maybe I will. There was no confusion about the direction. I just chose to ignore it, and provide all of my samples to the head of the infectious disease department at Maine Medical Center. As I told Ted, I felt a moral imperative to put the samples into his hands, not let them sit around my storage locker waiting for the next round of doomed negotiations between Biosphere and the government." *And, I kinda felt like sticking it to Ted.*

"I guess I still don't understand, especially given your military background. You're saying that the direction was clear, but you chose to disregard the policy anyway? To disobey a direct order?" she says. *Sounds like you understand it pretty well.*

Alex detects a shift in her tone. Although her corporate central processor gave her away after a few seconds of talking, her use of a condescending rhetorical question completely strips away the camouflage. Alex expects the phone call to deteriorate from this point forward, not that it really started on anything he would consider a high point.

"Yes, I think that sums it up,' he says, suppressing a desire to engage her sarcastically.

"Well Alex, I'm having a tough time with this one. My first instinct is to let you go immediately, but the company is committed to maximizing the effectiveness and impact of the PRP. So…"

"PRP? I'm not familiar with the term," says Alex.

"Pandemic Redeployment Program…" she clarifies.

"Got it. Moving us to Massachusetts," he interrupts.

"Right. As I was saying, because of Biosphere's commitment to this program, I don't think this would be a good time to weaken our sales force, by lowering the head count," she says.

"You mean like fire me?" he asks. *Right between the eyes please.*

"Well, yes. Under any other circumstances, I would initiate separation procedures, but Ted said that you seemed to fully support the PRP initiative, which surprised him since you routinely undermine his authority." *What authority?*

"He thought I was onboard because I didn't say much about it during this morning's teleconference. Everyone else beat me to it. Anyway, I feel really bad about dragging this out, so let me make this easy for everyone. I have no intention of abandoning my family during the pandemic, and relocating to Massachusetts…even temporarily. I don't really plan to leave my house until this whole thing has cleared up. So, would it be easier for company if I just resigned?"

The line remains silent for a few seconds.

"Is that what you want to do?" she asks.

"Yes, I would like to resign my position. Right now. It doesn't make any sense to continue this relationship. Do I need to send a letter to anyone? Or do anything officially?" Alex asks.

"No. I will initiate resignation procedures, and we should have you closed out in a few days. Ted will contact you with the details and a close out checklist," she states.

"At least the inventory should go smoothly," Alex adds, unable to resist the joke.

"This might not be such a laughing matter to you after legal takes a closer look at your actions. I've already brought the matter to their attention, and between you and me, I don't plan to let this slip away," she says.

"I'm sure I'll be fine. A legitimate sample transaction to a licensed physician. Head of the infectious disease department nonetheless. I'm not worried. Thanks for taking this personally though," he says, feeling the blood rise to his face.

"We'll just let the lawyers figure that out. I'm sure they'll find something, and we'll be sure to help them along," she adds.

Michelle's parting comment breaks down his remaining sarcasm barrier.

"Well, you better tell them not to drag out their investigation. I'd be willing to bet that in a few weeks, most of them will either be dead or hooked up to a ventilator somewhere in the greater New York metro area, if they're lucky. Good luck avoiding the flu."

He disconnects the call, initially satisfied with his retort. His satisfaction quickly dissolves into a bittersweet disappointment with himself for having descended low enough to invoke such a ghastly image and wish. Alex rises from the chair and steps into the mudroom. He opens the door to the garage and steps out onto the cement floor next to the Forerunner.

The bay door behind the Forerunner is open, and Alex steps out of the bay onto the driveway. He squints, immediately hit with blinding rays of sunlight. He brings his left arm up to his face, blocking the bright light. He sees that the bright orange mail flag is down, and starts walking down the driveway to the mailbox. While walking down the driveway, he see's Ed Walkers' Honda Pilot pull around the corner of the block, headed his way.

The garage bay door closest to Alex starts to rumble open and Alex stops. Ed's car pulls up into the driveway, but stops short of entering the garage bay. Alex waves, as Ed opens the car door. All three of his kids start to spill out of the back door, running for the house. The oldest daughter Chloe yells out a greeting to Alex, and he responds.

"Hey Ed. Home early today. Very nice," says Alex.

"Yeah, Samantha called me earlier. Said she was running late at the firm, so I figured I'd close up shop early and grab some Chinese on the way to pick up the kids."

Ed walks over to Alex and they shake hands. Alex moves next to Ed, so they can both talk without the sun blazing in their eyes.

"What about you guys? Abby said that Emily wasn't in school, and Chloe didn't see Ryan," says Ed.

"We've decided to keep the kids out of school until we're sure what's going on with the flu. Based on what we're seeing, I imagine they're going to close the schools at some point this week. But they'll wait till the flu is already in the schools before making that call."

Alex sees from Ed's expression, that he is seriously contemplating what Alex just said.

"I wonder if I could shift to working from my home office, and keep the kids home. I'd hate to take any chances with them at school. But…I don't know if I could pull that off. I still have to meet with clients…or I could reschedule for later…I don't know. Do you really think the schools are going to close? DHS officials sound pretty confident that this won't get out of control," he says.

"I wouldn't count on it. Based on several unbiased projections from other organizations, the number of cases in the U.S. will exceed 2008's total by the middle of next week. We're really concerned," Alex says.

"I'll have to talk to Sam about it. I know she can't work from home," he says.

"Well, if I were you guys…" starts Alex.

"Sounds like one of your famous plots brewing," he jokes.

"Oh, it's more than a plot. Anyway, if I were you, here's what I would do. I would get your home office gig rolling, and keep the kids home. Then, I would have your wife call in sick with flu like symptoms. You can wait a few days for this, just make sure Sam is really careful out there, avoiding public places, washing hands a lot, watching everyone around her. By the time she calls in sick, there'll be enough cases out there."

"It's not a matter of being questioned. She can take the next month off if she wants. She still has to meet her billable hours by the end of the year, or she loses money, and looks bad as a partner," he says.

"I know. Kate has the same issue. In a few weeks, this flu is going to fuck things up pretty good, and nobody's going to be worried about billable hours, year-end bonuses, or client meetings. The next few weeks will be critical. Hey, if we're wrong, then everything goes back to normal."

"What's Kate doing?"

"She called in sick, but told them she would work as much as she could from home. She can access most of her work from our office, so her firm shouldn't care."

"What about you. How long can you hide out? Didn't you say they track all of your transactions with that computer thing?" he asks.

"They can. However…it won't matter since I resigned a few minutes ago. Things were getting crazy with them. They wanted me to drive down to Lawrence tomorrow to boost the sales force there. I checked online this afternoon and the Lawrence/Andover area has been hit by a sizable outbreak of the Jakarta Flu. Upwards of a thousand confirmed cases in north east Massachusetts. Probably more. Lawrence General, Lowell General, and a few other bigger hospitals are taking most of the cases. Biosphere is sending nearly all of the Maine reps down there, probably New Hampshire and Vermont reps too. Indefinitely. I told them to go pack sand."

"Sorry man," says Ed.

"Actually, I feel kinda relieved. Biosphere was nothing like my last company. Things were dicey from the beginning. I have some good contacts at other companies if this flu thing fizzles," he says.

"So, I assume you guys are all set over there," he says, nodding with a gesture toward Alex's house.

"I think so. The kids are gonna be the biggest challenge, and possibly some of the neighbors," Alex replies, looking around at the houses on their side of the loop. "Who knows how this'll go down."

"What about you guys? You're all set right?" Alex asks.

"I think so. We have a decent amount of food stored up in the basement. Sam and I stocked up on canned food for a couple months after you guys scared the shit out of us with the Swine Flu, but that pretty much fizzled out. I'm not sure how long all of our stuff will last, but I think we have the basics covered. Our stove is propane and I have plenty of wood for the fireplace…"

"You should move that into your garage or basement. How much do you guys have?" says Alex.

"I had a half a cord left from last year, and I just had them deliver another cord in September, which we probably don't need. We just never seem to get around to making a fire. Fuck, I really don't want to move the wood into the garage. That'll be a massive pain in the ass."

"I know. I still have another cord or so to go. Pain in the balls for sure. Still, I wouldn't leave it outside. Not if this thing takes a turn for the worse," Alex says.

"You're probably right," he says.

"Every once in a while I'm right," says Alex.

"Not according to Kate. Anyway, we should be good. We grabbed plenty of groceries for the next couple of weeks. We should be fine," he says.

Alex looks at Ed.

"Ed, if you guys need anything, let me know. Seriously. Food, medical supplies, whatever. I don't think we're gonna have the luxury of running out to the stores for very long," says Alex.

"Hey, thanks Alex. It definitely makes me feel more secure about this whole thing. I just hope it all blows over."

"You and me both," Alex replies, breaking off the handshake.

"Hey, I gotta get these kids settled in the house," says Ed.

"Have a good one Ed," Alex says and turns toward his mailbox.

"You too," says Ed.

Alex walks up to the mailbox and opens the door. He pulls out a handful of assorted mail. Two magazines, bills, maybe a birthday invitation for one of the kids, advertisements. Alex looks at the mail and wonders exactly who, beyond their postal carrier, touched these items. Mail from several different parts of the country, each piece touched by at least a half dozen different people. Finally, the postal carrier, who handled every piece of mail in the Fletchers' mailbox, opened the mailbox door, and lowered the orange delivery flag. Dozens of points of contact. All of this now transferred onto Alex's hands, as he closes the door, and walks back to the house with the mail.

Alex decides that from this point forward, they'll wear gloves when they grab the mail, and then sort it in the garage. They'll leave it there for a few more days to make sure it's safe. *We'll get that going tomorrow.*

Alex walks into the house, straining not to touch his face, which for some reason is nearly impossible to resist. *Like the urge to throw your keys over the side of a bridge. Ridiculous.* He washes his hands thoroughly in the mudroom and then laughs quietly to himself.

"Now I'm going to open the contaminated mail," he whispers. *This is going to drive me crazy.*

Then he thinks about the door knobs, garage door button, and faucet handles, that in theory, he just contaminated on his way in. *In addition to the bench in the mudroom where the mail is sitting.* Alex grabs the mail and walks into the kitchen to see what Kate is preparing for dinner

■

Alex picks up the phone in his office, and starts to dial his brother's cell phone. *Smartphone Alex, not the same.* Alex does the math in his head. *Mountain Time, so it's 7:01.* He's probably still driving home from Denver. He stops dialing and hangs up the phone. He dreads calling Daniel. *Alright, here we go.* He dials the number.

"Alex! How's it going out there in Maine," he yells into the phone.

"Excellent, aside from all of this pandemic nonsense."

"Yeah, it's been crazy all around the country. Karla picked up some pizza on the way home from work. Maurizio's had a three hour estimated delivery time. Can you friggin believe that?"

"I can. I saw…"

"Your business must be booming! Anti-virals. Pfizer stock should be through the roof," he interrupts. *You mean Biosphere stock.*

"**You know, I haven't even checked,**" Alex says.

"You'll probably be able to retire early with all of **those stock** options. Hell, I'm thinking about taking those TerraFlu samples you gave us and selling them on Ebay. Make a fortune."

"That may not be such a good idea. You could be trying to buy those back in a few weeks, for a much higher price," Alex says.

"You don't really think this thing is going to be a big deal?" he says. *Here he goes.*

"Actually, that's why I'm calling."

"I know, I know. Mom called me earlier today, and they're thinking about a trip out East to see the Ryan and Emily. Frankly, I think you guys are scaring the hell out of mom and dad for no reason, and you need to ease off the drama. They can plan a trip out to see you guys in a month or two."

"It'll probably be too late by then," says Alex flatly.

"Like with the Swine Flu last year? Fucking bust man. Christ! When did you guys become so paranoid? Mom thinks you came back from the war all paranoid. I told her you were always a sweat about things."

"Thanks for the Dr. Phil moment," says Alex.

"Just telling it like it is," says Daniel.

"As always. Anyway, we're just taking precautions here. It's all pretty reasonable given the world situation," Alex replies.

"I don't know who got to you guys, but I watched a senior official at DHS tell the American people that our borders were secure, and that they were several steps ahead of the flu. I'm really not worried about this one, and I don't see any reason for you to try and scare mom and dad into jumping ship."

Alex feels his anger rising.

"Well, I'm going to keep pressing them, so I suggest you guys figure something out for daycare. It sounds like mom is seriously considering the trip, and you're the only one holding her back. If you guys aren't taking this seriously, then at least let mom and dad make their own decision. And all of you over there need to watch something other than FOX news."

"Hey, if we listened to NPR and read the New York Times like you guys, we'd be wasting our money on solar panels too," he says, muffling a laugh.

"Funny. Hey, you guys are all welcome to make the trip. Just don't wait too long. Do yourselves a favor and acquire some supplies too. Lots of food, medical supplies, anything you can buy up. Seriously, it'll make a big difference. Just take one small leap of faith, that's all."

"We'll keep it in mind. Mom said that dad got a whole bunch of groceries this morning, so we can always ride it out at their house until they get the stores up and running again. Karla saw a local news spot with one of Colorado Springs' biggest food distributors, and they planned to empty the warehouses tonight and tomorrow to keep the stores full. Mom's coming over in the morning, so Karla can hit the stores early." *Sounds like a load of bullshit.*

Alex didn't believe any of it. He'd be shocked if Karla actually made it to the store. Even if she did make it past the nearest Starbucks, and into a grocery store, she wouldn't know what to buy. He knew their mother did most of the grocery shopping for Daniel's family, and that most meals at his brother's house were take-out in front of the TV. They were too busy to cook, let alone make a meal plan. He really needed to get his parents out of there. Alex suddenly has a different idea.

"Hey Danny, what if mom and dad brought your kids out for the visit? All of the cousins could hang out. Mom and dad can dote over all four of them at once, and you guys wouldn't have to worry about daycare."

"I'll run that by Karla. Hey, that's her texting me now. 'Where are you? We're hungry.' Jesus, she can't wait another twenty minutes? I gotta let you go. Talk to you later."

The call is disconnected. Alex figures that Karla will oppose the idea. Alex knows exactly what she thinks about the pandemic stuff. She thinks it's asinine, and makes no attempt to camouflage her opinion. Alex thinks about his nephews, Ethan and Kevin, and how their parents' egos will put them in severe danger. *I really hope Dan sends those kids over.*

Alex pulls his chair up to the desk and jars the computer out of standby. The screen activates, and fills the room with bluish light. The screen is bright in contrast to the room, so Alex turns on the desk lamp to soften the glow of the screen.

Alex checks the ISPAC website, and sees that a live update is scheduled for nine tomorrow morning. He also sees the site updated to reflect the recovery of their lost team. Information from the team's debrief will be part of tomorrow's live update.

He scans all of the other websites and finds nothing worth keeping him awake any longer.

"That's it, I'm beat."

Alex puts the computer on standby, and sets his wristwatch alarm for 5:45AM. On the way to the master bedroom, he stops by both of the kids' rooms to check on them. Both kids are buried in their blankets. One of Ryan's windows is open about six inches, and his room is chilly. Alex quietly closes the window. Like Alex, Ryan likes his room to be cold at night.

Alex finds his way to the master bedroom in the dark. He takes off his sweatshirt and then his watch. He throws the sweatshirt on the floor next to his side of the bed, and places the watch on the nightstand. He climbs in bed and presses up against Kate's warm body, holding her tightly, and kissing her gently on the cheek. Although deep asleep, Kate responds to his embrace by burrowing herself deeper into his hold. Alex starts to drift asleep, when suddenly his whole body twitches. He is alert, briefly, until his mind settles again, and his body is carried away into a deep sleep.

Chapter Fourteen

Tuesday, November 6, 2012

Alex sits by himself on one of the brown leather love seats in the great room. He glances up at the flat screen TV and waits for the live ISPAC information update. The Today show cuts away to a live picture in a large conference room with stadium seating. The camera is focused on a podium to the left of a large wall mounted screen. The picture on the screen features both ISPAC and CDC logos, side by side. Another podium flanks the screen on the right side. The setup reminds Alex of the Iraq War briefings he watched when he returned from the war. The information at the bottom of the screen tells Alex that the broadcast is "Live from CDC Headquarters in Atlanta, Georgia."

A man and woman, both dressed in business attire, walk to the middle of the stage, shake hands and then separate, taking position behind opposing podiums. To Alex, it almost looked like the start of a debate. Alex recognizes Dr. Allison Devreaux, of the ISPAC, as she settles in behind the left podium.

"Ladies and gentlemen, thank you for your attendance. We have a lot to cover, but before we start, I would like to introduce Dr. Joshua Relstein from the CDC, who has an announcement. Joshua."

"Thank you Allison. I am proud to announce that the CDC and ISPAC are formally joining together to coordinate pandemic efforts abroad, and most importantly here at home in the U.S. This strategic partnership, formed in time of crisis, will better focus the world's best scientific resources against the growing pandemic threat. We have received a similar pledge from the European Union's European Centre for Disease Prevention and Control (ECDC), and eagerly welcome their cooperation.

Just as a note, this morning's update will run shorter than expected. Both Dr. Devreaux and I are scheduled for a 9:30 videoconference with the White House, which obviously takes priority. I just wanted to give you all fair warning. We will both be as brief and informative as possible, leaving time for questions. Thank you in advance for your understanding. Dr. Devreaux?"

"Thank you Josh. First and foremost, all of us here extend a heartfelt thank you to the sailors and marines involved in the rescue of our survey team. The team's families and friends are relieved beyond words, as are we at the ISPAC. Few details of the rescue operation have been made available, but from what we can ascertain, the rescue was conducted at considerable personal risk to those involved.

The importance of this rescue extends well beyond reuniting the team with loved ones. Information provided by the team confirms beyond a shadow of a doubt in our minds…that Indonesia, and specifically the area around Jakarta, is the epicenter of the H16N1 pandemic outbreak. I will give you a brief synopsis of the survey teams frightening ordeal.

Upon debarking their flight at the Jakarta International Airport, **they were immediately strong-armed into what they thought was a police van, waiting for them on the runway.** Apparently, the individuals involved had become aware of a government plot to detain the survey team. This small renegade group, comprised of health care professionals and sympathetic law enforcement agents, kidnapped the team in order to prevent their immediate incarceration at the terminal.

The survey team was shuffled around Java Island for three days, hidden by sympathetic civilians. They operated in constant fear of arrest. The team observed the general state of the pandemic's progress on the island, and conducted close observation of patients when possible. The web of locals, who hid the team and helped transport them, did so at great risk. The Indonesian government had no intention of letting our team confirm the extent of the disaster unfolding on Java Island. We extend our sincerest thanks and well wishes to these heroes.

As you may have seen on the website, our rough estimate for the number of flu cases in Indonesia is simply staggering. Our survey team saw entire hospitals filled to capacity with flu victims, soccer stadiums filled, indoor malls filled. Flu patients stacked in every conceivable location for triage and treatment, with scant medical supplies available to local healthcare providers. The scene was described by one of the team members as catastrophic, with no end in sight.

The team was finally smuggled aboard a fishing boat and taken out to sea, where they sent an international distress call over the boat's VHF radio. According to the team leader, it had become common knowledge on the streets that U.S. Navy ships were operating close to Indonesian territorial waters. Fortunately for the team, the call was swiftly answered by the U.S. Navy. The details surrounding the actual rescue operation are classified.

So, what are we looking at within Indonesian borders? Data given to the team by Indonesian health officials puts the estimated number of cases at easily over a million. We thinks it's closer to two million. The number of deaths is still unknown, but sources interviewed by our teams claimed that roughly one out of every three deaths seemed related to Acute Respiratory Distress Syndrome or some form of an acute pulmonary disorder. Dr. Relstein will handle this topic when I am finished, so please hold your questions."

Dr. Devreaux rightly anticipated an outburst from the auditorium, which quieted just as quickly as it started.

"The first outbreak occurred approximately seventeen days ago, right outside of Jakarta. The outbreak spread quickly to the rest of Java Island, and some parts of Sumatra. Java Island is one of the most densely populated regions of the world, especially since Indonesia became an Islamic theocracy in 2010, and a safe haven for Muslims worldwide. Without seeking any outside help, and with very little help available internally, the H16N1 virus spread rapidly with devastating effect. Dr. Relstein will share what we've learned about H16N1 and its behavior."

Dr. Relstein picks up the coffee mug he brought up to the podium, and takes a lengthy drink.

"Thank you Allison. So, as you have all noticed, the map which is now shared by both CDC and ISPAC websites, is very different today, than it was twenty four hours ago," he says, pointing to the projection of the map on the screen behind him.

A considerable amount of talking and mumbling erupts from the crowd, as nearly every person seated in the auditorium starts to check their cell phone or PDA. Dr. Relstein stops talking for a moment, and responds to the interruption with an annoyed look. He raises his eyebrows and looks at Dr. Devreaux, shaking his head. He steps forward of the podium, and addresses one of the closest journalists.

"What just happened?" he asks a young woman in a gray business suit.

"The WHO just raised the Pandemic Phase Level to Six," she states, looking stunned. Dr. Relstein walks back to the podium, takes another drink of coffee and addresses the group.

"Alright everyone. Please, we don't have much time for this conference, so if I could please have your attention," he says loudly into the microphone.

The crowd starts to quiet and Dr. Relstein gives them another minute to simmer the excitement.

"Thank you, I have to admit that as a senior spokesperson for the CDC, I didn't expect to hear that news from all of you first."

Laughter erupts from the room.

"Well, there is no doubt that the world is right in the middle of a pandemic with devastating potential, so let's get back to what we now know about H16N1. As data pours in from around the world, it is clear that this flu is spreading, and spreading fast. Further testing and observation confirms that H16N1 is super contagious. Sounds like a very non-scientific term, but I don't know any other way to put it. Upon infecting a host, H16N1 starts shedding virus in under one day. This is the shortest latent period I have ever seen among known flu strains, and I wish the bad news ended there. The shedding is also on a level we have never witnessed with known flu strains. H16N1 appears to be hell bent on spreading. It can survive on porous and nonporous surfaces longer than we originally calculated, and is easily spread by direct and indirect contact. You do not want to sit next to someone on the bus, who has this disease. More accurately, you don't even want to be on the same bus as this person.

"So, let's take another look at the basic timeline," he says, shooting a laser pointer at the timeline on the screen.

"The latent period lasts under one day, and this is the only time that the patient is not infectious. Once the disease starts shedding, the patient enters the infectious period. Remember, the patient at this point is still asymptomatic, and spreading the disease like wildfire. At some point within four to six days of first infection, the patient enters the symptomatic period. They are still highly infectious during this period, and may remain infectious for another six to ten days after first symptoms. Like H5N1, children can remain infectious for nearly a week longer than adults. Most of the ARDS deaths occur within a few days of first showing symptoms.

Yesterday I estimated that ARDS deaths accounted for one out of five total deaths. Today, we are revising the estimate to one out of three. H16N1, like the Spanish Flu and Avian Flu, seems to trigger an autoimmune cascade in a high percentage of healthy young adults. It's a cruel irony, that this syndrome specifically targets a cross-section of society with the healthiest immune system. We are constantly analyzing this data, and revising our projections, but honestly, I thought this number would decrease, not increase. We are still in the very early stages of the pandemic, and ARDS deaths will dominate the death tolls for at least another few weeks. I don't expect the ratio to go much lower than one to three.

As for deaths due to pulmonary or secondary complications, like diabetes or heart disease, these are seen starting from four days after first symptoms and lasting months. Obviously, these cases will dominate the death tolls, especially as time increases. Generally, the early deaths occur in younger and older patients, or patients with vulnerable secondary complications. Of course, a patient's prognosis varies significantly based upon the level and duration of care available.

Before I turn this back over to Dr. Devreaux, I want to emphasize again that H16N1 has several characteristics that make it a unique and deadly pandemic flu. It is highly contagious and demonstrates a longer than normal asymptomatic period, which presents a challenge to traditional health screening methods. This must be addressed by our government immediately. Strict quarantine and social distancing strategies will be critical to mitigating the spread of this disease."

He turns to Dr. Devreaux. Dozens of hands shoot up from the auditorium.

"Thank you Dr. Relstein. We are running short on time, so we'll start questions. We can only take a few. Yes. Dr. Perry? From Johns Hopkins. Is that right?" she asks.

"Yes, thank you Allison. So, my question concerns the transmission probability of H16N1. Do you have a rough estimate of secondary attack rate or reproductive probability? Sorry to get so technical in this forum," Dr. Perry says, and glances around at the sea of journalists and reporters surrounding him.

"Not at all Dr. Perry. I would be happy to show you those numbers once you sign all of the necessary paperwork to join our team here in Atlanta," Dr. Relstein replies.

Dr Perry laughs out loud, and sits down. The joke briefly lifts the somber mood of the room, though his Dr. Relstein's answer quickly sinks the auditorium back into the realm of gasps and shaking heads.

"I tried. So, transmission probability is the chance of a disease being transmitted from one person to another if they have been in contact, and secondary attack rate is a similar projection. To answer your question, we are still trying to establish a solid estimate for transmission probability. For secondary attack rate, we have been able to isolate data for smaller groups exposed to a single index case. In these cases, we are seeing a 35-44% secondary attack rate, which is indeed high.

"We need to wrap this up quick, one more question," she says, and points to a tall man standing in the back of the auditorium.

"Thank you. Have either of your agencies consulted with the Department of Health and Human Services, to start coordinating more aggressive pandemic response measures. From what you've described today, this sounds like a logical next step."

"I couldn't agree with you more. The purpose of our videoconference with the White House today is two-fold. First, to provide our most up to date data and projections regarding the pandemic. Secondly, to stress the paramount importance of escalating measures taken by DHHS to implement the national pandemic response strategy. We are also currently reaching out to the international community, to provide this same information and stress the importance of immediate action. We are working in close coordination with the WHO to this effect. Ladies and gentlemen, I am getting a signal from the sidelines here, that we must leave. Thank you."

She starts to back away from the podium, when someone yells a question loudly enough to attract her attention.

"What about a vaccine?"

She looks up at the auditorium and steps back up to the microphone.

"Several of the best vaccine research and development sites in the world are currently working on the vaccine. From what I understand, they will work non-stop until a vaccine is produced. Thank you, I have to go."

She abruptly walks off the stage to her right, followed by Dr. Relstein and Dr. Perry, who pushes through the crowd to get up on the stage. A man wearing a CDC badge helps Dr. Perry up onto the stage, and through the same door used seconds ago by Dr. Relstein and Dr. Devreaux.

■

Alex leads the last stretch of the run down Harrison Road, keeping a quick pace for the last half mile of the run. The beach loop already carried Alex and Ryan five miles, emptying out onto Higgins Beach about half way through their run. Alex loves this route, especially breaking out into the fresh ocean air. Occasionally, when the winds are off the ocean, and conditions are just perfect, the same unmistakable traces of salt air fill their neighborhood.

They had a strong breeze in their face the whole way out, which carried colder air than he expected, especially for shorts and T-shirts, which would have been appropriate yesterday. He knew that the late fall warm spell was over when he opened the sliding door to the deck this morning, but consciously decided to extend his denial by at least one more day. Luckily, the wind has been at their back for the return trip.

Alex let Ryan lead the first half of the run, which Ryan paced at what Alex considered to be an unsustainable speed. Not for Alex, but for his son. Despite young legs and seemingly boundless energy, Alex was pretty sure that the middle school cross country team's practice runs didn't exceed four miles. Five at the most, and only occasionally. He figured that Ryan would hit a brick wall early at this pace, so he took over the lead, and slowed them down a notch. He hasn't heard any complaints.

Alex glances back at Ryan, and sees that he is upright and running strong. Alex's mind starts to wander as he passes a huge neighborhood development to his left, which only a few years ago, was abandoned farm land.

Alex looks back again. *Still looks strong.* He decides they are close enough for him to pick up the pace. *Only about a quarter of a mile, with a nasty little hill right before the turn into Durham Road.*

Alex yells back to Ryan, "Ready to pick it up for the hill?"

"Let's do it," his son yells back.

Alex quickens the pace, and lengthens his stride. He immediately feels the impact on his body's oxygen needs, as he labors up the hill. The increased pace feels good, almost purifying, though Alex is glad that the burst of speed will come to an end within a few minutes. He can already see the turn onto Durham Road. Only a short, brutal hill stands in their way. They both hit the hill, and Alex feels his legs start to burn. His son is keeping pace behind, with a similarly anguished look on his face. Alex feels his heart thumping, as he reaches the top of the hill, and they both turn onto Durham Road. Ryan runs up beside Alex, and they both slow the pace down to a jog.

"Let's loop around a few times for a warm down," he grunts to Ryan.

"Sounds good to me dad," he replies, sounding a lot less worn down than Alex.

Alex's heart starts to slow down as they approach the fork in Durham Road. Alex plans to lead them left at the fork. He glances down the right side of the fork, toward their house.

He sees two cars in the driveway, both Foresters. His garage bay door is open, and the Forester directly in front of the bay is Red, which leads him to believe the car is his. He can't see far enough into the garage to be completely sure. The Forester parked behind his car is black. Alex picks up the pace again and turns right, toward his house.

"What's up dad?" Ryan asks, as he pulls up to Alex.

"I don't know, but...hey, when we get home, I want you to stay clear of anyone you don't recognize there. Alright?" he says, as he hauls past the Perry's house, still two houses away from his own.

"Ok. What's going on?" his son asks, keeping pace.

"I'm not sure, but this could be my boss, and he's an asshole, so just stay in the backyard. Ok?"

"Yep."

Alex suddenly slows down to a walk right in front of the Walkers', wanting to slow his heart rate when he runs into Ted. *If it's Ted.* Just as he finishes this thought, he hears the unmistakable sound of his wife yelling. She sounds frantic. Alex sprints ahead, yelling back to Ryan.

"Backyard!" Alex yells over his shoulder.

Alex runs between the two cars, noticing Massachusetts plates on the black Forester.

"Get the fuck out of here, right now! Don't you fucking touch me!"

Alex hears his wife clearly, as he passes between the cars and rushes up to the mudroom door. A large man dressed in tight khaki pants and an even tighter blue polo shirt moves from inside the mudroom to block the door. The man's biceps strain against the armholes of his shirt. Despite the smart outfit, Alex immediately categorizes him as hired muscle. *Fucking Ted. I'll kill him.* His wife continues to verbally assault someone deeper in the house, as Alex walks briskly toward the door. The man in the doorway looks alarmed.

"I think he's here," the man yells back into the house.

"Stay right there, everything is fine," he says, pointing at Alex.

Alex is still breathing heavily from the run, sweat pouring from his face. He wishes this encounter had occurred under different circumstances. He knew that he was running on pure adrenaline, and that it would soon run out.

"Alex! Get these assholes out of our house," Kate yells from the kitchen.

Alex suppresses his fury, and the urge to charge through the guy at the door. He decides to try a different strategy. *I just need to get into the house.*

"Hi, I'm Alex," he says, closing the distance with his hand out.

"Jeff," the man says, shaking Alex's hand with a bewildered look.

Alex purposely gives him an excessively firm handshake, and backs up a few feet, folding his hands in front to assume a non-threatening posture. *Plenty of time for that later.* He hears his wife yell out to him.

"Alex, where are you? These assholes have been all over the house!"

"Jeff, do you see any reason why I can't come inside and help calm my wife. She sounds pretty frantic, and quite frankly, she's not exactly stable. I really need to get in here," he says calmly. *Just get me in there, so I can break Ted's neck.*

"Uh…I don't really…"

Kate suddenly appears in the mudroom.

"I've got another meathead in the kitchen standing guard over me. Ted is searching the basement. Who the fuck do these…"

A massive hand connected to a huge, tattooed forearm, extends from the kitchen into the mudroom, and grabs Kate's right arm.

She shakes loose of the grip, "Get your hands off me."

She flashes a faint smile at Alex as the other man steps into the mudroom.

"Take it easy," he barks at her, turning his head toward Alex.

The man is not as tall as the guy playing bouncer, but he is clearly cut from the same mold. His muscles bulge through the khaki pants and blue polo. He has a thick goatee and a tattoo at the base of his neck, by his right shoulder, and both of them have crew cuts. He stops trying to grab Kate, and walks a few steps toward the door. Alex notices that he has two pouches attached to his belt. One looks like it could house a multi-tool, or knife. The other is bigger. *Pepper spray canister.* Alex notes the same set up on the guy at the door.

"Your woman is out of control. You'd better do something about her before she gets hurt," he says.

"That's what I've been trying to do. She has some problems. Can I calm her down?" Alex asks.

"Be my guest," he says, nodding to the guy at the door. *So he's the leader of team meathead.*

Alex steps through the doorway, inching past the bouncer's chest, staring at him intensely. The guy's expression changes almost imperceptibly, but Alex sees it. The guy just realized that they shouldn't have let him in until their job was done. Alex intends to prove him right. He walks up to Kate and hugs her.

"How long have they been here?" he asks, moving her into the kitchen.

Alex notices that all of his computer equipment sits on top of the kitchen island, along with Ted's briefcase and a few inventory sheets.

"About ten minutes. They pushed through the door, and searched most of the house for your company equipment. They've been in our bedroom, your office, the kids' rooms. Third floor. Fucking everywhere."

"Is Emily alright?" he asks, feeling his anger almost boil over at the thought of these guys barging into their daughter's room.

"She's fine. Really freaked out, but fine. They poked their heads in and left when they saw her. I told her everything's fine, and to lock the door," she says, clutching him tightly as the leader walks into the kitchen.

"Are you alright? Did any of them touch you, beyond the obvious case of criminal assault that I saw in the mudroom," he says, emphasizing the point for the tattooed guy standing with his arms crossed near the open door to the basement.

"They pushed through me at the door, and this guy's been trying to manhandle me ever since they got here," she hisses at the guy.

"Hey, I'm just doing my job here, and she's been out 'a control. Pushing my buttons...she's fucking lucky," remarks the tattooed guy.

"Lucky about what? That she just had three fucking idiots break into her house and assault her? Just doing your job ain't gonna cut it when they come to serve the warrant for your arrest," says Alex, letting go of Kate.

"Where's the king dumbshit?" he asks Kate, getting a laugh out of her.

"He's still in the basement," she says, and they both hear footsteps ascending the basement stairs.

"Hey Carl? We're going to need to bust open a door down here. I think that's where all the samples are hidden. It has two separate locks..."

Ted enters the kitchen and see's Alex. He looks surprised. Alex whispers to Kate, who walks heads toward the great room.

"Hi Ted. Looks like you have everything you need here, so where do I sign. I'd like to conclude this transaction in less than two minutes, and I'd like to conclude it in the driveway, so please issue the appropriate orders to your crew of Neanderthals. Right fucking now!" he says, taking a few steps toward Ted.

Carl unfolds his arms and cocks his head at Alex.

"Wait a minute right there Alex. I have every right to be here. Company policy. I am required to make a visual search of your residence to check for any product literature or company property."

"Let me get this straight Ted. Somehow, Biofuck's company policy trumps the Fourth Amendment? Don't worry Carl, I don't think Ted knows what I'm talking about either, so I'll explain. If the police can't search my house without a warrant issued by a judge, why the fuck do you think that Bioshit's company policy gives you and your butt buddies here a free pass to break into my house and search it. Carl, I don't think you've thought this through very well. You guys are breaking the law, and probably probation from the looks of you..."

"That's enough with the jokes pretty boy," Carl snarls.

"Ted. Get the fuck out of my house now!" Alex yells.

"I'm not going anywhere until you open the locked door in your basement. Nobody believes your bullshit sample transaction to Maine

Med. I know you have it all hidden down there, so you can sell it later. Don't even for one minute…"

"Ted! Get out!"

Alex starts walking behind the kitchen island to reach the cordless phone. Carl moves along the other side of the island.

"Where do you think you're going?" he demands.

Alex understands why. The phone is sitting in front of the knife rack.

"I'm just grabbing the phone to dial 911," he says, swiping the phone from the counter.

Carl moves his hand away from the pepper spray pouch.

"Last warning guys. Get that out of here, and…"

"Carl, I am required to see that room. If he won't open it, then we're going to force it open," Ted squeaks across the kitchen.

"Are you kidding me Ted? Hold on. Let me make this call, so the police can be here when you and your soon to be cell mates are smashing down the door. I'll be sure to mail you some lipstick Ted. You gotta look pretty for skull fuck Fridays. Right Carl?" says Alex, walking back toward the great room with the phone.

Alex notices a strong breeze blowing into the house from open patio door.

"I'm busting that door down, and putting those samples back into the regional inventory," says Ted with spittle flying from his mouth.

"The samples are gone Ted. Gone. And now, I'd like for you to be fucking gone. Last warning fucker!" says Alex, walking through the great room to the other doorway spilling into the foyer.

Alex stands at the foot of the stairs, and watches Jeff appear in front of the island next to Carl. Jeff doesn't look comfortable with the situation. Next to the two behemoths, Ted looks pathetic. Carl's forearms look bigger than Ted's neck. Alex shakes his head at the sight.

"Gentlemen, I have a phone call to make. I expect all of you to be gone when I get back down. And take all of that shit out with you," he says, pointing to the equipment behind them.

As he walks up the stairs, he hears them arguing in the kitchen. He hears Jeff ask if they think it's a good idea for Alex to be going upstairs. *No, Jeff, it's not a good idea at all for the three of you.*

Alex gets to the top of the stairs and Kate pokes her head out of Emily's room.

"Are they leaving?" she asks.

Alex sees that she's scared.

"I don't know. They're arguing about whether to break into the storeroom downstairs. He thinks all of the samples I gave to Dr. Wright are hidden down there, and he thinks I'm going to open up a stand on the corner of our street and sell them or something. He's lost it," says Alex.

"But you do have some Terraflu samples down there?" she says.

"Yeah, that's why I'm not calling the police. I have a lot of drug samples down there, from several different companies. All stolen really, so I'd rather not take any chances. I don't know exactly what laws come into play, and I really don't want to find out."

He starts walking to the bedroom. Kate and Emily follow him.

"I still can't believe they think they're entitled to force their way into the house. Did you know they might do this?" she asks.

"I knew I'd have to inventory all of the company's equipment with Ted, but I didn't think they'd try to search the house. Ted looks frazzled, like he hasn't slept in days. I'd be willing to bet that he's taken some serious heat because of the samples. And you know what…I hope he is. Sorry about all of this Emmie," he says, peeking into her room.

"Dad, those guys are really creeping me out," says Emily.

"I know, and I'm going to get rid of them. Sorry you had to hear all of that yelling, are you alright sweetie?" he asks her.

"I'm fine daddy. I was worried about mommy when you weren't here. They weren't very nice to her," she says.

He looks up at Kate, shaking his head. He can see tears forming in Kate's eyes.

"Do you feel better now that daddy's here?"

"Yes," she says, and hugs him.

"Good. I would never let anything happen to you or mommy," he says looking into her eyes and smiling.

"Or Ryan?" she says.

"Or Ryan. Hey hon, can you take our little sweetness into the bedroom and call out to Ryan in the back yard. Just tell him to stay in the backyard, and that everything's OK in here. I saw him stretching near the picnic table when I was on my way up the stairs. If you could do that now, I have some pressing business on the ground level. I don't think Ted will leave unless I can motivate him" he says, still hugging Emily, and giving Kate an urgent look.

"Hey Emily, let's make sure Ryan stays in the backyard, and we can watch some TV," she says, taking Emily's hand and walking into the bedroom.

Alex follows closely behind and slips into the walk-in closet, located to the left of the bedroom door. He reaches high up into the left front corner of the closet, and pulls his Mossberg shotgun down from the top shelf. He had moved the shotgun to the closet a few days ago, late in the evening, creating a nest for it behind a long stack of sweatshirts. He takes a key from a small hook along the inside of the closet door trim. He opens the trigger lock on the shotgun, putting the lock on the shelf, and places the gun against the door frame.

He kicks off his running shoes and pulls on an old pair of faded jeans. He slips the shoes back on his feet, grabs the shotgun, and moves with purpose toward the staircase. On the way, he hears the men still arguing in the kitchen. He can definitely hear Ted's unsettled voice, which reassures Alex that none of them are in the basement. He needs them all in one place for this to work.

He gets to the top of the stairs and stops for a moment. He removes all four of the shotgun shells from the stock of the weapon, where they are stored for a quick reload. He places the shells in his back pocket. The shotgun is unloaded, but Alex knows he can have it loaded in a matter of seconds if they call his bluff and escalate the situation. He contemplates leaving the shells in the kids' bathroom, but decides against it.

He can hear Kate and Emily calling out to Ryan, and he is pretty sure he hears Ryan respond. Alex needs to make sure that Ryan is out of the picture, so he steps into the kids' bathroom and looks out of the window into the backyard. He feels a strong gust of wind through the window as he spots Ryan on the picnic table, talking to the girls. *Feels like that front is moving through. Alright, here we go.* He walks to the top of the stairs and starts to descend them. About half way down the stairs, he hears Ted announce that he's going to grab a sledgehammer from the garage, and break down the door. Jeff protests the plan immediately. *This guy is amazing.*

He reaches the bottom of the stairs and takes an immediate left into the great room. The squabble in the kitchen quiets as they realize he is back on the ground floor of the house. His plan is to get behind them and force them out of the front of the house. He'd prefer to drive them toward the front door, and not the mudroom. By moving them toward the front door, they would be visible to him the entire time.

He assumes that the sight of the shotgun should scatter them pretty quickly, especially Ted, though he's slightly concerned about Carl. Carl strikes him as fearless, and Alex wouldn't be surprised if Carl declares bullshit. All of these thoughts float through his head again, as he rounds the great room corner, and confronts the bickering trio.

"I agree with Jeff. I think you should all leave. Right…fucking…now," he says in a conversational tone, keeping the shotgun pointed at the floor.

Jeff spots the shotgun first.

"Take it easy dude, we're on our way out," he says, raising his hands in front of him.

Ted's eyes widen to fill his glasses. Carl immediately puts his right hand down to his pepper spray pouch, as Ted gasps and falls back into Carl. Ted hits Carl's solid chassis and stops. Carl pushes him aside with his free hand, knocking him into the wall to the left of the group. He knocks loose a framed picture from the wall, which becomes lodged between Ted and the wall. Ted moves his hand behind him to catch the frame. He lowers it to the ground behind him, unbroken, never taking his eyes off Alex.

Alex moves into the dining area, and swiftly puts the kitchen island between him and the men. He raises the shotgun above the level of the island's granite surface, to keep it visible, but does not point the weapon at any of the men. He keeps it pointed toward the mudroom, hoping to dissuade them from moving in that direction. At this point, Alex feels that he has their attention.

"That's not exactly a good instinct you have their Carl. Sudden moves and shotguns? Not a good idea at all."

All three of them watch him intensely. Carl wears a look of sheer hatred, which worries Alex. *This guy can't stand the fact that he's lost control of the situation.* Ted looks paralyzed, which isn't ideal either. He had hoped that Ted would order them out of the house at the sight of the shotgun, but it appears that he is no longer in control of himself or the other men. Jeff shows a composed fear. He is edging toward the front door, which slightly eases Alex's concerns about the situation.

"Jeff here seems like the brains of this operation, so I recommend you all follow his lead and head out the front door. I'll place all of this equipment on the walkway, and then Ted and I can finish the inventory, while the two of you wait in the car. I'll leave the shotgun inside Ted, don't worry. Let's go. Out the front door…now," he snarls.

Finally, Ted manages to speak, his voice is cracked.

"This is legitimate company business, and you have no right to point a gun at us. I don't…"

"I haven't pointed a gun at anyone, right Jeff? I just wanted to show off my brand new shotgun to a couple of firearms enthusiasts. And regarding all of this as being legitimate? Give me a fucking break Ted. I'm sure Michelle wouldn't approve of your plan to bust down doors with a stolen sledgehammer. Then again, she's out of her skull too. Keep walking, all of you," he says firmly, moving around the side of the island to herd them toward the door.

Carl's eyes burn a hole in Alex's face, and his hand is still defiantly placed on the pepper spray pouch. All three of them continue moving down the hallway to the foyer. Jeff reaches the door first, and opens the glass storm door.

"Jeff, could you press the button down there to keep the door open?" says Alex.

Jeff nods, and pushes the button on the bottom hydraulic closer with his foot. He lets go of the door, and it stays open for the Ted and Carl.

"You know, it was Michelle's idea to hire these guys. She was pretty pissed at you. I told her it wasn't necessary, but she insisted," he tells him smugly.

"You're both fucking idiots Ted," says Alex.

Both Carl and Ted exit the house, and start walking down the walkway, toward the driveway. Jeff is well ahead of them, almost at Ted's car. Carl is walking away, still watching Alex. His hand is still on the pepper spray case. Alex places the shotgun against the wall on the inside of the house, and steps out onto the rough granite block steps. Carl covertly flips open the cap on the pepper spray, staring at Alex, and slowing his walk.

"Bad idea Carl. Bad idea. Ted, I want you to pull your car into the street. I don't want these guys on my property. Carl here has a death wish. I'll start loading the gear onto the porch, when these two are off my property," says Alex, stepping halfway into the house and keeping his eyes fixed on Carl's enraged face.

"We'll just have ourselves a nice talk with the cops about your shotgun," yells Carl.

"Oh, I didn't bother to call the police Carl," says Alex.

"What the fuck? You said…"

"That I was calling 911? Nope. Keep moving or the next town official on the scene will be the coroner," he says.

Alex watches as Ted moves both cars onto the street. Carl takes a seat on the hood of Alex's former car, and lights a cigarette from a pack he pulls from his back pocket. Jeff stands behind Ted's car, keeping an eye on the front door of the house. Momentarily satisfied that Carl doesn't plan to charge the house, Alex steps back inside to grab the gear off the kitchen island.

He calls up the stairs to Kate.

"Hey hon?"

"Yeah? Are those jackasses gone?" she yells from the bedroom.

"Yeah, they're outside waiting," he says.

He can hear her walking down the upstairs hallway. He sees her appear at the top of the stairs, and shiver.

"Wow, that's a chilly breeze. No more T-shirts, huh?" she says.

"Hey, the guys are out of the house. What's Emily up to?" he asks.

"She's watching the Disney Channel in our room."

"Is she OK?" he asks.

"She's fine, she got really worried when I was downstairs alone with those assholes."

Alex glances back outside. Carl looks relaxed on the hood of the car. Ted is standing next to Jeff, looking over some paperwork on the hood of Ted's car.

"Let's get Ryan inside and upstairs. I'm gonna carry all of the computer stuff outside and sign whatever papers I need to sign to get them out of here. I'm really sorry about all this. I had no idea this would happen. Fucking unreal," he says.

"Fucking unreal is right," she whispers, walking down the stairs to call Ryan inside. She walks to the sliding screen door and calls him into the house.

Alex checks on the guys again. *All in the same places. Good.* He walks into the kitchen and picks up the laser printer. He walks this over to the open door, and places it on the walkway in front of the granite steps. *I'm really going to miss that printer.* Ryan walks up to Alex as he returns for the rest of the gear.

"Everything OK dad?" he asks before he spots the shotgun leaning against the wall next to the front door.

"Whoa, what's that for? Is it real?" he says, pushing past Alex to get a closer look.

Alex grabs Ryan by the shoulder.

"Don't touch that. Just head upstairs. We'll talk about it later," says Alex, putting himself between the shotgun and Ryan.

"I didn't know we had a shotgun. What is that a Mossberg?" he says, peeking around Alex while backing up to the stairs.

"How do you know what a Mossberg is?" says Alex.

"Modern Warfare. Whenever I use a shotgun, I like to use the Benelli because…"

"Yeah I know, semi-automatic instead of pump," he says, ruffling Ryan's hair, "Get out of here. We can talk guns later."

"I'd rather you didn't," adds Kate from the kitchen.

Kate pours a glass of water from the sink and walks past Alex by the island.

"Why don't you all stay upstairs until these bozos are out of sight," he says.

"Sounds good to me," she says, walking to the stairs.

"Come on, does he have to sit there smoking in front of our house?" she says, standing at the bottom of the stairs, looking out at Carl.

"I'm just glad he's sitting out there where he won't make any trouble. That guy looked unstable, and he's not in the least bit happy that I got the better of him," he says, walking by Kate with a large stack of promotional material that Ted dug out of his office closet.

"He has a bad look to him," he whispers back to her, as he places the material on the walkway.

Kate looks out at Carl again and shakes her head before walking up the stairs. Alex makes three more trips, offloading the computer tablet and the rest of the peripheral equipment associated with the computer. The last item he handles is Ted's brown leather briefcase. He assembles the paperwork sitting on the island and stuffs it into the briefcase. He picks up Ted's cell phone from the island and starts to put it into a side pouch on the briefcase, when a better idea comes to mind.

He scrolls through the Blackberry's contacts and finds the regional manager's contact information. He selects her cell phone number and presses send. Michelle answers on the first ring. *Perfect.*

"Hey Ted, I assume the deed is done. Did you recover the samples?" Michelle asks.

"Actually it's Alex. I just killed Ted and the two thugs you hired. Shot them dead in my basement and beheaded them. I'm about to bury their heads in the backyard," he says, and waits.

A few seconds go by.

"Are you still there Michelle?"

"Alex? Is this some kind of a joke?" she says.

Alex can tell she's unsure.

"Yes, this is a joke Michelle. I didn't kill Ted. Or the two criminals you hired. I did have to eject them from my house, after they broke in and rough housed my wife and daughter. You might want to schedule a little HR review session for Ted. Somehow, he got it into his head that he could bust into my house, when I wasn't here, and have his thugs restrain my wife while he ransacked the house. This could have ended very badly Michelle," he says, and motions for Ted to come retrieve his gear.

Ted hesitates, and starts to edge around the front of the car.

"Come on man, I don't have all day! Don't worry; I'm not going to hurt you. Sorry about that Michelle. It seems that I gave Ted quite a fright. He looks a little scared," he says, stepping forward from the doorway, and away from the hidden shotgun.

"We should have this wrapped up in a few minutes Michelle, then you and Ted can chat. Unless you'd like to talk with him right now," says Alex.

"No, that's alright," she says, blankly.

"As for the samples, you can contact Dr. Wright at Maine Coast Internal Med, and see if he'd be willing to return them. Or, even better, you could hire ten more meatheads like the two here, and bust some heads over at Dr. Wright's office. Hey Ted, Michelle wants to talk to you," he says, and throws the phone to Ted, who is standing about ten feet away from Alex.

Ted barely catches the phone, juggling it a few times, before gaining control. He puts the phone to his ear.

"Michelle?" he says, and starts nodding his head.

Alex can hear her yelling over the phone.

"I know. I know. No, no, everything was done by the book…Look, the policy isn't exactly clear about the verification process…No, I didn't touch his wife…I don't know. No, I didn't see the….can we talk about this when I'm done here. He's standing right here watching…Yes, I'll call you as soon as I'm on the road."

He disconnects the call and closes the phone, cursing under his breath.

"That didn't sound like a career enhancing phone call," says Alex, standing with his hands on his hips in front of the pile.

"Fuck you," Ted mutters, barely making eye contact with Alex.

"Looks like it's all here, so let's get this over with. Where do I sign," says Alex.

Ted takes the paper work out of his briefcase, and locates the inventory sheet. He matches the listed items with the array of equipment sitting on the red concrete pavers.

"Looks like it's all here," he says, "except for the samples you stole."

Alex walks over and starts to sign the inventory. As he starts to enter the date, he catches movement in his peripheral vision, and spots Carl halfway across the front lawn, heading directly at the two of them.

Alex freezes for a few moments, unable to react, giving Carl enough ground to make it impossible for Alex to retreat into the house.

Shit. Carl's face is deep red, snarled in a malicious glare. His intentions are clear, so Alex pushes Ted directly into Carl's path. Ted's stiffened body collides with Carl, and causes Carl to stumble forward, off balance. As he pitches forward, he desperately aims the pepper spray canister in his right hand in Alex's direction, and activates the canister. Carl tramples Ted's body as he staggers.

The direction of the spray is not accurate, and the unit shoots a thick fog in his general direction, which, if aimed better, would have enveloped Alex's entire upper body in a caustic pepper spray cloud. Instead, the majority of the blast saturates the air to Alex's left, and gets caught in the strong breeze flowing through the front door. The wind disperses the pepper spray fog over all the three of them.

Alex instantly feels burning in his eyes and nose, as he rushes to neutralize Carl. He knows that he has to do this fast, before Jeff reinforces the group.

Carl whirls around; still unsteady, trying to aim the canister at Alex again, as Alex slides alongside Carl's right side. Carl is still focused on using the spray, which gives Alex an advantage. Alex slides his own right arm under Carl's right arm, and reaches up across his massive chest. Simultaneously, he places his right leg behind Carl's legs and twists his own core to the left. This topples Carl onto his back.

Alex quickly puts Carl's pepper spray arm into an extended lock, and pushes down on the elbow, creating an unbearable pressure on Carl's shoulder. Despite the size and strength of Carl's arm, he immediately drops the canister.

"Alright, that's enough!" he yells through the grass, coughing and rubbing his eyes with his other hand.

Alex starts to cough as the pepper spray makes breathing more painful. His eyes are burning, and nearly closed. Alex keeps Carl's arm under pressure with one hand, and picks up the pepper spray canister with the other. His hands, neck and face feel like they are on fire.

Pissed off and in pain, Alex aims the pepper spray canister at Carl's face near the ground, and releases a point blank blast of pepper spray fog. The effects are immediate, as Carl groans and starts to scream. Alex aims casually at Ted, on the ground behind Carl, and dispenses the rest of the canister. The fog envelopes Ted's body, and causes his former manager to start pounding the grass while squealing.

Alex disengages the arm lock, and runs toward the open front door, tossing the canister behind him. He looks back and sees Jeff walk slowly over to Carl and Ted, with his hands in the air in.

Alex closes the door, and watches the scene unfold, barely able to keep his own eyes open for more than a few seconds at a time. Jeff helps Carl back to his Alex's old Forrester, having to restrain him a few times from charging the house again. Ted continues to cry out in pain, and barely rises to his knees. His hands appear glued to his eyes. He looks pathetic on his knees in a crumpled navy blue suit, hunched over coughing. *I hope he doesn't have asthma.* Alex sees grass stains on the chest of Ted's blue shirt. *Maybe I shouldn't have done that to him. Now how am I going to get all of this junk off my property?*

Alex opens the front door and yells out to Ted.

"Ted, I'd like all of this trash out of here immediately." he says, coughing.

Alex shuts the front door and locks it. He does the same in the mudroom, and closes the garage door. Alex then runs over to the sink to get a drink of water, and to try and flush the pepper spray out of eyes. Alex was fortunate that he really just got a dusting of the pepper spray. He walks over to the door with the glass of water, and see's Jeff picking up all of the equipment and loading Ted's car. Alex bets they'll all have to sit there for a while before Ted can drive again. He'll keep a close eye on them until they're gone.

Chapter Fifteen

Wednesday, November 7, 2012

Alex gets up from the couch and walks into the kitchen looking for Kate. She got up to pour a cup of coffee and disappeared into the mudroom after they determined that today's joint CDC/ISPAC update had been cancelled. He hasn't heard her make any noise for several minutes. He feels a small burst of anxiety not knowing her exact location and his pulse quickens as he moves swiftly over to the mudroom. As he approaches the entry to the mudroom, he hears muffled voices followed by raucous laughter and Samantha Walker's unmistakable shriek. Alex knows they're laughing about him.

He opens the mudroom storm door and steps out onto the stoop.

"Uh, we like to keep the riff raff to a minimum around…"

Alex is interrupted by a coughing fit that lasts several seconds.

"Jesus. You were right," Samantha says and glances at Kate. They both look like they could break out laughing at any moment.

"Still tickling your throat?" she says, trying to look sympathetic.

"Tickling? More than tickling. I'll be tasting this shit for days," he says.

"Sorry. I really can't believe that happened," says Samantha, putting her arm around her waist.

Alex knew that he'd probably be coughing from the pepper spray until Saturday. Like tear gas, most of the pepper spray's effects are short lived, no more than thirty to forty five minutes, but the respiratory inflammation takes a few days to completely subside. Even though he despised Ted, he felt bad about giving him the extra blast of spray. If Ted is asthmatic, he could have serious complications for several days. Most deaths related to the use of pepper spray are caused by the severe respiratory complications triggered by massive airway inflammation.

"I was asking Kate how your little vacation was coming along," she says.

"Well, as you can see it got off to a rough start," replies Alex.

"And I wanted to find out what happened. Ed was pretty sure he missed the exciting part. He said that two of the guys needed help getting back to their cars. He didn't want to bother you last night," she says.

"One of the guys was a psychopath, and I had to convince him to vacate the premises. He tried to pepper spray me," he says, muffling a cough

"Sounds…and looks like he got you," she says, focusing on his eyes, "unless you just spent the last hour firing up some good stuff in the basement," she says, and both of the women start laughing.

"Funny," he says wryly, suddenly very self-conscious of his bright red eyes, another pepper spray gift likely to stick around for a few more days.

"You look like one of the guys in those pothead movies. What is it Kate?" she asks.

"Oh, uh…Harold and Kumar!" blurts Kate.

"Yeah, but he's like…Harold and Kumar join the Marine Corps!" says Sam, and they both double over laughing.

"I hope you two are enjoying this," he says, slightly laughing.

"Seriously though," she says, stifling a few more fits of laughter, "is everything OK? You're fine right?"

"Yeah I'm fine. Thanks. I received an indirect hit from the pepper spray canister, which is more than I can say for the two guys Ed saw limping back to the car. I'm sure Ed told you that I quit my job on Monday."

"Right before he was about to be fired," adds Kate.

"Thank you honey. For some reason, the regional manager, who also apparently hates my guts now, hired two meatheads to accompany Ted on his mission to retrieve my computer equipment…"

"Yeah, they show up when Alex and Ryan are out for a run, and push their way into the house, searching for company property," Kate interjects.

"Get out of here!" Samantha says.

"And they wouldn't leave until I threatened them with a shotgun," adds Alex.

"You have a shotgun?" says Samantha, with a quizzical look.

"Fortunately. They were talking about breaking some doors down in the basement to complete their search. Unbelievable," he says.

"I'm freezing. I'll be right back," Kate says, and disappears back into the house.

"So, are you going to keep the kids home with Ed?" he asks.

"I think so. I hate to have them miss school for nothing, but this thing is getting worse, and the number of cases in the area…they're really multiplying quickly. Ed didn't have any problems working from home, so

I think we're going to keep them home tomorrow and see how it goes. How has it been going for you guys?"

"Aside from this," he says, pointing to his eyes, "it's been going well. Kate's working from home, and her firm hasn't bothered her much, so she's just going to keep working out of the home office. What about you?" he asks.

"I don't think there's any way I can pull that off. I need to be physically present in the office. I'm keeping my eyes on the situation, and if it gets really bad, I'll call in sick, or, god forgive me, activate Operation Dead Relative, which, in my view is really one of your sickest ideas. Unfortunately, it's the only one I can think of to get me out of the office for any length of time."

"Just say you have flu symptoms. Nobody will want you to come in. It's as easy as that," he says, as Kate emerges from the house, wearing a thigh level dark blue coat with a hood.

"Anyway. I'll let the two of you laugh a little more at my expense. I'm headed back down into the basement to hang out with Cheech and Chong," he says, and opens his bloodshot eyes wide.

"Jesus honey. There's some Visine in the medicine cabinet honey. Please, don't feel like you need to conserve any," Kate says, shaking her head.

"See what I get from her. I leap in front of a cloud of pepper spray to save her, and all she does is make jokes…"

"They're just really gross looking hon," she says.

"I'm out of here," he says, and tries to smack her rear as she scoots away.

∎

Alex and Kate snuggle together on the couch to watch a recording of tonight's NBC Evening News. Alex stifles a cough and shakes his head. The anchor, Kerrie Connor, appears on the screen alongside a large flat screen monitor. The studio monitor shows an image of an American aircraft carrier plowing through rough seas. Alex stifles a cough and shakes his head.

"Good evening. Tonight's top stories. Tensions with China increase as the fate of several hundred World Health Organization health workers remains unknown. At least two more U.S. aircraft carriers and an additional battle group are dispatched to the region.

In Jakarta, the death toll rises as the killer flu burns unhindered throughout Java Island, and spreads to Sumatra. The first reporters on scene describe the sight as cataclysmic.

Worldwide, the Jakarta flu continues to spread. Reports of large flu outbreaks in Europe, the Middle East and Africa have world health officials concerned that the pandemic cannot be contained.

Here at home, the number of flu cases continues to rise, as the CDC and the Department of Human and Health Services race to stay one step ahead of the pandemic. Earlier this afternoon the CDC reported that the number of lab confirmed cases in the U.S. reached thirteen thousand yesterday, only six days into the crisis. **Several hundred deaths have been associated with the Jakarta Flu, mostly due to Acute Respiratory Distress** Syndrome. The high incidence of Acute Respiratory Distress Syndrome has raised serious concerns that the Jakarta Flu may have characteristics similar to the 1918 Spanish Flu, where apparently healthy young adults died of massive respiratory complications shortly after developing symptoms of the flu. Health officials are keeping a close eye on this potentially devastating characteristic, given the surprising fact that no treatment has ever been shown to be effective in halting or reversing the effects of the syndrome.

Shortages of food and medical supplies have caused considerable disruption throughout the nation, as most Americans hurried to the stores over the weekend to stock up on groceries and essentials. Most had to wait hours to buy groceries, or were turned away altogether. In Los Angeles, a disastrous situation was narrowly averted by Mayor David Gomez's swift deployment of the city's disaster supply package to Watts, where over a thousand angry residents had gathered to protest the city's inability to keep the food supply chain flowing to minority communities. A police officer at the scene confirmed that the situation was moments from erupting into a full scale riot. Law enforcement officials nationwide expect similar situations to develop as the flu worsens and shortages continue.

Major food suppliers and distributors responded to the criticism, blaming the shortages on a system adept at minimizing wasted product, but unable to cope with an unexpected and sustained rush. Federal commerce officials speculate that it may take a few weeks for the system to catch up with the demand. Pandemic experts from the ISPAC cast serious doubt on the system's capability to restore the nation's food supply under existing conditions.

First, a closer look at the crisis developing in China. Department of Defense officials acknowledged today that an additional carrier battle group comprised of ships from Hawaii and Southern California, will join naval forces already deployed to the South China Sea. A battle group centered on the nuclear aircraft carrier George Washington, based out of Japan, is already on station in the area. And rumors of another carrier being recalled from the Arabian gulf, for service off the coast of China, have not been confirmed by the Pentagon.

Chinese government officials protested the additional deployments to the United Nations. Jennifer Moskowitz reports from United Nations headquarters in Manhattan."

The screen changes to a picture of a blond woman with medium length hair, wearing a rather non-descript black ensemble, standing in front of a spectacularly illuminated United Nations Secretariat building. Several member nation flags wave in a light breeze, bathed in spotlights. The broadcast is live.

"Kerrie, I'm standing in front the United Nations Secretariat building, where the mood today can only be described as tense and desperate. Chinese delegates continued to deflect questions regarding the status of WHO teams within their borders, stating only that these teams are consumed by the task of containing and mitigating the pandemic within Chinese borders, and have no intention of abandoning their heroic efforts on behalf of the Chinese people. Tempers flared as delegates from at least a dozen nations accused the Chinese of holding the teams hostage. Delegates from Germany and Australia went so far as to blame China once again for exacerbating the pandemic situation, a reference to China's mishandling of the 2008 Avian Flu pandemic."

"Jennifer, was there any mention of sanctions against China, or the use of force to expedite the release of the WHO teams?"

"There was no discussion or suggestion of sanctions today by the assembly, however, it is no secret to any of the members that several nations have assembled outside of the U.N. to discuss options in response to China's actions. Chinese delegates repeatedly lobbied the assembly to formally denounce the growing coalition outside of the U.N. They are particularly alarmed by the deployment of an additional U.S. carrier battle group to the region, calling this an aggressive and warlike action."

"Thank you Jennifer."

The screen next to Kerrie shows a Google Earth map of Indonesia, which starts to slowly pan closer to the city of Jakarta, on the northwestern tip of Java Island.

"Reporters and a limited number of aid workers landed during daylight hours at Jakarta's International Airport, to assess the worsening situation on Java Island. Flights are unable to land during nighttime hours, due to a complete black out on Java Island. Initial reports passed through Indonesian health officials puts the official death toll at nearly 85,000, with over a million cases estimated on Java Island alone.

One health official stressed that these figures were only an estimate, since they no longer have any accurate way to track the sheer volume of cases, which grows by the hour. Health officials told reporters that they were shocked by how quickly the flu spread through the population. The first cases of the Jakarta Flu appeared less than three weeks ago.

Indonesian diplomats around the world pleaded with the international community for aid, in the form of food, medical supplies and infrastructure support. WHO officials hinted that no pandemic response assets are likely to be deployed to Java Island or Sumatra. An anonymous source at the United Nations stated that WHO resources are stretched thin, and are being reserved for locations where containment stands a better chance of success. For Java Island and Sumatra, it appears that little hope is on the horizon. We'll have more when we return,"

The screen cuts to a commercial, and Alex starts to fast forwards past them.

"I'm sure the Mullahs will blame the West for this somehow. Unfortunately for them, they'll be preaching to empty mosques. This pandemic is going to clear their bleachers."

"Honey, that's not cool. It'll clear the bleachers everywhere."

"I know, but facts are facts. Modernized societies with modern health care systems will suffer a much lower casualty rate than any of those shitholes," says Alex.

"It's still sad," she says.

"And they'll still find a way to blame it all on us somehow. I'm just glad there won't be as many of them to hear their nonsense," he says.

"That's enough. I don't want to hear any more about it. Are the kids up in the attic?" says Kate.

"Ryan was up there on the Xbox. They'll love the new games. I got a bunch we can all play, and a couple for Ryan and me."

"Let me guess, Call of Duty Future Warrior and Insurgency Three?"

"You peaked," he says flatly.

"The other games look fun I guess, but I'd have to be really bored."

"I don't think that's going to be a problem," he says, and stops fast forwarding.

Chapter Sixteen

Thursday, November 8, 2012

Alex walks up the stairs to the attic, and coughs several times on his way up the stairs, still feeling the effects of the pepper spray. He reaches the top of the stairs, and sees Kate walking on the treadmill. Her pace is slow, but Alex can see that the treadmill is set to the highest incline possible. Kate is wearing maroon running shorts and a black cutoff running top, which to Alex, resembles a bra. She is sweating, and breathing heavily, as she struggles to keep her pace on the incline. She shoots him an annoyed glance and doesn't say a word. Alex knows she doesn't like to talk during her workouts. Alex walks over to her and checks the time on the treadmill. *Four minutes left.* He decides to do a set of pull-ups. As he turns around, he hears the treadmill start to grind, as the incline is automatically lowered for her warm down.

Alex walks over to the freestanding pull-up bar, and begins a declining set, starting at twelve pull-ups. Halfway through the set, Kate interrupts.

"Hey, did you see that Portland's considering school closures next week?" she says, out of breath.

Alex finishes a few more pull-ups and hops down to the floor.

"No. Did they say anything about any of the other towns?" he asks.

"Falmouth closed today. They made the decision last night at an emergency school board meeting. They have six confirmed cases at the high school, and a few more at the other schools in town. School officials made the decision because they suspect that there might be a dozen or more unconfirmed cases present at the school. I guess one of the original cases identified last week was a guy from Falmouth, who travels back and forth from New York every week for business. He has a son and a daughter at Falmouth high school. Had a son and daughter. He died early in the week," says Kate.

"Was all this on the news?" Alex asks.

"Yeah, they just ran the story this morning," she says, pressing a few more buttons to slow the treadmill even further.

"What about Scarborough?" he presses.

"Nothing. Just Portland and Falmouth. The governor's office is looking into statewide school closures, but according to their spokesperson, Susan Michaud is probably going to wait for the feds to make the recommendation. It has something to do with emergency funding, but it sounds like it has more to do with politics," she says.

"It always does," he says, and hops up on the bar for a set of ten pull-ups.

"I still can't believe you haven't heard from Ted?" she says, stepping off the treadmill and onto a mat to stretch.

Alex finishes, hops down, and raises his arms above his head for a stretch.

"I just hope I didn't kill the guy. I did hear from HR. They left a voicemail on my cell phone letting me know that I am checked out, and should expect a final package shortly. God knows what's in that package. Probably a non-disclosure agreement for me to sign, or something equally as asinine."

"Nothing like a formal apology for the home invasion and pepper spray attack?" she says, incredulously.

"Not a mention. I really don't care either. I'm just glad to be done with them," he says, and hops back up on the pull-up bar.

"I'm gonna to be done soon if I don't come up with something better than diarrhea to keep me out of the office. I've cancelled several appointments already, and Jim left me a message yesterday asking when I could reschedule them. I'll need to call him today. Monday at the latest," she says.

Alex finishes several pull-ups and drops back down to the floor. He starts to cough again, which forces him to bow toward the ground.

"Damn it! I can't get rid of this," he says, exasperated.

"Maybe you need to take it easy," she says, and wipes her face with a white towel.

"Probably. Anyway, you just need to buy a little more time at work. The way things are looking, you won't have to hide much longer. They're starting to shut down the schools, and other steps will be taken by the state and the feds within the upcoming week. I'd just keep stalling them. Tell Jim you still have a fever, but you might be able to meet with clients. Trust me, they won't want to see you any time soon. Speaking of calls, I still need to call my parents," he says, and pauses.

"I haven't heard anything from them about bringing my brother's kids out."

Kate turns her head toward Alex and gives him a perplexed look.

"What do you mean?" she asks.

"What do you mean, what do you mean?" he replies, buying himself a few more seconds.

"I don't remember you mentioning anything about your parents bringing Ethan and Kevin out," she says sternly.

"Well, I'm pretty sure that's not going to happen. I was talking to Daniel a few nights ago, and getting nowhere with him, as usual. My parents are stuck there babysitting and raising his kids. That's why they won't leave. They can't. My brother won't let them go, 'without some advance notice.' Unbelievable if you ask me. 'Karla can't come home at three in the afternoon to babysit.' And of course, God forbid they actually have to dig into their own pockets to pay for babysitting. I thought that if my parents brought Kevin and Ethan, then there would be no babysitting issue for Daniel."

Kate waits patiently for his tirade to end.

"First of all, Karla would never go for it, and neither would your brother. Second, your parents will never make the trip. For the same reason you just ranted about, and many more. Same story with my parents. But that's not why I'm a little pissed…"

"Can I get a drink of water before we get into this?" interrupts Alex. *I just need a few more seconds.*

"You look like you'll live. So, I'm little pissed because we've talked about all of this before. Your brother and my sister are off the list, and have been off the list for quite a while. Things would not work out with them here, for any duration of time. Pandemic, long weekend, short weekend, Super Bowl party. It doesn't matter. It never worked before, and I can't figure out why you continue to press the issue with them," she says.

"I felt safe making the offer, because they'll never make the trip. I just feel that I have to at least make the offer," he says. *That's a weak excuse.*

"I know. I have the same guilt with Claire, but her husband can be an intolerable ass, and so can she."

"They're not that bad. Not as bad as Daniel and Karla," he says.

"I think they're worse. They try to take control of everything, and if you're not on the same page, well I don't need to describe the scene any further. Bottom line? We can't have them here in a quarantine situation. Plus, they think it's all a joke anyway," she says, shaking her head.

"If they were onboard with the whole idea from the beginning, I might have reconsidered and invited them, but they weren't, so I have never mentioned it to them. I don't know why you would even consider it for Daniel and Karla. They openly mock all of this," she says, waving her hands around.

"You're right, sorry," he says.

"I can't count the number of times you've lectured me about how important it will be to stick to our plan. 'In a quarantine situation, there is no room for error. We have to stick to the plan. No variations.'"

"Alright, you don't have to mock me. I'm sorry. They're not coming out anyway, so we don't have to worry," he says.

"That's not what I'm worried about. I'm worried that you didn't think about the dangerous situation you might have created. If your brother took you up on the offer, and sent the kids out with your parents, then what happens when your brother and Karla finally come to their senses about the pandemic all around them? Where do you think they'll be headed? Here to join their kids. How would we deal with that? Tell them it's too late. Sorry. Head on back to Colorado. Here's some TerraFlu. We'll take care of the kids. Not likely they'd leave. Do we let them in, and try to quarantine them for ten days in the mudroom area? Hope they're not harboring the flu? Would they leave if they showed symptoms? If they won't leave without their kids, do we send the kids out onto the streets with their parents and some supplies?"

She continues to look softly into his eyes. Alex has a hard time meeting them.

"You're right. It could lead to a disastrous confrontation. I really never thought of it this way," he says, as he leans over to kiss her forehead.

"Do you think we should just forget about trying to convince our parents to come out here?" he asks. "I don't feel like giving up on them, but you're right. At a certain point…"

His voice trails off.

"I don't know. I hate to give up on them too. I'm still trying to get my brother out here. He's only a few hours away, but I'm certain that he'll head to Princeton when things get bad. He's really tight with them. He always heads down there when they have something going on. If my parents won't come to him, he'll come to them. He still drags the family to Princeton for every holiday. They haven't celebrated Christmas or Thanksgiving in Concord since they moved in."

"He's a momma's boy. First child is always a momma's boy," he teases.

"You're not," she says. "I wouldn't have married you if you were."

He tightens his hug for a moment and kisses her neck.

"They should all be going up to New Hampshire. Your parents included. They could easily ride out the storm up north. It kills me to think that your brother would abandon the perfect mountain hideout for New Jersey," he says.

"My parents have the same problem as yours. They're stuck. I guarantee my sister will head up there when the flu racks the Baltimore area. She's probably on the way already with the kids," she says. "They'll all flock to Princeton. Trust me."

"Well, at least the mountain camp will be empty. If the situation got out of control here, we could always pack up as much stuff as possible and head up into the White Mountains. Does Robbie keep the place stocked in the winter?" he says.

"Not really. They have everything you'd find in a camp, but no food or stuff like that. I know he has enough firewood to keep the stove going forever, and a well, but that wouldn't work if the electric died. He does have a propane tank for hot water and the stove."

"We can keep it in mind. We can definitely get there on a single tank of gas," he says.

"Probably," she says.

"Well anyway, I won't push the issue with my parents. God knows I've pushed it enough," he says.

She squeezes his hand and he hugs her tightly.

"I think we made all of the offers we needed to make. I don't feel guilty at all about it. If they come, we'll have to deal with it. Within a few weeks, we're going to have all the guilt we can handle around here," she says, and they both head down the stairs.

Chapter Seventeen

Friday, November 9, 2012

Ryan and Alex sit side by side, on the edge of a dark brown couch, several feet in front of a 37 inch LCD screen TV. Alex is perched forward, intensely studying the screen. Both of them hold Xbox controllers.

"Don't do it dad. Use the remote optics on the rifle," his son warns him.

"I got it. I…shit! There's no way they could hit me," he says, flying back into the couch.

"I told you to quit peeking around corners. Use the gun camera. If you lose your rifle, you can pick up another one, or use your secondary," he explains.

"But I was quick peeking," he says, demonstrating with his head, moving it back and forth quickly.

"Everyone knows that trick," he says.

"Can we reset to right before I got my head splattered, I don't feel like fighting through the entire shopping mall again," Alex pleads.

The iPhone on the table next to the couch starts to ring.

"Hold on Ryan," he says, and grabs the phone.

He answers the call.

"Hey Mike, did they pepper spray you yet?" says Alex.

"Go ahead without me Ryan," he says, and Ryan nods his head.

Alex gets up and walks down the stairs from the third floor to his home office, as Mike responds.

"No, not yet, but probably soon. I just resigned about twenty minutes ago. I'm headed back up the turnpike."

"What happened man? You don't sound good," says Alex.

"I'm fine. I just can't believe I quit my job. Still in shock I guess. Anyway, it was unbelievable down there. So get this. I wake up this morning, and head down to breakfast at the Courtyard Marriot, and I run into one of the reps from Vermont, who's also temp assigned to the area, and she's hacking up a lung all over the fruit station. I made sure not to go anywhere near her. She sits down at a table with three other reps, and one of the guys looks like they just dug him out of his grave to work."

"Which could very likely be a new official Biosphere policy," Alex adds, causing Mike to break out laughing.

"No shit man. So I really start to rethink this whole thing. These people were fine at the beginning of the week. I remember seeing them at the orientation meeting. Now they look like extras from Night of the Living Dead. So, I head out to my assigned area, and start to make some office calls. Every office is like a scene from Night of the Living Dead. I went into an internal med office in Methuen, and walked right the fuck out. Three people in the waiting room were hacking and groaning. I'm not kidding, it was unreal. I sat in my car for a while thinking this over, after nearly taking a bath in hand sanitizer. I hope Biosphere didn't cheap out on that stuff like everything else."

"Have you been wearing a mask and gloves," Alex asks.

"At first, but you feel like a complete douche bag walking into an office with a mask on your face. The gloves aren't so bad, but what's the point. If you touch your eyes or mouth with the gloves on, it doesn't matter. The gloves only work if you throw them away after each office, and don't touch your face while you're still in the office. I quit using them after day one. My hands are so dry from washing and sanitizer, that I could use them as sandpaper."

"Dude, I'm glad you're on your way home. Load up your cars, and caravan out to Colleen's parents in North Conway. The number of cases is exploding. Did you talk to Michelle?" Alex asks.

"No, I talked to Ted. He didn't take it very well. He wanted me to get in touch with the district manager down here and transfer my samples to her. I told him that I was already half way home, and would drop the stuff off at my storage locker for him to inventory," Mike says.

"You better recon the parking lot at the storage locker. He might be there waiting for you. And tell your wife to keep the door locked. Did you tell her what happened to Kate?" says Alex.

"Yeah, she couldn't believe it. Shit, how am I going to caravan out to North Conway, if Ted repo's my car?" he says.

"Just pack up a load today and drive it out there tonight. It's only a few hours away. Even if you only had one car, you could make multiple trips. Gas is still available everywhere. I'd make as many trips as you can with the company car, and charge the gas to Biosphere," says Alex.

"Yeah, that's true. I keep thinking in terms of just making one final trip," he says.

"A few weeks from now, it might be a different story. One trip might be all you get," says Alex.

"From what I saw down in Boston, that version of the story isn't too far away. We were briefed by a Biosphere exec during a working breakfast yesterday. He proudly announced that Boston has one of the fastest growing numbers of cases. Almost three thousand confirmed cases so far, and the number of cases is expected to reach fifteen thousand by early next week. And that only takes into account the cases confirmed by a hospital lab. I saw at least twenty potential cases this morning alone and that's just in a few offices. Not even big offices. I think this thing is about to break wide open."

"How's Colleen doing? Today's Falmouth's last day right?" Alex says.

"She's relieved to get out of there. She didn't want to call in sick or make up a story, but with the cases floating around the Falmouth schools, she was starting to get hysterical. She's been off since Wednesday with the kids," he says.

"Good, good. Where are you now?" asks Alex.

"I'm coming up on the New Hampshire toll. I should be home in about an hour or so. Do you think I should skip the storage unit?" he asks.

"Do a drive-by and see. If he's not there, I'd get the samples out of your possession. You don't want him coming to your house looking for them. And make sure to tell him to stay clear of your house. You can tell him I'll be over there showing you my favorite shotgun," Alex says laughing.

"I'm gonna buy him some pepper spray as a farewell present," says Mike laughing.

"I already took care of that," says Alex, barely able to get the words out through his own laughter.

"Hey, I gotta let you go. I'm gonna call Colleen and set this plan in motion," he says.

"Alright man, good luck and take good care. OK?" says Alex.

"You got it man, same to you. Say hi to Kate and the kids for me. Salud," he says, and the call is disconnected.

Alex puts the phone in the front pocket of his jeans and returns to the attic to rejoin Ryan.

Chapter Eighteen

Saturday, November 10, 2012

Someone shakes Alex's right shoulder, and he involuntarily catapults back into consciousness, hoping everything is alright. His eyelids feel heavy, and he is disoriented, as he slowly opens his eyes. The room is dark, but not pitch black like the middle of the night. He hears the wind buffet the front of the bedroom, rattling the screens, as furious gusts of wind and rain blow in from the north. He turns his head to face Kate, the likely source of his premature awakening.

"You awake?" she asks, as his eyes adjust to her face.

"I am now. What's up?" he asks.

For a moment, he perks up at the idea that she might have woken him up for sex.

"I think the power's out," she says, "I was going to get up and do the treadmill, but I don't think the batteries are giving the house any power. Don't you need to switch over the power?" she says.

"Yeah, I'll get right on that. I thought you wanted to do me," he says, and rolls over to grab his wrist watch off the nightstand.

His black diver's watch reads 6:42 AM. He rolls back on his stomach.

"You're going to switch the power over. Right?" she says.

Alex doesn't move. "You're serious?"

"Uh, yeah. I committed to working out every day, and…I'd like to work out today. This morning," she says.

"Right now?" he asks.

"Within the next fifteen minutes or so. I don't want to have to worry about it later," she says.

"Because we have so much planned?" he says, laughing.

"I just like to exercise in the morning. Will you please go down and switch over the power. I'll make it worth your while later tonight," she says, and caresses his thigh under the sheets.

Alex flings off the covers, and stands up out of bed, stretching his arms and yawning.

"You better make this worthwhile," he says, "I'm thinking one way massage and another one way activity."

"Can't I get a little massage too?" she begs.

"We'll see. It'll be based on your performance," he says, grinning devilishly and walking over to the closet.

"Hey, that's sexual harassment," she says.

"Bring it up with management," he quips

"Great," she says, throwing him a sarcastic smile.

■

Alex hangs up the phone and yells up to Kate.

"Honey. The Murrays are on their way over. They're headed out to New York."

He arrives at the bottom of the stairs as Kate appears at the top.

"Right now?"

"Yeah. He said they were closing up the house. They should be here in a minute," he says.

"I can't believe they're leaving. I'm gonna throw on a sweatshirt. I'll be right down," she says and disappears.

Alex hears her yell to the kids as he opens the front door. He takes a few steps and glances at the Thorntons' house. *Wonder what that fucking nutcase is up to.* The Murrays' convoy materializes from behind the Thorntons' house, and glides around the corner, headed in Alex's direction. As they approach, he sees Greg in the lead, driving their red four door Honda Accord, and Carolyn picking up the rear in a black Honda Odyssey. Both vehicles have large, squat Yakima top carriers attached to the roof racks.

Alex walks back toward the top of his driveway, and stops near the walkway, as the two cars pull into the left side of the driveway. Greg opens the door of his car and hops out. Alex hears the mini-van doors slide open and the kids burst out onto the driveway. They run by him toward the house.

"Hi kids," Alex says mostly to himself.

Kate intercepts them in front of mudroom door, and redirects them through the garage to the backyard. Alex hears her say something about snacks and drinks on the picnic table.

"Loaded down for war here," observes Alex.

"Yeah, we'll probably get eight miles per gallon," says Greg.

"So how are you escaping from National Semi?" asks Alex.

"Vacation. I have over three weeks on the books since we never made it out to see Carolyn's sister in Virginia. They encourage us to use it up before the end of the year, and sales have been great this year."

Carolyn walks up to the two of them.

"How did you end up driving the loony wagon?" Alex asks her.

"I drew the short straw. We're gonna switch every couple of hours, supposedly. We're hoping the trip won't take much longer than eight hours, so it shouldn't be too bad. Plus, they have every electronic distraction available at Best Buy to keep them busy. Sorry we can't stay too long Alex," she says.

Alex steps out of her way, and motions to the mudroom door.

"No worries. We understand. Really. What's important is that you guys get over to New York safely. Kate's got all the kids out back. Dosing them up with sugary drinks and high fructose corn syrup snacks."

"Somehow I doubt there's any high fructose corn syrup in that entire house," she says, and walks through the garage to the door accessing the back yard.

"Sorry about your job. That really sucks," Greg says.

"I'm not sorry at all. That job had a limited half-life. Biosphere really sucked as a company, and my boss was fucking clueless. He's about six years younger than me and all he ever talked about was Biosphere. This is all he's ever done since college. I'll miss the pay, but that's about it."

"Hey, maybe you could take your story to the Portland Paper. They'd love it. Local hero stands up to big pharma. You could sell them all your juicy stories about the pharmaceutical industry."

"Unfortunately, there's not much to sell, and the last thing I want to do is draw any attention to myself. Hey, before I forget, let me give you the TerraFlu samples we talked about. I'm giving you enough for twelve courses of therapy, which should cover everyone in your parents' house," Alex says, walking toward the garage. Alex turns around.

"Remember, if anyone…"

"I know. If anyone shows flu symptoms, make sure we all take them. Got it," Greg interrupts.

Alex laughs, as he grabs a small plastic shopping bag filled with Terraflu samples from a shelf near the mudroom door. He hands them to Greg, who has followed him into the garage.   "What did you tell the kids about the trip?" says Alex.

"Not much. Just that we're going to visit my parents for a few weeks. I think the boys know what's going on, but the girls really have no idea."

"Yeah, same thing happening in our house, though I don't think even Ryan really understands what this might mean for us. I probably don't fully understand it."

"No kidding. I keep thinking…hoping that we'll be able to come back in a few weeks. It still hasn't sunk in that we might be gone for a lot longer. Carolyn said that it might take months to produce a vaccine."

"Longer maybe," Ales says grimly, as Greg shakes his head back and forth.

They spend the next ten minutes watching the kids run around the back yard, before Carolyn and Greg reluctantly direct all of their kids back to their assigned seats in the cars. They all walk around the side of the garage to the driveway, and Kate helps Carolyn get her kids settled into the mini-van, as Emily and Ryan say goodbye and start to walk back up the driveway to their house. Alex walks over to the open sliding door on the right side of the mini-van, and pokes his head in. He passes Kate, as she walks up the driveway to stand with her kids, who are up on the brick walkway, next to the front light post.

"Take it easy on your parents. We'll see you guys later," he yells into the van.

All of the kids have headphones, and are occupied by various portable electronic devices. James and Justin, sitting in the second row swivel chairs, give him a thumbs up, and he salutes them in return. The two younger girls are seated in the third row. Every conceivable inch of space between the kids and behind the third row is packed with gear. Alex walks up to Carolyn's window. He sees that the front seat is completely jammed with packages, nearly blocking Carolyn's view of the passenger side mirror.

"Good luck. I hope the electronic distractions at least get you through to Greg's shift," he says.

She laughs loudly.

"I was just hoping to get past the Kennebunk rest stop before the fighting started. See you later Alex. Thanks again for everything. I really think this is the right thing for us to do, and if it wasn't for you guys, we'd probably be making this trip three weeks from now, when it was too late."

"Hey, I've given this advice to dozens of other friends, and very few of them have taken it seriously. You owe yourself the biggest thanks. Am I sounding too much like one of those self-help books?"

"Yes, and I'm out of here before you really start emoting," she says, as she starts to back the car down the driveway.

Alex jogs up to Greg's car, and leans in the window. The entire back seating area, all the way to the roof of the car is filled. His passenger seat is similarly stuffed with bags and a large plastic crate.

"Good luck. Stay safe. And don't worry about the house. We'll keep a good eye on it," Alex says, extending his hand.

"You got it man. Keep the neighborhood under control," he says, shaking Alex's hand.

Alex salutes Greg, and walks back up the driveway to join his family. They wave to the Murrays, as their two cars pull out of the neighborhood. Kate's eyes are watery and red, and Alex puts his arm around her shoulder as they walk toward the house.

"Wash your hands!" he says, as the kids run past them into the garage.

When they get inside the mudroom, Alex hugs her fully, cradling her head in his chest and rubbing her back. Her hair smells like lavender shampoo, and he takes in a long breath through his nose. He sees the kids washing their hands in the mudroom bathroom. An argument breaks out over the towel.

"I have a terrible feeling we might never see them again," she says.

"They'll be fine," he says, as the kids tumble out of the bathroom, dripping water on mudroom tile.

Chapter Nineteen

Sunday, November 11, 2012

Alex walks down the stairs and into the great room, fresh from a shower.

"Wait till you see this," Kate says, without even looking up.

She hands a piece of paper up to Alex as he walks by the back of the couch. He takes the sheet and starts to read it standing up.

"What the ffff…a neighborhood meeting? Today at two. To discuss neighborhood plans to address the impact of the flu pandemic. Come with ideas. Bring your own snacks and drinks. Some topics of discussion will include. Organizing neighborhood daycare, resource sharing, neighborhood security, phone tree, information sharing. Let me guess who put this out…location, #4 Durham Road. Signed, Sarah Quinn. You can attend this one hon."

"You knew this was inevitable honey. If it wasn't Sarah, then Nicki Bartlett or Laura would have called the Durham Clan together eventually. You're the pandemic expert, and the closest thing we have to a statesman around here, so the honor is yours. Happy Veteran's Day."

"Yeah. Thanks. Happy Veteran's Day. Don't you think we could just skip out on this one? We are in quarantine you know," he says.

"Nice try, but everyone in the neighborhood has seen you out running, or me out for a walk. Plus, I think we need to keep pace with what's going on around here. The more we know what everyone else is doing, the better," she says, looking up at him as he walks around the couch to sit in one of the leather chairs next to the wood burning stove.

"I know. I just can't stomach the idea of standing around while Sarah blares at everyone through that Mr. Microphone thing she likes to use at the summer block party. It's obnoxious. Then Nicki will grab the thing, and broadcast her shrill voice," he says, shaking his head and exhaling dramatically.

"Yeah, or like how Sarah insists on passing the microphone around like the conch if you want to talk. She's super anal about it too. She doesn't like anyone addressing the group without it. It's sort of weird," Kate adds.

"Yeah. I got the conch!" he says, and they both break out laughing.

Still laughing, Alex speaks, "We won't be laughing in a few weeks when some real Lord of the Flies shit is going down around here."

"Easy," Kate says, nodding toward Emily who is lounging on the other chair.

"She's receiving input from one source only right now. Watch. Hey Emily?" he says, and waits a few seconds.

"Emily?" he says raising his voice.

"You hoo, Emily?"

Finally, she turns her head slowly, eyes still watching the show until it becomes physically impossible for her eyes to strain in their sockets. Her eyes catch up with the new direction of her head, facing Alex.

"What?" she asks, turning her head back to the show, and then back to Alex.

"What are you watching?" he asks, having no real reason for interrupting her.

"Gwen and Cam," she says, and turns back toward the show.

Alex nods his head, "Cool."

"See. They hear nothing, the see nothing, and they know nothing," he says.

"Kind of like you," she says.

He walks over and gives her a kiss on the forehead.

"I better go prepare my speech for this afternoon," he says.

"Oh hey, we need to set the clocks in the house back for Daylight Savings Time. That's your job," she says.

"You know, I didn't even put it together. I saw the computer time was different than my watch, and thought it had something to do with the power failure. I guess it's going to get dark pretty early tonight," he says.

"Yeah, probably around 4:30," Kate says, without looking up, "alright, can you go bother someone else now?"

"Yes ma'am," says Alex, as he head back to the kitchen.

■

Alex stands in the garage looking out at the Walkers' house. The sun occasionally manages to stab through the dense gray cloud cover, momentarily warming the air. The temperature sits in the high forties, with a light breeze.

Alex wears a dark blue winter parka, which he has owned for several years, and his head is covered by a tight brown knit cap. He wears a pair of sunglasses, mainly to avoid eye contact with some of his neighbors.

Where are you Ed? Alex checks his watch again. 1:52. *A few minutes late. No big deal.* He hears one of Ed's garage doors start to open. Alex pats his jacket pocket again; to make sure he brought his iPhone, just in case Kate needs to get in touch with him. After Ted's stunt last week, he doesn't plan to take any chances, ever again. He hasn't heard anything from Ted or Biosphere since Michelle's last voicemail. *All the better.*

He sees Ed emerge from the open garage bay, and starts walking across his front lawn to meet up with Ed. As he crosses onto the Walkers' property, Derek Sheppard opens his front door and starts to jog across the street toward them. Simultaneously, the McDaniels' garage door opens and Jamie walks out of the open bay door waving at them. She starts walking over to them. Alex and Ed stand in the driveway, waiting for Derek and Jamie to join them.

"Hey Ed. Alex," she says, nodding at them as they all meet at the bottom of Ed's driveway.

"Hey Jamie," says Ed.

"How did Matt talk you into representing the McDaniel clan? I tried everything in my power to push Kate out the door," Alex says, eliciting a laugh from Ed.

"Hell, there wasn't even the start of a negotiation in my house," said Ed.

Both Derek and Alex cackle quietly.

"No choice for me either. Ellen wasn't too keen on standing outside in the wind. Though it seems to have died down a lot from this morning," says Derek.

"Yeah. I went for a run earlier, and the wind sucked," comments Alex.

"I wish I had a choice, but Matt woke up this morning not feeling well at all. He's been dragging around the house all day. Don't you think Sarah's going to have this inside?" she asks, sniffling and clearing her throat.

Alex tries not to look alarmed, as he casually canvasses Jamie. She doesn't look nervous or worried about her husband's illness. He doesn't plan to get any closer to Jamie. She is clearly underdressed for the weather, having assumed that the Quinns would host the meeting inside. Alex doubts they will assemble indoors. There are thirty three houses in the neighborhood, which puts the total attendance a minimum of around thirty, more likely higher. Alex plans to return home if the Quinns try to jam everyone inside their house. Jamie already looks cold, standing in light brown corduroy pants and a waist level light blue fleece coat. Alex sees that she is already shivering. *She's going to freeze her ass off.*

"I hope not. I'm not going to cram my body into a flu incubator," says Alex, and they all start walking down the sidewalk.

"Does someone at the Quinns' have the flu?" asks Derek.

"No. I just don't think it's a good idea for a member of every household in the neighborhood to be jammed into a closed space breathing on each other, touching the same door knobs, and using the same bathroom,. If this is indoors, one of you will have to take notes for me," says Alex.

"I don't think you'll have to worry about that. I see a bunch of people on their driveway," says Ed.

Alex looks over at the turn in the road, and suddenly sees the Quinn house clear the Hopkins' house on the inside corner of the loop. At first glance, it looks like nearly fifty people could be milling around the driveway. He sees about two dozen lawn chairs and folding chairs in place on the driveway, mostly occupied. *She is certainly organized.* Several younger children are running around the lawn, kicking a soccer balls. A goal is set up on the other end of the front lawn, away from the driveway.

"Crap. Maybe I should grab a warmer coat. I'll catch a cold for sure if I stand out here in this fleece. I'll meet up with you guys in few minutes," says Jamie, as she turns back toward her house.

"Sounds good Jamie," says Ed, as Jamie starts to jog toward her house.

Alex lets about ten seconds of silence pass, as the walk in front of the Perry's house. Alex hopes Todd Perry doesn't come out to join them.

"Did you guys catch that about Matt?" asks Alex.

"Yeah," says Ed, flashing them a concerned look.

"What do you mean?" says Derek.

"Matt's not healthy enough to go outside? They both work in the schools. Now her husband's sick, and she's sniffling and coughing?" says Alex, looking at them with a face that says "not good."

"I didn't hear her coughing," says Ed.

"She cleared her throat several times, but it sounded more like a suppressed cough," says Alex.

"It could be anything. Anyway, I ain't planning to lock lips with her, so what does it matter," says Derek.

They all laugh.

"Good point," says Alex, still laughing.

"I guess all I'm saying is to be careful around her. You don't want her coughing or sneezing near you, and you don't want her touching you…"

"I wouldn't exactly object to her touching me," says Ed.

"No kidding," adds Derek.

"Gentlemen, I refuse to engage in this kind of banter. Based on the one in a billion chance that Kate is paying one of you to wear a wire. And I especially wouldn't engage in this kind of talk, because…"

He leans close to Ed's jacket collar and speaks up.

"I love and respect my wife more than anything on this planet," he says, and they all break out laughing.

"I don't know why you're laughing. We're still close enough to your house to set off Sam's radar. You'll come back from the meeting to a kick in the nutsack," says Alex.

Derek laughs harder.

Ed grabs the collar of his own jacket, and speaks quietly into it.

"As you just heard, Alex's love and respect pales in comparison to his fear of a ball kicking."

They all break out laughing.

"Anyway, I'd be really careful around anyone from the McDaniel house," Alex adds.

The trio approaches the bottom of the Quinns' driveway and the din of the crowd increases. Alex sees that Todd is present and sitting in the front row of chairs. A few more neighbors are walking down the other side of the Durham loop toward the group, and Alex looks behind him to see Jamie walking up the street with Mary Thompson, Alex's neighbor directly to the east, and John Anderson, from one house past Ed's, between the Walkers' and the Perry's.

They all stay at the bottom of the driveway. Alex turns around and scans the crowd again. He sees Sarah Quinn at the top of the driveway, playing with her loudspeaker system. Her husband George scurries toward her with what look like batteries for the microphone. She looks mad at George. *Poor George forgot to op check the system.* He glances at his watch. *And now the meeting is two minutes late. George is going to pay for this.* He chuckles to himself.

"I don't see any Cheetos," remarks Alex, still examining the crowd.

"I have a pack of gum in my pocket," says Ed.

"Is it sugarless?" says Alex.

"Probably," replies Ed.

"You can keep it. No nutritional value. You'll burn up more calories chewing it," he says, and smiles wryly at Ed.

"Speaking of calories. She looks like she could use a few," says Ed, looking at Nicole Bartlett.

Nicole Bartlett moves in their direction, handing a sheet of paper to everyone in the crowd. As she approaches, he notices that Laura Burton just finished taping sheets of paper to the card table in front of Sarah. *Sign-up sheets maybe?* Nicole reaches the three of them.

"Hey Nicki," says Alex, bracing for the excessive perkiness.

"Hey guys. Thanks for coming to the meeting. This is an agenda, and some topic ideas. You can also take notes on it. Did you bring any pens?" she says, handing a sheet to Ed and Derek.

"No, I didn't think we'd need pens," Ed offers, as Alex politely declines one of her agendas.

"No worries. We have some extra's floating around. You'll probably have to share one," she says. "Good to see you guys. Hey, you might want to move up to closer."

As she walks to the next group, Ed chimes in.

"Jesus, she's unbelievably skinny. She'd fit into a thirteen year old's jeans."

"Get this. Ellen ran into her over at The Gap. Nicki was shopping with her daughter Taylor, and Ellen overheard a weird conversation. Nicki was absolutely distressed that she couldn't fit into the same size blouse as Taylor. She heard Nicki say 'give me a few months, and I'll get into that.' Sick if you ask me," says Derek.

"How old is her daughter?" Ed whispers.

"She's one grade ahead of Emily. All Emily hears her talk about at school is her weight and her clothes fitting. She's starting to give Emmy a complex," says Alex.

"Emily's ten right?" asks Derek.

"Yeah. Ten."

"That's some sick shit man," says Derek.

"Well, I've heard a number of wives say that they think she looks great," says Ed.   "Yeah, well there's a lot of the anorexia going around the neighborhood, if you haven't noticed. Look at Stephanie. I can barely tell her apart from Nicki," comments Alex.

"Yeah, it's like single white female scary looking at the two of them together," says Derek.

"Sam's definitely noticed, and she'd like to figure out how to catch whatever they've got?" Ed says laughing.

"First she has to quit her job, because if you look around, you'll notice there's a direct correlation between staying home and emaciation, which I don't quite understand. I've spent plenty of days home with kids, and all I want to do on those days is eat," says Alex.

"I still haven't recovered from the toddler years," says Ed, grabbing his slightly bulging stomach.

"I saw your wedding photos Ed and I hate to break it to you, but…" says Alex, raising his shoulders and sporting a patronizing look.

"Thanks. Hey, at least I didn't deteriorate. Three kids," he says, and flexes his right arm in an overly dramatic muscle pose.

Alex spots Paul and Nancy Cooper in the back row of seats, with their chocolate lab Max.

"Gentlemen, I'm gonna say hi to Paul and Nancy. Keep my spot in the back," he says to Ed.

Ed nods and Alex walks up behind the Coopers. Stephanie and Eric Bishop are seated next to the Coopers. The Bishops' kids, Hunter and Evan are playing soccer with the other kids on the lawn. Emily and Hunter are in the same class, though Alex rarely hears her talk about him.

"You didn't bring me any snacks? How disappointing," he says, laying his left hand on Paul's shoulder. "But you did bring my good friend Max."

Both Paul and Nancy turn around, as Alex kneels down to hug Max. Alex's wonders if hugging Max is such a good idea. He considers his chance of contracting the flu from contact with a domestic pet. He's really not sure, but makes a mental note to research the topic on the internet. Offhand, he can't imagine any reason why the flu could not be transferred from a dog's fur to his hand. He'll need to talk to Kate about her trips around the neighborhood, visiting every dog free roaming dog.

"Hey we weren't sure you'd show up. Figured you'd be off limits by now," says Paul.

Alex stands up from petting Max.

"Believe me, I tried to get out of it," he says, and Stephanie Bishop gives him a strained look. He returns a slightly less strained smile.

"Hey Stephanie. Eric," he says.

"Why wouldn't you want to be here," she says annoyed.

"I just don't think it's a good idea for all of us to come together in one place, when there's a highly contagious flu virus spreading around Scarborough." he says softly, shrugging his shoulders.

"I don't think anyone's going to catch the flu at this meeting," says Eric.

"The whole point of getting together is to figure out how we can all help each other." "Sounds great, but the best way for us to help each other, is to stay away from each other. Hey, I'll catch you guys later," he says to Paul and Nancy.

"See ya Alex," they both say.

Alex catches Paul's glance. Paul makes a face signaling that he has no idea why Eric and Stephanie acted so oddly. Alex walks back to Derek and Ed, who are now joined by Jamie, Mary Thompson and John Anderson. Alex sees a few stragglers coming in from the north side of the loop. Dave Santos and Charlie Thornton. Charlie waves to Alex, and Alex returns the wave, smiling. *Cuckoo guy.* Alex stands next to Ed, glad that he didn't have to actively evade Jamie. Jamie is now wearing a black hooded winter jacket and a hat, but she is still shivering. *Probably has a fever.* Derek fidgets and looks uncomfortable standing next to her.

"Here comes Charlie," Alex whispers to Ed.

Ed glances over at Charlie.

"I think he's going to stand by us. Have you talked to him lately?" says Ed.

"Not since he interrogated me by the woodpile. Nancy Cooper said she heard him ranting and raving in his driveway last week. Food issues. I guess neither of them could find the time to wait in line for groceries. I hope they figured out something. He might be the last person you'd want scouring the neighborhood for food in a bad mood," says Alex quietly.

"You know who else is a loose cannon? Todd. I've hear him screaming a lot lately. Screaming at his wife. Kicking his car. Knocking shit around his garage. Every day something's going on over there," says Ed.

"Really? Jesus…hold on, here comes Charlie," whispers Alex.

"Hey Charlie," says Alex enthusiastically, keeping his hands in his jacket pockets.

"Can you believe what's going on in this country? Unreal if you ask me. I can't believe the government let it get this bad. Food rationing? What the fuck," says Charlie, he face turning red.

"Take it easy man, you're gonna explode," says Alex.

"Take it easy? That's the last thing any of us can afford to do. What do you think this little meeting's all about?" he asks.

Before anyone can respond, he continues.

"I'll bet this is an attempt at a little socialist share the wealth program… for those that haven't done shit over the past few weeks," he says. *He might be right.*

Charlie is in rare form, clearly pumped up on something.

"Everybody. Everybody. If you could grab a seat, or pull it in as tight as possible here, we'll get this started," says Sarah Quinn.

Nicki Bartlett and Laura Burton quickly move to stand near Sarah, behind the folding table. The kids continue to play on the lawn, as the adults not seated in the makeshift auditorium, start to crowd both sides of the seating.

Alex takes a quick inventory of the group. He sees Michael McCarthy seated in the second row, talking to Peter and Brenda Brady, who are sitting directly in front of them in the first row. Michael spends most of the week out of town, flying back and forth from New York and Atlanta, working onsite with a few large investment firms to troubleshoot and optimize their computer software. His wife Jennifer stays at home with their three children, Ethan, who is in the same grade as Emily, and two younger girls, Hannah and Sophia. Alex is not sure how old the girls are, only that their youngest, Sophia, just started kindergarten.

Standing next to the McCarthys is Michelle Hayes, who lives in the house between the Coopers' and the Murrays'. Alex figures her husband Ken is babysitting their kids. He wonders how Ken managed to dodge this one. The Hayes have two younger kids, a boy and a girl, right around the same age as the McCarthys' girls.

From his quick glance around, he can tell that most households are represented. He doesn't see Phil or Julia Rhodes, which is odd, since he saw Phil grab the newspaper this morning. With two kids in college, and one in high school, he can't imagine why at least one of them wouldn't be here. *Then again, I don't want to be here either.* He sees Sarah ready to start.

"OK everyone, we're going to get this started. First of all, thank you for coming together at such short notice. We've always pulled together as a neighborhood in the past, so when Nicki found out that the Scarborough schools would be closed this week…"

The group huddled on the Quinns' driveway erupted into a cacophony of whispers.

"Is that confirmed?" asks Todd incredulously.

"Yes. One of Jack's colleagues at the diabetes center is one the school board, and he confirmed that Friday was the last day," Nicole answers.

Sarah continues.

"Anyway, Nicki called me right away to see what I was going to do with my kids during the week, and to ask she could help out. This got me thinking that everyone in the neighborhood is facing the same challenge. Most of us have school aged kids, and few of us can afford to quit our jobs, when this might only last a few weeks. *Don't count on it.* So we got together and started talking about the daycare issue. Then we realized that daycare wasn't going to be the only problem out there. It's no secret that the stores are rationing food, and who knows how long the food will last. Then we started reading the CDC website, and found some links to articles about how essential services might be disrupted if things get really bad. Stuff like electricity, water, hospital service, phones, cable."

"The electricity isn't going to fail. A lot of experts are saying that this whole thing is likely to pass in a few weeks," says Mike Lynch, who lives right across the street and one house toward Harrison Road.

Mike is standing to the right of the driveway with Vicki and Tom Hodges, who are both nodding in agreement with Mike's statement. The Hodgeses live directly across the street from the Lynch's, and the two families seem tight to Alex, despite a large gulf in age between them. Mike and Katherine are in their early thirties, with two toddlers, while Vicki and Tom appear to be in their fifties, though Alex suspects they might be younger. Alex knows that the Hodges' daughter Anna just left this fall for Boston College, and that their son is still in high school. Mark and Beverly Silva, from the house directly across the street, are standing in the hostile group, but it is apparent that they aren't comfortable with Mike's statement.

"What a fucking idiot," whispers Charlie into Alex's ear. *I agree.*

"Well, the articles only mentioned that it could happen, but it didn't go into any details," Sarah says, looking to Laura for support.

Jamie sneezes next to Derek. Derek glances at Alex and Ed nervously. Alex can tell he wants to move away from her, but he doesn't move.

"Hey Sarah? Can I say something about the electricity?" offers Alex. *I can't resist.*

"Thanks Alex. Everyone knows Alex Fletcher," she says, relieved.

Every face in the crowd turns to look at Alex. Most of the faces still look friendly, though he detects a strange underlying current in the group. He can't determine the general aura of the group, but it makes him immediately uncomfortable, which is not a common feeling for Alex.

"Right. Anyway, so if the flu pandemic becomes widespread and attacks a large percentage of the population, then two things will happen. Either people will be unable to work because they're sick or dead, or people will stop going to work, because they don't want to become sick or dead. It's really that simple. This shortage of labor will affect every aspect of society, from policemen to doctors to truck drivers. If the trains can't deliver coal to the electrical plants, then eventually the electrical system will fail. God knows it doesn't take much to knock out one of those grids. And if a grid fails, who's going to repair it? If the electricity fails, the water pressure is soon to follow. You can apply the same logic to nearly every essential service. They all run on electricity. Hell, if a storm knocks out the power in the middle of the pandemic, who's gonna to repair the lines? They can barely get the power back up with a full workforce." *That's enough.*

"Yeah, but don't the power plants keep an emergency supply on hand for just this kind of a situation? Same with the water systems and cable companies. They all have back up power capability," challenges Mike.

"Sure they do. The power plants are required by law to maintain a six week supply of coal on hand for emergencies, however, these laws are rarely enforced, and the recent audits put the average emergency reserve supply for a power plant at about one and a half weeks. Compliance at all other levels is pretty much the same. You can thank the current and previous administration for that one," says Alex.

Mike Lynch looks pissed at Alex's comment about the administration, which doesn't surprise Alex, since the comment was designed to push Mike's rabid Republican buttons.

"Thanks Alex. So, the whole reason for us to get together is to figure out what challenges we might face, and how we can help each other out. Nicki has put together a few categories, and some signup sheets. Nicki," says Sarah, and gives her the microphone.

Nicole Bartlett takes the microphone from Sarah, and steps around the folding table. She's wearing a tight fitting pink quilted vest and a white skin-tight long sleeve turtle neck. Her head is covered by a thin light purple knit cap with a pink tassel falling to the left side. Her skin hugging dark blue jeans complete her look, which Alex has seen before in the youth pages of the latest LL Bean catalogue. Certainly well put together, but completely inappropriate for a forty year old. Nicole starts to address the group, in a tone appropriate for a room of elementary school kids.

"OK, I'm going to get started on my little portion. Thank you all again for braving the cold weather," she says, and executes a fake shiver. *Kate is going to pay for this.*

"So, what I have done, is put together some categories where we can all help out. I've made sign up lists for each one, and if we come up with any more categories, I'll make another list.

First, I think it would be awesome if everyone could update their contact information. You don't have to do it here. You can send me an email with your home phone and cell phones. We might need the cell numbers if the power goes out. My email is on the sheet I handed out. The phone list I have is a few years old, and we have some new neighbors, so it's important for everyone to update this. Please put your cell phones on the list too, in case the power goes out. I know a lot of us have digital phone service, which is useless without the power.

Alright, the first issue which many of us will face is daycare. Most of us will have to make alternate daycare arrangements or take time off from work," she says in a tone indicating that she might be in that same position.

"Why did she say that like she'll be needing daycare too? She doesn't work." whispers Alex to Ed.

"Probably because she's always had her kids in daycare, preschool, or public school. She had her first two kids in daycare at least three full days a week before they started school. Same thing with Grace. She keeps them in all day programs during most of the school breaks and the summer," whispers Ed.

"Wow, she's a piece of work. Kate's going to love this," says Alex.

"So, the daycare list is for both those who will need daycare and those who will be home and can help provide daycare services for their neighbors. Please fill in the times you need covered, how many kids, anything like that. If you can open up your home to help, please note your availability. Once we get all of the names and information, we'll put them together and try to find matches. We can even use this information in case someone in your family gets the flu, and you need to leave the house to take that person to get treatment. That way, you don't have to drag the entire family out where they could get sick." *Are you shitting me?*

Alex shakes his head and leans over to Ed. He surveys the crowd, and sees that the idea is popular, which doesn't surprise him considering the number of dual income families in the neighborhood.

"So, are you going to volunteer to watch Jamie's kids while she takes her flu ridden husband to the hospital? Or let your kids stay at Jamie's while you head out to the office? This has bad idea written all over it," he whispers.

"I agree," responds Ed.

"The next list is for volunteers to take sick people to doctor's appointments, or the hospital. If both parents are sick, and a child needs to be seen by a doctor, volunteers from this list would help out," she says smiling.

"This is right from the manual of how to guarantee a one hundred percent infection rate in your neighborhood," Alex whispers to Ed, who breaks out laughing and quickly contains himself.

Several heads turn in their direction, including Stephanie Bishop, who shakes her head and says something to her husband. Eric Bishop looks back at them and frowns.

"Did you have something to add?" booms Laura Burton, the other self-appointed pandemic coordinator.

Alex shakes his head, "Nope."

Most heads return to Nicki, though Mike Lynch draws out his glare a little longer than necessary.

"The next topic, which was suggested by Todd Perry, deals with basic necessities and supplies. As we are all painfully aware, food and other basic survival needs are in short supply at the stores. I tried to put together just one emergency kit earlier in the week, and couldn't find even a quarter of the things needed. CVS and Riteaid are wiped out daily. Same story with all of the hardware stores. Everyone is out there trying to assemble their own emergency stockpile from the federal disaster checklist," she says.

"I got all my stuff," whispers Charlie Thornton, who drifted over to Alex's right side, during Nicki's speech.

"Got it all the week before last. You're smart to hide your firewood in the garage. I didn't know what to make of it when I talked to you. I knew you were up to something, then it suddenly hit me. Of course. I moved all of mine in a few days later. I have to thank you. It got me thinking about the whole situation. I went on a few of the NRA websites and found a shitload of survival information. I got a jump start on those checklists. While everyone else was waiting in line for groceries, I spent the better part of three days buying up supplies and dried food. MRE's from the surplus stores, whatever I could get my hands on. I bet you have the same thing over there," he whispers with glee.

"I might have some supplies on hand," he says, studying Charlie's face. *Actually, he doesn't look too crazy.*

"So, if you could list on this sheet what supplies or food you have on hand, we can create sort of our own Durham Road stockpile. If someone needs a certain item, then they can get it, as long as they've put into the stockpile themselves. It's kind of like a swap shop idea," she says.

"I don't know. How would we manage this stockpile? Would it be located in one place? Or just a list of who has what, and you can trade? It sounds kind of complicated, and...I don't know," says Beverly Silva.

A majority of the crowd backs her sentiment, and there is considerable protest from all corners of the driveway. Alex focuses on Todd, whose face has turned a few shades redder since Beverly opened her mouth.

"Yeah, I don't feel comfortable taking what I have and putting it in a central location. Is that what you're suggesting?" asks Jamie McDaniels, who is visibly shivering.

"Uh, it's just an idea, but if we all have an idea of how much food is available, then...well, we can work on a system," says Nicki.

"The idea isn't to start a communal soup kitchen, but like Nicki said, it would help to get an idea of what we have here if times get really tough," says Laura Burton, looking to Sarah Quinn for support.

Oddly enough, Sarah Quinn does not look pleased by this agenda item. As one of the lead coordinators, Alex expected her to support the idea, but she appears to have grasped the true meaning of concept's design. That everyone else in the neighborhood would know exactly how much food she had on hand, and that she'd be expected to share some of that food in the very near future. Alex remembers that Sarah was one of the first people on the block to head to the Hannaford's when the massive lines formed.

"We can revisit this at the next meeting after everyone has had time to think about it. It's a lot to ask, given the fact that none of us are in great shape when it comes to food. If you want to put this information down now on the sheet, you're encouraged to do so," says Sarah.

Alex can tell that the meeting is about to break apart on its own. The last agenda item hit everyone deep, and it was clear that nobody relished the idea of giving up any of their food. Alex sees Todd stirring in his seat.

"Can I say something here," says Todd, standing and facing most of the crowd on the driveway.

"I'm not sure what everyone's problem is with sharing food. To be honest, it seems a bit selfish to me, and frankly I'm surprised. We've had parties at our house over the years, and we've always put out a nice spread for everyone. We're all neighbors right?" he says, his face reaching a deep red color.

"Yeah, but that's what you do when you host a party," says Michelle Hayes cynically. "This is a bit different. I agree with Beverly and Jamie. Don't take this the wrong way, but I don't want any of you knowing how much food I have in my house. That's my family's business."

"Well, I don't mind telling you how much food I have," Todd responds.

"How much food do you have Todd?" blurts Charlie.

Alex inches away from Charlie.

"You're on your own with this nut," he whispers to Charlie.

"What do you mean?" Todd responds, stunned by the blunt question.

"If you don't care, then tell all of us how much food you have on hand," Charlie demands.

"Well I don't know exactly. I'd have to take a good look, and figure it out," says Todd, flustered.

"Bullshit. You know exactly what you have. In terms of a regular grocery week. How many weeks do you have on hand," pushes Charlie.

"Probably…like, a few…I don't know. Not much," he says.

"Exactly. Now I know why you're pushing this socialist agenda so hard. You don't have shit. That's why nobody else likes this idea either. Because they don't want to start supporting other households from the very beginning of this crisis. I agree with Alex here. This pandemic thing isn't going to last a few weeks. More like a few months, maybe longer. And you want the handouts to start next week? You can still get food at the stores. It's rationed, but the lines are faster, and each member of your family with a driver's license can show up once a day. I suggest everyone takes full advantage of this system. There's just no excuse for anyone having nothing," finishes Charlie.

Alex puts his hand on Charlie's shoulder. "You alright man? I swear you're gonna explode."

"Look, I've got four kids at home…" starts Todd.

"You work from home Todd. The stores open at six AM. Figure it out!" says Charlie.

Todd moves around the chairs and is restrained by his neighbor, Daniel Lewis. *Thank god.* Eric Bishop stands up and turns around.

"Someone needs to slap a muzzle on him," Eric says, as his wife nods in agreement.

"What the fuck is your problem today Eric?" says Alex, and the entire crowd goes silent.

"What do you mean what's my problem? You and your friend came here with the wrong attitude. This whole meeting was put together so we could help each other. Todd's idea is just as valid as anyone else's," says Eric.

"Great, another communist with nothing to throw into the pile but empty hands," yells Charlie. *Great. How did I suddenly become this guy's champion?*

"Charlie, you gotta take it easy. OK?" Alex whispers to him.

Charlie looks composed compared to Todd, Eric and several other jeering neighbors. He appears at ease with the confrontation, which frightens Alex for a couple of reasons. Charlie is either slightly sociopathic or he's carrying a weapon. Neither possibility comforts him. *I need to diffuse this ASAP.*

"If you're not here to help, then get the out of here," says Tom Hodges.

Mark and Beverly Silva edge away from Tom and Vicki, as Mike Lynch echoes Tom's sentiment. Alex sees Charlie stiffen. *This is getting ugly.*

"Take it easy guys," Alex says firmly, passing glances at Tom and Eric.

"I happen to strongly agree with them. I don't want anyone else shopping at my house for food or supplies. I can tell you right now it won't work. I didn't exactly see a lot of enthusiastic faces when Nicki described the idea. Nobody wants to put an inventory of their house out there. I sure as hell don't. So don't get pissed at Charlie. He said exactly what most of us were thinking," says Alex.

"Maybe we should just forget about helping each other at all. You don't sound like much of a team player Alex," says Eric.

"I'm willing to help out, but we're all dealing with a very unique set of circumstances. When the power goes out after a nasty spring storm, I have no problem opening my house to all of you. Everyone here knows that. We've all done last minute babysitting for each other. This is going to be very different, and I think we all need to get a grip on that," says Alex. *Shut up please.*

"I guess I'm not getting it," says Andrew Greene in a hostile tone.

Alex guesses that Andrew is also part of what appears to be a growing faction of disgruntled neighbors from the northern loop of Durham Road. The Greens live next door to the Bartletts' house, and a just a few houses down from the Burtons', smack in the middle of what Charlie might now call the socialist side of Durham Road. Alex is not surprised at how quickly the neighborhood became polarized at the meeting. Each side of the loop tended to band together at social events, and even the kids' interaction is loosely bound by the north south polarization of the neighborhood. The neighborhood is no longer than one third of a mile, end to end, and there still exists a wide separation. What surprises Alex is how quickly animosity rose to the surface at this meeting.

Deep down, Alex really doesn't care how this meeting goes. His only goal is to keep his family alive and intact. Alex didn't lie when said that he is willing to help the neighborhood. His assistance will be guided by his own rules of engagement, and the first overriding rule is that he won't let anything jeopardize his family's safety. Keeping most of his neighbors placated for now might be an important part of this strategy.

"I can answer your question, but first let me say that I really meant what I said about helping. We all probably have something to offer. As most of you know, I work...rather, worked for Biosphere pharmaceuticals. The company that makes TerraFlu. It's like Tamiflu. When I left the company, I managed to retain about twenty courses of therapy. Enough for twenty people. I would be more than happy to relinquish these into a communal pool, and then as people get sick, they can be treated," he says, redoing the math in his head. *Twenty-eight to give out. Gave twelve to the Murrays. Sixteen. Close enough.*

"If...anyone gets sick," says Andrew.

"Which brings me back to answering your question. We all need to get a solid grip on the fact that some of you, maybe many of you, are going to get sick. Especially if you put some of these ideas into play," says Alex, and the group erupts into a verbal geyser of doubt and anger, all directed at Alex.

"Hey, hey...let Alex finish," yells Ed.

"Yeah, I want to hear the rest of this," calls out Michelle Hayes.

The group calms down, and Alex continues, though he seriously considers walking away. He's not sure if this is helping or hurting his situation.

"Don't shoot the messenger. My point is that the only way to guarantee that you won't catch the flu is to quarantine your entire family. That means zero or at a minimum, very controlled contact with anyone outside of your family. That's really the only way.

So, am I going to put my name down on the daycare list? No. Am I going to volunteer to drive potentially infected people to the hospital? No. Am I willing to be part of a neighborhood crime patrol when police service is no longer available? Sure. You all need to start thinking like this, or the flu is going to spread through the neighborhood like wildfire."

Eric and Stephanie Bishop are both shaking their heads, with disgusted looks on their faces. Alex makes a quick mental assessment of the scene, dividing the group into two groups. Those that think he's an asshole, and those that either don't know what to think, or seem to support his ideas.

Right away, he puts Todd Perry, the Bishops, the Hodges, Mike Lynch, Nicki Bartlett, Laura Burton, and Andrew Green in the hostile group. He leaves the Quinns out of the group, based on her reaction to the food sharing idea, and the fact that she didn't react either way to his last comments. Ed Walker, the Silvas, Charlie Thornton, the Coopers, and Michelle Hayes fall into the second group.

As he continues to scan the faces, he puts Peter Brady and Michael McCarthy into the hostile group. They are standing side by side, with loathsome faces, talking to each other and glancing up at Alex while shaking their heads. Mary Thompson and Jamie McDaniels appear to be quietly arguing with each other. Alex can't make a determination about either of them.

Todd calmly steps around the chairs, and approaches Alex, as the group continues to disintegrate into a chaotic mutter-fest. Todd's face is no longer swollen red, but Alex can tell by his bearing that Todd is about to get something important off his chest. Most of the driveway goes silent in anticipation.

"Let me handle this Charlie," he whispers to his left, as Ed puts a hand on his shoulder.

Todd stops about ten feet in front of Alex.

"You know Alex, you really surprised me today," he says.

"Not me," says Eric Bishop. *What is Eric's problem with me?*

"I used to think you were a stand-up guy. All that talk about the Marines. Band of Brothers. Looking out for the guy next to you. I guess that was all just a bunch of crap. I'm starting to put together a pretty clear picture of your situation. Put in a wood burning stove and some solar panels recently. Extra oil tank. You're not worried about a thing. You don't need anything from any us. I see exactly what kind of guy you are now. I guess my only question is why the hell did you show up to this meeting in the first place?"

Todd stands his ground with his hands on his hips, and waits for a response. Alex senses that everyone else is waiting for a response. Most of the adults are standing in a loose perimeter around the current epicenter of controversy.

"I'm starting to ask myself the same question, though I have managed to accomplish one important task. I've identified the belligerent assholes on the block," says Alex, letting his rising anger get the better of him.

Todd takes a few steps forward, and Daniel Lewis puts a hand on his Todd's shoulder, diffusing his lack of self-control.

"Well, my offer still stands. Sarah, I'll bring the anti-virals over to your house later this afternoon. You can all figure out how you want to distribute them. I'll catch you later Ed. Derek. Jamie, give me a call when you get home. It's important. Charlie," says Alex, nodding to them as he starts to walk toward the end of the driveway.

They all acknowledge him with various gestures and quiet responses.

"I wonder how much you're keeping for yourself," grumbles Todd.

"You just don't quit, do you?" says Alex, turning around to face Todd. *This guy needs a warning.*

"I guess not. I don't turn my back on friends, like some of us," says Todd in a strained voice that betrays an underlying fear of the situation.

"Well, that can be a positive quality in the right situation," he says lightly, taking a few steps toward Todd.

"Oh Nicki, could you do me a favor and put me on the security roster? Especially if we need any heavily armed patrols. You know, if looters become an issue. Thanks," says Alex, and turns to leave.

"That asshole's threatening us? I don't believe it," he hears someone whisper.

You're damned right I am. Alex hears Charlie call out to him. *Here's the real powder keg.*

"Alex," he says, and Alex turns his head while continuing to walk.

"What's up Charlie?" he says, as Charlie closes the gap.

"That was a nice finishing touch," he says.

"We'll see. I don't have a good feeling about Todd. I think he's going to need more than a veiled threat," says Alex.

"You might be right. I should have said the same thing. I know that fucker has it in for me too," he says.

"Well, you called it like most of us saw it," says Alex.

"Yeah, well I'm sorry to have gotten you involved in that little fiasco over there. Looks like half the neighborhood hates us," he says, and Alex senses that Charlie might be happy about his outlaw status in the neighborhood.

"Yeah, I'm a little surprised that so many people rallied against me. Jesus. I'm not making any of this up. If they execute their little daycare plan, then the neighborhood is screwed. How are you guys set?

It sounds like you've been doing some prep work," says Alex, as they pass Todd's house.

"Pretty good I guess. You're probably the expert. We have at least two months of military style MRE's and freeze dried meals. I couldn't believe these were still on the shelves. I guess no one thought about it at first. Now you can't find that stuff anywhere. Other than that, we have a bunch of dried stuff, like rice, beans, and nuts. A good amount of canned food. Some jugs of water. I can melt snow if I have to. I have a bunch of those water purification tablets, from our deep woods hunting trips. Propane stove. Plenty of firewood. I thought you were nuts putting in that solar panel system, but now it looks like a pretty damn good idea."

"Yeah, it's something we wanted to do for quite a while. For more than one reason," says Alex.

"Like sticking it to the power company?" says Charlie.

"In a sense. Unfortunately, it'll take another fifteen or twenty years for this system to pay for itself. But that's definitely part of it," says Alex, as the pass they pass the Walkers' house.

Charlie looks up at Ed's house. "Ed seems like a good guy. How are they set for this thing?"

"Alright, I suppose. Ed's biggest challenge will be keeping his distance from the rest of the neighborhood. Ed understands the gravity of the situation better than most around here, but he's not far enough along yet for me to say he's good to go. He's too nice. The best advice I can give you Charlie, is to steer clear of the neighbors. If you have to interact, keep your distance, and for god's sake, don't provoke anyone. You and I both could use some help with that one," says Alex.

"For a minute there, I wasn't sure if you were the pot or the kettle," says Charlie.

Alex laughs, and Charlie joins him. *I think I was wrong about this guy.* Alex and Charlie stand at the foot of the Fletchers' driveway.

"I'd shake your hand Alex, but..."

"Unfortunately, that's exactly how we all need to start thinking. I'd definitely steer clear of the McDaniels. Jamie said her husband Matt couldn't make it to the little soiree today because he was sick. He's head honcho for one of the Portland high schools, so who knows. Hopefully, he's got a bad cold, or a case of the seasonal flu. But with his proximity to the schools, I wouldn't take any chances. Jamie didn't look that great either," says Alex.

"I noticed. Sniffling, coughing and shivering with that winter jacket and hat. Do you really think it's going to hit the neighborhood hard?" he asks.

Once again, Alex gets a weird sense that Charlie might want the flu to break out in the neighborhood.

"If it's already in the schools, we'll definitely see cases in the neighborhood. If people keep going to work? If they implement that stupid ass plan to pass kids around the neighborhood? It's going to rage through the neighborhood," says Alex.

"Friday was the last day of school for the Thornton clan. For everyone I guess. I wish I had pulled them sooner. Is there any way to tell if they've already got the virus from someone at school?" he asks.

"If they show any flu-like symptoms, you could start them on anti-virals and take them to the hospital. Better now than later. At this point they can still get adequate care and treatment. In a week or two? Forget it. I can give you a few anti-viral treatment courses if they show any symptoms. Just keep it quiet OK," says Alex, wondering if it was a good idea to promise those to him. *I can use all the allies I can find or make.*

"Thanks Alex, that means a lot to me. If you need anything, don't hesitate. We should keep an eye out for each other. Never know what's going to happen around here. I have the ability to reach out and touch somebody, if you catch my drift. How about you?" he says, obviously referring to his hunting rifles.

"I'm set in that department," replies Alex, ending the topic.

"Good to hear that. Hey, I'll catch you later. Let me know if you hear anything," he says, and starts to walk down the block.

"You too man," says Alex.

He walks up his driveway, and looks down the street toward the Quinns', before stepping into the garage. He closes the garage bay, and squeezes by the Forerunner to get to the mudroom door. *Why does she park so far in?* He won't say anything to her about her parking job, because he knows what her response will be. "Why don't you walk around the back of the truck?" He opens the mudroom door and walks in the house.

"Kate?" he says, loudly enough to be heard throughout the first floor.

"In the great room," she responds.

Alex removes his shoes and stacks them in the mudroom closet. He hangs his coat up on a row of hooks next to the door, and stuffs his hat in one of the pockets of the coat. Alex smells freshly brewed coffee.

"Coffee? That's a treat in the afternoon," he says, walking into the kitchen.

He hears Kate shuffling through the great room. She appears, dressed in a thick gray turtle neck sweater and faded jeans.

"Yeah, I started to feel a bit chilly, and sleepy, so I thought I'd brew up some of that Bolivian coffee your doctor friend gave to you. I figured you could use some too after standing out there. How did it go?" she says.

"Well, the rest of the group is still out there," he says, pouring coffee into an oversized blue mug, and giving her an odd luck.

"That well?" she says, putting her mug down on the island.

Alex backs up from the coffee and takes a seat on a black kitchen stool. He leans into the backrest and takes a sip of straight black coffee.

"Well, it certainly could have gone better. I'm not sure how to describe the scene, but there is a definite divide between the other side of Durham and our side. Todd Perry is a nutcase, that's confirmed. He's gonna be a problem. He was pushing for everyone to disclose how much food they have on hand. Basic supplies too. Apparently, he doesn't have jack squat, and he was trying to institute a system of sharing food. I think. Anyway, a couple of people calmly voiced their concerns about this idea, and Charlie Thornton came at the idea with guns a' blazin…"

"That nutcase?" says Kate.

"You know, I think Charlie might be alright. A little unstable, but he really seems to understand what's going on with the pandemic. He says he's all set at his house. Food, supplies, everything. We had a nice little chat on the way back, since we were both sort of kicked out of the meeting," says Alex.

"Are you serious? They kicked you out?" she asks.

"Not really, but it was clearly time for me to go. Anyway, Charlie accuses Todd of being a self-interested communist…or socialist. Either way, this really set off Team Hostile, which includes, but doesn't appear to be limited to the Bishops, who seem to hate me for some reason; Mike Lynch, Andrew Greene, Laura Burton, and the uh…Hodges up at the top of the street. None of them really cared for my ideas, so we'll have to keep a close eye on these people as the situation deteriorates. Especially Todd. I think Mary Thompson hates me too now."

"Sounds great," says Kate sarcastically.

"Anything in particular you said to upset everyone?"

"Well, I didn't like the food disclosure idea, and I made that very clear. Though I have to say that a majority of the group didn't seem too keen about sharing food either. Todd and the Bishops were all fired up about it. Other than that, I told the group that if they didn't all stay away from each other, then the flu was going to run unchecked through the neighborhood, and kill a bunch of people. Nobody really liked that. This really hits the spot honey. Thank you," he says, taking another sip.

"Did you tell the group that we are off limits here at the house?" she says.

"Pretty much. That was part of the 'stay away from each other' speech. One of the big ideas forwarded by the pandemic committee was to organize a neighborhood daycare system. Oh, and a volunteer roster to drive sick people to the hospital, if the family can't do it. I told them that these ideas were the quickest way to ensure that the neighborhood did not survive the pandemic. This was not received well. Oh, and I'm pretty sure that the McDaniels' house is infected with the flu," he says.

"What? How do you know that? Is Jamie sick?" she asks, sounding slightly frantic.

"No…well maybe. Matt is definitely sick with something. Sounds a lot like the flu. It could be anything really," he says.

"Yeah, but with their exposure to the school systems? I wouldn't take any chances," she emphasizes.

"Well, it's not like we hang out with them," says Alex.

The phone rings, and Kate walks over to the kitchen desk to pick it up. She reads the caller ID.

"Matthew McDaniels?" she asks.

"That might be Jamie," he says. *This should be interesting.*

"Why would she be calling?" she says.

"I told her to give me a call. I wanted to convince her to take her husband in to be seen," he says.

He knows that this response won't quell Kate's instinctual suspicion of any attractive woman that interacts on any level with Alex. Jamie is probably at the top of Kate's list, simply due to her proximity in the neighborhood. Alex has sensed this before with Kate.

"Hello? Hold on, he's right here," she says, still maintaining a suspicious look.

"Thanks honey, now can you give us some privacy?" he says, covering up the phone's mouthpiece.

"Just kidding. Hey Jamie, thanks for calling," he says.

"That's fine Alex. God, I've never seen people act like that before. I almost got into a shouting match with Mary Thompson. I wouldn't count on getting a Christmas card from her," she says.

"Yeah, I saw the two of you going at it. What's her deal?" he asks.

Kate doesn't seem interested in the conversation any longer, and retreats to the great room. She grabs her iPad and sits in the leather lounge chair to the left of the wood burning stove.

"I really don't know. She asked me if I could believe what you were saying, about not helping each other out with food. I told her I completely agreed with you, and she started into me. Really weird," she says, and breaks into a cough.

Alex cringes at the sound and momentarily pulls the phone away from his face, as if he could catch the flu through it.

"Hey Jamie, the reason I wanted you to call, is that I'm worried about Matt, and maybe you. You said Matt was pretty sick, right?" he says.

"Yeah, it really hit him this morning. He woke up sweating, and could barely get out of bed. He felt really hot, and I could tell he was really congested. He's been on the couch most of the day," she says, alarmed.

"Is he coughing much?" Alex asks.

"Yeah, that's what woke us up so early," she says.

"Jamie, I think you need to take him to the ER, and have him tested for the Jakarta Flu. The hospitals aren't slammed yet, and if he has it, and you catch it early, he should be fine," he says.

"Do you really think he might have it? Oh my god, I don't…I'm not sure if I can take him in today. I have the kids home, and I'd…"

"Jamie, you should all go in and get tested. You don't sound so great either, and if both of you have it, there's a good chance your kids might have been exposed. The earlier you catch this thing the better. This may sound weird, but if you're going to get infected, then it's better to get infected now, while the hospitals can provide the right services. Seriously, you should all hop in the car, and head over to the Maine Medical Center. Pack an overnight bag for your husband."

"Really? I mean he was fine last night. I kind of feel like we'd be jumping the gun. Don't you think…"

"Jamie, you can't be too cautious with this flu strain. It's killing people, lots of people. Some within twenty four to forty eight hours. You don't want to wait around," he says.

"Alright. I'll uh…I'll talk to Matt about it. I don't know about taking the kids. That might be a little too much for them. I might make an appointment with their pediatrician for tomorrow," she says, and Alex can sense the hesitation.

"Your pediatrician might not have the field test yet. They'll probably send you over to Maine Med, or tell you to go home and call if symptoms develop. You're probably better off all going together…hey Jamie, I have Ed buzzing through. Think about what I said. You really need to go sooner than later. No later than tomorrow morning. Seriously," he says.

"Alright. Let me see," she says and the line goes dead.

Alex switches over to Ed.

"Hey Ed," he says, and the phone beeps. *Another call.*

The caller ID says Paul Cooper. *Christ. My own little sewing circle.*

Chapter Twenty

Tuesday, November 13, 2012

Alex works at pruning a large oval shaped flower bed to the left of the brick patio in his backyard. So far this afternoon, he has stuffed three large brown yard bags with dead perennial clippings and leaves. He still has two more flower beds to cut back, which should keep him busy until the sun starts to dip below the trees.

Alex pulls his brown knit cap down tighter on his head and continues to cut away at the dry branches. As the sun sinks lower in the sky, the temperature drops rapidly and a southerly winds picks up. Alex considers a warmer jacket. His hands are starting to chill through the thick leather garden gloves. Alex grabs the pile of leaves he collected, and stuffs them into a half filled bag. Just as he finishes, his iPhone rings, and he fishes it out of his pocket. Alex isn't familiar with the number, but he can tell it's a Scarborough prefix. He answers the call.

"Alex Fletcher," he says.

"Hey Alex, it's Ed. Kate gave me your cell," he says.

Alex looks up at the Walkers' house and sees Ed opening the sliding door to the deck. Alex waves to him, and signals with his hand to come over.

"Come on over. I'm not that paranoid. Unless you don't want to be seen in public with me, which I can understand," says Alex.

"I don't care what any of those assholes think. No, my wife just got a call from Jamie across the street, and I don't want her to see me scooting over to your house. And I didn't feel like low crawling in the drainage area. Jamie asked Sam if we'd watch the kids while she took her husband over to the ER. I guess he's having serious trouble breathing, and she's really freaked out. She sounded like shit too. I told Sam to tell her we'd call back in a few minutes. Alex, I really don't want to take the risk, but I feel like a real fucking asshole not helping her out," he says.

Alex pauses for a moment to consider his response. *I guess it doesn't matter how I phrase this. The answer is the same.*

"Ed, please don't consider watching her kids. Odds are very high that all four of them are infected. I told her Sunday to take the entire family in to get tested, and she blew it off. She needs to take all of them to the ER. All of them. You can tell her I said so, I don't care. I'll call her myself if you want," says Alex, walking over to Ed's house.

Alex hangs up the phone, and continues walking over to Ed's deck. Ed puts the phone back inside, and steps outside.

"Jesus it's cold out," he says, folding his arms.

"No, I'll call her back, but Sam seems to be considering the idea."

"The whole thing is a bad idea. If she's sick with the flu, they're not going to just let her drop off her husband and hang around for a while. As soon as they see she's coughing and wheezing, they'll put her in a hospital bed too, if they have any to spare. They certainly won't let her hang around the hospital if she's an infection risk.

According to the news, DHS just authorized active risk reduction measures, which means that they might simply detain her so she can't go back into the community and spread the flu. You could be stuck with the kids indefinitely, which would be fine if they weren't likely sick themselves. She needs to take them all in to be tested. I'll call her and explain it," says Alex.

"No it's fine. I'll take care of it. This really sucks," he says.

"I agree, but this is how it spreads. It's going to get worse around here, and the decisions are going to get tougher. Did Jamie even mention the conversation I had with her on Sunday?" says Alex.

"No, but she told Sam that she didn't think you guys would help, and that we were her last hope since they don't have any family around. Threw a guilt grenade on us," says Ed.

"Yeah, well that won't be the last one. Stand by for a few tactical nuclear guilt bombs. I look at this whole situation as a military operation. The main objective is to keep the Fletchers' safe from harm, in whatever form it takes. The flu, crazy neighbors, whatever…"

"Is this a long speech General Patton? I'm freezing out here," he says.

"You better get in before you freeze your tits off. Your lips are turning blue," says Alex.

"Yeah, I'll let you know how it goes," he says, grabbing the handle on the sliding door.

"Good luck man," says Alex, as he salutes Ed and walks back to his yard.

∎

Alex see's the McDaniels' Volvo station wagon back down their drive way and turn toward Harrison Road. As it heads down the street,

Alex gets up from the computer and walks to the office window, staring down the street as the station wagon approaches the Durham Road fork. Instead of turning left and heading directly toward Harrison Road, the car continues around the loop.

Alex keeps track of the cars headlights, as the lights disappear behind houses on the other side of the loop, and suddenly reappear. He catches the lights passing the McKinney's house, as they quickly vanish behind the edge of the Cohens' stockade fence. Alex quickly moves to the far left edge of the window to see if the car passes the Cohens' house. There is only a sliver of space between the other side of the Cohens' fence, and the Sheppards' house. Alex doesn't see the lights pass. He waits a few more seconds, then shifts to the right side of the window to check the visible stretch of road between the Santos and Barton houses. *Nothing.*

He calculates that the Bartletts live right across from the Cohens, and figures that the Bartletts' house must be the car's destination. *Jesus, she's dropping them off with Nicki.* Alex thinks about how she probably ended up at the Bartletts'. She probably called Nicki to check and see if there were any volunteers to watch the kids, and as one of the neighborhood "leaders," she stepped up to set the example for rest of the neighborhood. Alex grabs the phone from the desk, and dials Ed's number.

"Hey Sam, it's Alex, is Ed there?" he says, sitting in his office chair.

"Let me see if I can pry him away from the window. I assume that's why you're calling?" she says.

"Guilty. The McDaniels just took off. I was hoping they were all going to the hospital, but it looks like they made a stop on the other side of the block," he says.

"Well, I wish we could have helped them, but I'm beginning to think you're right about all this. I've seen a few lawyers and staff around the office that look and sound really sick. I'm really starting to get paranoid. I'm thinking about calling in sick for next week. Diarrhea sound good to you?" she says laughing.

"I'm telling you, it's the most underestimated illness out there. You won't even have to finish the sentence. Start to describe the contents of the toilet bowl and wham, end of discussion. Take as much time off as you need. At this point, you could probably just use the words, 'flu like symptom,' and nobody will question your decision to stay home. According to the evening news, absenteeism is on the rise in Maine," says Alex.

"I can imagine. Anyway, here's the other peeping tom. Take care Alex. Say hi to Kate," she says.

"Sure thing Sam," says Alex.

"Hey Alex. Did you see where Jamie went?" says Ed.

"I'm pretty sure it was the Bartletts'. I saw the car pass the McKinney's, which eliminates the Green's, and I'm pretty sure it didn't get past the Cohens'…"

"It didn't. I can fully see the Bishops house, and she didn't land there either," he says.

"Definitely disappeared behind the Cohens', at Nicki's house. Unbelievable. What is she thinking?" says Alex.

"Who, Jamie or Nicki?" says Ed.

"Either of them," replies Alex.

"Well, Jamie was pretty upset, but said that she understood why we couldn't help…"

"But she went ahead and pawned her kids off on another family. What the fuck?" says Alex.

"She said they weren't symptomatic, and she didn't want to risk bringing them to the hospital. She thought the state might yank the kids right out of the hospital if they she was infected too," he says.

"She might be right. I really didn't think of that," says Alex.

"Me either. It's a shitty situation for them," says Ed.

"Yeah, and it'll probably get shittier," says Alex.

"Way shittier."

■

Alex sits at the computer in the great room. He finally got an email response from Dr. Wright, almost a full week after he left him both a voicemail and an email, digging for any more inside information. According to the email, Dr. Wright had been contacted by Biosphere Pharmaceuticals to confirm Alex's transaction, which probably explains why Alex hasn't heard a word from Biosphere. Possibly the fact that he was attacked on his own front lawn also has something to do with Biosphere's silence.

Dr. Wright explains that the situation in Maine is fast approaching the breaking point, with a large percentage of available hospital beds unavailable to new cases. Local area hospitals have canceled nearly all elective and non-critical surgeries, to make room for the swiftly rising number of flu cases. Alex wonders about the McDaniels, who left for the hospital earlier this evening. Dr. Wright's email is terse and filled with spelling errors, giving Alex the impression that he is exhausted and overwhelmed.

Mike Gallagher left him an email announcing his family's arrival in New Hampshire at Colleen's parents' house. He finally met Ted at the storage locker, two days after abandoning his Biosphere post down in Andover. Ted arrived alone, and didn't mention searching Mike's house. Overall, Mike said that the close out was painless and cordial.

Alex hears a faint sound from upstairs. Sitting at the computer, Alex is located directly under Emily's bedroom. The thump he heard emanated from the other side of the great room, above the TV. Alex remains completely still, straining his ears in the silence. He hears the telltale creak of the first stair at the top. *Rookie error.* Alex doesn't hear anything for a few more seconds, then finally, he hears one more creak near the bottom of the stairs. Third stair up from the bottom to be precise. At this point, he figures Ryan could peer around the corner of the doorway to examine the great room. He had to be curious about the light radiating through the entryway. Alex risks a peek behind him, and catches Ryan peering into the family room.

"Hey buddy," Alex says, turning back to the computer screen.

"Oh, hi dad. I just came down to grab a glass of water," says Ryan, stepping into the foyer.

Ryan is dressed in navy blue sweatpants and a gray t-shirt, which allays any suspicion that he might have been creeping downstairs to sneak outside.

"Yeah, I got caught up checking email and scanning the news. I could use a glass of water too," says Alex, standing up from the computer.

"Anything big going on out there," he asks, walking into the family room.

"I just finished an article in the New York Times about the situation in the greater New York City area. Sounds like the healthcare system is close to the breaking point, and the food situation is worse. New York State's governor just called up the New York National Guard. I read that Massachusetts will be doing the same in the next few days. The rest of the states can't be too far behind," says Alex, walking toward the kitchen.

"Why would they need the National Guard?" asks Ryan, following him through the great room.

"Well, they call up the National Guard a lot during emergencies, and this is certainly an emergency. I think the real reason for the call up is that they expect the overall situation to explode. They'll need the Guard to handle civil disorder," says Alex.

Alex takes two thick glasses out of the cabinet, and hands one to Ryan.

"Like protests?" asks Ryan.

"At first, but if the government can't ensure basic food or healthcare, protests will be the least of their problems," says Alex.

They both drink a glass of water, and Alex puts his glass next to the sink, by the coffee maker. Ryan pours another glass and nurses it, clearly stalling.

"Are you headed up dad? I'll turn the stove light off if you're done," says Ryan.

"No, I'll turn it off. I'll probably be up for a while. I couldn't get to sleep tonight. Too much stuff zinging around up here," says Alex, knocking on his head.

"Alright dad, I'll see you in the morning," he says.

"Good night Ryan. Hey, we haven't been out for a run in a while. If the weather holds, how about we get out there?" offers Alex.

"Sounds good dad," he says, and turns around to walk back upstairs.

Alex decides to work on an idea that formed when he saw Jamie's car stop at the Bartletts' house. As he watched the car pull around to the other side of the block, and realized the implications of Jamie's decision, he came up with the idea to create a way to track what was happening on the block. He pulled a piece of white poster board from the office closet, and drew a rough sketch of the Durham Road loop. The schematic representation of the loop extended from one side of the poster board to the other, and he intended to graphically represent each house with a square. He would then put as much information as possible about each household, next to the respective square.

The idea is a product of Alex's military experience. Alex now considers the neighborhood to be his primary area of operation, and he wants to gather as much intelligence about the neighborhood as possible. He waits a few minutes for his son to walk up the stairs and use the bathroom. After he hears the toilet flush and the door to Ryan's room shut, Alex heads up to the office to retrieve the poster board. He brings the poster board back down to the kitchen island and lays it flat on the surface.

Using a retractable pencil, he draws each house, and labels them with their street number and family name. He draws a line for each member of the household. He'll add individual names later. The first round of information that he puts on his new "intel board" is a circled letter "S" above each house that sent kids to school. He'll add to this, as he gathers information regarding daycare.

He then fills in the names of the McDaniel family. Next to Matt he writes "hospitalized with flu." *A guess, but a pretty solid one.* Beside Jamie's name, he also writes "hospitalized with flu." He hasn't seen their car return, though he admits that she could have easily slipped back in without him noticing while they were watching the television. Next to the children, Amanda and Katherine, he writes, "direct exposure to flu." He circles the kids' names, and draws a line to the Bartletts' house. He puts a note above the Bartletts' house, next to the "S," "Both McDaniel kids dropped off Nov 6th."

He then takes a packet of markers from the kitchen desk, and pulls out a green, red and yellow marker. He puts a red dot above the houses he strongly suspects of being hostile to him. He does the same for the "friendlies", but uses green. Any unknown households get a yellow dot. Within the span of five minutes, Alex has developed a workable threat matrix. Finally, he circles the houses that are empty, which includes the Cohens' and Murrays'. He scans the poster one more time, and nods his head in satisfaction. He contemplates Kate's reaction to his poster and stifles a laugh. *Crazy and bored is what she'll say...and she won't be too far off the mark.*

Chapter Twenty-One

Friday, November 16, 2012

From the master bathroom, Alex hears the home phone start to ring. The call is cut short, leading Alex to believe someone in the house answered it. He folds the towel he used, and throws it up over the steam covered glass shower door. He puts on blue and gray striped boxer shorts, and stands up straight in front of the body length mirror. He turns a few times, examining different angles, and concludes that he still doesn't look bad for forty two years. His eyes are drawn to the loosely patterned, deep scar tissue spread along the left side of his chest and abdomen. He stares at the scarring for a few more seconds, and shakes himself free of a heavy thought.

He steps on and off the scale, satisfied with the fact that nothing had changed since yesterday. The scale scrapes the floor when he steps off, creating a sound that can be heard in the hallway outside of the bathroom.

"Still weigh the same?" Kate announces from the other side of the door.

"What? Are you spying on me?" he says, pulling on his jeans.

"Yeah, I don't have anything better to do. Ed's on the line, he said that Matt McDaniel died yesterday," she says, lowering her voice for the last part of the sentence.

"Hold on," he says, rushing to put on jeans and a dark green USMC sweatshirt.

He opens the door and see's Kate standing by the couch, talking on the phone.

"What happened?" he says.

"Ed can fill you in. Looks like it's starting to rain. You were smart to get Ryan up for an early run," she says, handing him the phone.

He takes the phone and Kate leaves the bedroom, shutting the door behind her.

"What happened man?"

"I just heard it from John next door. He was leaving for work, when Todd flagged him down in the driveway. Todd told him that he died late Wednesday night. The kids are over at the Bishops' for a few days," he says, sounding exasperated.

"What about Jamie?" says Alex.

"She's in ICU. Confirmed Jakarta Flu. From what Nicki told Todd, she's not doing great, but they consider her to be stable. It sounds like her husband died from the acute syndrome," he says.

"Yeah, from what you told me Tuesday, he had advanced ARDS symptoms. Respiratory issues usually come later as a complication of the flu. Jesus," says Alex.

"What a mess," says Ed.

"Yeah, and it's going to get messier. So, what's going on with Jamie's kids? Are they sick yet?" says Alex.

"I didn't hear anything about that, but John said that they were over at the Bishops'. Nobody knows when Jamie will be able to return home," he says.

"It really depends on how severe her case turns out to be. If she's in the ICU, and she's stable, she has a pretty good chance of survival. She could be home in a week, or it could be a month. Either way, she's going to feel like hell for quite a while. This may sound fucked up, but she's lucky she got into the hospital when she did. Looking at the news today, DHS officials estimate that all inpatient services will be slammed shut within two weeks. ISPAC thinks less time than that," says Alex.

"I saw that. Pretty unbelievable," says Ed.

"I don't think people are taking this seriously enough. The estimated number of confirmed cases in the U.S. is around 90,000, which doesn't sound bad, but it's slightly higher than CDC projections. 90,000 will be half a million next week, and then nearly three million the week after that. The case fatality rate worldwide is steady around fourteen percent, mostly from ARDS, but most experts agree that this number will climb as people start dying from complications. Fifteen percent of three million is 450,000. That's a lot of deaths," says Alex.

"Scary. Do you think it's safe to get more groceries?" asks Ed.

"Yeah, as long as you don't touch anything with your bare hands, and wear a mask. I think they're still just plopping pre-packed bags in your car and running your credit card. Honestly, it's probably very low risk, as long as you're smart about it," he says.

"What about the groceries," Ed asks.

"That's a little trickier. I don't think you'll get much produce, but I'd wash it thoroughly if you do. Everything else you could wash in the sink with soap and hot water. Wear gloves and don't touch your face. Hey, I have plenty of food and supplies over here. Seriously, we'll take care of you. You don't have to take any risks," says Alex.

"I know. I'd just feel better doing as much as possible until it becomes a necessity," he says.

"I hear you. Hey, if it comes to it, you could always go deer hunting with Charlie. He said that the conservation land back there is full of deer," says Alex.

"We might all need to remember that," says Ed.

"No kidding. Hey, thanks for the call. I don't seem to be on the neighborhood distribution list anymore," says Alex.

"Are your feelings hurt?" says Ed.

"Not really."

"I'll catch you later Alex."

"Sounds good man," Alex says and hangs up.

Chapter Twenty-Two

Saturday, November 17, 2012

What time is it? The phone next to the bed rings. *Seven? God damn it.* He reaches over to the phone. He can hear a heavy rain hitting the northeast windows of the bedroom. The bedroom is dark for seven, and Alex can see dark gray skies through the half opened shades on the front windows.

"Who is that," says Kate, in a groggy and annoyed voice.

"It's Ed," he says in a similar voice.

"Hello," he answers.

"Alex, sorry to wake you, but something weird is going on outside. I think you should take a look. Sam was up early in the office, and saw Eric Bishop and Todd Perry walk over to the McDaniels' house. She saw them walk up to the front door, and then walk around to the back of the house. What do you think they're up to?" says Ed.

"Maybe they're going to bring something over to Jamie at the hospital, or she asked them to take care of something," says Alex, standing up to look out of the window at the McDaniel house.

"Yeah, but I have the key to their house. Why wouldn't she have told them to get it from me? I don't like this. Why would they both need to be there?" he asks.

"I don't know. Are you thinking about heading over there? Wait. Hey, I can see them at the corner of the garage behind the house. It looks like Todd is trying to shoulder the back door open." says Alex.

"I'm heading over there to find out what's going on. I don't trust those two," he says.

"I'll be right out," says Alex.

"Thanks," Ed says, and the call is disconnected.

Alex heads toward the closet.

"What's going on?" says Kate, sitting up in bed.

"Nothing I hope. Todd and Eric Bishop are over at the McDaniels', and it looks like they are trying to break in the back garage door. Ed is heading over to see what they are up to. Maybe you should keep an eye on us out there, just in case. Call the police if something other than a fistfight erupts," he says.

"Are you kidding me?" she asks and sits up in bed.

"Not really," he says.

"You're not bringing a gun out there, are you?" she asks, standing up out of bed.

"I can't imagine that will be necessary," he says.

"That's not really an answer," she replies.

He looks at her, and considers her comment.

"No, I'm not. I can handle myself against those two yahoos. Bringing a gun out there would only complicate the situation. The last thing we need is the police in our lives. I'll be right back," he says, and heads out of the bedroom.

"Be careful," he hears her say.

"As always," he yells back, descending the stairs.

Alex reaches the mudroom, and puts on his old black leather combat boots. He grabs his blue winter gortex jacket and starts to put it on as he opens the mudroom door. He zips the jacket all the way up, pulls the hood over his head, and steps out of the protective cover of the porch. The rain and wind hits him hard as he walks across the driveway, pushing him slightly forward. He sees Ed already across the street, walking up to the McDaniels' garage. They acknowledge each other, and Alex jogs across to meet him. The rain is now pelting his face from the right. Alex hopes this doesn't last very long.

"This blows," says Alex.

"Yeah, it's pretty fucking miserable. You're used to this kind of shit, right?" says Ed, smiling.

"Nobody really gets used to this; they just get better at not bitching about it. And I'm almost ten years out of practice," says Alex, and Ed laughs.

Alex holds his index finger to his lips as they approach the corner. *No need to announce our presence.*

Before they reach the corner, Alex leans in close to Ed.

"Be careful. Either one of these guys could have the flu. Don't get too close," he whispers, and Ed nods.

They both round the corner of the garage together, facing down the length of the garage. The rain is at their backs again, and Alex is relieved. What he sees next dashes any sense of relief. Todd and Eric are standing on the bulkhead door, trying to open a window, oblivious to the two of them. Ed steps forward, and Alex follows. *These two are definitely up to no good.*

As they slowly approach, Eric notices them, and taps Todd on the shoulder. Todd turns, and steps down from the sloping bulkhead door. Alex resolves to let Ed do most of the talking.

"Hey, I have a key if that would make things easier?" says Ed.

"That would really help. As a last resort, I was going to bust one of the window panes on the garage door to get in," says Eric.

Alex keeps his hands in his jacket pocket, which he feels is a neutral gesture. The rain is hitting them in sheets, clearly bothering Eric and Todd, who are facing directly into the onslaught.

"What do you guys need?" asks Ed.

Eric's eyes dart almost imperceptibly toward Todd.

"I wanted to get the kids some new clothes. It looks like they'll be staying with us a little longer than expected. You heard about Matt right?" offers Eric.

"Yeah, that's tough. I hope Jamie recovers quickly, the kids are going to need her," says Ed.

"Have you told them yet," says Alex.

"No, I'm not sure how to handle it. I think we should wait until Jamie's home. The girls are worried, but doing ok. She should probably be the one to break the news," says Eric.

They all nod, and Todd breaks the moment.

"Hey, we can talk in the house. I need to get out of this fucking rain."

Ed takes a Patriots keychain out of his pocket, with two keys on it. He uses one of them to open the garage door. They all step inside, and into the empty bay, which is next to Matt's dark green Honda Pilot. A faint gasoline smell hits Alex as he steps into the garage. The air is dusty. Eric and Todd move to the center of the bay, near a large faded oil stain on the concrete deck. Alex and Ed stand in front of a waist level workbench along the back wall of the garage, next to the door.

Alex pulls back his hood, and Ed does the same. Eric and Todd stand there wiping the rain from their faces and hair. Todd is wearing a brown waist level hoodless fall jacket. The material is clearly not waterproof, and he looks miserable. Eric isn't faring much better, in a black wool pea coat, which must weigh twice its original weight from absorbed rainwater. The pea coat looks thick, which is probably the only reason that Eric isn't shivering like Todd. Alex's feels fine, aside from his legs, which are cold. The rain completely soaked his jeans by the time he got to the top of the McDaniels' driveway.

"That's better," says Eric.

"Anyway, I'm going to grab some more clothes and a few personal items. They gave me a list, he says, pulling it out of his pocket. I'll make sure to lock up on the way out. Thanks for opening up for us," says Eric.

"No problem. I was pretty sure it was you guys. My wife thought she saw you head over, and Alex couldn't be sure from his house. I'll stick around to make sure it's locked up, and check on the rest of the house for Jamie," say Ed. *Here comes the moment of truth.*

"We'll take care of that for you. Take a look around; make sure the windows are shut tight, turn down the thermostat, all that stuff. No reason for all of us to be out on a day like this," says Todd.

"I feel responsible for the house, and letting you guys in. I should be the last one out. I'd feel better that way. You guys can grab the stuff on the list, and I'll make the rounds," says Ed.

"Ed, we can handle it. Really, you're kind of making us feel like children. I'll check around, lock up and give you a call," he says.

"I don't see what the big deal is. We're already here. It'll go faster this way. You guys get the girls' stuff and we'll check out the house. We should all be out of here in five or ten minutes," says Alex.

"And why are you here?" asks Eric, starting at Alex. *Here comes angry Eric.*

"Why is Todd here?" counters Ed.

"Because I asked him to help," says Eric.

"Same with Alex. Hey, we're wasting time. Let's get this going and get out of here," says Ed.

"Ed, you're not the one watching her kids. OK? We're the only ones that really need to be here," challenges Eric.

"She gave me this key a few months ago, in case her kids got locked out, or for an emergency. I'd say that qualifies. I don't see anyone else with a key," says Ed.

"And I don't see anyone here volunteering to watch her kids either," say Eric, gesturing with his hands to Ed and Alex.

"Her kids know about the key. They didn't tell you about it?" says Ed.

"No," says Eric.

"How did you end up with the kids Eric?" says Alex.

"What do you care?" he replies.

"Let's just cut all of the bullshit. There's a reason you want us out of here, and it has nothing to do with that supposed list in your hand," says Alex.

Ed regards Alex with a surprised but satisfied look. Alex takes his hands out of his coat pockets and folds his arms in front of him.

"Fuck you," says Todd, and Alex flashes a mock smile.

Eric remains silent, with a look of rage on his face. He crumples the yellow piece of paper in his hand.

"I'll tell you what. You guys can get the stuff on that list, and check the house. Ed and I will stay here in the garage and lock up when you leave. I'll wait out in the rain. Doesn't matter to me, or does that still fuck up your real reason for being here? " says Alex.

"Look, we're going to get some more clothes for the girls, and…" Eric pauses to look at Todd, who shakes his head in response.

"And what?" presses Ed.

"It's none of their business Eric," says Todd.

"I'm not sure how any of this is yours either," says Ed, staring at Todd.

"Jesus. Will one of you just come out and say it. You're taking the food too," says Alex.

"Not all of it…" starts Eric.

"You don't owe them an explanation!" yells Todd.

"Now it makes sense," says Alex, pointing at Todd.

"Go fuck yourself Alex. I'm taking the kids next week," says Todd.

"And you need to stock up now? Makes sense," Alex says, shaking his head mockingly.

"Nobody is taking any of the food in this house," declares Ed.

"It's only fair that if we're feeding her kids, then we should be using their food!" yells Todd.

"Take it easy," says Alex.

Todd takes a step toward Alex, and Eric puts a hand on his shoulder to restrain him.

"It's fine Todd, don't let him push your buttons. That's what you're really good at, isn't it? Pushing buttons?" says Eric.

"Only when they need to be pushed," says Alex.

"I know you think you're the shit around here. Tough guy Marine. Decorated veteran. All that meaningless crap you and your wife have pushed on us over the past eight years. You may have impressed the rest, but your nonsense never worked with me or my wife," says Eric.

"I'm sorry, did I just land in the middle of a different planet. What are you talking about Eric?" says Alex.

"You may not have ever said anything directly, but you've made it pretty clear that you think you're better than the rest of us. Clear to me at least. You had most of us fooled until Sunday, when your true colors showed," says Eric.

"Turned out to be a gutless loser," says Todd.

Alex can feel his own blood rising, and figures that the two of them can probably see that his face is reddening. *I need to redirect this.*

"Hey, if you're watching the kids, you shouldn't have to dig into your own supplies to feed them. Do you agree Ed?"

"Barely, but I'm listening," says Ed, staring intently at Todd.

"So, what I propose is that you grab all of the stuff on that list, and then together, we'll figure out how much food you should take…"

"Who the fuck are you to tell me my business!" yells Todd.

"Exactly, I'm not having you guys stand over my shoulder like a prison guard," says Eric.

"Then get out of here," says Ed.

"You'd just be screwing over the kids by kicking us out of here," says Eric, and Todd sighs agreement.

"Fucking pathetic," says Alex.

Todd lunges for Alex, who steps aside and turns his body with Todd's motion, sending Todd toward the workbench behind him. Sent off balance, Todd stumbles full speed into the work bench with his hands and arms extended, which luckily absorb some of the impact. Despite the cushion of limbs, his chest hits the edge of the bench hard enough knock the wind out of him. He slumps to the garage floor, looking up at Alex, straining to breath. Eric remains frozen in the middle of the garage, and Ed steps clear of the potential melee zone.

"Do not try that again!" says Alex pointing at Todd.

"Here's the deal. Eric, you get the girls stuff, and Todd will cool his jets down here in the garage. Ed, why don't you put together some food for the girls. Find a suitcase or an athletic bag, something big enough to fill with plenty of food. The girls can carry it around with them until Jamie gets back, and we can refill the bag as needed," says Alex, moving out of Todd's immediate striking distance.

Eric nods at Alex, still dazed by the sudden violence.

"You OK?" says Eric, walking over to Todd.

"He's fine. He just lost his wind," says Alex forcefully.

Eric stops and backs up slowly into the Honda Pilot, which startles him and moves him into action. He scurries around the SUV and opens the door to the house. Ed starts to move in the same direction.

"Nice one," he says, looking down at Todd, who is still taking shallow breaths of air, and staring intensely at Alex.

"I'll deliver the food to the girls myself. I don't trust these heroes," says Ed, as he skirts around the back of the SUV to follow Eric.

"Hey, you should put together a package for the Bartletts too. These guys couldn't have gone about this any worse, but I see their point about feeding Jamie's kids," says Alex.

"Sounds fair, but I don't want to totally deplete Jamie's supply. She's going to need it for all of them when she gets back," says Ed.

"Don't worry about that," he says, and Ed nods over the hood of the SUV, and then disappears into the house, leaving the door wide open. Alex turns around to face Todd.

"I'm sure you have a few ideas swimming around in your head, and I can assure you that none of them are healthy for you right now," Alex continues.

Todd appears to breathe more easily, sitting with his back against a large green plastic bin stored under the workbench. Several tools sit in disarray on top of the workbench, knocked loose from their places on the peg board behind bench. Alex eyes a few of the tools warily, especially the hammer and a two foot long metal ruler. *I need to keep his hands from finding those.*

Several minutes pass in complete silence between Alex and Todd, punctuated only by the occasional sound of rummaging in the house or sudden sheets of rain slamming into the sides of the garage. Todd finally stands up and dusts himself off, still glaring at Alex. Alex may appear relaxed and aloof to Todd, but inside, he is anything but calm. Until Todd moves away from the potential weapons on the workbench, Alex will keep his mind and body on high alert. As Todd beams hatred at Alex, Alex struggles to keep his breathing under control as his heart races.

Todd moves away from the workbench, never looking at it, and resumes his original position near the center of the garage. Alex feels his body loosen and steps over to the bench. He leans his back against the same edge that took Todd to the floor, blocking Todd's view of the hammer and metal ruler. He hears something solid strike the floor in the mudroom, and leans forward to look through the doorway. He sees Ed moving around the mudroom. Eric walks past him and into the garage.

"I have everything. Let's go," says Eric, holding a large pink nylon duffel bag.

"Are either of the girls sick yet?" asks Alex.

"Why would you care?" says Eric.

"Asshole," adds Todd.

"You two still don't get it, do you?" says Alex.

"Get what?" says Todd, as they both move to the garage door.

"That their dad died from the Jakarta Flu and their mother is in the ICU. That the two of them are very likely infected. They need to be taken to the hospital and tested immediately for the flu. You're fucking crazy keeping them at your house. They'll infect everyone," says Alex.

"They're fine. We've been watching them off and on all week, and even the Bartletts' said they've been symptom free. Hey, someone has to take care of them. Certainly isn't going to be one of you two shit bags," says Eric, grinning at his own jab.

"Fucking losers," mutters Todd.

"Shut the fuck up Todd. Hey, are you still planning to take your turn watching the kids, or will you take a pass now that your free buffet ticket's been revoked?" says Alex, watching Eric closely for a reaction.

Eric looks to Todd for a response. Todd opens the door, and a wave of rain pours into the garage, soaking the floor and the end of the workbench closest to the door.

"I'm done with these assholes," insists Todd.

"Good luck Eric. Looks like the good Samaritan is even more full of shit than you," yells Alex.

Eric looks torn, almost confused, as if the possibility of being stuck with Jamie's kids never crossed his mind. Ed steps around the front of the SUV on the other side of the garage, pulling a medium sized red suitcase with one hand, and holding two stuffed plastic Target bags in the other. Everyone focuses on Ed.

"Eric. I'll drop this off a little later. The suitcase is for the girls. One of these bags is for you and your family, to offset any food you've shared with the girls. The other is for the Bartletts'. How long have they been at your house?" he says.

"Since yesterday morning," says Eric.

"Well, this might be a lot for just one day, but I know Jamie really appreciates what you're doing," says Ed.

Eric nods his head in what might be his first genuine non-hostile act of the morning. Todd doesn't look nearly so defused.

"What do I get if I take the kids?" says Todd. *This guy is relentless.*

"A good neighbor ribbon," interjects Alex.

"Alex," says Ed, giving him the 'take it easy' look.

"Fuck this guy. These kids aren't going to be passed around the neighborhood for a food dowry," says Alex.

Todd lets go of the garage door, and Ed moves up against him, shielding him from Alex. Alex glances at the tools on the workbench, and quickly determines that Todd is in a much better position to take possession of them than he is.

"Don't worry about him. We'll figure it out," says Eric, pushing Todd out of the door.

The two of them disappear into the rain, and Alex sees them both pass quickly by the garage's side window. Ed lowers the bags to the concrete and runs over to the door to close it. He turns around and faces Alex.

"Alex, you really need to dial it back a few notches," he says.

"I know. I'm really sorry about that. I didn't expect Todd to lose it that easily," says Alex.

"Well, he doesn't seem very stable, so I'd avoid sending him the wrong signals. Especially when I'm around please. Anyway, I think this should be enough for them, at least for a week or so," says Ed, and tilts the bulging suitcase.

"What does their food supply look like?" asks Alex, picking up the two plastic bags.

"Alright I guess. I really can't tell how many weeks, but it seems like a reasonable amount. Maybe I'm setting them up for problems with this suitcase," says Ed, putting his face in his hands.

"Let Eric know that he should integrate the food into the house's daily meals, and that the suitcase doesn't represent a restriction. More like an adjustment for two more people. If they run out, and he's still watching the kids, you can refill the suitcase. I think he'll understand the food idea.

Eric, or Todd, or most anyone on this block would be fair to those kids. I just didn't like the precedent that their home invasion might set. I think this will work out fine. I'm more concerned about Amanda and Katherine getting sick. After we drop this off at your house, I'm going to run home and grab some anti-virals to put in the suitcase. If they start taking them now, and continue the full course, then hopefully, their symptoms won't be as bad, and they might be spared the worst the flu has to offer."

"I'll make sure they start taking those. They should probably try to keep it a secret. Are they the same ones you gave us last year?" says Ed.

"Yeah, either TerraFlu or Tamiflu. Same thing really," says Alex.

Ed opens the door, and is hit with a pressure wave of wind and driving rain. He presses the button on the back of the door knob, and they both step through the doorway into the storm.

■

Alex sits at the corner of the sectional sofa, next to Emily who is kneeling on the floor next to the coffee table, putting away a board game.

"Well, that was fun. Next time we'll play Trivial Pursuit, the 80's edition, and your mother and I will be on the same team. Two decades should be a comfortable buffer for us," says Alex, ruffling Emily's hair.

"Dad, stop it," she protests, grabbing his hand.

"Hey, Cartoon Network is on all day long around here. How could you miss so many of those questions?" says Ryan.

"Oh, I do everything I can to shut that channel out of my mind," says Kate. "Most of the shows are either gross or confusing."

"We all know your mother is pretty easily confused," says Alex.

Ryan and Emily laugh, and Kate moves over on the couch toward Alex.

"Whoa, no need to resort to violence here. Third time today," says Alex.

"Yeah, you're an instigator, just like your son," she says.

"I don't instigate stuff," counters Ryan with a completely insincere look on his face.

"Right. You and your father," she says, and manages to get one of her hands through Alex's defenses.

She digs her hand into his lower right side, and he reacts by moving his lower body away from her hand. Alex is terribly ticklish around the waist.

"Alright, that's it! Stop it!" he says in between uncontrolled laughter.

Kate eases up on the attack, and Alex jumps off the couch, and runs behind it.

"I told you not to mess with me," she says, raising her eyebrows.

"I get the message. Kids, don't mess with your mother, or she'll tickle you," he says.

The phone interrupts them.

Kate reaches back onto the coffee table, and picks up the phone. She looks at the caller ID.

"It's your partner in crime, Ed," she says, and hands the phone across the back of the couch.

Alex answers the phone, just as Ryan turns on the TV.

"Hello. Hold on. Hey, can you guys turn that down! Sorry about that. What's up?"

"Hey, I just got back from Eric's. I got a good feeling from Eric and Stephanie about the food and the kids. I don't feel as stressed about it. I'll tell you what though; the Bishops' house is a zoo. Everyone was over there. The Green's kids, the Bartletts', the Perry's. He said they've been swapping houses back and forth all week, so the ladies could get a break."

"Jesus. They really don't get it," says Alex.

"No, they really don't. Plus, one of Jamie's kids doesn't look so good. Katherine. She wasn't coughing, but she had a nasty sniffle, and she felt warm. I put my hand on the top of her head, and her head was cooking. I told the girls that they had to take the pills, and keep the pills out of sight. I also told Stephanie that Katherine had a fever. She said they'd keep a close eye on it," he says.

"Ed, you've done your duty to Durham Road and mankind. You're a good man," says Alex.

"Thanks. I feel another one of your lengthy lectures coming on, and I really need to get out of these clothes. I'm soaked. I'll catch you later," says Ed.

"Am I really that bad?" says Alex.

"No, just bad timing. Later," he says, and the call is disconnected.

Alex sits back down on the couch as the kids disperse.

"Hey, how many sets of anti-virals do we have left now? I'm starting to lose track," says Kate.

"Twelve for us, plus three I kept for Charlie, if they need them. Minus two for the girls. Thirteen total," he says.

"Minus three for Charlie? That leaves ten for us. You're already dipping into our core supply," she says.

"Yeah, I know, but I had to do something for those kids. Ten is fine for us. The plan for twelve gives us three courses of therapy each, way more than we'd need. Ten is more than adequate," he says.

"I'm sure it is, but that's not the problem. You know what the problem is right?" she says, looking in his eyes.

"Yeah, I need to listen a little more to my lectures," he says.

"A lot more. This isn't going to be the last shitty situation on the block. Far from it…"

"I know," says Alex, stepping on the first stair.

"I think from now on, we need to both be in on any decisions like that. You can be a hard ass most of the time, but when you give in, you really give in," she says.

"I know. I have a few soft spots," he says.

She kisses him, and starts to walk toward the kitchen.

"That's one of the reasons I fell in love with you. You're a tough guy with a soft side," she says.

"Not that tough," he says.

"Tough enough," she says.

"I'm thinking about pasta with a red sauce for lunch…and dinner, and probably lunch again tomorrow. I'll make a nice bean dish too."

"Works for me," he says, continuing up the stairs.

Chapter Twenty-Three

Monday, November 19, 2012

"Good morning, this is Matt Lauer. Julia Williams is filling in for Meredith this morning. Our top stories this morning focus on the Jakarta Flu worldwide and at home. Simply put, the worldwide figures are staggering, with Asia in the middle of an uncontained, and apparently uncontrollable pandemic disaster, and Europe, South America and Africa following a similar pattern. Here in the U.S., the situation is deteriorating quickly, with labor absenteeism rates skyrocketing, and the total number of Jakarta Flu cases multiplying daily.

According to CDC figures, the total number of confirmed cases of the Jakarta Flu rose from around 90,000 last week to nearly 215,000 today, with a large majority of these cases centered near major metropolitan areas. Worse hit cities so far are New York City, Los Angeles, San Diego, San Francisco, Boston, Chicago, Dallas, Atlanta and Miami, accounting for over 125,000 of the total number of cases, with New York City alone reporting over 30,000 cases.

Keep in mind that this number only represents the cases confirmed by health officials through testing. As anyone on the street will attest, symptoms of the flu seem everywhere, and even CDC officials admit that the actual number of cases waiting to be confirmed could be three to four times the officially reported numbers.

Hospitals and medical facilities in the heaviest hit metro areas are operating at near full capacity. DHS officials estimate that the nation's hospitals will likely reach or exceed surge capacity by the middle of the week, and have taken steps to deploy all remaining Federal Medical Stations to the hardest hit areas.

Three of these stations have already been established in New York City and one is operational in Los Angeles. Furthermore, DHS officials have assured state governments that all remaining Strategic National Stockpile assets have been slated for the soonest possible delivery to individual states.

On Saturday, in a hastily assembled pandemic summit at the Department of Energy headquarters in Washington, officials from Department of Transportation, Energy, Labor, and Agriculture met with private sector food and energy leaders to develop and implement short term solutions to the growing food and energy crisis. High absenteeism rates have plagued both fuel and food deliveries nationwide, nearly crippling the nation's food distribution and supply system.

Coupled with weeks of unusually high demand, industry officials state that the system has been stretched to its limit. Several states have already taken steps to activate all of their National Guard units, though their roles in the pandemic response effort have not been announced. Department of Defense officials refuse to comment on the possibility of using active duty military personnel to augment reserve and National Guard roles.

On Sunday, Energy officials at the pandemic summit voiced strong concerns over the continued operation of the nation's electricity grid in the face of unreliable coal supply to the nation's network of coal powered power plants. Department of Energy officials and energy leaders have already implemented a plan to divert coal reserves to power plants feeding the grid's weak points.

DOE officials are close to announcing the launch of a nationwide effort to conserve electricity. DC insiders predict that this announcement will be part of a Presidential broadcast tentatively scheduled for later this week. The Presidential address is rumored to include several broad sweeping measures designed to minimize the pandemic's impact on the population and critical infrastructure.

Let's go to Maria Castelli for our international update.

"Thanks Matt. I wish I had better news here, but the situation worldwide is continues to worsen. Chinese health officials report over 30 million cases, warning that these numbers may be understated. Casualties in China are reported in the millions, with leading Chinese epidemiologists confirming a twenty percent case fatality rate. This rate has remained steady for the past week.

Outside of China, in Asia, the situation is equally grim. Japanese health officials report nearly 900,000 confirmed cases of the pandemic flu and nearly 200,000 deaths, stating that their healthcare system has been completely overwhelmed. Government officials report that they are now relying nearly one hundred percent upon stockpiled food and fuel reserves. Unfortunately, Japan relies upon foreign imports for nearly sixty percent of its food supply, and nearly eighty percent of its regular fuel needs. Japanese government officials cite increased delinquency of oversea food and fuel deliveries as the primary cause of their worsening crisis.

In Europe, governments brace for the worst, as the number of cases throughout the Europe Union increased nearly fourfold over the week, bringing the EU total to nearly 1.4 million cases. The death rate in the EU remains consistent with worldwide statistics, hovering around twenty percent. EU leaders expressed confidence in the power generation capabilities of most EU nations, attributing the stability to the EU's aggressive progress over the past five years to replace coal based energy production with alternative fuel sources.

News out of Africa bears a striking resemblance to the 2008 pandemic, with an escalating continent wide famine overshadowing the effects of the spreading flu. In areas dependent upon international aid shipments, like Sudan and Zimbabwe, malnutrition and dehydration related deaths have far outpaced flu attributed casualties, and little relief is in sight, as donor nations struggle with the growing pandemic threat within their own borders.

The Southern African Energy Grid suffered a devastating blow Saturday, when the South African government announced that it would limit the amount of power transmitted to the grid. South Africa's decision will likely plunge most of the southern Africa into periods of prolonged, if not permanent darkness, until reliable power generation can be reestablished in South Africa. South African military and reserve units have been mobilized to handle the anticipated flow of refugees from affected countries. Matt, back to you."

"It looks like no one is getting a break out there. After we return, we'll hear from…"

Alex mutes the TV and sips his coffee.

"This machine makes some damn good coffee," says Alex.

"Yeah, it's awesome," she says, taking another sip, "though I kinda feel like an ass sitting around making cappuccino's while the world crumbles around us."

Alex stifles a laugh.

"I don't know. We can't wrap every single thing we do around that kind of a framework. You could spend the entire day questioning everything. This is just how it is for us. No different than any other day of the year when we run water in the sink while millions of people worldwide struggle for water. You'll drive yourself crazy. This is no different," he says, not really satisfied with his own rationalization.

"I guess, I just keep thinking about all of the food and supplies we have downstairs, and I wonder if we're making the right decision. If we shouldn't make a hard core assessment of how much we'll really need to survive through the winter, and come up with a plan to spread it around the neighborhood. I'm just wondering what it's going to be like around here when the first wave of the flu passes, and everything starts to return to normal," she says.

"What do you mean?" he says.

"Well, I guess I'm looking at how we're going to fit in around here, if we choose turn our backs on the neighborhood. I think if we make a better effort…"

"No matter what we do, this neighborhood will be a vastly different place in spring. We have a lot of stuff in the basement, but nowhere near enough to make a lasting impact on the neighborhood. We have over thirty families here, and our stockpile can probably feed four, maybe five families comfortably for the duration of the first and second wave. If we open the stockpile to the neighborhood, it'll be like opening Pandora's Box. **The consequences of trying to shut it down, once opened, will be worse for us than never opening it in the first place. Plus,** I've already promised Ed that we'd take care of his family, and I plan to stock up the McDaniel house when Jamie is released from the hospital."

"How many of these promises do you have out there that I don't know about?" she asks.

"That's it. While we were at Jamie's, Ed packed up a bunch of food in a suitcase for the girls, and I suggested that he pack up more food for the Bartletts, to compensate them for feeding the girls for most of the week. He didn't want to stretch their food supply to thin, so I told him not to worry about it, and that I'd take care of it. I see it as a way to ensure the girls were treated fairly until she gets back and can take care of them," he says.

"You didn't say that in front of Todd or Eric did you?" she says.

"I don't think so…maybe. Things were pretty crazy in that garage. I might have," he says. *Why is she railing on me like this?*

"I really hope you didn't, because if you did, then Todd's going to be all over us when things gets really bad over at his house," she says.

"So, basically, we're supporting the Walkers and McDaniels unofficially, and the Walkers too?" she adds.

"No, not the Walkers. I just told him that if his kids got the flu from school, I would hook him up with some anti-virals. I think we would have heard from him by now. He'll be the least of our problems. He's set for food, and he seems to get it about the quarantine idea," argues Alex.

"Right, but if anyone in his family gets sick, you know where his first stop will be? And we're down to thirteen courses of anti-virals," she says.

"If we do this right, and don't get involved, we won't need to use any of the anti-virals. Why are we arguing about this?" he says.

"Because once again, you're out there making deals that conflict with our original plan," she says.

Alex sets his coffee down on the island and takes a deep breath. He knows she's right. His level of involvement within the neighborhood has slowly escalated, and may have already fostered enough negative sentiment toward them to jeopardize their safety. Alex turns in the chair and faces Kate, grabbing her hands.

"You're right. There's been a bit of a double standard…"

"A bit?" she interrupts.

"Hey, I'm trying to apologize here," he says.

She eyes him suspiciously, "Go on."

"Anyway, I'm sorry that I've been making decisions without you. You're right. I need to limit my involvement to matters directly affecting this house, and quit aggravating our neighbors. So, what I propose, is that we honor any promises already made, but I…we won't make any more promises. I wish we could help more people, but we can't without jeopardizing our own situation. Aside from that, we should still maintain enough contact with our friends to make sure we know what's going on around the neighborhood. We don't want to get blindsided," says Alex.

"Apology accepted. I was really getting worried. I know that it's hard to stick with a plan once you're faced with the complexities and realities of real world adversity. You've been through some tough spots, and probably know this better than anyone. We really need you to pull this off for us," she says compassionately.

Kate is talking about his time in Iraq. Unlike many combat veterans, Alex shared details of his combat tour with Kate. Though he excluded many of the grotesque details from his stories, Kate probably has a better understanding of his combat experience than most other veterans would allow. She definitely appreciates the fact that a combat plan rarely stands unchallenged, and that a successful leader will tweak the plan accordingly, staying on course and never forgetting the objective. Unfortunately, Alex has been subtly working against both the plan and objective, by creating challenges and hostility where it may not have existed.

"I understand what you're saying. I need to focus more on getting us through this safely, and not get distracted by the stuff that doesn't really matter," he says.

"That's easier said than done. There's a reason you're the one we're relying on to keep us on track. If I thought I could do a better job, I would have already taken charge, but I know I can't. We'd already have a line forming at our bulkhead door if I was the out there in the neighborhood," she says.

"True," he says.

"So, right now, we'll keep you in charge of managing all external aspects of our survival plan…"

"Wait a minute, who's we?" he says jokingly.

"You didn't think you were in charge of the whole operation did you? I, of course, am still in charge of everything. That has never changed. You just got a minor field promotion, which can be revoked," she says, easing out of her seat.

"Oh really? I didn't realize that I was still moving up the ranks around here. And what exactly is your rank in this organization?" he says.

"Supreme Commander. That's the highest rank attainable, and it's a life time position. I've held it for fourteen years. Actually, fifteen. I appointed myself when we got engaged," she says, hoping off the chair.

Alex gets up swiftly, and starts to move around the island toward Kate, who is laughing and circling the island.

"Every now and then, the troops need to rise up and teach their leaders a lesson," he says, closing in on her.

"Are you rising right now," she says.

"I could be," he responds, and makes a move to grab her.

Kate dodges the attempt, and runs toward the stairs. She takes the stairs quickly, with Alex in pursuit. Alex playfully remains a few steps behind her. She rounds the top of the stairs and turns around to face Alex, walking backward into the master bedroom. Alex follows her in and locks the door.

Chapter Twenty-Four

Friday, November 23, 2012

Alex sits at the great room computer desk, and scans the headlines from dozens of online newspapers. Since Wednesday, the situation nationwide deteriorated significantly.

The national pandemic data collection system, maintained by the CDC, reports a total of 460,243 confirmed Jakarta Flu cases in the U.S. The ISPAC revised their projections, stating that the current number of confirmed cases surpassed their original prediction by over 110,000 cases. They estimate the total number to reach three million cases by late next week, which in Alex's view, will be the nationwide tipping point.

CDC epidemiologists verified that the case fatality rate in the U.S. is still considerably lower than rates seen in Asia, 11% compared to 21%, but contend that the rate in the U.S. will continue to rise, as complications, beyond Acute Respiratory Distress Syndrome, start to claim lives in greater numbers. In Europe, where the flu's progression is approximately one week ahead of North America, the case fatality rate rose from 13% to 16.5% in the span of one week. ISPAC analysts predict that the rate in the U.S. will closely follow Europe, and will approach rates seen in Asia within two to three weeks.

From the computer desk in the front corner of the great room, Alex can see out of two sets of windows into the neighborhood. The skies overhead are completely clear, with some scattered, low clouds on the western horizon. The past few days have been in the fifties, and the days have been sunny and clear, representing a welcome shift from the seemingly endless series of storms racking southern Maine over the past week. The change in weather brought life back to the neighborhood, which Alex and his family mostly observed as spectators.

Alex sees Derek Sheppard in his backyard playing with his kids. From the corner window facing the street, Alex can see half of the Sheppards' enormous wooden play set, and over the past thirty minutes, he has spotted all three of Derek's kids and their dog, running around the play set. The only Sheppard he hasn't seen today, or over the past week, is Ellen. He hasn't spoken with Derek since the neighborhood meeting.

The break in the weather also brought a few visitors, which they kept at a comfortable distance. Nancy and Paul Cooper stopped by

Thursday morning to say hello while out for a walk with Max. Both of them took extended, unpaid leave from work, starting at the beginning of the week.

Charlie Thornton brought them some freshly cut venison steaks later that same day, compliments of the normally off-limits conservation land behind the Hewitt Park sports fields. Charlie said that the area was full of deer, and that he'd be willing to bring Alex out there on his next foray. Alex invited him around back to the deck, and produced a few chilled beers. Charlie looked thrilled by the invitation, and they sat there for about an hour talking about the neighborhood and the pandemic in general.

Alex was impressed by Charlie's level of knowledge, most of it gained over the past few weeks. As they parted, Alex considered explaining to Charlie that they didn't eat meat, but decided that it was better for him to accept Charlie's gift, than to risk insulting him. Kate almost passed out at the sight of the venison steaks on her kitchen island. Alex suggested they wrap and store the steaks in the basement freezer, for an emergency. Kate responded that it would take one hell of an emergency for her to eat deer meat.

He grabs the neighborhood status board from the side of the computer table, and turns toward the couch. Kate sits on the couch reading a book and sipping coffee. Her accounting firm closed indefinitely on Wednesday, and Kate didn't skip a beat adjusting to a life of full time leisure. Over the past two days, Alex mostly found her reading, napping upstairs, or taking a long walk with Emily or Ryan. Despite the milder weather, Alex remained indoors, feeling that this was a better strategy for him, given the high profile he had been developing among his more hostile neighbors.

Alex unfolds the worn, smudged poster board, and lays it on the coffee table. Alex has started to highlight the names of confirmed or suspected sick neighbors with a yellow marker. Several yellow lines cross the diagram, signifying known interactions with potentially infected neighbors. A red marker is used to indicate death. Currently, only one name is highlighted red. Matt McDaniel. He examines the diagram of the neighborhood and adds a line connecting the Thompsons' house to the McCarthys', the apparent babysitting hub on their side of the Durham Road loop.

While sitting at the computer, Alex detected some movement down the street to the right. He didn't have a good view from south east corner of the house, so he grabbed his binoculars and ran upstairs to the master bedroom, nearly knocking Kate over as she emerged from the bathroom.

With the binoculars, Alex saw James Thompson push a stroller, with another small child in tow, right up to the McCarthys' house, and then return by himself. A few minutes later, both he and his wife, Mary, left in their Toyota Sienna. Alex assumed that their third child was in the van with them. Judging from the stroller, he figured it had to be either Emily or Madison, since their baby Alex had to be in the stroller.

The Thompsons' departure made sense, given the information that been shared with him yesterday by Ed. Sarah Quinn continues to collect, verify and pass along information to the neighborhood regarding suspected or confirmed illnesses. Her latest download to Ed didn't surprise Alex.

According to Sarah, Mary Thompson has been fighting flu like symptoms for a few days, and based on what Alex just saw, one of their children is probably sick also. They were probably on their way to see a doctor. Alex highlights Mary's name in yellow, and randomly selects Emily, age three, for the other highlight. Alex finds it interesting that Mary and James would bring their children to the McCarthys', despite persistent rumors that Jennifer McCarthy and at least one of her children is also sick with flu like symptoms.

Sarah Quinn knows this, because four days ago, Jennifer asked her for two of anti-viral treatment courses that Sarah held for the neighborhood. Jennifer refused to give Sarah any details, but insisted that they needed the anti-virals immediately. According to Sarah, she didn't sound good over the phone, and Michael McCarthy picked up the drugs from Sarah just minutes after the phone call. She should have asked for five, one for each member of the family, but Alex is certain that neither Michael nor Jennifer have invested any time into researching effective pandemic anti-viral treatment strategies. Then again, it's unlikely that Sarah would have given her five courses of treatment without more information. This transaction left eleven courses of treatment for neighborhood, which didn't last long according to Sarah.

Owing to her close friendship with Nicki Bartlett, she also knows that Nicki and two of her children are sick with high fevers, muscle aches and worsening coughs. Nicki and her kids have been sick since the weekend, and Sarah gave them three courses of anti-viral therapy, bringing the remaining total to eight.

Nicki's husband Jack, an endocrinologist, insists that they can be adequately treated at home, under his care. Apparently, he has access to medical supplies from the diabetes center, though Alex couldn't imagine that the center had any antibiotics left in their drug sample closet, which would be critical for treating flu induced pneumonia. Few companies make antibiotics any more, and the only antibiotic Alex has managed to sparingly find in drug closets over the past few years is Levaquin.

Logically, since the Bartletts had been hit with the flu, Alex wasn't surprised to hear that both the Bishops and the Green's had been hit as well. Sarah delivered four courses of antiviral therapy to the Bishops on Tuesday, after Stephanie called to tell Sarah that her entire family had developed flu symptoms simultaneously on Monday morning.

All of their children have been closely intertwined since school was cancelled, and the McDaniel girls stayed among the Bartletts and Bishops for several days, nearly guaranteeing that the flu would be spread. Sarah asked about Jamie's girls, and Stephanie said that Katherine was still sick, but didn't seem to be getting any worse, and that Amanda had no symptoms at all. After delivering drugs to both the Bartletts and Bishops, Sarah was left with only four remaining treatments. Two of those went to the Greens, and the remaining two to the Burtons, who each reported two possible cases of the flu in their households.

Within the span of a week and a half, all of the anti-virals were gone, and as far as Alex knew, the only remaining anti-virals in the neighborhood sat in his basement, and somewhere within Ed's house. Alex had given Ed enough for his family nearly a year ago.

Sarah heard from Jennifer McCarthy that Ken Hayes might be sick. Michelle stopped sending her kids over to the McCarthys on the same day that Jennifer McCarthy called Sarah to ask for anti-virals. She told Jennifer that they had decided to stay home from work for a few weeks, and that nearly everyone in her husband's office was sick. Jennifer wondered if one of the Hayes' kids had brought the virus into their house. Alex highlights Ken Hayes on the chart.

The last piece of news from Ed hit Alex the hardest because he knew it meant trouble. Todd Perry's wife was sick, and had been refused treatment at Maine Medical Center. She was given a basic home treatment kit, with no prescription medications, only basic pain and fever relief medications. Worse yet, she had brought her nine year old son Michael, who was also suffering from escalating flu symptoms, and he received the same kit. Both of them were turned away without explanation. Alex expects a knock on his door at any time from Todd. Right after he knocks on Sarah's door to get some of the promised anti-virals, only to be told that Alex's original promise of twenty courses, materialized as thirteen.

Alex ensures that all of the highlights on the diagram are up to date, and then folds the poster board in half. He sits back on the coach and exhales deeply.

"Done with arts and crafts hour?" Kate quips.

"Pretty much. You want to check out the updates?" he asks.

"Can you just summarize them for me," she says, continuing to focus on her book.

"Annoying. Anyway, I saw James deliver two of his kids over to the McCarthys' house about thirty minutes ago, then take off with his wife and one of the kids in the minivan," he says.

Kate looks up from her book with a puzzled look.

"Isn't Jennifer McCarthy and at least one other person in that house sick?" she says.

"Based on my intel, I assume that's the case," he says.

"What the fuck is wrong with these people? Why would she send her kids over there? I saw Mary outside yesterday in the backyard playing with the dog. Why couldn't she drive by herself?"

"I don't know. Maybe she got worse, and can't drive. Either way, I'm surprised Jennifer agreed to watch the kids. None of it makes much sense," he says.

"Oh, I had meant to ask you earlier, but I forgot. Did the Carters leave town? I haven't seen anything going on at their house since last week, and Kelso hasn't greeted me on any of my recent walks," she asks, sounding more disappointed about not seeing Kelso than the Carters.

"You mean Kelso hasn't been rummaging around inside our house for the past few weeks?" he says.

"Yeah, well that's unusual too," she responds.

"I really don't know, but I think you're right. I circled their house on the board, and put a big question mark next to it for the same reasons you mentioned. Ed hasn't heard anything, so maybe they scooted out of town at night," he says.

"Well if Ed doesn't know, then nobody knows," she says, and lowers her eyes back to her book.

"Maybe if I had an extra set of eyes on the neighborhood, we'd catch things like this," he says.

"Nice try. Besides, you're doing a fantastic job right now, and it's keeping you busy. You should consider staking out another window, like maybe the one up in the attic. Hey, who knows what you might see from a higher vantage point. Didn't they teach you that in the Marine Corps?" she says.

"Among other things. Like when someone was trying to get rid of you," he says, as he picks up the poster board.

"Was I that obvious?" she says.

"Oh no. Not at all," he says.

Alex leans over and kisses Kate on the forehead.

"To the high ground," he says and walks toward the stairs.

■

Alex emerges from the mudroom and puts the phone down on the kitchen island. He walks over to the kitchen table and sits down without saying a word. Kate and the kids have already started to eat what has become a typical meal for the Fletchers since they exhausted most of their supply of perishable foods.

On a dark blue placemat in the middle of the table sits a bowl of seasoned pinto beans next to a small sauce pan filled with watery green beans. An open pressure cooker filled with a mixture of brown rice and barley sits on a separate placemat next to the beans.

The kids each have a glass of water in front of them. A half drained bottle of Syrah sits off to the side of the food. Alex starts to serve himself, still silent. Kate eyes him nervously.

"They don't seem to be able to resist calling us right before dinner," she says.

"Yeah," he says, still not committing to a conversation.

Alex sees Kate glance at the kids, who seem oblivious to the tension.

"How are your parents holding out?" she asks.

Alex takes a deep breath and feigns a smile, not wanting to upset the kids.

"They're doing fine I suppose. Plugging along like everyone else, but they claim to be healthy, which I believe considering the fact that if one of them gets even a splinter, I hear every detail," he says, forcing more of a smile.

Ryan does his best to generate a laugh, and even Emily muffles a snort, which tells Alex that the kids are better tuned in to his mood than he anticipated. Every time a call comes into the house from a relative, the tension level rises.

"How about your brother?" she says, and he quickly shakes his head, hoping the kids didn't see him do it.

"Sounds like they're doing fine too," he says, staring at her with a serious face and shaking his head imperceptibly once again.

He glances at the kids, who seem too preoccupied with eating to have caught his wave off. Alex is amazed at how well they eat at meals, now that snacks are more or less a thing of the past. Two months ago, the two of them would have stared at this dinner with disbelief.

Kate receives his message and doesn't pursue any more questions. Alex just found out from his parents, that his brother Daniel is hospitalized with a mild concussion and advanced stage pneumonia. Apparently, Daniel was spared Acute Respiratory Distress Syndrome, but continued to drive to work over the course of the past few days, with worsening flu symptoms, until his co-workers forced him to leave the office at around eleven Tuesday morning. He never made it home. At some point during the drive home, he lost control of his Land Rover and plowed into a guard rail on Interstate Twenty-Five, nearly jumping it. He was rushed to a hospital near Castle Rock, where he was treated for minor acute injuries, and admitted to the ICU for flu related pneumonia.

This wasn't the worst news. Alex also learned that his nephew Ethan was sick with the flu. Alex thinks about Daniel, and how he probably walked through the house, oblivious to the fact that he was getting sicker and sicker, and that he was highly contagious with a killer flu. *Gotta get to work. Make the deals.* Worse yet, Karla can't find the anti-virals Alex had sent a few years ago, so his parents were sacrificing theirs to give to both kids. Alex really wishes his parents had taken him up on the offer to bring the kids out here. Alex shakes his head at the table thinking about it, furious at his brother. They eat the rest of the meal in an awkward silence, punctuated by several unsuccessful attempts to jar Alex out of his gloomy mood.

■

Alex sits in his office scanning the Boston Globe website. He is focused on a late breaking story about riots breaking out in Dorchester and East Boston.

"For the third day in a row, major food stores throughout the greater Boston metropolitan area have remained closed, blaming a supply chain failure that has affected most of northern New England. Food shipments have been erratic at best for the past week, stopping altogether in areas like Dorchester, Roxbury, East Boston and Jamaica Plain. Fires and looting broke out midday, as residents in these beleaguered areas, already pressed for critical supplies, learned that food stores would not open for the third day in a row."

Alex skips down further.

"City and state officials have augmented National Guard and law enforcement presence in these areas, anticipating a worsening of the situation. One anonymous state official stated that the food and supply situation was not likely to improve, as absenteeism and flu attack rates continue to soar."

He keeps reading toward the end of the article.

"Several residents interviewed said that they would soon leave the Boston metropolitan area in search of less populated areas where the food supply chain was more stable, like the upper New England states."

Great. That's the last thing we need up here.

Kate walks into the office as he finishes the article.

"Did you see what's happening in Boston?" she says, walking up to him.

"It won't be long before people start to riot up here," he says, swiveling the chair to face her.

"I don't think there are enough people in Maine for a riot of any type. You've seen the anti-whatever rallies in Monument Square. Fifteen, maybe twenty people, even on the weekend. The biggest riot we've ever had here had something to do with American Idol tickets several years back," she says.

"That's right. It was like the Cabbage Patch frenzy of the eighties all over again. Remember that? Moms and dads slugging it out for a place in line to get those stupid Idol tickets. And I thought fighting over dolls was fucking crazy," he says.

"Hey, I'm sure Ethan will be fine," she says.

"I hope so. I really do," he says, grabbing her hands.

"Hey, look at Jamie's kids. They're still sick, but they seem to be doing fine. They got anti-virals early and it made a big difference. The same thing will happen with our nephews," she says.

"If Karla doesn't steal them for herself. She's planning to drive the kids north to stay in a hotel while Daniel recovers, so they can be close to him. Fucking clueless. I bet Daniel asked her to come. What does she think they're gonna eat while they're in the hotel? Take-out pizza? Thai delivery? The woman is dumber than a box of rocks, and she's going to drive them out there without enough gas to get back, just to watch Daniel expire. Gas delivery is already highly sporadic. Won't be long before that's gone too. I...."

Alex stops ranting and puts both of his hands on his head, grabbing his thick black hair.

"What's wrong with these people?" he says.

"I don't know. Maybe they don't feel like they have a choice."

"Choice to do what?" he asks, exasperated.

"To quit their jobs. To cash in their life savings to buy food. To stay away from their friends and family. We've been lucky so far.

Nobody sick has appeared at our door with one of the dozens of golden tickets you've handed out," she says.

"You handed a few out yourself," he responds.

"Sorry, I didn't mean it that way. But, we haven't been pressed by family or friends to compromise our quarantine. Would you be able to turn away your parents if they suddenly arrived at our steps? Sick?" she says.

"I don't know how I'd handle it, but I can tell you one thing. They wouldn't be sitting at the dinner table with our kids. I'd be applying every piece of information available to figure out the situation. The internet still works. It's not like I paid anyone for this knowledge. You just type 'home quarantine procedures' and bingo. How about your parents? They're still fine right?" he says, changing the subject.

"I suppose. My brother, Liz and the girls are with them right now. They're all still healthy. It sounds like my brother has been paying more attention to us than I thought. Mom said he showed up with all kinds of survival gear and has been pretty much running the show over there. She said that the food was tight, but they should be fine.

Claire still hasn't shown up, which worries me more than anything. I tried to call her the other day, but the machine picked up at the house, and I got the voice mail on her cell phone. She won't answer, because she knows I'm going to try and talk her out of crashing at my parents. She'll push her way right into that house, sick or not, and try to take over. Luckily, Robbie has never taken any of her shit, so I'm hoping he'll do what's necessary to keep them all safe."

"I'm more concerned about Claire making the trip up here. She's no dummy. I could see her bypassing your parents for a safer haven up in Scarborough. It's only a nine hour drive. One and a half tanks of gas, unless they bring the Suburban," he says, smiling.

"Thanks. Are you trying to sabotage my sleep tonight?" she says, squeezing his hands.

"Well, I thought you might want to stay awake a little longer for some action," he says, standing up from the chair.

"Are the kids out?" she asks.

"I haven't heard a peep since about nine," he says.

Holding hands, Kate and Alex head out of the office. The phone rings and Alex hesitates. 9:30 is a strange time for a phone call.

"Don't worry about it. Whoever it is can leave a message," she says.

"Uh…hold on a second. I just want to see who it is," he says and scurries back into the office.

The phone keeps ringing.

"Hey, this was your idea. If you're not in the bed within five minutes, I'm not playing," she says.

"Don't worry, I'll be there," he says, checking his watch.

The caller ID says "Walker, Edward."

Alex picks up, "Hey Ed. Make it fast, I'm about to get lucky."

"Well, I'm about to kill the mood. There's going to be another neighborhood meeting tomorrow at Sarah Quinn's house to discuss the matter of neighborhood security. Everyone is pretty worried about the rioting in Boston, and the possible flow of refugees into Maine. Sarah heard that there was a group going around looking for armed volunteers to man a roadblock at the Piscataqua Bridge to keep people from fleeing up into Maine," he says.

"That's nothing new Ed. Mainer's have wanted to do that for decades. They tried to stop Kate and me when we drove out here from San Diego, but we just told them that we were here to do some shopping in Kittery and then to hit Bean's. I don't think they realized California was on the other side of the country. Most of them have never been out of the state," says Alex.

"They should have checked your ID a little closer, and saved us all some trouble," says Ed.

"True. So what time does this little party start?" says Alex.

"Ten in the morning at the Quinns'," he says.

"Are you going?" asks Alex.

"Of course. Why wouldn't I?" he says.

"Why wouldn't you? Oh I don't know, maybe because half of the people who show up might have the flu. If you show up, make sure you wear one of those surgical masks and gloves. Seriously. This bug is all over the neighborhood. Eighteen households by my calculation," says Alex.

"Well, we can only see so much from these windows, and the phone calls with information have slowed to a trickle," he says.

"You're doing better than the Fletchers. Nobody calls us anymore," says Alex.

"Well, after the last meeting, most of the neighbors probably figured they'd be better off steering clear of the Fletcher-Thornton connection," he says.

"Of course, against my better judgment, I reluctantly decided to take my chances with you."

"Thanks for the loyalty Ed, you'll be rewarded handsomely. Actually, the less attention on this house the better. I don't even think

Kate would let me out to that meeting even if I thought it was a good idea. You'll have to be my eyes and ears out there. Sorry to cut this short, but I'm on a deadline. Give me a ring tomorrow," he says, and hangs up the phone.

Alex walks swiftly to the bedroom and closes the door behind him, locking it.

"Four minutes and fifty seconds. That's cutting it close…although I had planned to give you some leeway," she says from the candle lit area by the bed.

Alex jumps into the bed and burrows under the covers. He feels her warm naked body and forgets about the neighborhood meeting.

Chapter Twenty-Five

Saturday, November 24, 2012

Alex stares out of the dining room window, straining to see the small mob that followed Ed halfway down the street. The group, which consists of Todd Perry, Mike Lynch, Eric Bishop and a few others, stopped in front of Todd's house, but he lost sight of them as they wandered up Todd's driveway. Alex grabs the phone off the dining room table, and before he can start dialing Ed's number, it starts to ring. *Ed.*

"I know you can't get enough of my charming…"

"Yeah, yeah. Hey, there's a small crowd gathered in front of Todd's house, and they ain't happy campers. I was pretty much chased by back to my house by these lunatics. Todd started ranting and raving about you, and how you fucked over the entire neighborhood with the anti-virals and blah, blah, blah. I think they're about to head your way," says Ed.

"Are you serious? Sounds like it was a great meeting," says Alex.

"It was all a set up from the start. I think they were waiting for you to show up, so they could attack you or something. They turned on me as soon as it was clear you weren't going to make an appearance. Scared the shit out of me. Oh boy. Looks like they're on the move and headed our way," he says.

"What's going on? I see some people walking this way from Todd's," Kate says, having suddenly materialized on the stairs next to the dining room.

"Hold on Ed," Alex says, and muffles the phone.

"Honey, I'll be off in a second. It's nothing we need to worry about."

"Sorry Ed, Kate's freaking out…"

"Freaking out?" she yells, and grabs the phone from Alex.

"Thank you for the heads up Ed. Sorry to hang up on you, but I need to talk some sense into my 'it'll all work out' husband."

Kate ends the call, and puts the phone back on the table. She faces Alex, who stands staring at the hand that just moments ago held a phone.

"That's funny, I could have sworn I was having a productive, adult conversation with a good friend of mine, when…" he says.

"You'll get over it. So now we have an angry mob headed toward our house?" she says, walking toward the great room. *She's in driver, panic mode. Great.*

"Why don't we take a look. I'm not worried about these yahoos," he says, and follows her.

As they cross the great room, Alex passes Emily, who is sitting on her favorite chair, wearing earphones that are plugged into a portable DVD player opened on her lap. *Kate's solution to the great room noise problem.* Emily looks up and smiles at them as they walk by. Kate walks to the front of the great room and peers through one of the windows facing across the Walkers' yard. Alex joins her and sees the group walking down the sidewalk, in the direction of their house. The group is halfway across the sidewalk in front of the Andersons' house.

"Looks like you need to start getting concerned real quick. Those assholes are going to be at our front door in less than a minute. Emily, turn off the DVD player and go upstairs please," she says loudly.

Emily looks up, and shrugs her shoulders. Kate briskly walks up to her and reaches for the headphones. Emily takes them off annoyed.

"What? What's going on?" says Emily.

"I need you to go upstairs right now?" she says.

Emily doesn't stir.

"Why? What's..." Emily starts.

"Just get upstairs now! Go!" she says.

Emily closes the player, and hops out of the chair, mumbling a series of hushed complaints.

"Thank you," Kate says, as Emily exits the room.

"Thank you sweetie," adds Alex.

"Alright, when they come to the door, we'll see..."

"Come to the door? No way. We're not letting them get that close to our house. You want to know why I'm freaked out? I don't like the idea of these people just deciding to march on our house. We're going to meet them on our driveway and tell them to get the hell away from us. Let's go. They're already in front of Ed's," she says, and starts to walk back into the kitchen.

Alex pauses to think about the situation, then he follows her.

"Do you want me to bring the rifle?" he says.

"No, I don't think that would be a good idea. You still have the pistol on you right?' she says, and Alex nods his head as he pats the small of his back.

"That should be more than enough if this gets out of hand," she adds.

Alex and Kate rush to the mudroom and put on their shoes. They both grab jackets and head out of the mudroom door. As soon as they clear the mudroom stoop, Alex is glad they hurried. Six pissed off looking men are already halfway across their lawn, headed straight for the mudroom door. Kate leads Alex through the evergreen bushes, on a direct path to intercept them. Todd appears surprised by the sight of Alex and Kate.

"Can we help you?" Kate yells with her hands on her hips.

She looks irritated, and everyone stops. Alex moves next to Kate's right side, as the group pauses for a few seconds before Eric Bishop tries to respond. His words are cut off by a violent coughing spasm. He takes a knee and turns to Steve McKinney on his left, who backs away quickly with a frightened look. Mike Lynch and Tom Hodges move to in to help him, but withdraw as the hacking worsens. True to Ed's words, Eric looks like he is about to die. His face is ashen gray, his lips are purplish, and sweat is pouring down his face. Alex thinks he sees a small amount of blood on the corner of his mouth, but can't be sure. *Jesus, he didn't look this bad ten minutes ago.* Todd answers Kate's question.

"We're just out for a stroll. We all have the right to walk around the neighborhood," Todd says.

"Looks like you strayed off the sidewalk a little. I think you should all go home. You don't look so good Eric," says Alex.

"I'd be doing a lot better if you weren't hiding medicine from all of us. Fucking sneaky you two. Caught one of Jamie's kids swallowing some pills earlier this week. Looks like you managed to hook them up huh? Now they're doing just fine, while my entire family is sick," he says.

"What exactly do you want from us?" says Kate.

"I want a full inventory of your food supply and any medical supplies you have, so we can divide and distribute them to those families that need help," interjects Todd.

"This is ridiculous," says Kate

"It's alright honey. Really. I want to hear this," says Alex.

Todd looks confused by Alex's response, and looks at Eric, who shrugs his shoulder.

"So is that your plan? Just inventory everything and divide it up?" says Alex, trying to bring them back into the conversation.

"Yes, that's sounds right," says Todd hesitantly as if he is not sure how to answer the question.

"Just my house, or everyone's?" says Alex.

"Well…we should start with your…"

"But we're going to move on to every house? Right?" presses Alex.

"Sure, but I don't think most houses will have…"

"Have what? Any food? Any supplies? That shouldn't matter. Then what? Where will we store everything, and who will divide it up evenly?" says Alex.

"Look, cut all this bullshit speech and debate crap. I don't think we'll need to go any further than your house, or his…or his" Eric says, struggling to point at Charlie and Ed.

"So you just want to raid our houses, because you suspect we have enough food and medical supplies for everyone. How much food do you think I have Eric? Todd? Take a guess," challenges Alex.

"I don't know. That's why we want to see, so we can figure it out," says Todd.

"A year? Does that sound like a lot for one family? If we had a year, should we divide it up for everyone?" insists Alex.

"You're god damn right. If you have a year's worth of food…Are you fucking kidding me? I have less than a week," raves Todd.

"OK, so that's fifty two weeks, divided by thirty households. I've already done the math here. That's one point seven weeks per family, maybe more, maybe less. Twelve days. Not exactly a windfall. So, if I had that much food, which I don't, you'd be asking me to give it all up so that we could all be equally screwed as the winter descends. It's only the middle of November Todd. We have a long way to go. Probably until springtime when the roads are cleared and the trucks can move supplies again," says Alex.

"Clear from what?" demands Mike.

"From the snow. Do you really think the plows are going to keep up with the snow? When's the last time you've seen a police car, or heard a siren? Everyone is either sick, or not showing up to work, and we've only seeing the tip of the iceberg here. The worst is on the way and it won't get any easier. Especially if we sit on our asses and hope someone else solves our problems," says Alex.

"What the fuck is that supposed to mean?" says Todd.

"It means that I believe you had every opportunity to stock up on food, even after the food crisis started," says Alex.

"That's bullshit! Every time I tried, the store closed before I set foot inside!" says Todd.

"Are you kidding me Todd? I distinctly remember volunteering to watch your kids, at the ass crack of dawn, so you and your wife could get over to Hannaford's early enough to make it through the store. We waited, and we waited, and you never called." says Alex.

Todd looks uncomfortable with Alex's accusation, and Steve McKinney mumbles something to Mike Lynch. Mike Lynch fires back at Steve with a hushed "that's not the point of this." Mike steps forward.

"Look, food is no longer the issue. You made your point. You don't have enough food to carry the entire neighborhood along through the winter. Understood…"

"It's still an issue for me," yells Todd.

"I know, but we can deal with that later," responds Mike.

"So what exactly do you want from us now?" Alex says exaggerating an exasperated look.

Before Todd can answer, Eric, still on one knee, breaks into another coughing fit.

"Eric doesn't look like he needs to be out here in the cold. He needs to be breathing warm, moist air to help open up his airway. This cold air is constricting his lungs, making it worse," says Alex.

"He's fine for now," says Todd.

"And you're a doctor?" retorts Kate.

"I'm no doctor, but I'm pretty sure if he's received some of the drugs and medical supplies you're hoarding, he'd be doing a lot better!" says Todd, with a smug look.

"I already donated anti-virals to the community chest. That's it," says Alex.

"That's it? That's all you have to say?" says Todd, as his face reddens.

"That's it. And uh…from what I understand, Eric received one of those courses of anti-viral therapy. Sarah told me that she handed over four of the thirteen courses to Stephanie. Unfortunately, it didn't help him, which is not unusual," says Alex.

Todd looks down at Eric, barely able to contain his surprise. Alex also detects a hint of anger flash across Todd's face.

"Maybe he didn't take it," says Todd.

"Four doses. Four family members. You do the math. The flu affects everyone differently. Some get hit hard, some don't even get symptoms. Others get slammed and die within a day or two, like Matt McDaniel. Anti-virals are no guarantee of anything. The best way to fight this thing is to avoid it altogether. So like I said before, you should all separate and button up inside your houses," says Alex.

"If you're trying to talk me out of getting some anti-virals for my kids. Save the lecture," says Todd.

"This conversation's over," Kate says, and turns around to walk away.

"No it's not," adds John Hodges.

Kate turns back around.

"Get off our property right now. I say this is over, and that's it! I don't want to see any of you around here anymore. We have nothing more to say or give you. We're done here," she says, and pulls Alex's arm as she starts back toward the mudroom.

"Don't even look at them," she whispers, releasing his arm, as they both walk back to the mudroom.

"Talking just encourages them. We're through communicating with those jackasses."

Alex and Kate enter the house and close the door behind them, muting the verbal tirade launched by the group. Alex glances back out of the door and verifies that they haven't moved any closer to the house.

"Your problem is that you continue to engage these guys until they reach their boiling point. You have to cut them off and walk away. They want you to provoke them," she says.

"But I didn't even get a chance to threaten to kill them, or something good like that," he says, still watching the group.

"Yeah, that would have helped the situation immensely," she says.

"It doesn't matter what we do. He's an absolute raving mad cluster fuck. No food, no meds, and he's fomenting the idea that we're sitting on enough of these supplies to save the entire neighborhood."

"Christ. Could we give up some of our stuff, and make him happy? We have a lot of food down there. Way more than we need. We could put together a package for them. Just enough to get them off our backs," she suggests.

"I think it could only make matters worse. As soon as they run out of whatever we decide to give them, they'll be right back at our door, along with the rest of the neighborhood. Then we're truly fucked," he says.

"I don't know, but we need to do something. We can't sit here for months waiting for them to attack us. We can't live like that," she says.

"Hey, I lived like that for several months. It can be done," says Alex, as he steps into the kitchen.

"Yeah, but the rest of us can't. Let's figure out what we need to survive. I don't mind stretching our food supply thin if it will get them off our backs," she says.

"Off our backs for now," he says.

"Well, at least we'll have a clearer conscience," she says, following him into the kitchen.

Alex sits down at the kitchen island and pours a cup of steaming coffee into a brown mug. He waits for Kate to sit down next to him.

"My conscience is clear," he says, not sure he quite believes the statement.

"Really? You don't feel the slightest amount of guilt that we are sitting on enough food for six families to last well past the winter or spring? Or that we have essential medical supplies that could make a difference to at least a few households? Hon, we have a ton of stuff down there…"

"I know. Believe me. I've thought about it, and that's why I don't mind helping out Ed, or Jamie's kids…"

"Hon, we can't pick and choose who we help. That'll only make matters worse. We need to make an offer to those around us, but make sure they understand it's final. That it's all we can give up without…"

"Without sticking it to ourselves?" Alex says, and takes a long sip of coffee.

"Yeah, something like that," Kate says, her voice trailing off.

Kate leaves the mudroom and Alex hears her remove the coffee pot from the coffee maker. *Priorities.* Alex watches them through the mudroom door windows, and sees them confer with each other, obviously arguing about their next move. He see's Mark Silva shake his head furiously and hold up his hands, waving them. He then starts to walk back down the street.   Eric manages to rise to his feet by himself, and everyone keeps several feet away from him. *He'll be lucky if he makes it home.* Todd continues to gesture wildly to the four of them. Alex sees some agreement in the faces and gestures of Mike and Tom, but Steve is clearly not interested in whatever Todd proposes. Steve steps back out of the group and starts to head across the street. Alex watches as he walks between McDaniels' and Sheppards' house, soon disappearing behind the McDaniels' on what Alex assumes is a straight line through the backyards to his house.

The remaining four men start to walk down the sidewalk toward Todd's house, soon escaping Alex's view from the mudroom door. Alex hurries out of the mudroom and through the kitchen on his way to the great room, so he can keep an eye on them the whole way back. He notices that Emily isn't in her seat anymore, as he arrives alongside Kate at the front corner window.

"Did I miss anything?" he asks, embracing her from behind.

"Not really, just a bunch of bickering. Eric doesn't look good at all," she says, settling back into his grasp.

Eric keeps shaking his head and coughing. His left leg collapses and he falls to the ground in front of the Walkers' house, managing to break his sideways plunge with his left arm. He ends up on his stomach, with his head turned away from Alex's view. The other three kneel down around him, keeping back by a few feet. They don't appear enthusiastic about the prospect of lifting him back onto his feet. Todd stays down with Eric, who is coughing so violently on the ground that his body appears to convulse.

"Hon, you better call Stephanie and tell her to get over here. I'll let them know she's on her way," says Alex, releasing Kate.

He rushes over to the front door and opens it. He opens the screen door, and calls out to the group.

"Hey, we're calling Stephanie to come pick him up!"

The three of them look up at him, and he repeats himself. He hears Kate on the phone with Stephanie.

"Just get over here and pick him up," she says, and appears in the hallway from the kitchen.

"What's up?" he says, keeping the screen door propped open.

"Nothing…let's just say that she isn't a big fan of the Fletchers either," says Kate.

Alex shakes his head and continues to monitor the situation outside. A few minutes later, Stephanie Bishop pulls up in their gray Nissan Pathfinder. Stephanie, dressed in blue sweat pants and a light brown hooded winter jacket, gets out and runs to her husband. Todd helps her get him into front passenger seat of the SUV. Stephanie steps around and walks toward the Fletchers' house.

"Here it comes," he says to Kate.

Kate joins Alex at the front door. Stephanie gets halfway across the sidewalk in front of their house and launches into an outburst.

"You and your buddy over there," she screams, pointing at Ed's house, "can take care of Jamie's girls. I'm taking all…"

Stephanie breaks into a coughing fit that takes her at least thirty seconds to overcome.

"Jesus," whispers Kate.

"Yeah," Alex responds, never taking his eyes off Stephanie.

Stephanie continues a little more subdued.

"I'm taking my entire family over to the state triage center immediately, so the girls are going to have to find a new place to stay. I'm sending them over to your house in a few minutes. You and Ed can figure it out," she says and turns around abruptly.

Alex closes the door. Before he can open his mouth Kate speaks.

"They can't stay here," she says.

"I wasn't about to suggest that. They can stay in their own house. We can bring meals over to them, and keep a close eye on the house. They'll be fine over there. They can call us if something happens. Amanda is almost Ryan's age. She can take care of Katherine, as long as we help out. They have electricity, water, TV...they'll be fine," he says.

Alex isn't so sure about what he just said. The two girls will be terrified without their parents, or an adult at the house. Given all that they have been through over the past few weeks, Alex can't imagine how this can work. Still, he doesn't want them in the house, just in case they are still shedding the flu virus. It's been about two weeks since Jamie dropped them off at the Bartletts' house, and Alex thinks they were just getting sick at that point, so it's conceivable that they are no longer contagious, though he can't be sure about the timing.

CDC virologists confirmed that a patient exposed to the Jakarta flu will typically demonstrate symptoms within three to four days of exposure, and remain contagious for about seven to ten days after that. Alex does the math in his head. *They should be past the ten day mark.* However, as seen with most flu strains in the past, seasonal and pandemic, children can remain contagious for up to three weeks after showing symptoms. *No, we can't risk the exposure.*

"I don't think two pre-teen girls should be left alone like that, without their mother," says Kate.

"I know, but there's a possibility that they could still be contagious, so we can't have them here," says Alex.

Kate pauses, clearly struggling with the thought of the kids staying over there alone.

"I don't know. Could they stay in the basement, or...never mind, that's ridiculous. They'd be better off in their house with us checking on them," she says.

"I agree. We can't keep them locked up in the garage or basement like animals. They'll be better off in a familiar setting. I'll head over their later today and make sure the house is okay. They still have some food and snacks over there from what I remember, and we can bring them hot meals. It's not perfect for them, but it's the best we can do," he says.

"Alright," says Kate.

"I better call Ed and let him know what's going on," says Alex.

Kate follows him with a question, "Is it alright for you to be walking around their house?"

"You mean the flu?" he asks and she nods emphatically.

"Yeah, it should be fine. At the most, the Jakarta flu can survive for forty eight hours on a non-porous surface. Less on a porous one. I can't see any way that it could still be a danger in the house…however, I'll be sure to wear gloves and scrub down when I'm done. I'm calling Ed and going over right now. If the girls show up, explain the situation and keep them in the garage. They can use the camping chairs in the sports bin. I'd wear a mask just in case, and give them some leftovers," he says.

"Got it," she says, as Alex dials Ed's number.

Chapter Twenty-Six

Saturday, November 24, 2012

Alex dials Kate with his iPhone, as he makes his way across the McDaniels' lawn. Ed Walker waves goodbye and nods to Alex as he splits off and heads toward his own home directly across the street.

"Open sesame. I'm crossing the street," Alex says.

"What took you so long?" says Kate.

"I'll tell you when I get in the house," he says.

Alex jogs up to the mudroom door as Kate unlocks the deadbolt and door knob. He takes off a pair of surgical gloves and balls them up in his hand. Kate opens the door for him, and he walks in, careful not to touch anything.

"Can you do me a favor and open the door to the garage, I want to throw these in the trash," he says.

She opens the door and he walks into the garage, right up to the town garbage container. He uses his elbow to lift the hinged green plastic top and drops the gloves into the quarter filled container. Both this trash bin and the recyclables bin are located side by side to the left of the mudroom entrance inside the garage. The top of the recyclables bin is colored red to differentiate between the two. The town issued bins stand at around chest height on Alex and under normal circumstances would be full by this time of the week. Trash pickup is scheduled for Tuesdays in their neighborhood. Alex won't even bother to put the bins out tomorrow. The recyclables container sits emptier than trash bin.

Alex drops the lid and walks back inside the open door. He catches a glimpse of Ryan and Emily sitting at the island eating left over pizza as he ducks into the bathroom off the mudroom to thoroughly wash his hands. When he is finished, he sprays the sink's hardware with a sanitizing cleaner, and wipes them down with paper toweling that sits in the cabinet under the sink.

"All clean," he says, as he walks into the mudroom.

Kate is waiting for him to hear what he had to say. She walks over to him and they both sneak into the library.

"So, what's going on?" she says.

"I didn't want to freak you out earlier, but the reason I took longer than I expected, was that someone broke into their house through the back garage door and stole all of their food. Nothing else was touched, but every last bit of food is gone and shit was everywhere. Nothing broken, but clearly the house was searched for hidden stashes. Every room. I wanted to put the house back in order before we let the girls in," he says.

"Gee, I wonder who did that?" she whispers, "Do you think it's safe for the girls to be over there?"

"The girls will be fine. I did what I could to patch up the garage door window. Their mudroom door has a dead bolt, so they shouldn't have to worry about it. Those dickheads came back and finished the job. I am done messing around with them. If they show up here again, I promise you I'll put an end to their game," he says, fuming.

"Alright, let's calm back down and have some lunch with the kids. They were really curious about the girls being over here," she says.

"I wish they could stay here, but it's too risky. I'm just glad to see that they look fine. They're both still pretty beat from the flu, but not as bad as I expected. They aren't coughing, or anything, so I think they'll be fine. They just look exhausted. I can tell they're relieved to be back in their house. Katherine was already playing with her Barbies by the time we left. We'll keep a close eye on them," says Alex, and they join their kids for reheated pizza.

■

Alex hears the doorbell ring. He stands up from the couch and puts his book down on the coffee table. He picks up his pistol and tucks it into his jeans. A dozen scenarios flash through his head before the doorbell rings again. The timing between rings doesn't alarm Alex. Perfectly normal delay. He checks his watch and walks over to the bottom of the staircase. He looks up just as Kate appears.

"Can you see who it is?" she whispers.

"No," he says, leaning over to peek through the windows on each side of the front door.

"Not from here. Mudroom. I'll check it out. I'm sure it's fine. Doesn't sound too insistent," he says, as the bell rings again.

"Three rings qualifies as insistent. Be careful," she says.

"As always. I'll be right back," he says, and starts for the mudroom.

He walks through the dimly lit kitchen into the mudroom. He keeps the light off in the mudroom and peers through the mudroom door. He recognizes Derek Sheppard immediately and his tension level drops. He opens the interior door, keeping the storm door between them. He quickly scans the area around the mudroom stoop and determines that Derek is alone. *Hopefully.*

Alex cracks open the door and speaks.

"What's up Derek?"

"Nothing really. I'm just really sorry that I was shitting on you earlier today. I got caught up with Todd and his crew. I said some bad stuff to Ed about you. I've really felt terrible about it. I...my youngest two are sick, and I...I'm sorry, really. You've always been a good friend. Both you and Kate," he says softly. *Jesus. He's apologizing for something I didn't even know about.*

"No problem man. I wasn't even there to hear it. This is a bad time for everyone. Seriously, it wasn't on my radar, but I appreciate you coming over. Sorry to hear about the kids. How long have they been sick?" Alex asks and steps outside.

Derek steps back off the stoop onto the walkway.

"I don't want to get you sick. I feel fine, but you never know. The kids...not long, about three days. It came on kinda slow. Slower than we would have thought, so we hoped it was maybe just a cold or something, but then it picked up pretty fast with the fever and coughing. The fever's scary. Nothing's really cutting it. The coughing hasn't been so bad, but it's been miserable and we can't take the kids anywhere for treatment."

"Have you tried to get any help?" says Alex.

"They won't see new patients at any of the flu triage sites right now. We sat on the phone for hours trying to get through the DHS patient care line with no success, so we drove around for a couple of hours trying to find a site that would help. Everything's locked down hard by the National Guard. Really creepy, like right out of a horror movie. All we got were some homecare instructions, which quite frankly aren't very inspiring. I can deal with the fever, but the coughing has me worried."

"How's Ellen?" Alex asks.

"She just spiked a fever yesterday, and she's having a nervous breakdown. I honestly don't know which is worse. She's got Owen on the third floor, away from Gavin and Taylor. We've all been exposed, right? I mean, is there any point to keeping Owen separated?" he says.

"She has the right idea to keep Owen separate. Again, how long since they started with the fever?" says Alex.

"Three days, tops."

Alex pauses to consider an idea that just materialized. *I need to talk to Kate about this first.*

"I'm gonna call you in like ten minutes. I'm thinking about something that could help. I need to...let me call you in a few minutes," he says.

Derek looks confused.

"Alright Alex. Sounds good. Hey, I'm really sorry I didn't stand up for you, but...it just wasn't a good night with the kids. Fucking sad excuse I know, but..."

"Derek. Seriously, I know it's gotta be scary for you guys, especially with Owen and Ellen getting sick. Really, I'm not pissed at all. I appreciate you coming over here like this, really."

"I would've come by earlier, but Todd and those guys scare me. Enough to wait until dark. I thought about sneaking around back to your deck, but I didn't want to get shot," he says.

Alex suppresses a laugh. *He's probably not joking.*

"I'm not at the point where I'm shooting people yet, but it's probably a good policy not to be sneaking around at night," says Alex.

"Be careful with those assholes. It's not over for them," he says.

"I know. Believe me. Hey, I'll be in touch in like ten minutes," says Alex.

"Alright. Thanks again for being cool about this. I really feel bad."

"No need man. Talk to you in a few," Alex says, and steps back inside.

Derek turns and walks briskly back to his house across the street.

∎

Alex removes his dark blue winter jacket and hangs it in the garage, on a row of hooks adjacent to the mudroom door. He lifts his right elbow and uses it to press the garage door button. He hears the garage door motor engage, and the subsequent creak and squeak of the garage door as it slides along its infrequently lubricated track. Kate opens the door to the mudroom and Alex steps inside the house to commence his usual decontamination procedure, which basically just consists of him washing his hands and wiping down the faucet hardware with a disinfectant wipe. Once finished, he opens the bathroom door and steps out into the mudroom to take off his shoes. Alex just returned from delivering anti-virals to Derek Sheppard. He also stopped by Jamie's house to check on Amanda and Katherine, who seemed to be handling their situation well. While inside their house, Alex smelled the meal prepared and delivered by the Walkers. He didn't ask, but it smelled a lot like lasagna.

Kate pokes her head into the mudroom.

"How did it go?" she says.

"Uneventful, which is how I like it. The girls seem fine. Whatever the Walkers cooked up for them smelled a hell of a lot better than what we had tonight. It was some sort of Italian dish, and I swear I smelled cheese," he says.

"Really? Cheese. Huh. How about the rest of your journey?" she says.

Alex steps into the darkened library and removes a walkie-talkie radio from the left cargo pocket of his tan desert camouflage pants. He places it on a high, unused shelf, along with his pistol and a spare clip of ammunition.

"Good. Derek's doing alright given the circumstances. I gave him three courses, and he'll be using two of them tonight. Owen's been sick for about three days, started off really rough, but Derek thinks he might be doing a little better. .

His wife's a different story. She just started with the high fever, and she's already extremely congested. Having trouble breathing. He's really worried about ARDS, and I agree. It's been hitting mostly healthy young to middle aged adults, taking a lot of them down within a few days," he says standing up from the mudroom bench.

"Why would he use the drugs on Owen, if he's getting better?" she says.

"I don't know. I recommended he wait and watch. If he's stabilized, and hasn't been hit with pneumonia, then I think he should save the drugs. It's a tough call. I gave him some antibiotics too. Just in case. What are the kids up to?" he says, and moves into the kitchen to sit on one of the island stools.

"They're both up in the attic watching a movie on demand. Would you give Derek more drugs if he needed them?" she asks, settling on to a stool across from Alex.

Alex meets her eyes, as she takes a sip of tea.

"I don't know. We have ten courses left. I'd have a hard time refusing him," he says, casting his eyes down and exhaling in resignation.

"Hon, you shouldn't feel like that's the wrong answer. I feel the same way. I wish we could help more people," she says.

Alex looks up at her and sees a warm compassionate smile that eases his regret.

"I know you do. Sometimes I think about all of the drugs I gave to Dr. Wright. If I had just kept more of those, we could have made a huge difference around here," he says.

Kate leans forward, sliding her cup of tea across the island with both hands.

"Giving those to Dr. Wright was the right thing to do. Keeping them for yourself at that point would have been totally illegal, and would have yanked the moral and ethical chair right out from under you when it came to your final dealings with Biosphere," she says.

"Yeah, well I was already teetering on that chair. I'd hardly call it a moral or ethical high ground," he says and laughs through his nose.

"You've never done anything clearly out of bounds. Taking a few samples here and there. So what? Every other rep out there does it, and so do the doctors and their staff. Please don't tell me you think that all of the Terraflu samples sitting in those office bins went to patients. You and I know exactly where most of those samples went. You could have kept most of those samples, and forged Dr. Wright's signature, but you didn't. You delivered them to the right place, at exactly the right time," she says.

"I still kept an extra case from that load," he says.

"And you think Dr. Wright didn't? He's got a family too," she says.

"We have ten more courses of therapy left. Four of those stay here for us. That's non-negotiable, no matter who crawls up onto our porch. The other six we can give out. I have no problems with that. Hon, I don't want you feeling guilty about this. You've been doing an unbelievable job with all of this," she says and gets up from her stool.

"I've been doing what I think is right, given the circumstances," he says.

"And you've done an amazing job," she says and wraps her arms around his chest from behind.

Kate nestles her head over his left shoulder and leans her body into his, squeezing him tightly. Alex nuzzles his head against hers.

"I'm just worried that the situation out there is going to deteriorate as the winter gets worse. God forbid the power goes out. The decisions will get tougher, and they'll have to be made quicker. If things get really bad in the neighborhood, we need to be prepared to make some tough calls, right on the spot. My mission is to keep you and the kids safe at any cost. I need you to understand what this might come to mean," he says softly.

"I'm a mother, believe me when I say that I understand what it means to protect these kids unconditionally," she says.

Alex believes her every intention, but is still not convinced that she truly understands the full scope of what each of them might have to do in order to ensure survival in the face of a worst case scenario

"Nobody messes with the momma bear?" he says.

"Damn right," she says, and gives him and extra tight squeeze.

She lets him go, and walks around the island to grab her cup of tea.

"What are the kids watching?" he asks.

"I don't know. Probably something borderline inappropriate, like every other movie they want to see nowadays," she says.

"Still no Nightfall on demand?" he says.

"No. They haven't put a new movie on that feature for a couple of weeks now. Not since the theatres closed," she says.

"I hope she's forgotten about it," he says, wincing.

"No, she had another emotional blow out earlier today about it. She checks the on demand menu like three times a day for it," says Kate, grabbing her book.

"Great. Is she still blaming me for not seeing it?" he says.

"Of course. I've made sure to keep the blame focused on you," says Kate.

"Thanks. Hey, I think I'll head up and watch the movie with them. You coming up?" he says.

"Why, you still worried about me sitting down here by myself?" she says.

"I'd certainly feel better if you were at least in our bedroom, or somewhere a little closer to the rest of us. Pleeeeeease." he says.

"Don't you want to watch the evening news? It's recorded," she says.

"Not really. I'll catch up with everything later on the internet. Anything really big going on?" he says.

"Department of Energy officials estimate that most coal fired power plants are already operating on their emergency reserve supply. The white house and energy secretary is calling for a nationwide conservation plan to extend the coal supply until the whole system starts to come back online. Coal mining, transportation, all of it is nearly shut down," she says.

"I guess we should turn off some of these lights, and sit upstairs with the kids watching a movie," he says, glancing around the kitchen and giving her a smirk.

"Nice try," she says and walks to the bank of switches next to the sink.

She turns off the under cabinet lighting, which darkens the kitchen. The soft glow of a lamp in the great room casts more than enough light into the kitchen for them to see. Alex looks out of the wide window over the kitchen sink and stares at the numerous lights in the windows of the several houses within his view.

"Looks like nobody else cares," he says and nods toward the window.

"They'll care when the power fails," says Kate, walking over to the great room. "It's a good practice anyway…pandemic power failure or not. We keep way too many lights on around here. The kids turn on every light, in every room or hallway they use. I think your Marine protégé is still afraid of the dark," she says.

"He respects the dark," he says.

"Then according to your weird logic, shouldn't he be learning to embrace the dark? Like maybe using one less light at a time until he is walking around the house in the pitch black?" she says.

"Alright, whatever…he's afraid of the dark. Nobody likes the dark. Like I always say, most of the bad shit usually happens when it's dark. You coming upstairs?" he says.

"Yeah, I'll join you guys after I close up down here," she says.

"See you in a few," he says, and starts to walk toward the staircase.

He remembers the pistol and turns around. The light in the great room goes out and Kate meets Alex in the kitchen.

"Forget something?" she asks, and Alex detects a cheeky tone.

"Maybe," he says, standing between the island and the kitchen desk, hoping that she'll head upstairs.

"Last week I put it in the nightstand for you," she says.

"I know. Thanks," he says.

"Don't worry. I got your back around here," she says, and slaps his butt.

"Can you make sure the doors are locked?"

"Yeah, I got it," he says.

■

Alex sits bathed in the soft glow of his office computer screen, examining the ISPAC world pandemic map. Alex places the cursor over the United States.

"United States. Population 310,810,109. 1,920,341 reported cases. Borders closed. Uncontained."

Before opening the ISPAC site, he read several articles confirming that the national healthcare system's surge capacity had been exceeded nationwide. This assessment included all of the available mobile Federal Medical Stations, which as of late last week, had all been deployed to major metropolitan areas. At this point, almost no effective inpatient or outpatient care is available for the treatment of new cases.

Alex moves the cursor across the Pacific Ocean to China.

"China. Population 1,350,678,400. Massive outbreak. 152,843,000 reported cases as of 11/26/09. Further case reporting to be based on data samples and mathematical estimates. Borders closed. Uncontained."

Reluctantly, he pushes the cursor over Maine.

"Maine. Population 1,415,484. Large cluster outbreak. 88,434 cases confirmed. Uncontained. Surge capacity exceeded."

"Portland. Population 66,144. Large cluster outbreak. 21,400 cases reported. Uncontained. Surge capacity exceeded."

Alex resists the urge to analyze Boston. He knows it'll be worse, and that way too many of those people are already on their way up to Maine. He was mostly concerned with eastern Massachusetts, specifically the densely populated areas around Boston. Headlines throughout greater Boston strongly indicated that the area was on the brink of exploding into a full scale civil riot. If that happened, the city would turn into a war zone, further escalating the refugee situation, and the desperation of those fleeing north. *That's when the real fun'll start around here.*

Alex puts the computer into standby mode, and turns off the screen, which darkens the room. He stands up from the chair, and kneels down to peer through a two inch opening at the bottom of the office window shade. With the lights out in the office and the adjoining hall, he can scan the neighborhood unobserved.

He sees only a few scattered lights, mostly on the second floors of homes in the neighborhood. He stares at a fixed point above the Sheppards' front door for about one minute, relying on his peripheral vision to detect any movement in the neighborhood. *Nothing. No creepers yet.* Before standing up, he stares at the McDaniel house, wondering where Amanda and Katherine bunked for the night. Hoping they took his advice to stay in the same room and barricade the door with a folding chair. He told them to call either his house, or Ed's, if they heard anything unusual inside or outside of the house. He felt bad that they were alone without an adult, but not bad enough to risk bringing the flu into his own house. Alex pulls the shade down to the window sill and walks out of the office.

Chapter Twenty-Seven

Tuesday, November 27, 2012

Alex is startled out a shallow sleep by the home telephone on his night stand. Without looking, he reaches over to grab the handset out of its charging cradle, knocking his iPhone onto the floor. He hears the iPhone bounce off the carpet and hit the nightstand. *Damn it.* He finds the phone and brings the light blue LED illuminated handset to his face. Edward Walker. Alex stares at the name and number for a few more seconds and answers the call.

"Hello? Ed?" he says.

"Alex, someone forced their way into my basement, through the bulkhead door. I heard it creak open. I think they might still be here. I have the kids in our room. I don't want to…"

"Just stay where you are Ed. I'll be over there in less than a minute," says Alex, shooting up out of bed holding the phone.

"Should I call the police? I don't know if you…"

"You can try, but I don't think we're going to see any cops around anytime soon. Ed, stay in your bedroom, away from the door. Open one of your back windows. I'll be right over. I'm hanging up now," says Alex.

Alex rushes over to his closet and pulls on a pair of jeans that were lying in a heap on the closet floor. He grabs a gray sweatshirt and the Mossberg shotgun. He pulls down a box of double odd buck shot gun shells and opens it. He stuffs several shotgun shells into the front pockets of his jeans. As he emerges from the closet, he hears Kate's voice emanate from the bed.

"What's going on," she murmurs.

"Ed thinks someone has broken into his basement. I'm going over to investigate," he says.

"Why doesn't he call the police," she mumbles.

"Because it'll take the police hours to respond…if they respond. You should bring the kids into the bedroom, or at least lock their doors. I'm heading out right now," he says.

He doesn't want to waste any more crucial time talking to someone that he knows won't be capable of a lucid conversation for at least another ten minutes. Right now, he doesn't have time to brew the coffee necessary to speed up the process.

Alex reaches the mudroom and grabs his keys. He sticks his bare feet into his running shoes and takes a powerful, compact LED flashlight off the same shelf as his keys. He tucks this into his right back pocket along with the keys, and opens the door to the garage. He locks the door as he slides through and closes it behind him. He skirts along the Forerunner and performs the same action on the back door of the garage.

Alex slips into the frigid air of a dark overcast November night, and tests the door to the garage. *Locked.* A violent shiver overtakes him, as his body registers the change in temperature. Alex immediately regrets the decision to ignore the wide selection of fleeces and jackets available to him in the mudroom. Pushing the self-pity aside, he moves swiftly across his backyard to the concealment of several squat pine trees near the back of his lot. As he runs to the darkened shapes of the trees, he keeps his eyes trained on Ed's house.

High in the western sky, Alex can barely perceive the moon's glow, which casts no useful illumination through the thick layer of clouds. As he reaches the trees, the open bulkhead doors materialize from behind the Walkers' deck. Alex takes a knee behind one of the trees, extending his head out far enough to monitor the doors. Alex takes a shotgun shell out of the speed feeder in the stock of the shotgun, ignoring the shells in his pockets, and loads it into bottom of the shotgun. He repeats the procedure two more times.

Alex pumps the shotgun, loading a shell into the chamber. He stiffens at the sound of the pumping mechanism, hoping that the sound didn't carry all the way to the Walkers' house. In close proximity, the sound of the pump action is unmistakable, and usually enough to stop even the most stubborn adversary. At this distance, he doesn't think the sound would be loud enough to elicit the same response. He ensures that the safety is engaged, and starts to move swiftly toward the Walkers' deck. *With my luck I'll trip on some frozen dog shit and set this thing off.*

He crouches slightly, carrying the shotgun by the receiver with his right hand. He is struck by the absolute silence of the night in the late fall. Halfway to the deck, a dark figure darts out of the open bulkhead door, sprinting toward the Andersons' backyard. A second figure emerges from the evergreen bushes on the border of the Andersons' and Walkers' property, and runs to join the intruder toward the back of the lot. *A lookout?* Alex changes his own direction to match the two figures, and starts to sprint toward them yelling.

"Stop! Police! Stop! Don't move!"

One of the figures slows down and turns around, but Alex can't tell in the blackness if it's the intruder or the lookout. Both figures merged at the edge of the Walkers' property, and he lost track as they dodged between evergreens. Either way, one of the burglars has no intention of stopping, and Alex doesn't want to lose either of them. Alex yells another warning, as he approaches the closest figure, who is now at a standstill.

"Stop or I'll shoot!"

The runner doesn't slow, and Alex fires the shotgun straight up into the air. The man in front of him takes a few panicky steps backward and falls over a railroad tie into the hard dirt of the Andersons' empty rectangular vegetable garden. The runner slows down considerably, and Alex fires another deafening shot into the air, which stops the man in his tracks. He pumps the shotgun again, chambering another shell, and starts walking toward the downed figure in the Andersons' garden. His ears ring from the two blasts.

"Get back here now, or I'll blast your friend all over the yard! Now!" Alex says, aiming the shotgun at the figure on the ground.

"Don't move," says Alex.

Alex draws a deep, but quiet breath, straining to regain his wind after the brief sprint. He'll keep drawing quick shallow breaths through his nose until he feels more steady.

"Hey, don't shoot me, you don't have to shoot me," says the man, panicky. *I know that voice.*

"You better call that fucker back over here. He looks like he's going to bolt, and if he does, I'm going to blast one of your legs off, and then hunt him down," says Alex, pointing the barrel at the man's right leg.

"Todd! Todd! This guy isn't fucking around. You need to get back here!" says Mike Lynch, twisting his body far enough to face Todd.

Alex hears the distant figure muttering, still considering his options. He then starts to walk back across the Andersons' yard toward Alex. Alex shifts the shotgun from his right shoulder to his right hip, keeping it trained on Mike.

"Are either of you two armed?" says Alex.

"No, just a walkie-talkie. We didn't…we weren't trying to hurt anyone. We were looking for…"

"Don't say another fucking word Mike!" says Todd, approaching the group nonchalantly.

Alex sees what looks like a radio in his hand.

"You might want to take this a little more seriously," says Alex, pointing the shotgun towards Todd's head.

"Don't point that fucking gun at my head!" says Todd, waving his hands uselessly in front of him.

Alex can see that he's holding a small radio with a thick, stubby antennae.

"I'll do whatever I want right now. Stop right there. If you take more than two steps in my direction, I'll fire on you. And keep your hands where I can see them," says Alex.

"You're not gonna fire at anyone," says Todd.

Alex points the shotgun back at Mike.

"What do you think Mike?" says Alex.

Mike looks up at Todd and shakes his head.

"I wouldn't mess with this guy. I think he's a little…off right now," says Mike.

"Off is a good term. Right now I'm looking for any reason to permanently erase the two of you from my list of worries," says Alex, shifting the gun's aim back at Todd.

"Quit pointing that thing at me!" he says.

"Or what?" he says, shaking his head at Todd.

Mike starts to slowly get up from the dirt, clapping his hands together to clean off the dirt.

"Stay where you are Mike," says Alex, keeping the gun aimed at Todd.

Mike lowers his body back down into the dirt. *I don't have to worry about Mike. He's under voice control now.* Alex hears one of the Walkers' windows open, but doesn't turn to look.

"Alex! Who are they? What's going on?" Ed yells in a whisper from above. *I just fired a shotgun twice, and he's whispering.*

"It's our good friends Todd and Mike! Out for an evening stroll!" he says.

Alex scans his two neighbors. Both of them are dressed in blue jeans and hiking boots. Their jackets are dark colored. Alex guesses Todd's is dark blue, and that Mike's is a natural shade of green, like pine, although he can't be sure. Mike wears a dark blue ball cap, with what Alex is pretty sure is a reddish B on the front. Todd has a black watch cap pulled tightly over his head, covering his ears. Neither of them appear to be carrying or hiding anything.

"Didn't find what you're looking for?" says Alex.

"I'm out of here," says Todd.

Just as he finishes his sentence, a woman's voice emanates from the direction of Todd's house. Through the darkness, Alex perceives movement in one of the windows above Todd's garage. Alex suddenly feels exposed standing out in the open. He moves to his left, putting Todd between himself and the open window. *No reason to make this an easy shot for anyone.*

"You stay right there, or your wife is going to remember this night for the rest of her life," says Alex, raising the shotgun to his shoulder and aiming directly at Todd's head.

Todd raises his right hand out in front of his face.

"Don't bother, you'll lose the hand and your head," says Alex.

"I don't really give a shit Alex. My wife probably won't have the memory of you killing me for very long. I just hope she passes before one of the kids does. That's a memory I don't want her to carry for even a minute," says Todd.

"I'm sorry Todd," says Alex, truly meaning it.

"Are you?" Todd says, and shakes his head.

Alex lowers the gun barrel, pointing at the ground between Mike and Todd. Todd's wife is still yelling out of the window, but Alex can't figure out what she is saying. Todd looks back at the window, then turns his head slowly around to Alex.

"If you're planning to shoot us, now would be a good time. Otherwise, I'll see you later," he says, and starts to walk toward his house.

Mike remains on the ground, eyes darting back and forth between Alex and Todd.

"Last warning Todd. If I find you on either of these two lots again, I will kill you on sight. Same with the McDaniels' house. Actually, if I find you sneaking around anywhere in the neighborhood, you're a dead man. Keep to yourself. The same goes for you Mike. Do you understand me?"

Mike acknowledges him immediately with a vigorous nod and a weak "yes." Todd mutters "whatever."

The sudden deafening detonation of the shotgun drops Todd to his knees. As Alex's hearing floods back, he picks up screams from Todd's master bedroom window. Todd is frozen on his knees and doesn't look back. Alex racks the slide of the shotgun again, although the shotgun's ammunition cylinder is empty. He points the shotgun at Todd's back.

"I'll ask you that question one more time. Do you understand my terms?" says Alex quietly, over the relentless screams pouring out of Todd's house.

Todd nods his head and mutters "yes."

"Good. Now get out of here. Both of you," says Alex, lowering the shotgun.

Both of them rise up quickly and sprint toward the back of Todd's house. Alex watches them disappear behind Todd's house, and turns toward the open window on the second floor of the Walkers. He engages the safety on the shotgun.

"You need to keep your bulkhead door locked," says Alex wryly.

"Yeah, like I haven't checked my bulkhead thirty times since this started," replies Ed, suddenly appearing from the bulkhead steps.

"Does it look jimmied?" says Alex, taking the flashlight out of his back pocket.

"Hold on," he says, descending the stairs.

Light pours out of the basement a few seconds later as he reemerges to examine the locking mechanism. Alex activates his flashlight and points it at the locking bolt.

"Jesus, what do you have a million candle power coming out of that thing?" says Ed, shielding his eyes.

"Sorry," Alex says and shuts off the light.

He leans down by the mechanism, which consists of a thick metal bolt, curved on both ends to keep it from falling out of the sliding mechanism. There really wasn't much to it, and from casual observation, it looked intact and undamaged. Alex glances over his shoulder toward the Andersons' yard.

"Sure you locked it?" he says.

"Positive," replies Ed.

"I'd hate to think it's that easy to manipulate one of these. I have the same thing at my house," says Alex.

"I don't know. It's not exactly a complicated system, and the bulkhead itself isn't exactly airtight. I'm gonna try and jam some wood between the bolt and the door, wedge it in place better," says Ed.

"That should do it."

"Did you have to fire that thing three times? What was going on with them?"

"I needed to convince Todd that I was serious," Alex replies.

"What about the last shot? It looked like you were aiming at him," says Ed.

"I was aiming between them, plenty of room on either side. I was just using bird shot anyway. I needed Todd to escalate his level of care at that moment. He was a little dismissive, which wasn't the tone I was looking for," says Alex.

"Well, I think you got his attention. He was running sort of funny on the way back. Like he pissed his pants."

"I hope so," says Alex.

"I need to find the three expended shells. I can see Todd's wife calling the cops. So if you have everything under control here, I need to remove the evidence from your backyard."

"Have at it. I'll be down here jamming wood into this stupid door," says Ed.

"Maybe there's a place where you could put a padlock or something, and jam the mechanism shut," says Alex, backing up out of the light.

"I'll let you know if I figure something like that out. Happy hunting," says Ed.

"Yep," Alex says, and turns on his flashlight.

Ten minutes later, he unlocks and opens the door to his garage. He opens the green garbage bin lid, and tosses the three expended shells into the bin. He moves one of the trash bags near the top to make sure the shells filter down a little further so they are out of immediate sight. Alex plans to reload the speed feeder with three more birdshot shells. He makes a mental note to find a better way to carry around the double ought shells, just in case he needs more than the bird shot.

When Alex decided to keep the shotgun in his closet, he opted to keep four birdshot shells loaded in the stock's spring loaded speed feeders. To Alex, this made sense on several levels. First, in the unlikely case that he is forced to discharge the weapon inside the house, the birdshot would not pass through the walls with enough kinetic energy to kill or significantly hurt someone on the other side. This was an important consideration for Alex with children in the house.

His secondary reason for the selection is lethality, or in the case of birdshot, reduction of lethality. In Alex's opinion, birdshot in a confined space is more than adequate to instantly, and wholly incapacitate an intruder, without annihilating them.

Alex opens the door to the house, and is greeted by a well-lit mudroom. Kate is sitting at the kitchen island, just out of sight of the mudroom door, and pokes her head in view briefly. The kitchen is dimly lit by the stove's under mounted light.

"Hey hon," he calls out, slipping out of his shoes. *Rather not get stabbed in a case of mistaken identity.*

"What happened out there? I heard some gunshots, so I rushed down here to check on you. By the time I got out into the backyard, I could see you and Ed chatting by his bulkhead. Seemed like everything was under control," she says.

"Mike and Todd pulled off a little B and E at Ed's, through the bulkhead, so I put the fear of Mossberg into them…hon, the hammer's back on that gun," he says dryly, leaning the shotgun against the kitchen desk.

He steps around Kate to examine the pistol lying on the kitchen island next to her tea cup, "Which means that just about four pounds of pressure on that trigger and…"

Alex picks up the weapon, keeping it pointed toward the mudroom, and depresses the de-cocking lever with his thumb. The hammer falls lightly. He then presses the magazine release mechanism at the base of the trigger guard. The magazine slides out into his left hand, and he places it on the island. He then racks the slide and the chambered .45 caliber round pops out of the weapon, hits the island and rolls off. Alex hears it hit the seat of a stool, then the floor. Kate looks tense as the bullet rolls off the island onto the floor

"Don't worry hon. You can't set one of these off by dropping it. You can, however, set one off by keeping the hammer cocked while you traipse around the backyard in the dark. Good way to trip and shoot yourself in the head," he says, moving to retrieve the bullet from the floor.

"Yeah, well I got a little worried when I heard gunfire in the backyard. You know, I don't think it's such a great idea for you to be charging through the dark either," she says, nodding at the shotgun.

"You're not the only one around here with guns. You have no idea what might have been waiting for you in Ed's backyard. You're lucky it was only those two idiots. What did they want?"

"Food, medicine…both. I'm sure they're convinced that Ed has a huge stash of drugs too," he says, and sits on the stool next to Kate.

"Do you think they'd try the same thing here?" she says.

"Not after tonight, although Todd does seem to have some sort of death wish. I don't think Susan's doing well at all. He made a comment about how she won't be around much longer," he says, shaking his head.

"The more desperate everyone becomes…who knows what'll happen around here."

"Not much else we can do at this point," she says, kissing him on the forehead and standing up from her stool.

"That's it, I'm done. I don't want to be a zombie all day," she adds, and starts shuffling toward the staircase.

"Big day tomorrow?" he says.

"You know it," she says, laughing softly.

"What day is it tomorrow? Today actually."

"Tuesday. Not that it really matters," he says.

"Yeah. No kidding. I Love you" she says, and starts up the stairs.

"Love you too."

Chapter Twenty-Eight

Tuesday, November 27, 2012

Alex walks across the darkened kitchen into the great room, and is pleasantly surprised to find everyone quietly reading. The shades have already been pulled shut, and the room is bathed in the soothing glow of a few strategically placed reading lamps. Kate is on the leather sectional couch, staring at the screen of her iPad, which is propped up against her bent knees. Ryan occupies the other side of the couch, holding Alex's iPad. A few days ago, Alex showed Ryan how to find and download books, and Ryan found several science fiction books that interested him. Alex encouraged him to keep searching and ordering books. If the power grid failed nationwide, he wasn't sure how long they would have internet access. And without books, they would all be facing an extremely long winter.

Alex steps into the family room and puts his hand on Emily's head, softly stroking her hair. Emily is curled up in one of the oversized leather chairs right inside the great room entrance, eyes closed with a book weakly grasped in her right hand. She opens her eyes slowly as he pets her head.

"Hey sweetie. Whatcha reading?" he says.

She stifles a yawn, and stretches her shoulders back.

"Just one of the Explorer series books. I still have like four or five more in the series that I haven't read yet," she says.

"You still like those, huh?" he says, kneeling down next to her chair.

"Yeah, I forgot how good they were," she says.

"Even without vampires or the undead floating around? Hard to believe," he says.

"Even without vampires daddy," she says, dejected.

"Sounds good cupcake. Why don't you close your eyes and go back to sleep," he says.

She nods and starts to drift away. Kate looks up from the iPad.

"How is everyone?" she asks quietly, glancing at Ryan who appears undisturbed.

"Not bad overall," he says and signals her with his head to meet him in the other room.

He walks back into the kitchen and she joins him shortly. They both walk over to the den. Alex turns one of the lamps on and they both plop down into the leather club chairs. They keep the door open.

"This is a nice room. We should spend more time in here," Kate says, and takes a deep breath.

"Yeah, it is sort of a sanctuary," he says and pauses.

"So it looks like my brother is going to be fine. My parents picked him up from the hospital in Castle Rock this morning, and brought him to their house. He still has pneumonia, but I guess he responded well to antibiotics and the intensive intervention that was still miraculously available at that hospital. Lucky bastard. Broke his arm in the car crash."

"Why did Karla make your parents drive over an hour out to Castle Rock?" says Kate angrily.

"Karla died at the Fort Carson flu triage center last night. My parents had a long day yesterday," he says flatly.

"God, those poor kids. I can't even imagine. Did you know she was sick?" she says.

"No. I haven't talked to them for a week. Just a few emails to make sure they were OK. Mom said she came down with symptoms really fast. The kids were already sick, but never got worse. They all took the anti-virals. My mother tore Daniel's house apart and found the drugs stashed in one of the bathroom closets, still in the original box I sent. Unopened," he says, shaking his head.

"Anyway, Karla's dad still lives in C Springs. Made it to Colonel before retiring right outside of Ft Carson. He pulled some strings to get her into the triage center on base. It sounds like she went fast. Complete respiratory breakdown within like a day and a half. Ethan and Kevin are staying with my parents, along with Daniel. It doesn't sound like Daniel is not out of the woods yet. They gave him some strong antibiotics to take home, but he really needs to stay on an antibiotic drip. I don't know. Sounds like they were actively clearing hospital beds and ventilators for other patients," he says.

"I'm really sorry to hear about Karla. I can't believe it. So fast. She was the world to those kids," she says.

"That's why we can't take any chances here. This thing really seems to be annihilating younger, healthy adults. Karla, Eric Bishop, Joe Burton. All you hear on the news are reports of healthy adults being taken down in the course of a few days. Gone. That's why we can't afford a slip up," he says.

"I know," she says, nodding.

"Should we say anything to the kids?" she adds.

"No. It would just freak them out," he says.

"Alright. I'm so glad your parents are watching them. I don't think they would stand a chance if it wasn't for them," she says.

"That's what I told them. I also told them to go ahead and take the Terraflu I gave them. They each have two courses of therapy. I forgot I gave them more than one. With the kids in the house and Daniel, they're bound to get sick. If Terraflu is in their system before they show symptoms, then they might not even develop more than a mild fever or cough."

"Good. Your right, they'll be fine. I know they will. I am going to work on some dinner," she says and starts to get up from her seat.

"Your clan isn't still considering a migration up to your brother's place are they?" he says.

"No, I got an email from them this morning. Too many moving parts. Three cars, barely enough gas to pull it off. They've stockpiled a lot of stuff over there, and they'd have to move that too. Princeton is still pretty quiet, but the mayhem is getting closer, spilling out of Phillie…New York…northern Jersey. They're nervous about it, but they're way better off staying put. God only knows what could happen to them on the road. They'd be forced to transit some highly populated parts of Jersey and Mass…places that look like borderline warzones right now," she says.

"I think they made a good call," Alex says, following her out of the mudroom.

"How does pasta and sauce sound? Throw some beans in there maybe?" Kate says, opening the pantry door.

"Works for me," he says, leaning over to dig an onion out of a red net bag on the floor of the pantry.

"How many more of those do we have?" she asks.

"Four more in this bag, and we have another bag of about twelve in the bunker," he says standing up.

"We do?" she says.

"We do. You should spend a little more time down there. You might find all kinds of nice little surprises," he says.

"Maybe I will," she says, taking a box of pasta and a large can of crushed tomatoes to the counter next to the stove.

Alex follows behind her and takes a large squat knife out of the knife rack. He puts the knife behind his back in a reverse commando grip and moves behind Kate, never exposing her to the blade. Just as he reaches the wooden chopping block, their phone rings. Alex puts the knife and onion down and grabs the phone from the island.

"Ed," he says and answers the phone.

"What's up? More funny noises in the basement?" says Alex.

"Now that it's clear that I have Rambo guarding my house, I highly doubt we'll see either of those two again. Thanks again, I guess. At least you didn't blast a hole in my house," says Ed.

"Nice. Any time Mr. appreciative," says Alex, smiling at Kate, who is watching him.

"Hold on Ed, while I seek some privacy," he says.

"Who is it dad?" Ryan calls out from the family room.

"It's your girlfriend's dad, Mr. Walker," says Alex.

"Great," sighs Kate.

"Dad! She's not my girlfriend!"

"I'll be sure to tell him that," he says, and slides the pocket door to the mudroom shut to add a layer of soundproofing, in anticipation of the uproar he may have ignited.

He hears Ryan still grumbling to Kate about what he said, and he shuts the door to the den, locking it to prevent intrusion by an embarrassed twelve year old.

"I'm sure Ryan was happy to hear you say that," says Ed.

"Yeah, it was like setting off a bomb in the kitchen for Kate to clean up. What's going on?" says Alex, switching on the overhead light, which does not please him.

"I think Jamie's home. We saw a car pull away from the house about ten minutes ago. Never saw it pull up. Now there are lights on over the garage in the master bedroom. The girls never turned those lights on," he says.

"Should we go over there and make sure everything is alright?" says Alex.

"I think I'll call first. Maybe it's a relative, her parents or something," says Ed.

"I thought their families were pretty far away," says Alex.

"Midwest somewhere. That'd be a long trip," says Ed.

"Really long. I doubt it's a relative," says Alex.

"You're probably right," says Ed.

"Yet to be wrong," quips Alex.

"Keep running around the neighborhood with a shotgun, and that might change," says Ed.

"That's what my wife thinks."

"She's might be on to something," says Ed.

"Anyway, I'll give her a call. If she's home, we could bring over some supplies for them later tonight."

"Keep me posted," says Alex.

"I'll call you later," Ed says, ending the call.

Alex reenters the kitchen and briefs Kate on the most recent development.

Chapter Twenty-Nine

Wednesday, November 28, 2012

Alex lies awake in bed, on his left side, staring at the alarm clock on the night stand. Kate's arms are wrapped around him and her body is pressed snuggly into his back. Alex hears Emily breathing deeply on the other side of Kate. Having both of the kids in the master bedroom makes him feel better. More at ease given the unstable climate in the neighborhood. Their rooms seem so far away at the other end of the house, and with the staircase emptying in front of the entrances to both of their rooms, he worries about being able to reach them in time if they have an intruder. *More worries.* As Alex starts drifting back asleep, he hears the doorbell ring.

"Who's that," mumbles Kate.

Alex sits up slowly, feeling exhausted by the unplanned two hour interruption to his sleep last night. He slides out of the covers and walks over to the front window. He raises the shade half way and sees a police cruiser parked on the street in front of their mailbox. Alex can read Scarborough Police on the side of the car.

"It's the police. Stay in bed, I'll see what's up," he says, and pulls a pair of dark brown corduroy pants out of the closet.

"If you insist," she says.

He arrives at the mudroom door dressed in the brown pants, a thin gray long sleeve shirt and bare feet. Alex looks through the mudroom door window and sees a police officer standing on the stoop. Another officer stands back several paces on the walkway. The furthest officer takes a deep breath, exhaling through his mouth, and Alex can clearly see his breath. *Nasty cold out.* Neither looks particularly contentious or alarmed, and Alex feels only the typical apprehension anyone might experience finding two police officers standing outside their door. *Travelling in pairs? Things must really be going to shit out there.* Alex slips on a pair of Crocs and opens both the interior and storm doors to greet the officer. He is met by an expected rush of bitterly cold air.

"Good morning gentlemen," says Alex, stepping out onto the stoop with the officer.

"Morning Mr. Fletcher?" says the officer on the stoop.

The other officer nods a friendly, but stiff greeting. Alex considers the officer standing a few feet from him. From inside the house, the officer like any uniformed law enforcement official he had seen before, prior to the pandemic, but on close inspection, Alex immediately spots the considerable strain these officers must be facing.

Officer Hale, as he reads from the name badge, looks like he hasn't shaven in at least two days. Combined with dark circles under his blood shot eyes, Alex figures he hasn't slept much either in the past few days. The condition of his uniform betrays the same ordeal. Although still far from unserviceable, his uniform is no longer the crisp, heavily starched and pressed navy blue uniform he wore just a month ago.

Glancing furtively, Alex sees that one of his knees is dirty or possibly just worn through. He's not sure, and he doesn't plan to take another look. The last thing Alex notices ';;po is that the officer is definitely wearing some king of enhanced body armor under his cold weather parka. Whatever he's wearing underneath, it doesn't resemble the typical vest. This one is much thicker, giving his upper body a significant barrel like appearance. *Probably fitted with some ceramic trauma plates. Stop an AK-47 bullet. These guys aren't taking any chances.*

"Alex. Just Alex. How can I help you guys?" he says.

"Mr. Fle….Alex, we're looking into the possible discharge of a firearm in your neighborhood. Happened two nights ago…and…"

Officer Hale is having trouble forming the words, probably due to sheer exhaustion. The other officer helps him out.

"One of the neighbors reported several gunshots coming from over there. Shotgun," he says, pointing the general direction of Ed's house.

"I didn't hear any gunshots last night. Pretty quiet around here," says Alex, as they gather near the mudroom overhang.

"Actually, the report came in two nights ago," says Hale, stealing a glance at Downes.

"Nothing all week actually," says Alex, starting to feel a warmth creep over his face.

"Well, the person who called insisted they saw you in the backyard, behind the Andersons', right about the same time as the gunshots. Around two thirty in the morning," says Hale.

"And they're sure it was me?" says Alex.

"The report makes it pretty clear that they thought it was you," says Hale.

Alex shrugs, "Well, I can guarantee you that I don't make a habit of running around the neighborhood in the wee hours of the morning with a gun. Especially these days. Did anyone else report the shots?"

"We got a call from the street behind you and two more from your street. Just reporting what they thought was gunfire. Mr. Fletcher…Alex. Do you own any firearms?" says Hale.

"You guys want to step in the garage? I'm freezing my nuts off out here. I'd invite you in the house, but we're enforcing a strict quarantine until the flu tapers off," says Alex.

Officer Hale looks at Downes, who nods.

"Sure," says Hale.

"Let me open the door. I'll be right back," says Alex.

Alex opens the far garage door, and the officer's step into the empty space, which is considerably warmer than the open air. Alex meets them in the empty bay and leans against the Forerunner's rear passenger door. The two officers stand several feet away from him, in the middle of the empty bay, with their backs to the double stacked woodpile. Both officers cross their arms, almost in unison, taking what Alex interprets to be a neutral, yet interrogative stance.

"That's better. Anyway…uh, yes, I own a handgun, which you guys probably know already. I have a concealed carry permit filed with the town," says Alex. *What's the chance they'll stop the questions here?*

"No shotguns or rifles?" says Hale, and Alex feels the heat building up in his face.

"I'm not a hunter, so I don't have any need for a long gun," says Alex.

"Well, the reason I brought it up is because one of the other officers at the station remembers seeing you with a shotgun at the Fish and Game club. Said you're pretty handy with a shotgun. Mossberg he thought," says Hale, glancing briefly at Downes.

"I have a few friends that are really into guns, and I've taken them to the range before. He probably saw me with one of their shotguns. One of them has a Mossberg. My personal favorite. Defender model very similar to the one I trained on and used in Iraq," says Alex, feeling like every motion he makes is betraying his lie.

Alex feels uncomfortable lying to the officers, but he doesn't want to give them any more reason than they already have to enter his house. Neither one of them appears sick, but they're in constant contact with the public, so Alex doesn't want to take the chance. Plus, with the level of violence escalating region wide, he certainly can't risk having his firearms confiscated, which is a course of action he can envision them taking.

The last thing the police need is a loose cannon running around any of the neighborhoods, and Alex's behavior last night stands a good chance of landing him on the loose cannon list. Alex is certain that if these guys could verify with one hundred percent accuracy that he owned a shotgun, they'd take measures to remove it from the premises, along with every other weapon in his gun safe. He decides that his best strategy is to continue to play dumb about a shotgun.

"When did you serve?" says Downes.

"94' to 04'. Got out after the invasion of Iraq," says Alex.

"Small world. I was Army. Five years. Left as a sergeant in 2009. I'm still in the reserves. 94th MP detachment down in Saco," says Downes.

"Oh boy, here we go," says Hale, smirking.

"What unit were you with on active duty?" says Alex. *I need to drag this on as long as I can.*

"2nd Brigade Combat Team, 4th ID..."

"Out of Fort Carson?" says Alex.

"Yeah, you been there?" says Downes.

"My folks still live in C Springs. My sister-in-law's parents live right outside Ft. Carson. Her dad's a retired Colonel. His last post was at Ft. Carson, I think. Anyway, she died a few days ago," says Alex.

"Flu?" says Hale.

"Yeah. She went quick." says Alex.

Both officers put on somber faces, probably more out of courtesy than anything else.

"Sorry to hear that," says Hale.

"Yeah, that's tough," adds Downes, "there's too much of that going around."

"I imagine you guys are running into it all day," says Alex, not sure if that was the right thing to say.

"We're too busy to respond to those calls. Hell, you'd be lucky to get an ambulance out at this point. EMT crews got crushed by the flu. At this point, the department is at less than half strength. We're lucky to have two cars out at any given time, and those are usually twenty-four hour shifts. It's a real fu...friggin mess. We're pulling strictly volunteer duty to try and clear up any notable reports of violence or civil disorder, which brings me back to the point of our visit," says Hale.

"We've seen too many neighborhood disputes escalate over the past week or so. People are getting desperate. My best advice is to keep to yourselves, and if anything happens, avoid confrontation, try to make an ID, and give us a call. We might not respond right away, but we'll do our best to get to the bottom of it. Sometimes just our showing up and asking a few questions goes a long way," says Hale.

Alex grins, knowing that Hale's last statement was directed at him.

"Nobody likes having the police pay a visit," says Alex, as they all start to walk out of the garage.

"Unless they call 911," adds Downes.

"So, how bad is it out there? I mean beyond Scarborough? Those vests aren't standard issue. Pairing you guys up when they could double the number of cars out on patrol?" says Alex.

Both officers stop and turn around just short of leaving the garage. Hale wears an exhausted expression that betrays a concerned caution.

"It's not too bad up here yet, even in Portland or South Portland. Just the usual stuff. Lots of break-ins, vandalism, minor fights…some major ones, but nothing crazy yet," says Hale.

He touches his vest, "Tri-City Special Response divy'd up all the gear last week. Not enough trained guys left on the roster to field a response team. Everyone that goes out on patrol has the option to take one of these. We got some assault rifles too, though nobody's really been trained by the department to use one, other than the Special Response guys. Officer Downes is the only member of the team from Scarborough still fit for duty," says Hale, glancing at Downes.

"We only contributed two guys to the team. Most of them were from South Portland, so we didn't get a lot of the gear. Four sets of body armor, some night vision, other goodies. I hope we never really have to us any of it," says Downes.

"Amen," says Alex.

"Alright, we have to get moving here. Lots of ground to cover before one of us passes out. Do you have a radio that can scan police channels?" asks Hale.

The question catches Alex of guard, and he pauses, not really sure how to answer his question. He has a Uniden multi-channel radio with this capability in the basement, but he hasn't yet considered using it to eavesdrop on local law enforcement. His silence crosses over into discomfort, as he continues to ponder what he should say. *Is it illegal? I think it might be.*

"We don't care if you have a police scanner. They're perfectly legal in Maine. It's amazing how everyone clams up around us," says Hale.

"Well, it's not like you guys are here for beers. It's like when you're driving, and suddenly you see a cruiser in your rearview mirror. You could be driving your grandma back to the nursing home and your ass would still pucker," Alex says, causing both officers to briefly laugh.

"That's a scary thought. Anyway, if you have one, you should start scanning local and county channels. We haven't seen too many refugees from Mass up this far, but they're coming. They've been slipping into the state slowly, mainly up the turnpike, but we think that's all about to change," says Hale.

Downes leans in a little close, like he's about to share a secret.

"We've heard from a few sources that the situation down in Boston is about to go critical. They've already seen limited riots and fires, but from what we've been hearing, they're on the brink of a complete breakdown. Once that happens, we can expect a lot of people streaming north. Most of them with nothing. All of them looking for something," says Downes.

"Yeah, this has already caused some problems down in York County. These folks drive up with just the fuel in their tanks, and whatever they thought to jam in their cars. No plan. No contacts up here. Just the misguided idea that Maine wasn't hit as bad. They get here and quickly figure out that nobody's really keen on having them up here, and that's when it starts to get ugly. On both sides," says Downes.

"Where do they end up staying?" says Alex.

"Some check into hotels, if they have the cash. Credit cards are almost useless now. No one accepts them. Most just live in their cars until they can figure something out, which won't be an option for very long," says Downes, glancing up at the sky.

"Either way, none of them have enough food to last more than a week. Many have way less than that, so they start scoping out the neighborhoods during the day, maybe stopping to ask questions about food or the possibility of a vacant houses on the block. Then they return to cruise the neighborhood after dark, looking for houses with no lights. They'll just break into those houses outright, and you'll wake up with new neighbors. Once in place, they'll make you wish you had Jehovah's witnesses for neighbors," says Downes.

"Can we do anything to keep them off the block?" says Alex.

"That's where it's gotten ugly down state. Even if you blockade the entrance to your loop, they'll pour in on foot from the other streets, night and day. It's almost better to have them inside their cars. At least that way you can see them, and you don't have people sneaking through your yards at night. We've heard reports from some York County Sheriff's deputies about night time battles erupting in neighborhoods down in Kittery and York. Some reports from Sanford too. Way too many guns in Maine, and way too many people eager to use them." says Hale.

"Yeah, but if someone's breaking into your house, and the police can't respond...I mean, it's not your fault, but..." starts Alex.

"Most of these aren't break-ins. Some for sure, but there's been a lot of indiscriminate shooting. Blasting away at shadows. Even a few cases of pre-planned ambush. Anyway, nice talking with you Alex. Pull out that scanner and keep any guns you own inside the house. You'll be better off that way. Good luck," Hale says, and starts to walk toward the cruiser.

"Keep it safe guys," says Alex.

"You too," says Downes.

Alex watches the two officers walk back to their patrol car. Neither looks very enthusiastic about returning to duty. He's pretty sure he could end their voluntary shift pretty quickly if he offered them a beer, even at this early hour. He feels the cold penetrating his Crocs again.

"Hey, Officer Downes! Were you with Ironhorse?" he yells, as he backs into the garage.

"Yeah! How did you know?" yells Downes, as he reaches for the passenger door handle.

"I was in Iraq as a company commander when the war started. Rolled all the way up through Baghdad. I've read everything written about the war. 4th ID rolled in late 2007. Task Force Ironhorse. You guys did some incredible work out there," yells Alex.

"Thanks, I just hope we can all survive this!" says Downes, glancing around the neighborhood.

"We've seen worse," says Alex.

"I don't know. I don't think we've seen anything yet!" says Downes, as he ducks into the car. Alex watches the patrol car drive in the direction of the Thorntons' before walks over to shut the garage door.

A few minutes later he stands in front of their Espresso machine, at the far end of the kitchen counter, waiting for the green indicator to illuminate. He hears one of the top stairs creak, and guesses that Kate is coming down to check on him. Several more steps confirm his guess, as Kate's unmistakable stride brings her to the bottom of the stairs. She is dressed in pink and gray flannel pajama bottoms, and a thick, oversized maroon Boston College sweatshirt.

"So, are you under arrest?" she says, walking toward him.

"No, I traded some information for my freedom. They'll be back to haul you away after you've had some coffee. I told them you'd go quietly that way, or at least quieter," says Alex.

"Damn good call on your part. So, what did they want?" she says.

"To talk about my possible involvement in the discharge of a firearm," he says still looking at her.

"Please tell me you didn't admit to it," she says and walks over to the pantry.

"I told them I didn't hear a thing that night," he says.

"Did they buy it," she says, laughing a little as she walks up to the counter next to the stove with a container of quick oats.

"They really didn't seem to care," he says.

∎

Alex turns the last light off downstairs and heads upstairs to the office. He passes Emily's room and hears Kate and Emily talking, but can't figure out any of their conversation. As he moves down the hall, he starts to hear sounds of computerized violence and mayhem emanate from the attic doorway near the office. He enters the office and closes the door to drown out the sounds of simulated automatic weapons fire, screaming and explosions. Even through the door, he can hear the muted battle raging across the flat screen in the attic. *A full scale war could break out in South Portland and I wouldn't hear it.*

He turns off the overhead light and switches on the desk lamp. He picks up his iPhone. *No messages.* Alex hasn't received a message on his iPhone in several days. Barely any calls to the house either. Even email traffic has slowed to a near halt over the past week. At first he wondered why. He reasoned that people should have nothing but time on their hands. Plenty of time to stay in touch. *But for what, really?*

It didn't take him long to realize that his own situation certainly didn't resemble anything close to the most typical scenario out there. Most people are probably just barely getting by. Sick or not, supplies of everything are low. Even households untouched by the flu must be quickly coming to the realization that they are about to enter dire straits.

Alex sits down at the computer and sees that Kate had been checking out the weather forecast. He sees that the national weather service has predicted a major storm for the weekend, estimated to arrive on Sunday. "Mixed ice and snow. Possible ice storm followed by periods of heavy snow." *That doesn't sound very promising.*

He clicks over to one of the local news channel's websites and checks their storm center predictions. Their prediction is more detailed, and outlines the conditions meteorologists believe will likely cause a severe ice storm. Alex starts to talk quietly out loud, paraphrasing the prediction.

"Remnants of late season tropical storm from the Gulf of Mexico encounters polar high pressure zone over New England early Sunday morning. Persistent polar air mass could result in a stalled warm front and enduring precipitation in the form of frozen rain. *Great.* Freezing temperatures on the ground will make situation worse. Eventually moist air will push through stationary cold front. Possible transition to intense snowfall if warm layer thins before leaving the region.

Alex navigates back to the news station's homepage. One article catches his eye above all of the standard pandemic news. "Maine Civilian Defense Group plans to barricade I-95 bridge." *Fucking nut jobs.* As he reads the rest of the article, he starts to think that these guys might have the right idea.

"**The Coastal Defense Group consists of an informal network of several dozen volunteers. Group organizer and leader, Jerry Campbell, of** Kittery, says that the group is growing in response to the threat from outsiders. 'We've been subjected to an out of state invasion for decades. Property taxes are driving Mainers out of their homes, and there's new construction everywhere. Hardworking Mainers can't make a living in their own state anymore. Now they're gonna all stream up here and ransack the place? We're barely hanging on up here, and there ain't nothin to share. Our organization was founded under the same spirit as the original Minutemen. We'll respond to the call to defend our borders again.'

York County sheriff's officials stated that they would likely station their own deputies at the bridge, in anticipation of the group's action to barricade the I-95. An anonymous source within the sheriff's department casts serious doubt on the department's ability to remove the group from the bridge, pointing out that the deputies are already stretched to the breaking point around the county. Kittery police officials declined to comment on their planned reaction to a standoff on the bridge."

"Sounds like the makings of a regular goat fuck down there," Alex says out loud.

"Do you always talk to yourself in here," says Kate from the doorway to the office.

Alex is startled by her sudden appearance.

"Jesus! What is it with all of you people scaring the shit out of me?" he says.

"Who's you people?" she says, walking over to the desk.

"You, and that son of yours," he says.

He swings the chair around to face her.

"Did you see the storm warning?" she says.

"Yeah, I hope it's just a snow storm. An ice storm will take down the power," he says.

She is staring past him at the article on the screen.

"What's that all about?" she says, squinting to try and read it from where she is standing.

"Some nutbags are planning to barricade the bridge," he says.

"What about the Route One bridge?" she says.

"I don't know. What, do you want be on their planning committee?" he says.

"Someone has to keep the refugee situation under control," she says.

"Yeah, somehow I think that's a job better suited for the Army reserves or National Guard. Not a bunch of gun toting nuts who believe they are the reincarnated spirits of the Lexington and Concord minutemen," he says.

"Who do you think makes up the guard and reserves?" she says.

"I have several friends in the Guard, and they run a quality operation," he says.

"I didn't mean it that way. I'm just saying that regular civilians from all walks of life make up the Guard. Same people who are part of that group," she says.

"True, but either way, an untrained and undisciplined gaggle of armed civilians barricading a bridge is a recipe for major disaster," he says, turning back to the screen.

"Yeah, but I can't help thinking I'm glad they're doing something to keep these people from creeping into our neighborhood," she says.

"I know. I feel the same way," he says.

"Speaking of the Guard, they fully mobilized all Maine units. Same for New Hampshire, Massachusetts and the rest of New England. I think there was a national mobilization ordered by the President. I caught a bit of it on the TV in our room a little earlier," Kate says, lingering in the doorway.

"I didn't see that. Hold on," he says, and starts a search.

"Jesus, you're right, it was a presidential order. Christ, they're talking about the deployment of units to areas outside of assigned states," he says.

"Can they do that?" she says, stepping back in to the office.

"Do what? Fully mobilize or send units out of state?" he says.

"Both," she states.

"I've never heard of them mobilizing every single unit, but I know units travel out of state to augment disaster efforts, like major floods, or something like the disaster in New Orleans. Still, I'm pretty sure that's usually authorized by the state governor as a courtesy. I can't imagine any of the state governors volunteering to send any units out of state. This is unprecedented as far as I know," he says.

"The President, or the Secretary of Defense must have taken control of the National Guard. Not sure how, but I can guarantee this'll just add to the mess out there," says Alex.

"I wouldn't show up. Not with my family's safety on the line. I'm gonna take a shower," Kate says, and leaves.

Alex mumbles agreement, though fundamentally, he doesn't agree with her sentiment. He felt no qualms ditching his job at Biosphere, but military service was a different story. He could never refuse an authorized and legitimate call to duty, which is why after nearly ten years on active duty, Alex resigned his commission, and did not register with the Individual Ready Reserve (IRR).

President Bush had already exercised his right under the Presidential Reserve Callup Authority to reactivate members of the IRR, and by the end of 2003, Captain Fletcher, USMC, couldn't imagine any scenario in which the United States would be able to leave Iraq within the next ten years. With specialized Arabic language training from the Defense Language Institute documented in his service record, he felt certain that he'd once again choke on the stench of Iraq if he remained in the IRR. He was surprised that the Marine Corps let him resign, though he suspected that his last Fitness Report (FITREP) helped seal this deal.

The battalion's Executive Officer, Major Rogan, had an overly heavy hand influencing battalion FITREPs, especially for the officers he despised, and Captain Fletcher imagined he was at the top of the major's list. Major Rogan had a problem with Alex from the beginning, but after the An-Nasiryah disaster, Alex validated his position at the top when he openly suggested that the major might have underestimated the potential for communications problems during the attack.

He never directly blamed Major Rogan for the high casualty count at the bridge, but the implication was inescapable in the sun baked, sand blown canvas tent. Discomfort enveloped the exhausted Marines, and Alex felt the kind of sinking feeling one might expect after signing their own death warrant. His departing FITREP didn't contain any overt career ending statements, but it certainly didn't contain the prose needed to skyrocket him to the rank of general, or even the next rank of Major. In the eyes of the Marine Corps, he was at the end of his career, which suited him fine.

Alex chuckles to himself. He was wrong about the ten years. It only took eight years to effectively get out of Iraq. Of course, most of military units only moved a short distance over to Afghanistan and

Pakistan, where they had just recently finished up the remaining members of the Taliban that hadn't fled to the newest Islamic fundamentalist safe haven, Indonesia.

Alex laughs to himself again at that thought. *They move their fundamentalist core from the caves and tribal areas of Afghanistan to Indonesia, effecting one of the quickest and most brutal fundamentalist uprisings in recent history, and their new home turns out to be the epicenter of the greatest pandemic in recent history. They need to scout out their locations better. Then again, you can't hide from bad karma.*

He thinks about that for a moment, and wonders if the Taliban leadership looks at the coincidence as a curse or providence. He can picture them in a press conference declaring the pandemic as punishment for the world's infidel ways, spreading outward from the new holy land to cleanse the world.

Unfortunately for them, a vast majority of the world's estimated 1.8 billion Muslims live in third world conditions. Once the Jakarta Flu settles, many demographic experts project that the Muslim population will emerge at pre-1980's levels. In essence, the Jakarta Flu will put an end to Islam's 21st century resurgence. *I wonder what the Taliban think of that?*

Alex navigates to one of the major Boston newspapers. He sees a disturbing article featuring the sudden decline of civil order within the major Boston metropolitan area. He checks the submission time of the article, and sees that it was filed online only several minutes ago. *Here it goes.*

He skims the article, and sees reference to similar problems in all major cities along the north eastern coast. The article cites growing civil unrest as the primary reason for the nationwide Guard recall. *Sounds like they needed to put the Guard into action a few weeks ago.* The articles author goes further to blame the civil disorder on a "now nearly complete breakdown of the food and essentials supply chain in the northeast, compounded by an overwhelmed healthcare system that has far exceeded its capacity to handle the flu pandemic." *This is going to get way worse, really fast.*

Alex navigates to the Portland Press Herald website, and is slightly ashamed to find himself disappointed when he doesn't see a similar story describing large scale riots and fires in the greater Portland area. In truth, he really doesn't expect any large scale civil problem. Nothing ever happens on a large scale here. *Not enough people packed into one place.* And with the winter closing in on Maine, he can't imagine the streets filling up with rioters. He has no doubt that the police and Guard will have their hands full, and that there will be some fires and looting. Just not on a scale to cause more alarm or damage than the flu itself. Alex puts the computer into standby and heads toward the bedroom and possible a shower with his wife.

Survival

Chapter Thirty

Friday, November 30, 2012

Alex stares through one of front windows in the great room. He's counted three cars so far, all moving slowly through the neighborhood. Right now, he is distracted by the bright gray and white sky, which wasn't here yesterday. By all accounts, it's a pretty standard late November sky, complemented by a stiff northerly wind, but to Alex, it portends more. If the storm lives up to meteorologists expectations, it might be impossible for any more refugees to get through to Portland. He didn't think the Turnpike Authority's snow plows could work at anything close to full capacity. Fuel and personnel shortages would ground the monstrous fleet of orange behemoths.

As Alex continues to stare at the solid mass of clouds, he spots a minivan turning onto Durham Road. He shifts a pair of binoculars to his face.

The vehicle is a white Toyota Sienna. "White Sienna," he jots onto a legal pad balanced sideways on the window sill. He has to bend down slightly to write. The minivan turns right at the fork, lumbering slowly down the street in Alex's direction. He focuses the binoculars on the front license plate, and then scans for occupants.

"Massachusetts," he mumbles.

He sees a man in the driving and a woman in the front passenger seat. They are both scan the houses to each side of the mini-van while talking to each other. The car edges past Todd's house, and then the Andersons', almost stopping in front of the Walkers'. *Wonder what they saw there?* Just before the minivan reaches the Fletchers' house, Alex puts the binoculars down to scan the vehicle with unaided eyes. He confirms two adults in front, and possibly one more adult in the second row. He also catches the silhouette of a smaller person in the driver's side second row seat as the car passes directly in front of his window.

"Three adult, one pre-teen," he writes.

The minivan was in good shape, and through the binoculars, the man and woman looked normal. No different than anyone else on the block. The three other vehicles looked a bit sketchier, and the people in the cars gave Alex an uneasy feeling. Certainly not people he'd ever expect to see driving around their neighborhood, or any of the other neighborhoods around Durham Road.

Short of using force, he doesn't see how they can stop these people from occupying the empty houses on the block. If it's inevitable, maybe they could at least decide who stays in the houses. Maybe flag down the normal looking ones, and tell them which houses are empty. He thinks about the four car loads of people he's seen so far, and who he'd choose. He decides to scrap this new idea for now.

∎

So far, none of the cars have stopped on their block. He expected most cars to make a few passes, and then disgorge their inhabitants onto the sidewalks for some door to door action, but he hasn't seen any "feet on the ground" yet. He's not looking forward to this, and he hasn't really come up with a plan to handle the inevitable summons. Even with his coldest, iciest frame of mind, he can't bear the thought of opening his door to a family with kids, and then telling them to beat it out of the neighborhood. Even thinking about it makes him cringe.

As he stares pointlessly at the rear gate of yet another minivan, he detects motion in his peripheral vision to the left. He shifts his gaze and sees a light blue sedan approach the fork at the top of the street, and turn left toward an inevitable encounter with the minivan. Alex wonders if there is any informal nomadic etiquette already established between all of these travelers. *Probably not. And as this storm closes in, any etiquette will be out the window.*

As he waits for the car to appear to the right, his thoughts drift to yesterday's Thanksgiving Day meal. They had both completely forgotten about Thanksgiving until Wednesday night, after they had settled into bed for the night. Alex had just returned the bedroom thermostat to sixty two degrees, from the sixty five degrees mark, and was preparing himself to endure some guaranteed harassment from Kate, when the local news channel aired a story about how families plan to celebrate Thanksgiving.

They suffered through one progressively depressing interview after another. First at the Preble Street homeless shelter, where surprisingly there was still food to distribute.

Then, they entered the home of a large family that had lost two of five children to the flu, and proceeded to interview the entire family right before their meal. Alex didn't hear a word they had to say. He blocked it out the best he could, but he couldn't stop staring at the table.

He saw some sort of casserole, baked in a white corning ware dish, bread, and two or three dishes filled with an enormous amount of what he assumed had to be canned vegetables. At least two cans each. Judging by the modest apartment, it had to represent a sizable portion of their food supply.

The mother of the house told the reporters that they had used up most of their stored food supply for the meal. She said they didn't want the kids to be hungry on Thanksgiving, and that they would all eat a good meal and pray for a quick end to the entire world's suffering. Alex remembers thinking that only a stray comet could provide a quick end to the world's suffering at this point.

He figured that most people would find her decision to celebrate with a gratuitous meal as inspirational, but to Alex, it signified a complete surrender. They were giving up. Going out with a bang. He felt sorry for the kids. Sorry that their parents had given up on them. Or did they? Alex knows he'll never understand their situation.

Just when he thought it couldn't get any worse, the segment ended with a family that didn't have any food for Thanksgiving, and didn't know where they would get their next meal. Of course, there were children involved, and he kept expecting the Channel 6 news crew to provide them with a gift basket, or something. Anything really, to thank them for depressing everyone, but there was nothing for the family. Just a few awkward questions for a lethargic, nearly catatonic nuclear family of four.

Alex didn't say anything to Kate when he crawled into bed. He had watched the entire segment standing up. He had been too mesmerized by the TV to move. Kate didn't say a word either. She just hit the off button on the remote, and turned onto her left side. Alex slid under the covers and snuggled in closely, kissing her softly on her neck. She sobbed for a few minutes, and then announced that they would be having a nice meal for Thanksgiving. He agreed and kissed her again, telling her how much he loved her.

The meal itself was great. Even without a proper main course, they worked from noon until nearly two to prepare the meal, which consisted of several dishes. The meal's theme materialized mid-morning as "everyone's favorite side dishes," and they ate with ceremony on good china in the formal dining room. They grew more self-conscious as the sun faded, and thin cloth curtains grew more and more transparent.

Halfway through dinner, and most of the way through a bottle of Cabernet, Alex got up and ran upstairs without saying a word. He returned with a spare dark blue comforter from the kid's bathroom closet, and wedged the edges of the comforter into the curtain rod without saying a word. Lying in bed that night they both agreed not to watch the news. Neither one of them needed to feel any guiltier about their huge meal.

Alex snaps out of the reverie when the blue sedan pops into view around Charlie's house. He lifts the binoculars and scans the license plate. 'Beat up blue Honda, Mass' he scribbles. "5 poss 6 occup," he adds after scanning the windows. *Jam packed. I hope they don't stop here. They don't look right.*

The car crawls past the Fletchers' house, and Alex is spooked by the look on driver's face, which nearly fills his view through the binoculars. *Sheer desperation.* Alex drops the binoculars to his side and continues to watch the car as it moves down the street, back toward the entrance to Durham Road. 'Poss danger,' he writes next. *They all pose a danger. I don't want any of them on the block. Maybe I need a sign out front or something.*

Alex wishes he had a cup of coffee. He fully intended on making some when he walked downstairs, but the first car of the morning caught his eye, and he raced to grab the binoculars to take a look. He's been standing here ever since. He decides that if he wants coffee or breakfast within the next two hours, he'll have to take a break from watching the street. Kate's wake up time has slowly drifted more toward ten or ten-thirty, and they were lucky to see the kids before eleven or eleven-thirty. Alex could barely drag himself out of bed before eight, especially since he had all day to do nothing.

Cook simple meals, workout, read, check the internet or email, watch some news, scan the neighborhood, watch a movie with the family, play some video games, nap, stand on the deck for some fresh air, check the garage, calculate how long their supplies could last, talk about the same stuff over and over again with Kate. He had an infinite number of choices, most of them padding to get him through to the next night, where he could fall asleep again holding Kate, and wake up to repeat the process.

Boring, but with a key purpose hidden away under thick layers of apathy. Survival. And the key to their survival would be to never let those layers permanently dull their senses. Alex knows from experience that dullness lead to carelessness. And he's seen carelessness kill more people than he'd ever care to admit.

Alex shakes himself out of this existential drift. These mental strolls have almost completely replaced his flash backs, and he often finds himself attached to a string of thoughts, staring blankly ahead, seeing nothing, and barely hearing anything. Alex figures they're a product of his boredom, but he doesn't welcome the change. His flashbacks were infrequent, mostly at night during dreams. This new phenomena occurs more frequently, too frequently for his comfort.

His eyes squint as the rust spotted Honda turns right at the fork and does not leave the neighborhood. The car makes one more turn through the neighborhood and leaves. Alex waits a few minute and takes a break to make coffee and reheat Thanksgiving leftovers. He anticipates a long morning.

■

The doorbell rings for the eighth time, and Alex can barely stand it. *What the fuck is wrong with these people!*

He peaks through the slats of the plantation shutters. After the first group started walking through the neighborhood, Alex ensured that all ground level shades or shutters were put to good use. For the first time in four years, he was happy that Kate had insisted on putting curtains over the small windows on each side of the front door. Alex even moved the blue comforter in the dining room over to the sliding glass doors, and nailed it in place to cover the wide glass opening. The doorbell rings again, and Alex feels himself start to shake. *I'm gonna throttle this asshole.*

None of the previous three groups rang the doorbell more than four times before moving on, and Alex had felt a small wave of relief wash over him as the groups moved from smartly from house to house. The wave quickly recedes into a massive sea of gloom as he watches a rusted, 80's vintage, wood paneled station wagon stop in front of the Perry's house.

The driver of the car, a rough looking, no necked scruff, walks around to the rear passenger door and yanks a young girl out of the back seat. The girl, dressed in a light purple jacket more suitable for early fall, nearly falls onto her knees, and starts to pull away to get back into the car. Without taking his eyes off the Perry's house, the man nearly pulls her emaciated arm out of its socket, and forces her to walk compliantly with him to the Perry's, where they spend several minutes.

Alex can't see the interaction on Todd's mudroom stoop, but he smugly muses over how this idiot picked the worst starting point in the neighborhood. Alex's smug look fades as the skuzzy looking child abuser appears walking through the Andersons' yard, picking up speed as he heads in his direction. The smug look morphs into a painful grimace, as Alex come to understand why the guy didn't stop at the Walkers' either. *Todd sent them here.*

The doorbell sounds again, but this time it's a triple tap, signally clearly to Alex, that he's not the only one losing his patience with the situation. *He can ring the doorbell all day.* Just then, he hears Kate from the top of the stairs.

"Jesus Christ, what is going on?" she yells.

Alex hops up from his crouched position and walks swiftly through the doorway leading to the foyer, and starts up the stairs. He sees Kate at the top in a thick white bathrobe, her wet hair spilling over the shoulders.

Alex cuts her off with a wave of his hands and points at the door. Through the white curtains, he can see that the man outside is trying to peer through any possible opening in the curtains. Kate is startled by a sudden banging on the door. Alex walks up the stairs to her.

"He's been at it for a while. I saw him come straight here from Todd's house," he says.

"That asshole," she whispers, forcibly shaking her head.

"Yeah. Who knows what he's telling them, but judging from this guy's persistence, it isn't good," he says.

The doorbell rings repeatedly.

"Hon, you're gonna have to do something, or say something. We need a better plan than ignoring the doorbell," she says.

"I know," he says, with no clear plan forming.

"Just get rid of him. What if he thinks we're not home, and tries to break in later tonight?" she says.

"I'm pretty sure he knows we're home. Don't worry, I'll take care of it. I'll be right back," he says and turns around to go downstairs.

Alex walks down the stairs and turns toward the kitchen. He plans to walk out of the mudroom door and address them from a distance. He reaches behind the small of his back and pats the USP pistol tucked snugly into his blue jeans. He pulls down on the back of his hunter green fleece to make sure the gun is concealed. He opens the inner mudroom door slowly and then the storm door. He steps outside and eases the storm door shut without making a sound. He can hear the doorbell continue to ring on the inside. He peeks around the corner, and is immediately spotted by the younger girl.

"Daddy, over there," she yells excitedly.

The man lets go of the girl and jumps off the granite steps into a sea of evergreen bushes.

"Stop right there," Alex barks, still keeping most of his body behind the cover of the house.

The man falters as he struggles to push through the evergreens, but ultimately ignores Alex's warning. His face is pulses red, and Alex sees a dangerous combination of persistence and vacancy in his bloodshot light blue eyes.

"Shit," Alex mumbles, and steps back to retreat inside the house.

The man hurls himself around the corner, just as Alex finishes locking the storm door. Alex takes a few steps back into the mudroom, ready to shut the inner door if the guy tries to take down the storm door. If it goes any further than that, Alex resolves to shoot the man dead. *I'll leave the body there too, as a deterrent. Maybe I'll move it to the bottom of the driveway, with a sign.*

While he processes this internal dialogue, the man puts one hand on the door handle and the other on the glass, and Alex is suddenly sure that he'll have to shoot the man. So sure that his right hand moves behind his back to clear the shirt from the top of his pistol. Alex notes the worn Red Sox logo on the front of the man's sweatshirt, which is now pressed against his storm door.

"Whoa! Red Sox! Take it easy! And get away from the door before you get hurt!" he says.

As if suddenly possessed by a little logic and reason, the man takes his hands off the door and back up a few steps, leaving a fresh fog mark from his breath on the storm door glass.

"Why the fuck didn't you answer the door? I've been out here half the morning ringing that god damn doorbell. What's the fuck's the matter with you," he yells out in a thick Boston accent.

"I just woke up thanks to you. You need to move on. There's nothing in this neighborhood for you," says Alex forcefully.

"Bullshit you just woke up. I saw you moving around in there from the start, and I know you got a ton of food and supplies. Your friend down the street said you've been handing out food," he says, putting both hands on his hips and staring intensely at Alex.

I want to shoot him and leave him there for the others. He shakes the thought, and moves his hand away from the gun. He doesn't want to kill this man, at least not yet, though everything is still moving in that direction.

The man's daughter comes around the corner, and Alex finds himself once again fighting the urge to shoot the man dead on the mudroom stoop. The girl's hair is matted and her face is filthy. , but he can't be certain. Stark signs of neglect and abuse make it difficult to determine her age, though Alex guesses she is no older than Emily. Dark circles ring her unfocused blue eyes, frighteningly contrasted by bright red rims. Alex's eyes are immediately drawn away to a large bruise on her right cheek, and then another on her neck.

"Stay the fuck out of the way Skyler," he says, and steps off the stoop to reach out and grab her.

He misses, and Skyler retreats behind the front corner of the house. Not wanting to lose ground, he steps back on the stoop under Alex's murderous gaze.

"There's nothing for you here. You need to leave now," says Alex, shifting his gaze between the two of them, and becoming more enraged every time he sees her condition.

"Well, I'm not going anywhere until you dig around..."

"You'll be leaving right now," Alex yells in a controlled, forceful way.

The man is surprised by Alex's sudden change, and a flash of genuine concern washes over his face. He pauses and backs up a few steps without looking behind him. One more step and he'll toppled off the stoop. Alex continues to stare at him with intense hatred. After a few seconds, the man turns around and steps off the porch.

"Let's go you little bitch," he roars at the girl.

The man turns around and grins, flashing crooked, nicotine stained teeth.

"Well, maybe we'll be seeing more of each other. We could be neighbors soon," he says with a jack-assed smile, as he looks around the neighborhood.

The man turns around to leave, and Alex opens the storm door.

"Hey Red Sox!" Alex says, and lowers his voice when the man turns around.

"If I see you around this house again, I'll blow your fucking brains out of your head. Understand? The same deal goes for my friends' houses," says Alex.

"Which ones are those?" the man says snidely.

"You won't know until your brains hit the ground," Alex says, and closes the storm door.

Alex shapes his fingers like a gun and points them at the man. "Bang," he mouths silently, while the mock pistol in his hand recoils. The man's face goes slack, and Alex smiles. *What am I nuts?* Alex continues to grin as the man grabs his daughter and hurries her back to the station wagon. They pile back in and the car lurches forward, picking up speed and passing the Fletchers'. Alex traces its progress around the block and watches as it leaves the neighborhood. He closes the door and goes back to his post in the family room.

As soon as he slides the shutters open a few inches, he sees two more cars enter the neighborhood. He doesn't recognize either of them.

Newbies. Numbers twenty-six and twenty-seven. He watches as they follow each other around to the other side of Durham Road, then emerge from beyond the Thorntons'. One of the cars, a black Suburban, comes to a halt in front of the McCarthys' house, and the other, a dark blue domestic sedan, keeps cruising down the street, and eventually stopping in front of the Fullers house up near the turn. *I better start working on a sign for the front yard.*

■

Alex stands in the far left corner of his front yard with a large rubber mallet in his left hand and a makeshift sign in the other. His AR-15 is slung across his back with the barrel pointing toward the ground. His favorite blue winter coat fights against the bitter wind that followed the clouds. He feels the wind burn against his cheeks and ears, and wishes he had brought a hat. *I won't be out here very long.*

Right after Red Sox left, he proceeded to the garage to construct three semi-sturdy signs to post in the front yard. One for each end of the sidewalk, and one to be placed in a conspicuous location near the entrance to the driveway, in case these people decide to start driving their cars from house to house. Given the frigid temperatures and exacerbating wind, he's not sure why any of them would want to walk around anyway. *Maybe to save gas?* He dismisses this idea just as quickly. Most of the cars parked on the street have been left running.

The Carters' house received a lot of traffic for some reason, and he's seen at least two groups walk around to the back of the house, probably trying to confirm that it's empty. *Won't be long until some tries to break in.*

Alex stares at the sign in his left hand, which looks like a piece of junk. Like the kind of sign you'd expect to find marking the entrance to the Little Rascals hideout. Alex wasn't known for carpentry detail work, or any woodwork for that matter, and he didn't feel like trying to get fancy on this job. He wasn't even sure he could pound the stakes into the ground. It was late November and the ground felt pretty damn solid under his feet.

He selects a spot right next to the sidewalk, on the border between Ed's lot and his own. He tries to work the stake into the frozen ground, which initially resists. He manages to twist it in a little, and then straightens the sign for the mallet. He brings the mallet down on the top of the stake, and it drives an inch into the hard ground. *Maybe it's not as frozen as I thought.* He continues to slowly inch the sign into the ground until it feels solidly imbedded. *This ain't going anywhere.* He looks up to see Ed walking down the driveway from his house.

"What's up man? It's been a few days," says Ed.

"I was enjoying the peace and quiet until all of this shit started," says Alex.

"Yeah, the door's been ringing all morning. We've been ignoring it. Kept a few lights on inside so they know we're home. Nothing crazy yet," he says, folding his arms around his chest.

"We've been doing the same, but I had one guy about forty minutes ago that wouldn't give up. I saw him come straight from Todd's. Guy said that Todd told him I had plenty of food to hand out…or something like that," says Alex, shaking his head and glaring down the street at Todd's house.

"I figured some signs might help," says Alex, demonstrating the sturdiness of the sign with another light shake.

"The kids help you with those? What does it say? Keep away?" he says, staring at the other two rickety signs, then up at Alex with a thin smile.

"They'll do the job jackass."

"At least you have signs. I should probably put something together," says Ed, shivering again.

"Yeah, let me know when you're ready to post them, so I can come out and take a look at your expert handi-craft. I have some tools you can borrow," says Alex.

"Tools? Jesus Christ, I could use my teeth and come up with something better than that," he says, and Alex breaks into an outright laugh.

"I mean, is that magic marker, or crayon? I'm surprised you didn't use finger paints," he says, and Alex's laughter intensifies.

"That's it man. That's it. You're killing me," Alex barely says through continuous laughter.

As they finish laughing, a black SAAB sedan passes the Lewis's house, quickly moving down the street toward them.

"This is probably the wrong day to be outside yucking it up," says Alex.

"You better hope they have kids to decipher your sesame street project," says Ed, and Alex stifles another laugh.

"Knock it off man. Let me do the talking if they stop," says Alex, barely composing himself.

A steely grimace washes over Alex's face.

"Jesus, you changed your face like a schizophrenic," comments Ed between his teeth.

"You're killing me...Connecticut plates," Alex whispers back, as the sedan pulls up to the two of them.

Alex drops the rubber mallet on the ground, and reaches back to shift his rifle into a position that he can quickly transition to the offensive if necessary. He doesn't plan to take any chances. Especially after Red Sox. Through the windows he sees a younger couple.

"Yuppies?" he whispers to Ed.

"That's probably what they're thinking about us," he mouths back, as the passenger window rolls down.

An attractive, angular faced woman with dark brown hair appears from behind the window. At first glance, Alex can tell she is wearing makeup, which surprises him, given the likelihood that they were pretty far away from their starting point. She doesn't exhibit any of the signs of malnutrition or exhaustion that he's seen on most of the refugees' faces over the course of the morning. To Alex, she looks to be in better shape than most of his neighbors.

Alex peers in further, and sees a man with medium length jet black hair, olive complexion wearing thin black rimmed glasses. The woman suddenly puts her right arm over the edge of the open window, and Alex tightens. His left hand reacts by swiftly moving across his stomach to grab the hand guard of the rifle, and if necessary, pull it forward into a firing position.

"Sorry. Sorry. I didn't mean to...sorry," she says, and puts her hand back in the car.

"It's fine. Everyone's just a little jumpy around here," says Alex, easing his hand back to his side.

"We're really sorry to ask you this, but we're looking for a place to stay. We left the Hartford area late last night, and took back roads all night to get up here. It's a disaster down there, pretty much everywhere further south. I hate to do this. I'm sure you've been dealing with this for days, but we're just looking for a place that's safe..."

"I wouldn't exactly call this neighborhood safe," says Alex, keeping a completely neutral look on his face.

"Maybe we should move on honey," says the driver.

"Did you two bring any food?" says Alex.

"Yeah, honey, I think we better move on," he says, panicky, and starting to fumble with the gear shift.

"We're not going to take your food. I just want you to know that the stores have been empty for quite a while, and the spirit of sharing has long since left the neighborhood. Maine is not the Shangri-la everyone seems to be expecting," says Alex.

"What did you guys see on the way up here?" asks Ed.

The guy leans across the center console of the SAAB, suddenly enthusiastic.

"It was scary. People out of control everywhere. We tried to avoid bigger towns, but couldn't avoid all of them. Some fires. People out on the streets. We left at midnight, figuring the streets would be clear, but they weren't. It's like another fucking world," he says.

"How did you guys get across the state border? We heard that the bridges from Portsmouth might be barricaded," says Alex, finding himself more at ease with this couple.

"We heard the same rumors on the internet, so we eventually caught up with the ninety-three, and took that north, then east on side roads across the border, trying to avoid any towns. We eventually made our way to the twenty-five and then here. We rented a place down in Higgins Beach last year. We remembered this area. This looks a lot like our neighborhood..." she trails off.

"Our neighborhood was a little too close to Hartford, and a little too well off, if you know what I mean? We had to leave in a hurry when the looting started, because it sure wasn't confined to the business districts like the news might have you thinking. They were starting to ransack the suburbs. Sorry to bother you guys, looks like this place is wrapped up pretty tight," he says, and starts to shift the car out of neutral.

"Hold on. It sounds like you brought food with you, right?" says Alex.

The woman hesitates to answer, and looks at the driver, who also looks skeptical about answering the question.

"Really, we're not planning on taking your food. I'm just trying to figure out if you're gonna become a problem if you stay here. We've had some problems, and most of them have been related to the food shortage," says Alex.

Ed looks at him approvingly.

"What have the other problems been related to?" asks the driver.

"Medical supplies. Most of the houses on the block have been hit with the flu. There have been some deaths. I'm not sure how many," says Alex.

"Well, we have both. My husband is a surgeon..."

"I wouldn't exactly say I'm a surgeon. One year into a general surgery fellowship..."

"You're a surgeon. Anyway, he managed to stockpile some anti-virals and other medical supplies when this whole thing started. We both collected groceries while the stores still had food. We're set for now. We just need somewhere safe to stay until things cool down enough to head back to Connecticut," she says, her voice cracking.

She looks like she's about to break down.

"So, first things first. I'm not going to point, because everyone's watching everyone around here. If you look down the road toward the right, two houses past mine, you'll see a yellow house, with blue doors. That's the Carters' house, and they vanished a few weeks ago, maybe earlier. Nobody really knows where they went, but I haven't seen any signs of anyone living there, and I keep a pretty tight eye on the houses in the immediate vicinity. You should go around to the garage, and bust a window to open the door. Then pray that the door from the garage into the house isn't locked. If it is, you might have to force your way in. Make sure to patch up the window with something. Cardboard, wood, anything," says Alex.

"Thank you so much. I really can't tell you how much this means to us," the woman says.

Ed leans toward the car and peers into the back seat, his eye caught by something. Alex sees this and feels his body start to tense.

"Hey, looks like they have a golden puppy stuffed back there between the boxes," says Ed, easing back from the car with a smile.

"Yeah, her name is Karma. She's really friendly. You guys can go ahead and open the back door and…"

"Not a good idea out here. Anyway, the Carters' house has seen a lot of traffic this morning. Some people have gone around back to take a look. If you see any windows broken, or any doors busted, someone might be there already. Drive on back and I'll point you in the direction of another house," he says.

"Also, keep to yourselves, and don't get involved with anyone on the block. Definitely don't mention the fact that you have medical supplies and food, or that you're a doctor. Your neighbors to both sides have been hit with the flu, and some of the neighbors are not very stable at this point. The last thing you want anyone to know, is that you have anti-virals or medication," he says, and the couple nods.

"I can't stress the importance of staying out of sight. Don't answer the door for any of the people you see driving or walking around, and get your car in the garage immediately," says Alex.

"Sounds good. Thank you again. I'm Ben Glassman, and this is my wife Hannah," says the driver.

"Alex and Ed," says Alex.

"I'm Ed," he says dryly.

"And this will probably be the last time we talk until this whole thing blows over. Nothing personal, but we pretty much keep to ourselves. You're on your own when you get into the Carters' house," says Alex.

Hannah looks hurt by his statement, and Alex truly doesn't care. He allowed himself to like them only enough to justify using them as a block for any future interlopers in the neighborhood. He'd much rather have this couple in the Carters' house than Red Sox.

"Thank you again guys. Really, if there's anything I can do for you. If anyone gets hurt, or sick. Really, you uh…you know where find us," says Ben.

"Thank you," says Hannah, and she rolls up her window as the car moves forward and stops one house past the Carters'. *At least they didn't pull right into the driveway. That would have been way too obvious.*

Chapter Thirty-One

Friday, November 30, 2012

Kate sits down at the kitchen table as Alex surveys the remains of yesterday's Thanksgiving Day feast. Barley mixed with dried cranberries and sliced almonds; Green bean and fried onion casserole; Sweet and sour lima beans; Chickpea soup with dried dill; Homemade wheat bread and mashed potatoes with gravy. The only thing missing was the main course.

"What are you thinking about?" she says sitting down.

He pauses and chuckles. The kids start to fill their plates and pass the dishes around. Alex takes the beans from Emily.

"I was thinking about the last time we had Turkey for Thanksgiving," he says, still smiling.

"We've had turkey?" says Ryan.

"Not really, maybe when you were like one or two. Could that be right?" he says.

"No...well...no, I think I was making fish at that point. Maybe at one of our parents' houses? I was well into pushing my meat free agenda on you when Ryan was born, and I know for a fact you haven't eaten meat since you got back from Iraq," she says.

"Daddy ate meat before the war?" says Emily.

"Yes, daddy was a disgusting meat eater at one point," says Kate.

"So were you...at one point," he says.

"Why did you stop after coming back from the war?" says Ryan.

Kate looks at Alex, clearly signaling him to tread carefully.

"Well, let's just say that I saw people eating things over there that really made me think hard about what it means to eat animals," he says, looking to Kate for approval, which he can tell that he just barely won.

"Like what," says Emily.

"I really don't want to think about it sweetie, and neither do you," says Alex, setting down the last dish being rotated.

"Alright, let's all close our eyes and take a moment here," he says.

They all stay silent for several seconds. Emily interrupts the silence.

"But I can't stop thinking about it."

"I know sweetie, but daddy is really bothered by it, so we don't want to upset him. Let's eat everyone." says Kate

"I think I know what happened. Probably the same stuff that's happening in the big cities. They're talking about on the internet No food, and…"

"Ryan," Alex says forcefully, "not another word on the subject. We can talk about this later. Just you and me. But not now. Understand?"

Ryan looks hurt by Alex's sudden reprimand.

"Yes dad," he says, and starts to eat.

"What, like eating other people?" Emily blurts.

"No. No. Nobody's eating other people. That's crazy. I never saw that in Iraq…and that was a really messed up place," says Alex, warning Ryan with his eyes.

"Where do they get these ideas?" says Kate.

"From zombie movies," says Emily.

"I didn't let her watch any of those movies. I haven't seen any myself," Ryan interjects.

"Nobody said you did, but since you brought it up so quickly," says Kate.

"He didn't let me see it, but I snuck upstairs when he was watching one during a sleep over with James and Justin…"

"You freakin tattletale," says Ryan, throwing down his fork onto his plate.

"Easy there Mr. Ryan, I knew you guys were watching that. I crept up the stairs far enough to hear what you guys were watching," says Alex.

"So you knew they were watching rated R movies up there?" says Kate.

"Why am I the one that always ends up in trouble?" says Alex.

"Because you're the adult that is supposed to be making appropriate decisions for our children, and you sanction the watching of zombie movies," she says.

"Well, I didn't really sanction the movies. They didn't know that I knew what they were watching, and if they didn't know, then it's impossible to sanction. Sanctioning is more of an active type thing," Alex says, wondering if that made any sense.

"That didn't even make sense. Anyway, I think it's time that we cut the cable service on the third floor down to basic cable. God knows what they'll be watching and ordering next," she says.

"But mom, that's the only movie we watched that was rated R," says Ryan.

"And that'll be the last. So there's no problem. Just be happy you're still hooked up to Xbox Live. Start eating everyone," she says, ending the argument.

Ryan continues the argument by mumbling between forks full of food.

"You barely watch any TV up there anyway," she adds, feeding back into the argument, "and you'll still have all of the other channels, just no movie channels or OnDemand."

"Pretty much cuts out all of the cool movies…"

"Hey, you can watch all of the movies you want in our room, or down here. Anyway, we'll be lucky to still have cable after this weekend's storm. Did you see the forecast for Sunday?" he says, directly the question to Kate.

"Yeah. They're still calling for an ice storm Sunday morning, followed by a decent snow storm later in the day. I guess we don't have to change the cable right now, but I don't want you watching rated R movies without asking us first. There are some pretty disturbing movies out there," she says.

"Some of his games are pretty disturbing. Like most of the war games," Emily says, and continues eating.

Alex castes Emily a quizzical look and lightly shakes his head in disbelief. To the casual observer, her comment would pass as an innocent remark made by a child incapable of plotting to foment further criticism of her brother. But Alex has closely studied her behavior and tactics over the past few years, and has concluded that his beautiful, sweet, smiling daughter is a highly intelligent, self-aware, and fully competent agitator. Unlike Ryan, she holds back and waits for just the right moment to launch one of her nearly imperceptible time bombs into the fray. Emily averts her dad's gaze, and stares at her plate. He suspects that she is on to him.

"Yeah well, that's another problem…" starts Kate.

"Are you kidding me? Now you're gonna sweat the games I'm playing? Dad thinks they're fine."

"That doesn't mean they're fine for you. Maybe for him, though I'll go to my grave not understanding why a grown man enjoys playing video games," she says.

"They're fun, and it's not real. End of story. I'm on to you little one," he says, and stares at Emily, who continues to deflect his gaze.

"What?" she mumbles and takes a long drink of water.

"How bad do you think the storm will be?" asks Ryan.

"Well, it doesn't look terrible. The ice aspect is the problem. If we get ice and high winds, the whole area could lose power. But for us, it won't really make a difference. We can make our own power with the solar panels…at least enough to keep the lights and heat going. And the TV's . Don't worry, I know what's critical to you guys," he says, and both kids laugh a little.

Alex looks at them as they laugh. *Amazing. Almost thirty days into this, and they don't look any different than they did in the middle of September.* He quickly glances at Kate, and catches her watching both of them. She smiles slightly and Alex knows that she is happy to see them both laughing.

"We really don't have anything to worry about guys. We're going to be fine, and at some point in the spring, or maybe earlier, this whole thing will be over, and we'll all be able to go back to our normal lives. Jobs, sports, friends…and most importantly, school," says Alex dramatically.

"School isn't that bad dad," says Emily.

"Yeah, I'd trade this quarantine for school any day," adds Ryan.

"It takes a pandemic to get my son psyched for school," says Kate.

"I'm not psyched about school mom. Just more psyched than this," Ryan says, and sports a forced smile.

The phone rings, and Alex glances over his shoulder at the receiver on the kitchen island. Calls to the house were pretty rare at this point.

"You should answer that," she says.

Alex gets up from the table and walks over to the phone.

"Ed," he says, and answers the call.

"What's up?" he says, and starts walking toward the mudroom.

"I don't know. I've had my eye on this one car for the past hour or so. Just circling the neighborhood, over and over again. Really slow like the rest of them…"

"They all do that," he says and steps into the library.

"Yeah, but this one stopped in front of the McCarthys' house like thirty minutes ago, and hasn't moved. Nobody got out. It's just sitting there under the street light. I think they're planning to spend the night there," he says.

"That's ridiculous. They're probably going to canvas the neighborhood on foot in a few minutes, or something," says Alex.

"Is everything alright?" calls Kate from the kitchen.

Alex covers the receiver on the phone.

"Yeah. Everything's OK honey. Just talking about a car that's still cruising the neighborhood," he says.

"Sorry. That was Kate," says Alex.

"How's she holding up with all of the visitors?" says Ed.

"Fine. Just a little jumpy having people crawl around the neighborhood. We've had a few groups walk up onto our deck in back and try to peer inside. Not sure how they missed my signs, but who knows if they even speak English. How's Sam doing?"

"Same thing. Nervous about these people. I'm nervous about them too. Sarah Quinn called about an hour ago to talk to Sam. She heard from Jack Bartlett that a family moved into the Cohens' house," he says, and recalls exactly who Ed and Alex guided to the Cohens'.

"The balls on these people. How are the Quinns' doing?" says Alex.

"Not bad given the circumstances. She's not looking forward to losing power. Says if the storm doesn't kill it this weekend, the grid probably won't hold up for another week anyway. Have you heard that too? I saw it on a couple of sites, but I haven't heard word one on the news."

"Which news channel? They're all mostly broadcasting national coverage and federal updates, and I think the feds are trying to keep the national coal reserve numbers under wraps. I've seen estimates that fall in the week to two weeks range. Once the coal reserves at any of the power plants are depleted, say adios to the grid. We'll be lucky to get past this weekend. Did Sarah say anything about the Bartletts?" says Alex.

"Yeah, I guess they're doing OK. Their little girl Grace got hit the worst, but she's doing better. The rest of them didn't hit nearly as bad. Jack didn't get it at all, which is weird," says Ed.

"Who knows. He might still come down with it. One of Ryan's friends…his family got the same thing. Mild cases. Lucky if you ask me, but all well within the realm of statistical probability I suppose," says Alex.

"Yeah, they're pretty sure about the case fatality rate at this point. Right around twenty percent, with a clinical attack rate of forty percent or so. Odds are definitely in your favor if you get this thing," says Ed.

"I'm still not rushing out to get it," says Alex.

"Neither am I."

Alex hears what sounds like a solitary firecracker explode.

"Did you hear that?" says Alex, rushing out of the den into the kitchen.

"What was that?" asks Kate sharply from the dining room.

Alex walks swiftly back into the kitchen, and tries to conceal his panic. *Not a firecracker, that's for sure.*

"Honey, why don't you take the kids down into the basement for a few minutes. Follow you mom guys. Ed? Did you hear that?" he repeats, and moves around the house shutting off lights.

"Hold on. Look at that. Fucker just shot the light out," whispers Ed.

Alex hears Ed tell his own family to get into the basement. Kate and the kids disappear down the stairs, with Kate last. She leaves the door open and Alex walks to the head of the stairs.

"Just in case someone is shooting. I think everything is fine," he says to her.

She nods and turns the corner with the kids.

"Ed. Did you say someone shot out the street light?"

"Yeah. I ran to one of the windows and saw someone getting back into the car that's parked under the streetlight. The light is out now. I thought the guy had a gun, but I can't be sure," he says.

"Are you sure the light was on before?" says Alex.

"Yeah, I was wondering why he would park under that street light," says Ed.

"How many people are in the car. Were you using binoculars?" says Alex.

"Yeah, I have a small bird watching pair. I couldn't see how many people were in the car," he says.

"But when he opened the door and the lights went on, could you see other people?"

"The lights didn't go on. It's pitch black over in that corner," says Ed.

"Are you sure the lights didn't go on? What kind of car is it?" says Alex, heading upstairs with his own binoculars.

"I'm sure the lights didn't go on. It looks like a gray or maybe blue Volvo station wagon. One of the new ones. I couldn't see the guy very well in the dark, but it looked like he was carrying something. Why would he park under a light and then shoot it out?" he says.

Alex continues up the stairs and turns left to the master bedroom.

"Hold on," he says, as he walks across the bedroom to one of the northeast windows facing the Thompsons' house. He chooses the one closest to the street, and opens the shade an inch. He peers through and has an unobstructed view of the car. Even in the dark, he can tell that the car is parked on the wrong side of the road, facing his own house. *Interesting.* He studies the car for a few seconds and closes his eyes to create a mental map.

"You still there? This is freaking my wife out," says Ed.

"Yeah I'm here. I have eyes on the vehicle…"

"Eyes what?" he says.

"Eyes on the vehicle. Don't you watch any military or police movies? I'm watching the vehicle. My eyes are on the vehicle."

"Why can't you guys just talk like normal people and just say I'm watching the vehicle," says Ed.

"Because it doesn't sound as cool. Anyway, a couple of things disturb me here…"

"Like the gun?"

"If he has a gun. But yes, that's number one on my list," says Alex.

"Let's assume he has a gun," says Ed.

"I'm with you on that. But here's what's really creeping me out about this guy. He turned off the internal lights on purpose. He thought that one out. He knew that if he shot out the light, someone might take a look, and he didn't want them to see into the car when he hopped back in. I'm not sure I would have thought of that. This guy's either really smart, or he has some experience not wanting to be identified at night. Both scenarios bother me…"

"The last one worries me the most," says Ed.

"Yeah, it's not good news. He also picked a good spot to watch over half of the neighborhood. Notice he's parked on the wrong side of the road to be facing this way. But parked over there, he can see all the way down our road, and all the way to the Murrays'. Plus, he's far enough back in the neighborhood to avoid any attention from Harrison Road. I think this guy has some experience with this kind of activity. Shooting the light out leads me to think that this guy doesn't give a shit. We're looking at a bad combination of traits my friend," says Alex.

"No kidding. How long until he figures out that the Murrays' house is unoccupied? It's the only one left," says Ed.

"Not long. The signs I put up won't deter him if the lights don't go off. I should have put that doctor and his wife in the Murrays'," says Alex.

"We got some decent people in here," says Ed.

Alex considers his comment. They did the best they could with the choices they had. The Carters' house was filled first, though in retrospect, he would have been better off putting that couple in the Murrays' house. The Fullers' house went to a family from Connecticut driving a BMW sport utility vehicle, and the Cohens' to a family with kids, from somewhere just west of Boston. The parents looked preppy and drove an Audi station wagon. Alex and Ed didn't ask them many questions, just directed them to the Cohens' house. At that point, the sun was setting, so they both gave up their valet duties for the night, leaving the Murrays' house unfilled. Alex doesn't recall seeing the Volvo station wagon during daylight hours.

"Yeah. I just think it might have been a mistake not to fill all of the houses. There were some cars that didn't look too bad. Fuck. I'm gonna have to sneak out tonight and turn off the lights inside the Murrays'," he says.

"Do you really think it's necessary?" says Ed.

"I have a bad feeling about that car. I think I might have to hang out in the house for a few hours, and progressively turn the lights off like a family retiring for the night," says Alex.

"And leave your family alone with those nutbags camped out on the street? I wouldn't. We might be totally over thinking this. They might be just fine. Maybe it's just someone like you, smart and just covering all the angles. You know, keeping their car in a safe spot," he says.

"Where do you feel the safest at night? Under lights or in the pitch black?" says Alex.

"Uhh. I guess in the light, but I don't know..."

"Your first instinct is right. We've been conditioned since birth to fear the dark. Most people would feel safer in the light, unless they've been reconditioned, which takes time and experience using the dark to your advantage. Trust me, if this guy gets into the Murrays' house, or any house, we're going to have a serious problem on the block," says Alex.

"Do you think we could get them to leave?" says Ed.

"I don't know. But I do know that approaching that car in the dark is probably not a very good idea," says Alex.

"And leaving your own house is an even worse idea Alex," replies Ed.

"If I don't make it look like someone's in the Murrays' house, we might as well start baking cookies for their welcome party," says Alex.

"How many lights did you turn in the Murrays' house?" says Ed.

Alex shifts knees, keeping his binoculars trained on the car.

"A few on each floor. Enough to fit in with the rest of the occupied houses," says Alex.

"I wouldn't leave the house. Can you see anything with your night vision?" says Ed.

"Hey hon. Can we come up now?" yells Kate from downstairs.

"Hold on Ed."

"Yeah. I think it's fine. Let's keep everyone on the second floor for now. In their rooms away from the front windows please," he yells back.

"Sorry about that. Night vision. Hold on. Let me grab them," says Alex.

Alex takes a few steps over to his nightstand, and opens the top drawer. He moves the empty black nylon pistol holster out of the way, and grabs a stubby black night vision scope. He takes it back to the window, unscrews the lens cap and activates the 4X scope. *Let's see.* He hears Kate and the kids come up the stairs talking.

"**You still there?**" says Alex.

"**Yep?**" replies Ed.

"Alright. I can see the front seat. One man...or woman in the driver's seat," says Alex.

"You can't tell?" says Ed.

"This is a cheap Russian knock-off of a field scope. 4X magnification. You get what you get with these. Anyway...I can't see into the back seat due to the downward angle. Maybe if I move down..."

"Only one in the front?" says Ed.

"Hold on," Alex says, and squints through the eyepiece, searching the green image. *He's right. No, it's this piece of junk night vision. There's gotta...*

"Hold on," he says again.

"Do you see anyone else in the front seat?" says Ed.

Alex suddenly feels the weight of the HK USP tucked into the back of his jean. He craves heavier artillery.

"No," he whispers flatly. *Someone else is out there.*

Alex's phone handset suddenly glows orange and illuminates the side of his face. He pulls the phone away from his ear, and the phone's LCD bathes the front corner of the bedroom in a deep orange glow. *Shit.* Alex slams the phone down to the floor, face down. He puts the scope on the window shelf, and lies down to check the caller ID on the phone. *Charlie.* He hears Ed through the phone and puts the phone back to his ear.

"Charlie's on the other line. I'll call you right back," says Alex.

"OK," Ed says, and the call is disconnected.

Alex switches over to Charlie.

"Hey Charlie. You watching too?" says Alex.

"Did you see him shoot it out?" says Charlie.

"No, but Ed saw him get back into his car immediately after he heard the shot. Thought he saw a rifle in the guy's hands," says Alex.

"I think I spotted someone creeping around the Murrays' house. Might be the guy missing from the front passenger seat of the car. Car's jam packed with people, except the front. One of them is out scoping houses. If I see a gun on him. He's dead. I should take out the guy in the front seat of the car right now," says Charlie.

"Don't go shooting into the car. Never know who you might hit. Bullets bounce around," says Alex.

"Not when I'm using a 10X night vision scope on my Remington Milspec. The only thing that'll bounce is his head," says Charlie.

"Please don't shoot into the car," says Alex.

"I'm not gonna shoot into the car...unless I have to," says Charlie.

"What can you see in the car?" says Alex.

"I see...in the driver's seat, one male with what looks like hair coming more than half-way down his neck. He's either a hippie or that's a mullet. My guess is mullet. In the back seat, I counted four people. One more adult male, but I can't see him very well. He's on the far side from me. In the middle are two kids. I can't tell the ages, but I'd guess under ten. One boy and one girl. And...one female adult in the rear passenger side seat. This one talks to the driver a lot. Back and forth between the two of them. There's a third row of seats, and I can see one more kid. Looks like a young boy...elementary school age maybe. And...another adult female. Looks like the woman is holding something. Could be a baby...but it looks like something bigger. Like a young toddler aged kid. I can't tell very well. The back row seats are blocking my view."

"Are you pointing your rifle at them?" says Alex.

"Yeah. Linda's got the spotting scope looking around for the other one," he says.

"Just be careful and keep the safety on. You don't want to accidentally shoot any kids," says Alex.

"This gun doesn't go off by accident. Have you ever seen the 5R Milspec? It's modeled after the M24 sniper rifle used by the Marine Corps. Beautiful weapon. Hard to get your hands on one. I could find you one if you wanted. Mine's fitted to shoot 300's instead of the standard .308. I use it deer hunting. Unbelievable accuracy. It's a Remington 700 on steroids," says Charlie.

"Those are pretty nice weapons...but I think the Marine Corps sniper rifle is called the M40-A3. They're all modified versions of the 700, but the Marine version is hand crafted and built in Quantico. Either way, you have a nice piece of equipment there," says Alex. *How many rifles does this guy have?*

"That's right. The Army uses the 24…Hold on a second," Charlie says, and Alex can hear some yelling in the background at Charlie's house.

"Linda just saw a guy dodge between the Hayes' and Coopers' house," says Charlie.

Alex hears the floor creak inside the bedroom and turns around briefly to see Kate standing in front of the closets.

"What's going on out there," she whispers.

"Not now. Hold on," he says and turns back to look through the night vision scope.

He directs the scope at the opening between Coopers' house and the McCarthys'. He figures this is the closest and darkest approach to the car.

"Charlie. I'm watching the opening between the Coopers' and McCarthys'. You keep a tight watch on the car," says Alex.

"Roger," says Charlie.

Alex feels his chest tighten, and his pulse quicken. Within the span of a few seconds, a thin film of moisture starts to form on his face. *There he is.*

"Got him. Coming between the Coopers' and McCarthys'. Moving right toward the car," says Alex.

His senses are acutely focused on the scene developing through the scope, distracted only momentarily by Kate kneeling down next to him. Alex watches the man as he jogs to the driver side of the car and kneels down next to the window. The driver motions angrily for the man to get into the car, and the man with the hat quickly crosses in front of the Volvo and enters the front passenger side door. *Ed's right. No light.*

"They have the interior lights turned off. Sneaky fuckers," Charlie mutters into the phone.

"Yeah. This crew worries me," says Alex.

He watches as the man with the hat starts to point with his left hand, in the direction of the Murrays' house. The driver immediately pushes the man's arm down, and nods toward Alex's house, talking at the same time. *He saw the phone. This guy knows what he's doing. I wonder if Charlie would really be willing to take them out.*

"I think you've been made buddy," says Charlie.

"Yeah. My phone lit up when you called. Nice orange beacon for him. Hey, can you see the license plate?" says Alex.

"Already checked it out. Maine for sure. Hold on…looks like they're leaving."

Alex's right eye is blinded by a green flash in his scope, as the Volvo's headlights bath the street with light. He closes the eye and puts the scope on the window sill next to his binoculars.

"I'll let you know where they go," says Alex.

"Good, because I can't see out of my right eye," says Charlie.

"Me either," says Alex.

The Volvo's headlights start to move toward Alex's house. Alex moves to a front window and watches as the car moves slowly past his house, and heads down the street toward the Perry's. Alex expects the car to continue around the loop to the Murrays', and is surprised when the car turns toward the neighborhood exit.

"Huh. He's headed back out onto Harrison Road," says Alex.

"Who?" says Kate.

"Maybe he didn't like the idea that some of the neighbors are watching him," says Charlie.

"I don't know. He might be driving over to Everett Road to park and walk his family through the backyards over to the Murrays'. Or, he might just come back at three in the morning. Either way. I expect to have new neighbors in the morning," he says.

"I hope not. They look like bad news. Car's jammed full of people, but that's about it. I didn't see any supplies, or anything that even looked like a bag," says Charlie.

"Do you think it's strange that the car had Maine plates?" says Alex.

"I don't know. Maybe their house got destroyed, or burned. Who knows. Maybe they stole the car a bit further south. They didn't look like Volvo station wagon types," says Charlie.

"That's what I was thinking," says Alex.

"Well, I'll keep an eye on the Murrays' tonight. See if anyone shows up. I'll give you a ring if I see anything," says Charlie.

"Right. I'll probably be up all night too watching for those yahoos too," says Alex.

"I see them running around at night again, and I might make them one fewer," says Charlie.

"I wish I could say that I didn't like the sound of that…have a good night Charlie," he says.

"You too Alex."

Alex disconnects the call and puts the phone back in its receiver.

"What was going on out there?" asks Kate.

Alex jumps onto the bed and lies down. Kate follows him and they both lie staring at the ceiling, side by side, arms hooked together.

"A Volvo station wagon parked under the light, and the driver shot the light out..."

"Jesus," she whispers.

"And Charlie saw a guy snooping around the Murrays'. We both saw this guy emerge from the McCarthys' backyard and get in the car. Then they left. I'm pretty sure they're coming back for the Murrays' house. These guys seem to know what they're doing. Like they've cased houses before. I think they had a close look at the Murrays', and weren't fooled by the lights," he says.

"What makes you think they've cased houses before?" she says.

Alex explains his theory about the interior car lights, the position of the vehicle and the license plates.

"I don't know," she says.

"The guy brazenly blasts out a street light? Trust me. These are not the kind of people we want in the neighborhood," he says.

He leaves out the likelihood that the driver spotted him, not seeing any reason to escalate her anxiety.

"You don't think they're from Maine?" she says.

"I doubt it, and I'd hate to think about what happened to the owners of that car. I hope Charlie does some hunting tonight," he says.

"We don't need Charlie shooting at people in the dark. You and Ed have made some night time trips. You're lucky nobody took a shot at you," she says.

"Maybe. Either way, I don't think there's any reason for anyone to be alone on the ground floor after dark from this point forward. At least until we figure out what's going on with these guys. OK?" he says.

"Sounds reasonable," she says.

"Did you lock the door on the way in?" he says.

"No, should I have?" she says defensively.

"Not if you're OK with our kids walking in on some steamy sex," he says, and rolls over onto her, grasping her hands.

"A little presumptuous aren't we? What if I wasn't in the mood?" she says.

"I figure you're playing hard to get days ended several years ago," he says.

"Nice. This is what it comes down to after fifteen years?" she says.

"Pretty much," he responds.

"I'll lock the door," she says and jumps out of bed.

Chapter Thirty-Two

Saturday, December 1, 2012

Alex kneels in the dark and peers between a small gap between the window sill and the bottom of the pull shades in his office. He scans the block in both directions, first with the naked eye, and then with his night vision scope. He has alternated between the window and his computer for the past three hours. So far, the computer has proved more interesting.

Maine Medical Center and Mercy Hospital are no longer accepting any new patients. This decision was announced late Thursday, prompting protests outside of Mercy Hospital that required National Guard intervention.

Several state funded triage centers were established over the past week around the greater Portland area. These centers filled with patients before they officially opened on Thursday, leading to more protest, and a near takeover of the triage center located at the Maine Medical building in Falmouth. Local law enforcement and State Troopers kept the situation from escalating out of control until elements of an Air National Guard unit could be airlifted into a nearby strip mall parking lot.

As of Friday afternoon, most Guard units have been reassigned to provide security for area hospitals and state triage centers, leaving local authorities to handle any civil unrest within Portland.

Portland's situation seemed no different than that of the rest of the nation. Every treatment facility is overwhelmed, understaffed, and days away from exhausting any critical medical supplies. Federal and state emergency supply packages can't meet the demand, and will likely be exhausted within the next few weeks. The country is on the brink of a complete breakdown, and New England now faces a storm system that most meteorologists agree will be a uniquely devastating early season storm.

Alex stops his scan and focuses in the direction of the Murrays' house. The scope's green picture is different on this scan. His last good scan of the neighborhood occurred about thirty minutes earlier.

"Alright. What's going on here?" he whispers, half asleep.

He squints into the scope. The area doesn't appear to be as bright as before. Alex turns off the scope and opens the battery compartment. He takes two spare AA batteries from a half empty value pack on his desk, and replaces the batteries. He tosses the old ones into an empty black metallic waste can, making way too much noise for two in the morning. He cringes from the noise, and listens intently for any signs of disturbed sleep throughout the house. *Nothing. It would take a string of firecrackers to jar these people out of their sleep. Or a rock to the head.*

He turns on the scope and resumes his inspection. The scene is slightly brighter, but still darker than before. He stares at the scene for another minute, and then suddenly lowers the scope. *The lights are out at the Murrays'. They're in.*

"God damn it, they're in," he whispers.

He considers calling Charlie or Ed, but is pretty certain that neither household would appreciate a call at two thirty in the morning.

"This is not good."

"What's not good?" Ryan says out of nowhere.

Alex barely holds on to the night vision scope as he takes in a short quick breath and whirls on his knees to face the direction of Ryan's voice.

"Ryan," he whispers forcefully, "please do not surprise me like that. Jesus…I swear you guys are trying to give me an infarction."

"What's an infarction dad," Ryan says groggily.

"A heart attack," he says.

Ryan smiles.

"Sounds like a technical term for farting," he says.

"That's flatulence," says Alex.

"So what's going on out there? I don't think mom likes it when you do this kind of stuff," says Ryan, kneeling next to him.

"What kind of stuff?"

"Going tactical," says Ryan.

"What do you mean?" Alex says, though he has a pretty good idea.

"I think she gets worried when you get too into the military stuff. Like staring through night vision in the middle of the night. She doesn't think it's healthy for you," says Ryan.

"Does she talk about it with you?" says Alex.

"Sometimes. Mostly when you space out. Like at the beach this summer. She was really worried for a while," he says, and Alex can immediately tell that Ryan is unlikely to say more on his own.

"What was she worried about?" Alex prods.

"I don't know. Just worried," he says, and Alex knows that he doesn't want to talk about it.

Alex never suspected that she talked to the kids about his problem. He just assumed she'd treat it the same way that he treated it, and not talk about it. Now he wonders if this bothers her on a daily basis.

292

"Buddy. I know you really don't want to talk about this, but I need to know something, and I'll never bring it up again. And I won't be mad at anyone. Alright?"

He looks at Ryan, who nods his head, but is clearly struggling with this conversation.

"Was mommy worried that I might hurt one of you?" says Alex.

"No," he says, and shakes his head, "she was…"

Alex puts his arm around Ryan, and hugs him

Ryan hesitates to answer, and castes his eyes down again. His head turns back toward the window shade.

"Really buddy. Does mommy think I might hurt you guys?"

Ryan shakes his head, still staring at the shade in front of him. Alex feels an uneven wave of anger wash over him. Anger directed at Kate. He can barely stomach the thought that she believes him to be capable of hurting the kids, or her. He barely suppresses the thought and has to press his lips closed to keep the words from escaping.

He wonders if Ryan can sense his anger. The anger is immediately doused by a rush of guilt. His flashbacks have increased in intensity and duration over the past three or four years, and Kate has pleaded with him to see a counselor at Togus, or a private psychologist that specializes in PTSD. *I've blown it off for years, and now my family is terrified of me.* This realization starts to sink in when Ryan answers.

"Mommy knows you'd never hurt one of us. She always tells us that."

He hesitates and Alex senses that he's not finished.

"But you're not sure?" whispers Alex.

"I know you wouldn't do anything to us like some of the guys that came back, but…"

Alex lets Ryan's long pause go uninterrupted. He hears Ryan start to softly sob, taking in several quick breaths through his nose.

"But Mommy thinks that one day you'll go down into the basement and not come back up."

Alex hugs him tightly.

"I would never leave you guys like that. Ever," he whispers by Ryan's ear.

Ryan hugs him even tighter and Alex feels tears drop onto his neck.

"But that's what happens to a lot of guys who come back," Ryan barely says between sobs.

"Very…very few soldiers take their lives when they come back. It's extremely rare, and when it happens, it happens pretty soon after they return. I've been back for eight years, and I'm not going anywhere. Shit, I finally got you mowing the lawn. I enjoy listening to the lawn mower from the couch way too much to make an early exit," he says, and Ryan's sobs are stitched with a few stifled laughs.

Alex loosens his grip and holds Ryan in front of him by his shoulders.

"Seriously, I love you guys too much to do that, and I swear to you that I've never considered it once since I returned from Iraq. I can't remember ever thinking about suicide. Ever. I just don't think it's part of my programming. I can't envision any circumstance under which I would do it. Here, before, ever," Alex says.

"Like, even if you were captured by terrorists, and they were going to torture you in the worst way possible and then cut off your head on TV?"

"Well, if it was an Al Jazeera pay per view event, and all of the proceeds went to Muslim fundamentalist terrorists…then, I might consider ruining their show. Where did you get that crazy idea?"

"I don't know. From the news. I can never understand why the people in those internet videos just let them hack their heads off," says Ryan.

"You haven't watched any of those videos? Right?" says Alex.

"No. No, but they showed one of them on Fox news, right up until the terrorist started hacking, and the guy in the video just let it happen," Ryan says.

"I'm not sure those guys really, truly believed it would really happen to them. Or, maybe they just didn't want to give the terrorists the satisfaction of reacting at all. We'll never know. I get what you're saying though. I'd make it miserable for them if I knew what was coming," says Alex.

"Really miserable," he says and nods with an overly tough and dramatic squint, still staring down at the window sill. *He has no idea what he's talking about.*

"I'm sorry about telling you what mommy said. She really didn't want me to say anything, but I get scared thinking about it," Ryan says, finally looking him in the eye.

Alex can see that his eyes are still sad, though the tears have stopped.

"No, you really have nothing to be sorry about. I'm fine, but I've been acting a little strange at times. I can see why you guys are worried. Really. You don't need to feel bad about this. You guys are looking out for me. That's what a team does, and we're a tight team here. Task Force

Fletcher. You guys take care of me, and I'll take care of you. We're all doing a pretty good job so far. Don't you think?"

"Yeah. You're doing an awesome job. Mommy tells us that all the time. I feel bad for everyone else out there, but I'm really glad we're safe in here," says Ryan.

"My job is to keep us all safe, and I'll do anything to accomplish that mission," says Alex.

Ryan nods at the night vision scope.

"What are you checking out?"

"Here, take a look," Alex says and gives him the scope.

"First take an unaided look over toward the Murrays' house. Can't really see much because the Sheppards' house is blocking most of the view, and the houses on the other side of the loop aren't helping either. At most, you can see part of one garage bay. Now that you have a wide frame of reference, aim the scope in that direction and try to find that same garage bay."

Ryan searches through the scope for nearly a minute until he settles in on one point.

"I have it. I love this thing. It's like daytime," he says.

"Yeah. There's a lot of ambient light out there from the street light a few houses down. That's all this scope needs to turn the block into daylight. If that light was out, it would still work, but not this well. So...I've been keeping an eye on their house for the past few hours, and even though you think it's pretty bright over there through the scope, it's definitely darker than it was about thirty minutes ago. I left some of the lights on at the Murrays', and although I can't see the windows from here, I could sort of see the ambient glow of the windows from here. I don't see that anymore. If that makes any sense," says Alex.

"Yeah, kind of. So why aren't the lights on anymore?" says Ryan, looking up from the scope at Alex.

"That's the million dollar question. Who turned out the lights?" says Alex, taking the scope to take a look for himself.

"That's why dad is up at two in the morning staring at the neighborhood through night vision."

"You think it's those people in the car?"

"Yeah, that's my guess."

"And you're pretty worried about them," says Ryan.

"Yeah. Something's not right about them. That's really why I'm up past the witching hour. What are you doing up?" says Alex.

"I had to go to the bathroom, and I heard you talking to yourself in here. Kinda freaky," he says.

"Yeah I don't blame you. It is kinda weird. Well, I think I'm done here for the night. Not much else to see out there. You need to get to bed too. Busy day tomorrow," says Alex.

"Really?" exclaims Ryan.

"No. Not really, but you should get your sleep anyway, so you'll be rested up for your afternoon nap," he says.

"Nice," Ryan says dejectedly, "you had me hopeful there for a second."

"Hopeful for what? Until the pandemic lifts, all we should hope for are uneventful, boring days. Safe days. Task Force Fletcher's mission is to make your life as dull and unmemorable as possible."

"Mission accomplished so far," says Ryan.

"Thanks. Now get back to bed. Love you buddy," says Alex, still kneeling in front of the window.

Ryan surprises him with another hug.

"Love you too dad," he says and walks out of the office.

Alex takes another look through scope. He hears Ryan close the bathroom door.

"Unfortunately, I don't think it's going to stay boring for very long," he whispers, staring through the scope toward the Murrays' house.

Chapter Thirty-Three

Saturday, December 1, 2012

Alex sits up in bed exhausted. He hears the doorbell ring. The doorbell rings again, several times in fast succession. Kate stirs next to him.

"Are you gonna check that out?" she murmurs.

Yeah, I'll get right on it. I wasn't up all night, while you snored away ten solid hours of sleep. Jesus!

"Yeah. Give me a minute. How long has that been going on?" he says softly.

"A while I think. I fell back…"

"Hey dad. Someone's been ringing the doorbell for like the last five minutes. Nonstop," interrupts Ryan, suddenly appearing around the corner of the bathroom with Emily in tow.

"Yeah, they woke me up too. Is it the police again Daddy?" says Emily.

Alex rubs his eyes and starts to get out of bed.

"I don't know guys. I'll check it ou…"

His sentence is involuntarily cut off by a huge yawn.

"Sorry…I'm zonked. I'll check it out guys. Why don't you jump in here with mommy and go back to sleep or watch some TV," he says, as the doorbell rings again repeatedly.

Alex frowns in the direction of the sound. He grabs Emily as she passes him.

"Give me a hug sweetie," he says, squeezing her and kissing the top of her head.

"I love you," he says.

"I love you too," she says, squirming away to get into the warm bed.

"Stay in bed. No wandering please. Let me check this out," he says.

He watches them settle into bed with Kate, burrowing for warmth, one on each side of their mother. Alex stares at this for a moment, as another burst of doorbell blasts reaches his ears. Alex moves over to the window to check the front yard. He raises the shade a few inches and peers outside cautiously. He doesn't see any cars in the driveway. He looks down as far as he can and sees nothing in the driveway or walkway.

"See anything," says Kate, sounding a little more awake.

"No, whoever's ringing the doorbell is standing right on the mudroom porch. No worries. I'll take a look," he says, and starts to head over to the closet.

"Careful honey," she says.

"I know. Keep the kids up here. Love you," he says.

"Love you too."

Alex hustles over to the closet and dresses in a pair of faded blue jeans and a gray USMC hooded sweatshirt. He walks back over to his night stand and removes his USP pistol, tucking it into his waistband. He walks back across the bedroom as the doorbell erupts again, sending his frustration and blood pressure sky high. He passes the closet on the way out, and stops suddenly. He ducks back into the closet and grabs the shotgun, which he doesn't bother to hide on a high shelf anymore.

Alex arrives at the bottom of the stairs and glances at the front door curtains. He doesn't see anyone. *Mudroom for sure.* He heads toward the kitchen area and sees the shadow of a figure under the blanket covering the slider door to their deck. *Son of a bitch!* Alex rushes into the kitchen and ducks down behind the kitchen island. He peers over the top of the island and sees the figure moving around on the deck. The figure moves toward the kitchen window, which is partially covered with a flimsy, semi-transparent lace curtain. Alex ducks back down as the kitchen darkens slightly from the shadow cast by the figure's head. The doorbell rings again and Alex wonders if he could move fast enough to blast the head peeking through the window and still catch the guy on the front porch. *Probably not.*

The kitchen shadow vanishes, and Alex slowly peeks up over the island. Alex doesn't see any movement on the deck, so he raises himself up and moves toward the mudroom. He deactivates the shotgun's safety, and leans it up against the pantry door, just inside the kitchen from the mudroom. He feels for the pistol behind his back, tucking the sweatshirt between the pistol and his back so it won't get in the way of a quick draw. *All set.*

Alex steps into the mudroom and stops a few steps from the kitchen entry, well within grabbing range of his shotgun. He examines the figure standing in front of the door, and is glad the shotgun is nearby.

The man stands a few feet back from the door, and is dressed in a worn black leather jacket with a blue hooded sweatshirt underneath. His dark brown hair is shoulder length, stringy and matted. He wears a brown and gray camouflage patterned baseball cap. The outfit alone disturbs Alex, but not as much as the man's face.

Alex stares into the man's lifeless, bloodshot eyes. Alex has seen these eyes before, but no for a long while. The man's eyes flick to the left, returning quickly to Alex. *This man is capable of anything.*

He doesn't need to know anything else about the man. Alex considers his next move. Having stared at the man for fewer than five seconds, he knows that the best outcome for the entire neighborhood would be for him to shoot the man between the eyes right now. Alex knows that sooner or later, he'll be weighing this option again. *Probably sooner than later.*

Alex decides to remain silent and let the man initiate first contact. He continues to stare at the man, with what he hopes appears to be completely uninterested eyes.

The man doesn't react to Alex's silence, and he starts to second guess his strategy. Alex examines the man's face closer. His skin is pale, almost grayish, mottled with angry acne scars. Broken blood vessels track across his reddish purple nose. Hollow blue eyes sit underneath thick eyebrows and deep wrinkled forehead.

"Is this how it's gonna to be around here?" the man utters loud enough to be heard through the two doors.

"How's what going to be?" Alex replies, and hopes that he sounded convincing.

"This," he says with a minor hand gesture and a queer smirk, "nobody answering their fucking door. We're gonna need some help. It was a long trip up from Mass.

"Had to change cars a few times?" says Alex.

The man cracks a sly smile.

"The Murrays didn't exactly leave anything useful behind," he says.

"I don't think they were expecting house sitters," Alex says and crosses his arms.

"So, are you gonna help us out, or not?" the man says, and his smile dissolves.

"Look, you're not going to find any help around here. Everyone's struggling, and there's nothing to go around," says Alex.

"You don't look like your struggling," he says, never taking his eyes off Alex's. *I don't think he's blinked yet.* The man's eyes suddenly dart to the right. A bolt of fear hits Alex, as he remembers the other guy out back. He glances to his left, at the door to the garage. He knows this door is locked and dead bolted. Same with door to the garage. *No way for anyone to sneak up on me without making some noise.*

"You'd be better off heading further upstate. Trust me. No one's happy to see you here. You, or your friend back there," Alex says, and motions with his head toward the back of the house.

"So you're not gonna help?" the man presses.

"No," says Alex, shaking his head slowly.

"I'll remember that," the man says nodding his head.

He pulls a folded sheet of slightly crumpled yellow legal paper, and a pen out of an interior jacket pocket. Alex recognizes the green and yellow pen. *TerraFlu. Must have lifted it from Greg's.* He unfolds the paper and starts writing. *He's making a list and checking it twice. Gonna find out who's naughty or nice. Shit ball man is coming to town. He knows if you've been eating, he knows if you have heat...* Alex starts to smile as the tune plays out in his head.

"Something funny?" the man stops writing to yell.

"Nope," he says and pauses, "I don't want to see you guys around this house again."

"Or what?" the man says, and folds the paper back up into his jacket.

Alex just shrugs his shoulders. He considers telling the guy to stay away from Ed's house, but decides against it. Alex isn't exactly sure why, but his gut tells him that it would be a mistake. That it could possibly have the opposite effect. The man stares at Alex with dead, cold eyes for a few more seconds, before he turns around, and leaves the mudroom stoop. *Emotionless, but calculating.*

Alex watches him walk through the bushes in front of the walkway toward Ed's yard. A second man dressed in black jeans and a faded woodland patterned camouflage jacket joins him as he reaches the far left edge of Alex's house. The second man's bright red and blue knit cap stands in stark contrast to both of their outfits. *Patriots fan? Come on in boys!* Alex scrambles back into the kitchen, nearly knocking over the shotgun, and grabs the cordless phone. He dials Ed's number and waits.

"What's up man," Ed answers.

"I don't have time to explain, but whatever you do, do not answer the door in the next couple of seconds. Don't even go downstairs. Nutcases we saw last night just cased my house, and rang my doorbell for like ten minutes. The guy I talked to at the door looks like a pure sociopath. Fucking scary," says Alex.

"I've been watching them work their way around the block. One guy goes to the front door, and the other guy snoops around the back. I don't think anyone's answered their door," says Ed.

"We need to start calling around the block to make sure no one does. I'm telling you man, the guy at the front door looked scary. I've seen his look before and it scares me to see it again. This is not the kind of guy you want setting foot inside your house. Trust me," says Alex.

"I believe you man. I didn't plan on letting him in…"

"I wouldn't even show your face. A guy like this feeds on fear. If he senses hesitation, a lack of confidence…any weakness at all, he'll act on it immediately. At the minimum, he'll exploit it later, when he's truly desperate, which might not be too far away. I don't think they brought any food with them," says Alex.

"Shit, he's already ringing the doorbell. Alex, I'll call you in a little bit. I need to make sure no one answers the door," says Ed.

"Gotcha. I'm gonna let them know you're not going to answer. That nobody is. Start making calls to everyone on the outside of the loop. I'll take the inside," says Alex.

"Ok, will do. Later," he says and hangs up the phone.

Alex returns to the mudroom and contemplates what he just told Ed. *I'm going out there?* Alex deliberates for a few more seconds. He has two main concerns. His first consideration is the third male adult that Charlie saw in the car. If a third guy is following a few houses behind the first pair, he could be taken by surprise from behind. Ed only saw two guys, but Ed probably wasn't looking for a third. *He doesn't think like that.* Alex reaches behind his lower back and adjusts the sweater to cover the pistol, just in case the third man is watching.

The other concern is less immediate, but no less troubling. He's fairly confident that he's already made this man's shit list, but by drawing even more attention to himself, he's likely to end up at the very top of the list. *If I don't do this, someone will get robbed or killed today.* Alex slips on his sandals and unlocks the mudroom door's deadbolt. He steps through both doors onto the mudroom stoop.

Wow that's cold. A frigid wind whips into the semi-enclosed stoop, biting into his hands and stinging his face. *Once again under dressed.* He looks down at his feet.

"At least I have socks this time," he mutters.

He steps down onto the walk way and turns left, facing the Walkers' house. The Walkers' mudroom stoop is blocked by their garage, so Alex moves several meters into his own front yard. He can see the backside of one man standing at the Walkers' mudroom door. The man's outfit confirms that he is the same man that rang Alex's doorbell. *The other guy's already peeking through windows.*

"Here we go," he says to no one.

"Hey Manson!" he yells over the wind.

The man turns around slowly and takes a few steps toward Alex. Alex is not sure exactly how he'd react if the man continued to move toward him. The man doesn't answer. He only nods his head upward once, and stares at Alex. .

"The words out, and nobody's gonna answer. You'd be better off moving on to happier hunting ground," he yells.

"And I have you to thank for this hospitality," he says, reaching quickly into his coat pocket.

Alex stiffens and fights every impulse to grab his pistol. In a fraction of a second, Alex's logical side overrides the irrational. His hand only manages to move a few inches back along his right leg during the mental battle. He knows that if the man draws a gun, he can negate the man's advantage by darting to either side and pulling his own weapon. At that point, it'll be an even shooting match, or maybe not. The man could be an excellent shot, or he could have no experience at all. Alex figures it more likely that the man knows his way around firearms. Either way, Alex's instinct is to actively avoid a pistol duel at twenty meters with anyone, especially out in the open.

A flash memory of the man's yellow legal paper, located on the same side of the jacket settles the struggle, and his hand stays alongside his leg. The man pulls the note pad and pen out of a pocket inside his jacket, and Alex feels his body start to relax.

The man starts to write in the notepad again. *He's making a list, and checking it twice. Gonna find out who's naughty or nice. Manson Claus is coming to town.*

"You gonna give me a ticket for my lack of hospitality?" Alex says with the start of a grin.

"Just keeping track," he says, and puts the notepad back inside his jacket.

Alex watches his movements closely, and decides to head back toward the house.

"Not much left here to go around. You might have better luck up north. Less people, less problems…"

"We ain't go'in nowhere. Not with a storm coming in," he interrupts, looking up at the thick gray sky.

Alex's eyes follow skyward as another gust of frigid northern air washes over the neighborhood, and bathes him in arctic air. He fights the urge to shiver, and thinks about the impending storm, a low pressure burst of warm, tropical air, soon to collide with this stationary high pressure system. *Disaster for sure.*

Alex shrugs and starts to back up toward his mudroom door, never turning his back on the man. Just as he reaches his mudroom, the second man comes into view from around the far side of Ed's house. He walks up to Manson, and they start talking. They both stare at Alex with intense hatred for several seconds before walking across Ed's yard to the Andersons' house. *I hope Todd already warned them.* Alex walks back into his mudroom and locks both doors. He then enters the garage and verifies that the garage door is still locked and dead bolted. He then tests the three windows to make sure they are secure. *Don't need any surprises.* Satisfied with the garage, he walks back into the mudroom and locks the door behind him, door knob and deadbolt. Then he walks back over to the mudroom entrance door, and checks the locks again, despite the fact that he locked them less than two minutes ago. Alex looks at his watch.

"Captain's log. 8:27, Saturday, December 1st, Alex Fletcher is officially declared paranoid," he states.

Just as he finishes his proclamation, an overwhelming urge to recheck the garage rises within him. He glances at the garage door again and shakes his head. He kicks off his sandals and heads upstairs to check in with Kate. Then he'll start making some calls to the neighbors on the inner loop. He rounds the bedroom corner and sees Kate and the kids burrowed under the covers. Alex hears Kate's voice surface.

"What was going on out there?"

"Oh nothing. Just the new neighbors. The Manson family replaced the Murrays," says Alex.

"That bad?" she says, poking her head out of the covers.

"Maybe worse. Their front man looks extremely dangerous. I haven't seen a wild look like that in a long time. We'll need to have a serious talk about night time security around here. Hey, I gotta make some calls. Ed and I are warning the neighbors not to open their doors to these guys," he says, and starts walking out of the bedroom.

"How about some heat before you start riding your horse around the block? The kids are frozen," she says.

"Just for the Paul Revere reference alone, I give you heat," he says, and adjusts the thermostat before he leaves the room.

"Not because I'm the love of your life?" she says.

"Let's not wear that one out," he says and vanishes down the stairs.

Alex peeks out of the right most window of the family room and scans down the street toward the right, then the left, peering between houses, and letting his eyes settle on stationary objects to activate his peripheral vision. He sees nothing out of the ordinary beside an increasingly menacing dark gray sky. The neighborhood is once again lifeless after the surprisingly brief influx of refugees from the south. *Maybe they blew up the bridge.* Alex had convinced himself early on Friday that they would be forced to deal with slow moving vehicle traffic for days. He's pretty sure the forecast has something to do with the absence of travelers. He hears footsteps on the staircase. *Must be Ryan.*

Alex turns toward the foyer opening just as Ryan steps down off the stairs.

"Grab a seat buddy," says Alex.

"What about?" Ryan asks and rolls over the back of the couch onto Emily.

"Ouuuch. Cut it out jerk!" she cries and kicks out both legs simultaneously.

Ryan catches two feet directly in the chest while upside down, and is propelled off the couch, landing on his back. He springs back up to retaliate, but is brought right back down to the ground by Kate, who springs out from her cozy leather chair a few feet away from Ryan. Alex watches Kate take Ryan off balance, and gently ease him back down to the floor.

"That's enough for now," she says calmly.

Ryan doesn't physically protest, instead he verbally lashes out at Emily.

"That's not fair. She had no right to kick me for real. I was just playing and she could have paralyzed me!"

"Quit being a baby!" says Emily.

"Take it easy both of you!" says Alex.

"But dad, she's such a little…"

"That's it! I'm not kidding. If she doesn't want you crashing into her ten times a day, then lay off. And you need to be more careful. This isn't an ultimate fighting arena," says Alex.

"But dad, someone needs to beat him down," says Emily.

"Nobody's beating anyone down except for me," says Kate, still holding Ryan to the ground.

"If I let you go, do you promise not to attack your sister?" she says.

"Yes, mom," he says unconvincingly.

"I think you should just sit on him for the next few minutes," says Alex, eliciting a shrill laugh from Emily.

"Dad, you told her to knock it off, and now she's laughing in my face," cries Ryan.

"Promise your mother you won't retaliate, and mean it," Alex says forcefully.

"Alright, I won't bother her anymore. Sorry," he says.

"Thank you," Kate says, and releases Ryan's sweatshirt, "now grab a seat away from your sister. We just need to go over a couple of new rules for the house. Something has changed and we need to be more cautious."

"Is it those skuzzy people that moved into the Murrays'?" Ryan asks, and walks over to the other leather chair.

"Yeah. Your mom and I are a little concerned," says Alex.

"What's wrong with them?" says Alex.

"Are there any kids?" adds Emily.

"Uh, I'm not completely sure…about the kids. There might be some, but the problem is that one or more of the adults looks dangerous. Not the kind of people we're used to having around here at all," says Alex.

"Remember the guy that we didn't like this summer after the Red Sox game," says Kate.

"The one that asked daddy for money, then followed us to our car?" says Ryan.

"While his buddies trailed us too," adds Alex.

"Yes. This guy reminds your dad of that guy. Something's wrong with him, and without food or supplies, we think he might be a danger to the neighborhood, and to us," says Kate.

"Worse than some of our neighbors?" says Ryan.

Alex laughs, not sure if Ryan is serious or joking.

"I think this group is way worse," he says.

"Can we give them some food daddy," says Emily.

Kate smiles at her.

"That's a nice thought sweetie, but it's probably not a good idea…" says Kate.

"Why?" Emily presses.

"Because I think they would want more, and if we couldn't give them more, they would cause trouble," says Alex.

"How do you know?" says Emily.

"They're scummy looking," yells Ryan.

"Well, it's not just that they look scummy," Alex says, and glances at Kate. *I'll let her handle this one.*

"Your dad talked to them this morning…"

"Twice," interrupts Alex. *Like that justifies my conclusion.*

"Twice, and his gut instinct is that there is something seriously wrong with them," says Kate. *That won't satisfy her.*

"But you always tell us not to judge people by how they look, so how can we know that they just don't need a little help?" says Emily.

"Sweetie, under normal circumstances you're right. It's not fair to judge a book by its cover, but in this case, we have to make an exception. I can't explain it very well, but I don't want to take the risk with them. I think the consequences could be disastrous, and I'm not willing to take a chance with your safety," says Alex. *That might do it.*

"You should have said that in the first place daddy," she says with a completely happy and innocent look. *Unbelievable.*

"She's unbelievable," comments Ryan.

"That's enough. She's on the right track," says Kate.

Alex steps back over to the front corner window and stares down the street toward the Perry's for a few seconds, then down the other side of the street. He thinks about all of the doors and windows in their home as he walks over and takes a seat next to Emily. *Locked for sure.*

"So what we're going to do is be a little more cautious around the house. Pretty much what we've been doing before, but a little different, especially at night. First, like always, nobody answers the door for any reason. Mom and I will take care of answering the door. Second, I want you guys to have one of us with you when you're downstairs. Day or night, OK?"

"But what if I just want a drink of water?" says Ryan. *Always Ryan.*

"Then you keep a cup upstairs and get a drink from the bathroom," says Alex.

"But mom doesn't like us to drink from the bathroom faucet. Something about poop particles in the air," says Ryan.

"Mom will make an exception in this case," says Kate.

"But what…."

"Just get one of us to go down with you alright? One of us is down here most of the day anyway, just be a little flexible about this. I don't know what these people might try, okay?" says Alex.

"Okay," says Ryan, barely convincing Alex.

"All shades are open during the day. All shades are closed at night. After dark, kids upstairs, and we keep lights inside to a minimum. The other thing that will be different is that I will be visibly wearing a handgun, and you might see a few of my rifles around the house, and under no circumstances are you two to touch them. Don't knock them over, don't move them at all. They will be loaded with real bullets. Here's what you might see."

Alex stands up and moves over to Kate's chair. He reaches behind the chair and pulls out his shotgun and assault rifle.

"Cool," whispers Ryan.

"Great, those were behind my chair?" says Kate.

"This is a shotgun and this is a rifle. Don't touch either of them. I may have one of them sitting up against the island, next to one of the doors, or in my lap on the couch. No matter where you find them, or see them, do not touch them. Understand the rules Mr. Ryan?"

"Why am I being singled out?" he says with an overly incredulous look on his face.

"Because you're the only one in the room that said 'cool' when I pulled these out, and I know Emily could care less about guns," says Alex.

"Guns are stupid and dangerous," says Emily.

"Exactly," adds Kate.

"You want me to break them apart and bury them in the backyard?"

"Not today," says Kate.

Alex raises an eyebrow and smirks.

"They might be stupid, but still, don't touch them. Are we all clear?" says Alex,

"Yes daddy," they say in bored unison.

Alex looks at Kate.

"You're including me in your solemn swear?" she says.

He nods his head slowly.

"I gotcha," she says.

"And if you see something outside that doesn't look right, let one of us know right away. Like someone peeking from the trees, or even just walking around the neighborhood," says Alex.

"What's weird about walking around the block?" says Emily.

"It's weird because nobody does it anymore. Nobody just takes a walk for the sake of getting fresh air. If they're out, they have a purpose, and I want to figure out what that purpose is," he says. *And that's about the most paranoid thing I've said so far this year. They must think I'm nuts.*

"That's it for me. You got anything mommy?" says Alex.

"Nope, this was your show," she says. *That sounded a little patronizing.*

"Anything else from the peanut gallery?"

"What's for lunch mommy?" says Ryan.

"Tuna salad on crackers, with left over peas and carrots," she says.

"Sounds like a feast," says Alex.

"Sounds like…"

"Don't even think about continuing that sentence little man," says Kate.

"Like the best lunch ever," Ryan says, flashing a sly smile across the room.

"I'm keeping a close watch on you," says Kate.

"Lunch of course, is self-serve," she adds.

Ryan gets up and heads back up stairs. Emily moves over to her favorite chair and turns on the flat screen TV. Before Alex or Kate can vacate the family room, the silly screams and sounds of the Cartoon Network fill the room.

Kate and Alex meet in the kitchen at the island. Alex hops on one of the stool while Kate grabs a glass from the cupboard and fills it with water.

"How bad do you think it will get?" she asks.

Alex sits up from leaning the rifle and shotgun under the granite overhang, against the woodwork just next to his leg.

"I don't know. I'm not sure I made it clear enough that screwing with us would be a costly idea for them," he says.

"Well, if you're not sure, then assume you didn't. You're not exactly the best at making things clear. What's the plan then?" she says, and leans over the granite with her glass of water.

"Stay vigilant. Make sure we see them before they see us."

"What are you going to do if they show up again demanding that you share the bounty Todd probably told them we have?" she says.

"Tell them to pack sand," he says.

"Pack sand? I don't think these guys are going to respond to an ancient nautical insult. In the interest of direct communication, you might want to think of a more modern one," she says.

"I'll probably stick with something closer to fuck off," he says.

"God I hope they don't mess with us. Do you really think Todd screwed us over like that?"

"He did it a few times the other day. He picked the most unstable looking people, and sent them on down. I have little doubt that we'll be hearing from our new neighbors soon. Ed saw them spend a considerable amount of time at Todd's. My biggest concern is exactly how we'll be hearing from them. We have to plan for the worst case scenario," he says.

"Which is what?" she asks, and gently clasps his hands across the island.

Alex glances into the family room. He sees Emily in the oversized brown leather chair, intently watching the TV. *Not that she could hear me over that racket.*

"She can't hear us. I can barely hear you over the TV," she says.

"I know. Old habits. Anyway, we need to be ready for a direct assault on our house. Probably after dark. If I were planning this…"

"Which sounds scary. I wish you couldn't even do that," she says and releases his hands.

"Do what?"

"Think like they do. This isn't good for you," she says, with a pained look.

"What do you mean not good for…never mind. I know where you're going with that. We can talk about it later. I have to try and plan this out from their perspective, so we can prepare ourselves. Alright?" he says.

"I'm sorry. You're right. So what do you think they'll do?" she says.

"I think they're watching us right now, looking for some kind of pattern. Something they can use. I'd look for an opportunity to take one of us down, and storm the house. They can't see into our house during the day, but we can see out. This gives us an advantage during daylight. As the sun sets, we need to shut the shades before the reverse occurs. At night, they can see in…if we have lights on. I'm going out a little later to put up the Christmas flood lights. We have enough for the front and back…maybe one of the sides," he says, pointing to the side of the house next to the family room.

"I'll put them out a little farther than usual so they cover more space. If we keep the inside dark, we'll see shadows if they come between the lights and the house. We also have the motion lights on the garage in front and back. If it's dark in the house, we'll see those trip too,"

"What if they cut the wires, or just unplug them?" she says.

"Then we'll know something's wrong pretty quick. The lights will go off. Plus, they'd have to approach the house to unplug the lights," he says.

"Can the battery system keep this going all night? After this storm, we might be on our own for power." she says.

"I don't know. I doubt it, but the outdoor sockets can be turned on and turned off from the switch in the foyer hallway, so if we lose power, we can use the lights if we hear something outside, or at random intervals. But until then, I think we should have them on all night," he says.

"And we all stay upstairs after dark?"

"Yeah, once the shades are shut, we're blind except for the outside lights. Even then, they might be able to crawl and not cast a shadow. The ground floor will be their point of entry, maybe the basement. If they burst in while all of us are down here, it'll be chaos, and I won't be able to effectively protect us.

"What about dinner?"

"We're gonna have to eat earlier. Three thirty or four at the latest, or we eat upstairs. We've been shutting the shades at about four, so we should be fine if dinner goes on the table at roughly three thirty."

"That's workable. We'll eat and close the shades. Send the kids upstairs and finish cleaning up. Then what?" she says.

"We turn off the lights downstairs; maybe keep the stove light and the mudroom bathroom light on. The interior lighting scheme on the second and third floor should stay the same throughout the night, so they can't track our movements through the house. Turning lights off is fine, but turning lights on is not."

"What about when we all go to bed. Won't they know that we've all turned in when all of the lights are out?" she says. *Man she's the perfect devil's advocate.*

"It's not a perfect plan by any stretch. Ideally, we would keep the same lighting profile all night. We could keep one small lamp on in each bedroom all night. Shouldn't suck too much energy out of the batteries. One on the third floor too. Four light bulbs should be fine," he says.

"I don't think it'll matter. They know we're all gonna fall asleep eventually. I don't think the lighting scheme will be that important. They'll figure it out pretty quickly. We need to set up some kind of early warning system in the house, so you can wake up if something happens," she says.

"I wish we had a dog, or an alarm system. I can set up some beer bottles or cans, but it's no guarantee. I hate to say this, but I think I might have to change my schedule around. Nap during the day, and stay up at night. At least until they go away, or we're pretty sure they don't plan on trying to cut our throats in the middle of the night," he says.

"Do you really think they would try to break into our house? I mean, that's crazy. What kind of psycho would do that?" she says.

"You should see this guy. He looks like he's doesn't need a reason to kill you. Hungry, cold, sick family? I don't think we should take any chances. I'll visibly wear my pistol at all times, and if I have to go outside, I'll sling the assault rifle. I'll take it out with me when I set up the lights a little later. If they're watching, it might be enough of a deterrent for them."

Kate walks over to the pantry and pulls out a large can of tuna fish. She places it near the sink.

"Maybe they'll bother Charlie enough that he'll just shoot them from his bedroom window," says Alex.

"Charlie's all talk and no action. I'm sure he's perfectly comfortable blasting away at helpless animals, but I wouldn't count on him to line up his crosshairs on a human," she says.

"He's all we've got at this point," says Alex.

Alex walks around the island and starts to pull down some plates to help with the meal. Kate starts to open the can with a hand operated can opener that Alex hasn't seen in years.

"Where'd you find that antique?" he says.

"Stuffed into one of the island drawers. I figured I'd get used to it," she says, and cranks at the can again, sloshing tuna can juice on the counter.

"I think we'll be able to run the electric can opener if we need to," he says.

"I suppose. It just seems ridiculous not to use something like this, if we have it at our disposal. Why don't you call Ryan down for lunch," she says.

"Sure," he says and kisses her on the lips. He takes a few steps toward the stairs and turns around.

"You alright with all this?"

She looks down at the pistol in his hip holster.

"I guess so. I haven't seen this guy yet, but I trust your judgment. Seeing you this worried makes me pretty nervous," she says.

"This guy is a piece of work. We'll be fine if we stick together, and keep to our plan. Nothing to it," he says.

"Maybe you should go over the basics of that pistol you bought for me," she says quietly.

"I'll dig it up later. You can dry fire it, and get used to it. It's not a bad idea at all. You never know," he says and turns around.

He yells up the stairs and hears Ryan's faint reply from the attic.

"Here comes the tuna on crackers stampede," he says.

"This is his favorite lunch. Watch," she says.

Two seconds later Alex hears thumping from above, as Ryan hurtles down the stairs.

Chapter Thirty-Four

Saturday, December 1, 2012

Alex tips a cold bottle of pale ale into a pint glass, and stares at the golden beverage as the foam settles. He concentrates on the bubbles rising from various locations on the glass, temporarily mesmerized. His concentration is broken when Kate places a steaming pot of spaghetti on the table in front of him. Alex smells the olive oil tossed with the pasta. He turns and looks back into the kitchen to see Kate grab a large green ceramic bowl with oven mitts. *Careful with the sauce.*

"It smells awesome mom," says Ryan.

"Thank your dad for the sauce. There's enough here for a couple days," she says, cautiously edging her way over to the table.

A heavy gust of wind buffets the house and Alex's mind drifts back to the windows as he takes a long swig of beer. He's nervous about nightfall. The sun will set a few minutes after four, and there will be ample light outside for at least another half hour, even under overcast skies. He's not sure sitting here together is a good idea at all, and his second beer in twenty minutes isn't helping to ease his anxiety.

He expected to hear from the Manson's earlier in the afternoon, but as the afternoon grew longer, and the sky darker, Alex came to the uncomfortable acceptance that the Manson's wouldn't tip their hand so quickly. He takes another oversized swig of beer.

"No wine with your sauce?" Kate says as she places the bowl of sauce on one of the red placemats in the center of the table.

"No, it makes me too sleepy. Might be a long night," he says.

Kate gets up and grabs a bottle of red wine from the counter. Alex scans the open windows again and swallows hard. *I have a bad feeling. I would go for it right now before it gets completely dark.*

"You alright," Kate says and places the bottle on the table with a serious look.

"I guess so…I just don't know about this light. Something…"

"There's still plenty of light, right?" she says and takes an unusually long sip of wine.

Alex looks at the kids, who appear oblivious to their concerns, as they slurp down their pasta. A pile of peas, broccoli and olives grows on the corner of their plate.

"Eat the veggies too guys," he says.

Ryan makes a weak gesture with his fork toward the veggies. Emily ignores the request altogether. Alex looks back up at Kate smiling thinly.

"The whole neighborhood is starving, and my kids are picking at their food," he says.

"They'll polish it off, don't worry," she says.

"Anyway, the light's fine, but we were always cautious when the sun set. Your eyes have to constantly adjust to the changing light, and they're easily tricked. I always felt more comfortable when the dark completely settled," he says.

"They'll have the same problem," she says.

Alex sees that Ryan is listening to their conversation and nods.

"What? It's not like you're in a private forum," says Ryan defensively.

"We didn't say anything," says Kate.

"So are we alright having dinner now?" says Ryan.

Now Emily focuses on the conversation. *Great.* Kate raises her eyebrows and gently blows air out of her mouth, which is her patented non-verbal 'here we go.'

"Now that we're all part of the conversation…let's just finish eating and get upstairs. Everyone's in our room tonight. All night," says Alex.

"What? Come on, I don't want to sit around your room all night watching her stupid shows. Why can't we sit on the third floor? She can watch TV on the other side," says Ryan.

"Then all I'll hear is your stupid machine gun games," says Emily.

"I'll use headphones," he says.

"Is anyone still playing online?" says Kate.

"Earlier in the month it slowed down a lot, but it's starting to pick back up again. A bunch of my friends are on, and their fine," he says.

"Good, let's finish eating, so we can close up down here and…"

Alex's sentence is interrupted by a hard knock on the mudroom door.

"Everyone upstairs immediately. Let's go," he barks as he slams down the half empty pint glass.

Alex shoots up from the table and moves over toward the refrigerator. He pats his pistol and grabs the AR-15 assault rifle leaned up against the kitchen desk. He pulls the bolt handle back and lets it slap forward, chambering a round. He checks the safety and slings it over his back. He edges over to the doorway and peaks through the mudroom at the door. He meets Manson's lifeless eyes.

"I thought we were done here," yells Alex.

"You gonna open the door and talk to me civilized?" the man says, never blinking.

"No. You need to move along," Alex says, as a powerful burst of wind fills the mudroom stoop and buffets the man standing there.

"There hasn't been a lot of help for us around here. Fucking rude ass people mostly…"

"I hear it's a lot friendlier up north," says Alex, stepping into full view of the man.

Alex notices a slight change in the man's eyes, as he registers both the hip holster and the rifle.

"Who is it Alex?" Kate yells from the kitchen.

"Nobody we know. Just some drifters. You should head upstairs," he says firmly, but calmly.

Alex feels composed and in control of the situation. Openly carrying these two weapons reminds him of an era filled with supreme confidence. Only body armor, a helmet and immediate access to a dozen similarly equipped Marines could boost him up higher.

"Don't you think that's a little over-kill?" the man yells, nodding toward Alex.

"Not in my experience," says Alex.

The man momentarily laughs under his breath.

"And what experience might that be?" he demands.

"Enough to know that your arrival here is bad news. You guys aren't planning on shooting out all of the streetlights are you?"

The man snickers at the comment.

"Look, I know you're holding out on me. Your good friend Todd told us you have a ton of food stored away in there and that you've been handing it out to some of the neighbors," he says, and glances over his shoulder at another man who suddenly appears on the sidewalk in front of Alex's house, near the driveway.

"We just want our cut of this charity, and we won't bother you after that. We've got two families, so we'll need at least…"

Alex's glance drifts to the man near the street. Same type of clothes, hats, shoes. *Something's off. Fuck, it's not the same guy I saw before. No long hair. Stay calm. There might be another guy out there.*

Suddenly Alex doesn't feel very secure. Behind the door, he can't see below Manson's mid stomach, or below his elbows. *The guy could be holding a sawed-off shotgun down low, and I'd never be able to react in time.*

His eyes dart out beyond Manson and the man on the sidewalk, to the numerous bushes and evergreen trees within view across the street. *The other guy could be sighting in on my head right now.*

He glances back into the library, at the window. *Or hop up on the bulkhead door under the window and blast my head off.* Alex feels queasy, but maintains his posture and focus. He reaches back without looking and closes the door to the library. He glances through the kitchen at the family room. *They could blast me through one of the side family room windows from here.*

All of his attention was focused on the front door. Alex can't believe he made such an elementary mistake. He steps forward into the mudroom, eliminating the great room windows as an opportunity to take him down. He starts to refocus on what the man is saying. *Something about getting his share of the bounty?*

"I gave away all I had to spare. That's it. I need you to get the fuck out of here. Now!" he says.

"That's bullshit! You got plenty hidden in there…" the man starts, with his right hand pointed accusingly at Alex.

"Someone's in the backyard!" screams a panicked voice from the deep inside the house.

He instinctively slings the rifle around with his left hand, twisting his body slightly to the right. The AR-15 rifle points high on the man's chest within the barely discernable flash of a second, and disengages the safety before the barrel settles. The man starts to grin and show his brown stained teeth. Alex can see what looks like blackened decay on one of his incisors.

"Get that fucker around front where I can see him, or I'll kill you where you stand!" Alex hisses.

"Ten seconds! Ten…nine…eight…"

The man raises his hands to his mouth, and Alex almost pulls the trigger. He takes a few shallow, controlled breaths, and eases all pressure off the trigger, shocked at how far he involuntarily pulled it. The man whistles three times. Three short, sharp whistles.

"Seven…six…five…"

"He's running around front!" Kate yells from somewhere near the top of the stairs.

Alex keeps his own focus just to the side of the scope. At this range, he won't miss, even without sighting in. The man stares at him impassively.

"four…three…"

Before Alex reaches 'two', Manson barks something toward the driveway, and the third man suddenly appears. Manson yells for him to join "Rick," and he starts to walk over to the sidewalk. Alex watches as the third man walks over to "Rick" near the top of the driveway. The man tries hard to conceal a weapon on the right side by his body. Alex can't determine the weapon type, but guesses it to be a modified shotgun, with either a shortened barrel or no shoulder stock.

The phone rings and Alex ignores it. He needs to focus on the man standing on his mudroom stoop.

"Charlie Thornton's calling!" he hears from upstairs.

"See what he wants!" he yells back, shifting his gaze from the man on his porch to the two men standing on his sidewalk.

"He says the man that just ran out has a shotgun!" she says.

The man on the porch doesn't appear to hear what she says, and continues to stare at Alex. *This guy's fucking crazy.*

"You gonna quit pointing that thing at me mother fucker?" he grunts.

Alex lowers the barrel a few inches, but keeps it aligned with vertical center of the man's body.

"Not until you're out of my sight. Come back again, and I'll kill you. If I see you approach this house with that shotgun your friend is carrying, or any other weapon, I'll kill you."

"Don't worry Alex…you won't see us next time," he says and turns to leave.

Alex considers shooting him in the head, and then gunning down the other two. He'd probably get one of the others right away, hopefully the guy with the shotgun, then pop out of the mudroom door and tag the other one. Alex knows it would all be over in a matter of seconds, but something stops him. The pressure eases off the trigger, and Alex is once again surprised by how close he came to killing this man.

Manson walks straight across the landscaped bed, pushing through tightly spaced, waist high evergreen bushes, and trampling the remnants of a large, decayed perennial. The gunman no longer makes any attempt to conceal the short barreled shotgun, and brazenly slings it over his shoulder. *I know I should take them out now. All standing in a pile like that. I'll never get a chance like this again.*

"Charlie thinks you should start blasting away. He'll back you up!" Kate says from what sounds like half way down the stairs. *What the fuck is she talking about? This isn't a video game.* Alex knows she's right. If he opened up on them while they stood in a tight group like this, he would most likely hit them all right away.

"Get back up with the kids and keep them away from the windows. All shades shut. I'm not starting a gun battle in the middle of the street. I'll end up sending bullets through Derek's house," Alex yells.

"I'll call Derek and tell them to get in the basement if that's what's really stopping you. He was sneaking up on us with a shotgun Alex. Charlie has the guy with the gun sighted in," she yells.

Alex runs through the kitchen to the foyer, yelling at her as he moves to the formal dining room for a full view of the street.

"Tell Charlie to cool it! They got the message!"

Alex kneels down a few feet back from the window ledge and aims his rifle at the group standing on the street in front of his driveway. The tip of the rifle's barrel scrapes the glass and Alex slides back a couple of inches along the hardwood floor.

He takes in the view of the street. This new position will allow him to watch the group walk all the way around the bend near Charlie's house. This assumes that they head back toward their newly acquired residence. Charlie can visually escort them the rest of the way.

"Tell him yourself," she says, and walks down the stairs to hand him the phone.

"God damn it hon, I don't…," he protests as the phone is forced into his trigger hand.

"Can you get me the binoculars and then get upstairs. I don't want the kids near any of the front windows," he says annoyed.

"Sorry about that Charlie…" he starts.

"The kids are on the third floor. They're fine," she interrupts.

"Just check, and get me the bino's from the kitchen, and a pad of paper. Pen too," he snaps, and nervously glances at the Manson's out front.

The trio starts walking northeast down the middle of the road in the direction of the Murrays' house. Manson looks back at the house, points his finger and grins wickedly.

"They're on the move," Charlie whispers excitedly into the phone.

"This is our chance Alex. We may not get another."

"We can't just start ambushing people walking down our block."

"They just tried to sneak up on your house at sundown with a shotgun. That's it in my book. What else do you need?" he says, emphasizing the last part of his statement.

"They're heading back. Keep an eye on them, and call me if they don't park it back at their new digs. The storm's gonna cool them off.

Looks like it's gonna hit late tonight, and continue through most of the day. They won't be playing outside for a while."

Kate walks back into the dining room with the requested items and a full glass of water. She sets the binoculars on the window sill, and the pad and pen on the dining room table. The water is not meant for him.

"I'm going to check on the kids," she says coldly, and mumbles something about them being on the third floor.

"Thank you honey," he says with a thin smile. *Don't do me any favors.*

"Charlie, I need to take some notes here. Keep an eye on them," Alex says and disconnects the call.

Alex sets the rifle against the white trim of the windowsill and grabs the binoculars. He sights in on the three men walking away. He wishes they were facing him, so he could take in more of their details. He made an easy, but nearly fatal error earlier that he didn't intend to make again.

To a casual observer, the man standing on the sidewalk looked like the sidekick Alex saw earlier in the day. Same type of clothing. Same rough look. Pretty much everything was the same except for the hair. *I should have noticed that immediately.* Alex can't afford to be a casual observer anymore with this crew. He takes a long look and then grabs the paper and pen from the table. He starts to write under the Terraflu logo as he talks out loud.

"Alright, we have three guys. Let's name them Manson, Daryll and Rick. Manson wears a brown patterned hunting baseball cap and has brown shoulder length hair. Brown leather jacket. No facial hair, blue eyes. Brown work shoes. Daryll also has long hair, but it's distinctly lighter, almost blond. Red and Blue Patriot's winter hat. Jeans, leather boots. Green camouflage patterned field jacket. Goatee. Didn't notice that when he was sneaking around the houses. That leaves Rick. Faded OD green Vietnam era field jacket. Black watch cap pulled tight. No hair showing under hat. Faded black jeans, black high top sneakers. Huskier than the other two and taller."

Alex picks up the binoculars again and focuses in on the shotgun.

"Let's see, pump action, barrel shortened all the way to the feed cylinder. Looks like a full stock…"

"The kids are fine up on the third floor. I told them to stay clear of the windows," Kate suddenly announces from the staircase.

She sits on the stairs, just below the first floor ceiling level.

"Thank you for checking on them," he says, and puts the binoculars back on the sill, "and I'm sorry for barking at you. I was just a little frazzled…a lot frazzled."

"I'm not mad either really. I just…" she pauses and starts to shake her head slowly.

"Wanted me to kill them in the middle of the street?"

"I guess so. I lost it when I saw that guy in our backyard. You know what they tried right?" she says softly.

"Yeah. Exactly what I predicted. He kept me pretty distracted in the mudroom. If you hadn't seen that guy, we might not be having this conversation," he says, keeping an eye on the group meandering down the street.

"Lucky I chose to close Ryan's shades first. I just barely saw him darting through the trees," she says.

"But you saw him, and that's all that counts. Help me shut all of these shades. We'll get the lights on and hunker down for the night. Storm's gonna hit a few hours past midnight. I highly doubt we'll hear from them again tonight, but we'll be ready just in case," he says.

Alex picks up the assault rifle and engages the safety. He removes the thirty round magazine and slides back the bolt handle, which ejects the .223 caliber bullet onto the hardwood floor. He picks up the bullet and pushes it back into the rifle magazine. He reinserts the magazine, engages the safety, and slings the rifle over his shoulder. He checks on the Manson's one more time and sees the disappear around the block. The branches on an evergreen tree in Charlie Thornton's yard sways in response to a powerful gust of wind.

Chapter Thirty-Five

Sunday, December 2, 2012

Alex shifts on the great room couch, and drifts out of a shallow sleep. He opens his eyes to the pitch dark room, and quickly re-orients himself within the house. He remains motionless and listens intently. He feels certain that something woke him, but he can't be sure. He's been drifting in and out of sleep on the couch since the rain started pounding just after midnight. He checks his watch and put's his hand on the pistol grip of the assault rifle lying across his chest. *Something's different.* He stays in place under the wool blanket for a few more moments, and scans the house for sounds. *Nothing.*

Before lying down on the couch, he had checked on Kate and the kids in the master bedroom. Kate and Emily were snuggled together in bed, and Ryan was in his sleeping bag on the floor next to Kate.

After checking the family, he proceeded to check the sound traps he had set earlier in the evening. The traps were basic. In front of the doors to the mudroom porch, garage, front stoop and basement, he placed one of the four kitchen stools. On top of each stool, he placed a short two by four plank from his remnant pile in the garage, pushing one end of the plank up against the door. On the planks, he arranged several empty vegetable cans, which would hopefully tumble to the hardwood floor if the plank was moved. Given his shallow sleep tonight, Alex is confident that none of the traps have been triggered.

Alex sits up and squints. His eyes have still not adjusted to the darkness. *It's really dark in here.* Alex hears another wave of rain pummel the great room windows. Frequent, unpredictable gusts of wind and rain have kept any semblance of restful sleep far from Alex's grasp. *Something else woke me up this time.*

He rises off the couch and stands, letting the blanket slide to the floor between the couch and the round coffee table. Alex glances at the table, and glares at the mug of coffee. *A lot of good that did me.* As his eyes continue to adjust to the darkness, his brain labors to figure out what put him on alert. He fights the urge to whisper his thoughts.

The lights are out. Alex turns his head toward the front and back of the house. *Jesus! How did I miss that? Brilliant.* The last time he remembers being awake, the outdoor floodlights cast thin beams of light through the minute openings along the sides of the shades, creating a lattice work of beams high up on the walls and the ceiling. Now there was nothing. Alex's mind runs through several possibilities in the matter of seconds, starting with the worst and most unlikely scenario. *Doubtful in this storm, and they'd have to pull two plugs. One by the mudroom door, and one on the side of the great room. Simultaneously.*

Alex stops the mental process and stares toward the flat screen TV and home theatre system. *Nope, the power is out.* He sees nothing that would indicate energy flowing to the electronics. No green clock on the cable box, no red "off" indicator buttons on any of the electronics. Alex steps forward toward the kitchen and the whole picture falls into place. The blue LED on the microwave is gone. *Same with the stove.* All around the house, the small, unobtrusive signs of electronic life have vanished, and a pure silence punctuated by sheets of rain blankets has descended. *Very unlikely that they cut the power to the house.*

Alex creeps into the kitchen and glances left at the basement door. The plywood and cans remain balanced on the stool. Alex continues past the basement door to the hallway leading to the foyer. He can feel his heart pump faster, creating the only perceptible sound that competes with his shallow breath.

He stares down the hallway toward the front door. His eyes have adjusted enough for him determine that the trap is intact. *Two more to go.* Alex doesn't expect to find anything out of order in the mudroom. He moves silently across the kitchen, past the granite island, and approaches the entrance to the mudroom. He can already see from the kitchen, that the cans are still propped up on the plank set against the garage entrance. He slowly moves his head around the entrance corner and spies the contraption set against the mudroom door. *Intact.*

Alex steps into the mudroom, and walks up to the mudroom entrance door, taking care not to bump into the plank. He stares out into the night. *Nothing.* He can barely distinguish the Sheppards' house directly across the street, through the wintery mix of sleet and rain. He sees no ambient light from any source near his neighborhood. *I wonder if this is localized?* He stares out above the houses, but given the thick weather conditions, he doubts that he could see any of South Portland's lights on the northeast horizon, even if they were still energized.

Alex doesn't look forward to fumbling around the basement, not that it'll be any darker than where he's currently standing. Just the thought of going down into the basement at night makes him feel uneasy. His first order of business down there will be to make sure the bulkhead door is still locked, and that none of the telltales he left near the bulkhead entrance have been disturbed. Once he convinces himself that the bulkhead door has not been breached, his worries will be reduced to the occasional spider web, and the ever present, completely unreasonably feeling of panic and hysteria that accompanies him on every foray into any dark basement.

"I hate going down there without the lights," he whispers, and pulls a powerful compact LED flashlight from his right front pocket.

■

Bright sunlight pours through the sliding doors behind the kitchen table, and Alex sets a steaming mug of coffee down on the kitchen island. He looks up at the microwave clock, which blinks the letters PF. He forgot to reset that one before making coffee. Alex starts to walk around the island to change the time, but is once again distracted by the backyard. *Simply amazing.* He moves over to the sliding doors and stares out into the yard.

The scene before him is ethereal. The sun sits between the two closest houses behind the Fletchers' yard, blazing rays of sunlight through the crisp early morning air. The ground shimmers with color and light as the sun's rays scatters through millions of ice encased blades of grass. The sensation mesmerizes Alex again. Larger reflections sparkle from the ice that burdens the branches of the bare trees and empty bushes, pulling them closer to the ice encrusted ground.

The evergreen trees sag, and Alex sees several snapped evergreen branches throughout the yard. Most of the maples and birch appear intact, aside from the loss of some smaller branches. He imagines the heavy damage to the trees Across Harrison Road, which have stood for nearly half a century, and tower over the homes there.

Without thinking, Alex moves the wooden bar jammed into the sliding door's track, and opens the glass slider. He takes in the cold air for a few seconds, and takes a step out onto the deck. The step is treacherous, and Alex holds onto the door frame for balance. The entire deck is covered by a one inch thick slab of ice. *Don't be stupid here.* Alex tests his footing, and decides that the icy surface is rough enough for him to slowly walk across to the railing on the opposite side of the deck. He reaches the other side and uses the railing to navigate the steps down to the grass.

Alex steps down into the grass and kneels down to take a closer look at the grass, which resembles a crystallized shag rug. The grass crackles under his weight. Every blade is individually encased in ice.

Alex hears a distant cracking sound, followed by a crash, which makes him instinctively duck down a little further. *Maybe this isn't the best idea.* Last night it sounded like a firefight.

Alex stands up and scans the horizons. The eastern sky holds a thin, white layer of high altitude clouds barely visible over the distant tree line. The western sky tells a different story. A solid mass of dark gray, extending north and south along the horizon, looms nearly overhead, making it clear to Alex, that the sun's rays will probably never get a jump start melting all of the ice. Alex starts to walk carefully back up the stairs.

■

Alex watches his son from the kitchen island. He finally came down from his room to get some breakfast, and has been staring out of the great room window into the backyard for the past ten minutes. Alex turns his attention to the kitchen window. The snow started falling steadily about an hour ago, and picked up intensity over the past twenty minutes, joined by sporadic bursts of wind.

"You gonna grab something to eat?" says Alex.

Ryan slowly turns his head toward the kitchen, still in a daze.

"Uh…yeah. Can I make toast? Or does that use up too much electricity?" he says, and starts to walk toward the kitchen.

"You could make toast if we had any bread left," says Alex.

"Oh yeahhhh," he says, and plops down on one of the island stools.

"Or if your mom ever dusted off the bread maker in the basement. We have everything we need to make it," he says.

"How long do you think the power will be out dad?"

"Pretty long time. Longer than we're used to. I'd be willing to bet that the ice knocked down a bunch of lines. With the flu out there, I'd be surprised if CMP had the manpower to make a dent in repairing the downed lines," he says.

"So…can I play Xbox?"

"Not all day. We're gonna try to figure out how much battery power basic stuff like that will drain from the system. Right now, let's shoot for an hour of playtime, then we'll see about adding time. Who knows, we might be able to run the TV up there all day, and not have to worry. Right now all we're running is the fridge, which we really don't need, the furnace and some computer equipment. Everything else is unplugged for now," says Alex.

"Have you tried the cable?"

"Sorry buddy. Cable TV is dead. Good news is that the internet still works. I'm still running power to our router," he says optimistically.

"Good, I can still go live on the Xbox," he says.

"I don't know how many other people will be on there anymore," says Alex.

"There should still be a bunch of people outside of New England. There's usually people from all over," he says.

"Maybe, but probably not for long. Most experts estimate that large portions of the country's electrical grid will fail within the next few days anyway. Fuel deliveries to the power plants has been sporadic or non-existent for the past few weeks, and most plants are using up all of their reserve coal to keep operating," says Alex.

"We're really gonna be here for a long time, aren't we?" replies Ryan, staring out at the near blizzard conditions.

Alex nods his head.

■

Alex puts the last empty tin can on the plank resting against the basement door. Several minutes earlier, he finished a sweep of the basement, checking the bulkhead door, and taking a look at any of the basement nooks that could conceal an intruder. He then opened the door to the bunker and removed the Uniden scanners. The scanners now sit in his office, charging. New information from internet sources and the radio was sparse at best.

From what Alex can tell, the power failures are widespread throughout New England, sparing few communities in southern or central Maine. All efforts to return power were directed toward the reestablishment of permanent power links to hospitals, triage centers, and local law enforcement systems, which meant that the populace was extremely unlikely to see power any time soon.

Finished with the cans, he turns and looks at the kitchen window, which is now covered by an old dark blue towel. Alex nailed the top corners of the towel to the trim just before dinner. This was the last window on the ground floor that needed to be covered. He finished a similar project on the mudroom door earlier in the afternoon. He glances around at the kitchen and great room, which is scarcely illuminated by the stove light's lowest setting. He plans to turn it off later tonight when everyone is asleep.

He heads upstairs and sees empty tin cans, assorted wood planks and a folding chair to the left of the railing, sitting in the darkened hallway to his office. Alex plans to create another early warning trap on the stairs.

He turns left toward the master bedroom, which is faintly lit by a small lamp on Kate's dresser. He hears the shower running as he approaches the bedroom door. He thinks about joining Kate in the shower, and starts to feel excited, but the stirrings are immediately quelled as he steps up to the bathroom door.

"Hi daddy. Mommy's taking a shower," he hears from the bedroom.

He turns and walks toward Emily, who is reading a book, buried under a pink and purple checkered fleece blanket on the couch. *So much for that.*

"Sweetie, you can turn another light on in here. I don't want your eyes to fall out of your head," he says, and pats her head.

"I don't want to use up all of our electricity. Mommy said we could all watch a movie later if the batteries are charged up," she squeaks.

"Right now the batteries are fine, and we most certainly can still watch a movie together in here," he says.

"But not on cable," she states flatly. *All they're worried about is the cable.*

"Nope. The cable probably won't be back for a while. Tomorrow, we can bring the DVR box up here from the downstairs. We have a ton of shows and movies stored on it, and as long as it has power, we can watch those shows," he says. *At least I hope so.*

Alex looks around at the room. He sees two inflated air mattresses, and a large assortment of sleeping bags and blankets. From this point forward, the kids will stay in here at night, with no exceptions. Even if an intruder tripped two of the alarms downstairs, Alex isn't convinced that he could react in time to put himself between the intruder and the kids' rooms. With the threat of the Manson's looming, they both agreed that the best strategy is to keep everyone in the same place, with the door locked.

"I'm gonna check on a few things, then we'll get Ryan and watch a movie together," he says.

"Sounds good daddy," she says without lifting her head from the book.

"Be back in a few," he says, and heads out of the bedroom toward his office.

He turns into the dark hallway leading to his office, and almost trips on all of the junk he dropped there earlier. He walks forward to the only window in the house that isn't covered. He looks behind him to make sure that the background is dark enough not to create a silhouette of his body. There was barely enough light in the hallway to keep from stumbling, so he's not overly concerned.

He leans on the window sill with both hands and stares out into the complete darkness. He senses heavy snowfall passing the window, blown by steady gusts of wind, and sees a crust of snow forming on the screen outside of the glass window. Through the Cimmerian murk, he strains to identify barely discernible dark patches in his front yard, where he remembers the trees to stand. He laughs to himself at the thought of anyone staking out his house tonight. Still, he won't take any chances, because if he had to plan and execute an assault on one of the houses in the neighborhood, he'd pick a night like tonight.

Chapter Thirty-Six

Monday, December 3, 2012

Alex listens to Kate's deep rhythmic breathing, and stares up at the dark ceiling, unable to find sleep. Despite feeling exhausted from the previous evening's scattered sleep, he's still too anxious to drift away. Every time he feels himself start to slide into an unconscious haze, he involuntarily forms another paranoid thought, which triggers a small adrenaline rush. He continues to repeats this cycle, unable to sink under.

The paranoia comes in several forms, but mainly materializes as a desire to check and re-check the doors, the windows and his jury-rigged alarm system. He knows that if he gets up and actually checks, he'll start an even worse cycle of paranoia. So he lies there, accepting the finite amount of rest granted by almost falling asleep, over and over again.

He starts to drift off again, but jerks awake, fully convinced that he heard a noise from the downstairs. He peels away the blankets and comforter, careful not to wake up Kate or Emily. He sits on his side of the bed, and stares at the pistol on his nightstand. *There's nothing down there. I know it.*

"I'll just listen at the top of the stairs," he whispers to no one.

Twenty minutes later, convinced that nothing is wrong, he sidesteps the alarm contraption next to the railing, and enters his office, leaving the door open. He turns on the swing arm desk lamp, and lowers the arm until it's several inches off the desk. Most of the light is cast directly onto the desk, and not the rest of the room. *If I can't sleep, I'll surf the web until my eyes fall out.*

Alex spends the next hour alternating between staring at his computer screen and listening intently to a completely silent house. From the computer he manages to assemble an ominous picture of the situation in the Northeast. The storm swept along the eastern sea board and tangled with arctic air north of New Jersey starting late Saturday night. Gradually over the course of the Saturday evening and early Sunday morning, the arctic air dominated most of the Northeast, wreaking havoc on New England.

Widespread power outages are reported from Stamford to Bangor, and state authorities offer little hope that the power will be restored any time soon. ISPAC officials expect regional power grids to fail within a week, as critical power plants cease to generate power. Rolling blackouts prior to permanent darkness can be expected on a regional and then national level. ISPAC officials urge the Department of Energy to take steps to regionalize blackouts and prevent a nationwide failure.

CDC and ISPAC officials predict absenteeism to peak this week, topping 90% nationwide, as the population isolates itself in fear of the H16N1 virus. *It'll be higher up here with this storm.* He can't imagine anyone beyond the National Guard, medical community, or police leaving their homes. Beyond that, even if you wanted to go to work, he can't imagine a business that was still open at this point. *Hospitals, triage centers, police stations, radio stations? Casco Bay Ferry lines? What would be the point of leaving one of the islands?*

Alex turns off the computer screen and lifts the window shade up a few inches to stare out of the window. *Nothing.* He's astonished that he can't see the trees less than forty feet from the house. He's only seen nature conspire to do this once before, on the other side of the world. He remembers being engulfed by thick sheets of red, impenetrable sand, as his entire battalion lie sealed up and silent along an unpaved road north of the Euphrates River. The glass view ports on his armored vehicle afforded him a dark red view of nothing.

Visibility was limited to five feet in the worst surges of sand, and fifteen to twenty feet under the best circumstances during the storms. Vehicles were stacked within yards of each other along the road, and the Marines rotated through perimeter security duty while they weren't huddled inside their light armored vehicles.

The infantry fought off several scattered waves of confused Fedayeen loyalists that had somehow eluded the battalion's thermal sights, and stumbled right into the Marine's fighting positions. They were dispatched quickly, but the brief firefights generated confusion and paranoia. The Marines fired on a lot of "confirmed" enemy that day, and Alex tensely listened to the battalion communications net, for the friendly fire report that mercifully never materialized.

Alex drifts back to the sheer impenetrable darkness in front of him. He thinks about the criminals hunkered down at the Murray's, burning Greg's firewood, or maybe his furniture. *I don't think he ever got a delivery of firewood this fall.* Alex envisions the Manson's sawing apart Greg's dining room furniture to toss them into the fire. He slowly shakes his head. *They'll run out furniture in a day or two, and then they'll be on the prowl again.* He shuts the shade and resolves to get some desperately needed sleep.

■

Alex feels Kate stir in the bed. She gets out of bed several seconds later, kisses him on the forehead and replaces the covers. Bright sunlight pours into the bedroom from the transom windows, and Alex struggles to move, fighting the grogginess to check his watch. *Ten. Jesus.* Alex isn't surprised to see the time. He seems to vaguely remember glancing at his watch around three in the morning. He hears the toilet flush in the master bathroom, followed by the sink, and Kate emerges from the bathroom. She walks over to the front windows and raises the shades.

"Hey, looks like the plow made a run down the street. It's all clear. We got a lot of snow," she says.

Alex rises up onto his elbow and squints at her over the blankets.

"Two feet they thought. Is the street really cleared?"

"Yeah, but you're gonna have to do something about the driveway. The plow made a wall at the end," she says and turns toward the open bedroom door.

Alex knocks off the covers and sits on the side of the bed facing the door.

"I never heard it come down the street. Usually sounds like a 747 crashing into the neighborhood," he says

"None of us had a chance to hear it through your snoring. You were dead to the world this morning. The kids got up early and went back to their rooms it was so bad," she says.

"Sorry. It's been a long couple of nights," he says.

"You should really crash out some more. You need the rest," she says, and starts to walk back.

"No, that's ok, I need to get up and move around. If you get some coffee started, I'll cook up some pancakes," he says.

"You read my mind. I'll get everything going," she says and disappears through the door.

Alex stands at the side of the bed and raises his arms in the air, stretching his hands toward the ceiling. He leans over and reaches for the floor, coming nowhere remotely close to the carpet. *I need to start stretching again.*

"Hey hon?" he hears from somewhere down the hallway.

"Yes?" he says and pushes the stretch further.

"Am I gonna get hurt trying to take this thing apart?" she says.

Alex straightens his back and walks toward the door. Down the hallway, he sees her standing at the top of the stairs.

"No, just take the cans off, and step over the trip line. I'll move the line in a minute," he says.

"OK, I just didn't want to get hit in the head with a paint can or something," she says, and he sees her start to walk down the stairs cautiously.

"Very funny," he says.

She stops a quarter of the way down. Alex can still see her head.

"Any other new surprises down here?"

"No, but before you do anything down there, check all of the doors and make sure nothing is disturbed," he says.

"Alright," she says, and Alex detects a shift in her tone, from playful to cautious.

Chapter Thirty-Seven

Sunday, December 9, 2012

Alex stares out of the front great room window as the second snowstorm of the season tapers to a wispy indecisive powder. He sips lukewarm coffee and tries to gage the amount of fresh snowfall lying undisturbed on the street. He can't imagine any circumstance that could bring one of the town's few operating plows out to Durham Road again. He takes another sip, and looks in both directions down the street. *Nothing.*

He walks toward the stairs in the foyer, and steadies his coffee for the ascent. He reaches the top just as Kate emerges from the master suite bathroom wearing a white knee length cotton robe. Her black hair, still wet from a shower, drapes over the robe and behind her shoulders. She nods to him, and walks over to meet him at the bedroom door.

"Nice shower?" he says, and hopes that his tone didn't come across wrong.

They haven't seen more than a few hours of solid sunlight since the first storm, and Alex has watched the Power Cube battery status shrink at a predictable, yet slightly alarming rate. As of last night, the Power Cube's LED showed the battery reserves at fifty three percent, which was a marginally comfortable level for Alex, given six days of impenetrable cloud cover. With two or three clear days in the forecast, the system should regain most of the lost charge. Either way, Alex plans to make a few suggestions to stretch the battery life during long overcast stretches time. Robbing Kate of a long, relaxing hot shower is not one of his immediate suggestions.

"Beyond excellent. It's amazing how good a hot shower feels after going a few days without one," she says.

"Yeah, we're pretty lucky. They're won't be many hot showers in this neighborhood for quite a while," he says, and kisses her lips.

He pushes his binoculars over to the right, and under his armpit, as he moves in further to hug her.

"I'm not hugging your rifle," she says, holding his shoulders and avoiding the AR-15 rifle slung barrel up behind his back.

"Don't worry. She doesn't like anyone handling her but me," he says, and kisses her again.

"I guess I have more in common with her than I thought. She still sleeps on the floor though," she says.

"Fair enough. Besides, there's no more room in our bed with the kids," he says and starts walking toward the front window next to the office.

"No kidding. I keep expecting Ryan to crawl in next. How much snow did we get?" she says.

Alex reaches the window and stares down at the street.

"Easily another foot. Foot and a half maybe? It's hard to tell from the house," he says, and peers between the Sheppards' and Bradys' houses with the binoculars.

He can finally see the Murrays' roofline, which had been obscured by the thick snowfall for most of the early morning hours. He zeroes in on the chimney visible to the far left of the roof. *Nothing. No smoke. Well that doesn't mean anything. It's still early.*

"What are you staring at?" she asks, moving up next to him.

"Murrays' house. See the other houses with chimneys? How most of them are puffing white smoke?" he says.

"Yeah."

"Well, there was smoke coming from their chimney yesterday afternoon, and now there's nothing," he says.

"Please don't harass me when I ask this. So what?" she says, and winces.

"So what? So what?" he says mockingly, "Just kidding. I really don't know actually. I'm so bored that this is the kind of shit I keep track of now. However, I do have a theory if you want to hear it," he says.

"Of course you do."

"I think they're out of wood, and if they're out of wood, then there's going to be trouble. I saw the Coopers out yesterday with Max, and I'm pretty sure they were moving their wood indoors. I guarantee they're not the only ones that have spent a little time over the past few days safeguarding their only source of heat, especially after the Manson's daylight wood gathering foray," he says.

"We're really going to be dealing with them for the rest of the winter, aren't we?" she says and shakes her head.

"Pretty much. I don't see them going anywhere."

"They've really changed things for us," she states flatly.

"Look on the positive side, maybe they've scared Todd and any of the remaining Fletcher haters out there. The loop has been pretty quiet," he says.

"Yeah, but I feel like more of a prisoner than I did before. It was bad enough when it was just the flu and Todd's crew, but now we can't go outside, or stand near our windows without worrying about being shot. It's ridiculous," she says and starts to walk back toward the main hallway.

Alex follows and wonders if they were both visible from the street. He doubts it, especially with the screens still in place. Kate stops and turns around to face him.

"This doesn't bother you? You spend most of the day and night dressed like a commando, spying out of our windows, and talking to all of our equally stressed friends. How long do you want to live like this?" she says and puts her hands on her hips.

"I don't really see how I have a choice. Shooting them in cold blood on the streets isn't the answer. It might solve the problem for now…" he says.

"I think it would completely get rid of the problem," she says.

Great.

"Temporarily it might, but we'd still have a house full of women and children over there. We can't exactly walk them at gunpoint to the end of the block, and tell them to beat it," he says.

"They can drive out of here," she says.

"Nice. At some point we'll have to answer for it," he says.

"Answer to who?" she says and starts walking to the master bedroom.

Alex follows her and whispers.

"I just can't justify it. Deep down I want to do it, but I can't get past the fact that it would be murder," he says.

She stops at the door and faces him.

"More like a preemptive strike. You said it yourself that it was only a matter of time before they kill or hurt someone around here. Nobody would hold it against any of you. Charlie…or Ed," she says.

"I wouldn't involve Ed," he says, "and I'm not sure about Charlie. I'm worried that he's way more talk than action."

"Hey, you go to war with the army you have, not the army you want," she says, and cracks a smile.

"Thanks Rummy. Right now, I'm gonna keep watching, and we'll figure something out. I don't want to keep doing this all winter either," he says, and adjusts the rifle sling on his shoulder.

"I just don't think you should wait much longer. They have to be getting more and more desperate by the day, and it scares me to think that our house would be the ultimate prize for them," she says.

"For anyone. That's why I don't think it'll matter. Even if we get rid of them somehow, we won't be able to let our guard down," he says, and gives her a quick kiss on the cheek.

"You'll be able to let it down several levels. Before they showed up I think you were just keeping yourself busy, and having some fun with it. It's completely different now," she says.

Alex grimaces.

"Yeah, it's very different," he says.

"You should enjoy a hot bath or a nice hot shower, and then take a long nap. You look terrible hon. I don't know how long you can keep this up, but it's starting to take a visible toll. I'll rub your back too," she says with a concerned face.

"I'm good for now with the shower. I still need to clear the snow. But I'll take a little siesta after lunch," he says.

"Don't worry about the battery. We have a few days of sun coming our way. Take the shower. You need it," she says, and with a devilish smile adds, "plus, you're turning a little ripe."

"Nice. Always an ulterior motive," he says.

"I do what I can to survive around here," she says and heads back into the bedroom.

Chapter Thirty-Eight

Wednesday, December 12, 2012

"Dinner's almost ready," Kate says to Alex as he opens the door to the basement.

Barley and bean stew again? Don't wait for me.

"I'll be right up," he says, and heads down the stairs.

The smell of baby powder hits his nose, as he flips on the light, and heads straight to the bulkhead door. A paint can tied to a shoelace hangs precariously from the end of the crude lock mechanism's bolt. Even if an intruder managed to relock the door on the way out, there was no conceivable way for them to re-hang the paint can from the outside. Plus, the paint can's lid was loosened, and would likely open if the can was tipped, making a complete mess. The baby powder on the floor around the bulkhead door stairs serves as the final, unavoidable telltale. A fine layer of powder extends in a rough six foot circumference around the base of the short abbreviated stairway. *Undisturbed.*

Alex walks over and unlocks the bunker door. He steps in and turns on the light. He glances around quickly. Everything is the same as yesterday. He moves to the Power Cube and reads the LED status indicator. Sixty eight percent. Not as much as he had hoped. Three predominantly sunny days gave them about 15% of their charge back. Six days of constant cloud cover drained nearly fifty percent of the charge, and Alex felt like they had been pretty conservative with their power use. *A few more weather cycles like this, and the system will hit bottom.* And every time it hits bottom, the batteries won't hold as much charge during the next charge phase. *It's all a luxury anyway.*

Alex steps away from the Power Cube, and glances at the oil tanks. *Plenty in those.* One more glance at the supply shelves, and he heads toward the door. He locks both the door handle and the deadbolt before heading upstairs to dinner.

He steps into the kitchen and admits to himself that the stew smells pretty good. The bowls are already arranged on the table, along with Kate's recently invented pancake style biscuits. Alex sees what is now known as the obligatory canned vegetable side dish in a small sauce pan that is set on a mat in middle of the table. *Dinner has come a long way.*

He can't imagine what their neighbors are eating, and he doesn't want to think about it for very long.

He follows Kate to the table, and sits down. The kids are seated and look eager to eat. Just two months ago, they would have had to hire a bounty hunter to get them down to eat barley stew. Now the kids mill around the kitchen and great room before dinner. The days of unlimited snacks, fruit and juice drinks are long gone. The kids are actually hungry at meals, and eat without the constant prodding that had become a daily dinner ritual for Kate and Alex.

"Everything set downstairs?" Kate says as she starts to ladle out the chunky brownish-tan stew.

"Yeah. Good to go. The batteries are almost back to seventy percent," he says, "smells great hon."

"Kinda looks gross, I know, but the lentils give off a brown brothy color. Not much I can do to dress it up. I threw in some carrots, but the orange chunks aren't really helping," she says.

"Looks good mom," adds Ryan reassuringly.

"Thank you my favorite little man," says Kate and gives him an appreciative smile.

Emily can't contain herself.

"He just said it looked like dia…"

"Never mind sweetie. It'll be delicious, and we are very, very lucky to be eating this. Let's thank the chef," interrupts Alex.

Everyone thanks Kate at pretty much the same time.

"Let's eat up. Dinner's a little late, and we need to close up shop down here," she says.

Alex hears spoons hitting soup bowls as he gazes at the long shadows cast by a few of the trees at the rear of their property line. He turns his head and looks across the table, past Kate and out of the great room windows. The sun has already ducked behind the Walkers' house. Even without seeing the sun, he knows that it is probably only a few degrees over the artificial horizon formed by the thick trees to the southwest. They have about fifteen minutes to finish eating.

"Is seventy percent enough for the batteries?" says Ryan.

"Yeah. We'll be fine. I think we have a small storm brewing for later tomorrow and part of Friday, then some decent weather for the weekend. We should all make sure to take showers tonight, clean off. We might set the thermostats a little lower to keep the furnace from running as much," he says.

"They're already set pretty low. Fifty seven in our room," says Kate.

"I know. I don't want to set that one any lower, but the heat keeps coming on at night. I can feel it seeping out behind our bed," he says.

"Our room's cold because it's over the garage," she says.

"I think if we take it down to fifty four we'll be set. I got up to check the room temperature last night when the heat kicked on, and it hit fifty six. I've never seen it below fifty five in our room, even with the heat off. We'll have to burrow in a little deeper under the covers," he says.

"We can try it," she says. *She's not buying into it.*

"So what are the two of you up to?" Alex says, and digs into his bowl of lumpy brown stew.

"Nothing," says Emily, "just reading a book on mommy's iPad."

Ryan shakes his head, "Nothing. Xbox. Pretty much it."

"Anything good sweetie?" he says.

"Mommy downloaded like five of the Alissa Storm series books. I just started reading the series at the beginning of the school year," she says.

"That's the series where Alissa can time travel in her sleep, or something like that?" says Alex.

Ryan gives him a look.

"What?" says Alex.

"She sees the future in her sleep, like a dream, and she learns to control how far in the future she sees, and also what she sees. She solves mysteries, prevents disasters, stuff like that," she says.

"Sounds cool sweetie. Not a word from you," he says, and stares at Ryan, who was on the verge of what Alex can only presume was a statement likely to drive Emily to tears.

"The books are middle school level reading. She's really doing awesome. I'm going to download as many as possible before the service is interrupted," says Kate.

"You might want to get them all tonight mom. I keep losing my Xbox live connection. I think the internet is close to dead," says Ryan.

"Doesn't surprise me. We might be living on whatever is recorded in the two DVRs," says Alex.

"That would kind of suck," says Ryan.

Alex just raises his eyebrows. Kate doesn't even notice a word that would have been censored from the kids' vocabulary a month ago.

"Maybe we should download some books for you too. After dinner, we'll sit down and you can pick some books," says Kate.

"Cool," he says.

The light continues to drain from the room as the sun sinks further below the tree line, leaving an orange glow on the horizon to each side of the Walkers' house. *Not much time left here.*

"Let's eat up, and secure the perimeter. We can chat upstairs later. If the internet and cable is down, we're gonna have more quality time together than either of you ever dreamed possible," says Alex.

"More scrabble?" says Emily.

"And we might start to allow bad words, though that might put your mother at an unfair advantage," he says.

"Nice," she says.

"Keep eating guys. Upstairs in a few minutes please," says Alex.

Alex catches Kate's warm smile and they both relax for a few moments.

■

"Your cell phone's ringing!" Kate yells over the sound of automatic weapons fire and military radio transmissions.

Alex puts down the game controller and gets up from the couch in their attic.

"Pause it," he says, and flies down the carpeted stairs.

Kate stands at the bottom of the attic stairs.

"I don't think you guys should have that on so loud. Especially at night," she says with an acutely serious face.

"Yeah, I know. Where's the phone" he says in a "what the fuck" tone, glancing from her empty hands to her face.

"On your nightstand. Where's your machine gun?" she snaps right back. *Great.*

Alex starts walking briskly toward the master suite.

"It's upstairs. I'm headed right back up," he says, then mutters, "Couldn't bring the god damn phone…"

"Do you think playing that game with the volume so high is a good idea?" she says, following him.

"Why are we fighting?" he says.

He hears the phone's ring tone.

"Because I've been calling you from the bedroom, and you're up their blasting the volume and blasting away with your son on that stupid Modern Warfare twenty five game," she says.

The phone stops ringing as he reaches the bed. He turns around to face Kate.

"Sorry. You're right. We got carried away. It's not a good idea, given our circumstances. Sorry. Seriously," he says.

"Thank you. Sorry to be a bitch," she says.

Alex grabs the phone and checks the caller ID. *Charlie, and he called twice.*

"Charlie. And it's three," he says.

She sits on the bed.

"What are you talking about?"

"Modern Warfare. They're only up to number three," he says.

"I know very well they're only up to three. I was just giving you a glimpse of your very sad future. You'll be playing Modern Warfare Twenty Five when you're in your seventies, and hopefully your son will have moved out by then," she says and flashes a victorious grin.

"I thought you wanted him to stay home forever?" he says with a similar smile.

"Not so the two of you can sit upstairs all day and night playing video games," she says.

"Don't worry. By seventy five I won't be able to make the trip. We'll have to move the whole set up down here into the great room. Probably be in 3D by then. Surround sound. Some of those nice leather gaming chairs for my bad back," he says and touches his lower back.

"I think we need to consider the energy impact of running the Xbox and TV," she says and lies back on the bed.

"Actually, that's not a bad idea. Right after we consider banning hot showers," he says, and playfully pinches her left foot.

She yanks her foot back with a stifled scream. Kate is deathly ticklish. The cell phone starts to ring again.

"You better pick up, or your redneck rampage buddy might fire a signal flare at our house to get your attention," she says.

"Be nice to our friends," he says.

"Are we gonna have to hang out with them when this is over?"

"They might be the only friends we have left on the block. I foresee hunting trips and bison burger barbecues," he says and answers the phone.

"Hey Charlie. Sorry I missed your first call. Busy with something," he says.

Kate shakes her head as Alex walks out of the room.

"Alex, did you hear anything weird about few minutes ago?" he says.

Charlie's voice sounds distant, almost muffled.

Hear what? Are you guys alright?" says Alex as he walks down the hall to the attic stairs.

"Did you hear gunfire?" he says.

"No, I didn't hear anything. To be honest, I was upstairs playing a video game with Ryan. The whole neighborhood could have erupted in a gun battle, and I wouldn't have heard it," he says.

"You shouldn't..." Charlie starts.

"I know. We got carried away. Kate already read me the Riot Act. What did you hear?" he says and starts walking up the stairs to the attic.

"Well, the girls were watching Iron Man 3 in the bedroom with the volume kinda low, and I thought I heard some kind of popping sounds. Like when you're driving up the road at the fish and game club. I jumped up and turned off the TV, and by the time the girls quit bitching... I'm pretty sure I heard a shotgun blast."

He reaches the top of the stairs and turns the corner. Ryan lifts up from the couch and nods. Alex holds out a finger and whispers.

"Go ahead. I have to take care of something. And turn the volume down. Way down."

In the muted glow cast by the paused TV screen, Alex sees Ryan mouth OK and nod.

"Did you see anything outside?" says Alex.

"No, I rushed everyone down stairs into the basement. I'm starting to think we should just stay down here at night," he says.

Alex grabs his assault rifle, and backpack, which are both leaned up against the back of the couch. The backpack contains his binoculars, night vision scope, and spare ammunition for both the rifle, and the pistol. He starts back downstairs, headed to his office.

"Probably not a bad idea if you think you heard shots? I don't mean this to sound condescending Charlie, but are you absolutely sure you heard gunshots?" says Alex.

"I'm pretty sure about the last two. It was pretty quiet in the room at that point...aside from some bullshit hysterics," he says, raising his voice.

His twin twelve year old girls were obviously within earshot.

"My dad was reading in his room. He said it sounded like the Tet Offensive out there."

"Your dad was in Vietnam?" says Alex.

"No, and he can't hear squat, but he swears he heard a gunfight. Small and hard calibers he says," says Charlie.

"Hard calibers? What does that mean?" says Alex. *Did he ride with Jesse James too?*

"Hold on…what?" Charlie yells.

Alex hears someone yelling in the background, and then Charlie's muffled voice. He yells something about someone not being able to hear anything.

"Sorry about that," he says, then lowers his voice.

"My dad is driving me fucking crazy. Anyway, he heard booming shots and smaller ones, like sharp cracks. It's what I thought I heard over the TV. Small pops followed by louder thumps. Shotguns."

"Alright, we should take a look around. Use your night vision. I'll take a look too. I can't see the Murrays' house, so you should concentrate there," says Alex.

"Sounds good. Call you in a few," says Charlie.

Alex presses disconnect and digs into his backpack for the night vision scope. He raises the shade in his office a few inches, and pokes the scope through. He aims toward Charlie's side of the block and starts to scan the area. He increases the magnification, and starts to comb the area for more detail. He focuses on the houses that he can see from his office window. The Coopers', Bradys', McCarthys' and part of Charlie's. He can see the house occupied by the surgeon and his wife, but the angle is shallow, and only two side windows face him. *Nothing unusual. Flickering lights in most of the houses. Candles.*

He pulls the shade down and calls Charlie.

"Hey. I didn't catch anything on scope, but I don't have much of a view from here. Did your dad say how close he thought it was?" says Alex.

"He said it had to be across the street, but with my dad's hearing loss, it could have been in the kid's bathroom. Either way, it had to be pretty close for him to hear it. His room faces the street. Could have been from down your way, or up past the Barton's. I don't know, but I don't plan to sit on my ass and wait for those criminals to bust into my house and shoot it up," he says.

"I don't think anyone's shooting up houses Charlie," says Alex.

"You didn't sound very convincing Alex."

"Let's sit tight and observe. In my experience, when there are more unknowns than certainties, it's the best course of action."

"Sometimes sitting around and doing nothing is the worst thing you can do. We need to take the offensive. Bring the fight to them, on our terms…"

"Charlie. Come on. We can't just storm their house commando style and blast anything that moves," says Alex.

"Maybe we can set up an ambush outside their back door. Catch'em by surprise when they head out," Charlie says and clears his throat.

"Too many unknowns. We'd have to set up on their turf, on their timeline. It's way too risky. These guys may be psychotic, but I don't get the sense that they're stupid. Too many things can go wrong."

"We should at least start going door to door and checking on people. Make sure they're alright," he says.

"And stand out in the open knocking on the door of a possible murder scene. That's definitely not a good idea Charlie. We need to step up our observation and gather more information," says Alex.

"We'll see. I'm not gonna sit around forever."

"I agree, but we need more to go on here. Let me know if you see anything," says Alex.

"Alright. Later."

Alex disconnects the call and walks over to the bedroom with the backpack and rifle. He finds Kate lying on the couch with Emily. A recorded movie plays on low volume. She makes eye contact and raises her eyebrows.

"What's up?" she says and props herself up a little more, shifting Emily.

"Not too much," he says, and signals for her to follow him.

Kate apologizes to Emily and gets up from the couch. She follows him into the darkened hallway outside of their bedroom. Alex leans the rifle against the wall and drops the backpack.

"Charlie is pretty sure he heard some gunfire in the neighborhood…"

"Are you sure he didn't just hear you guys playing Xbox?" she says.

"Ha ha ha. Seriously, his dad heard it too. Two distinctly different guns. Probably a pistol, and Charlie thinks a shotgun."

"Well if anyone knows the difference, it's probably Charlie. Did you guys take a look around?" says Kate.

"With night vision. Neither of us saw anything."

"Did you check all of our doors?" she says.

"Yeah, and I set all of the noise makers. I'll set up the one on the stairs, and then we should all head into the bedroom. I really hate that we have to live like this in our own house," he says.

"Really sad is what it is. I wish we had a real alarm, or a dog. I just can't see us hearing anything asleep with the door shut," she says.

"I'll hear any noises downstairs. Don't worry hon," Alex says and kisses her on the forehead.

"You haven't heard yourself snore lately. You're sleeping harder than I am now," she says.

"What are you guys whispering about out there?" Emily says.

"Nothing sweetie," he says.

Alex puts a hand on each of her cheeks and looks her in the eyes. He doesn't see any fear. Kate can be pretty resilient in a crisis.

"We'll be fine. I'll grab Ryan, and you make something up so Emily's not worried," he says.

"Did you call the police?" she says.

"No. Not yet," he says. *What's the point.*

"You need to call the police and sit on the phone for as long as it takes to get through. Even if they can't respond right away, it might set the wheels in motion to get someone out here to take a look at the situation. Maybe they'll get booted from the house, and out of our neighborhood," she says.

"I don't know. I'll call...again, but I even if I get through, I don't see the police taking any action. I'm sure rooting out squatters is pretty low on their priority list. I don't even know how they'd get out here."

"That's not your problem to fix. Make the call, and start the process. If the situation deteriorates further, and the police can't do their job, then you'll have a clearer conscience to take action," she says.

"I guess it would also cover our asses with the cops if something happened," he says.

"Exactly," she says.

"Alright. I'll call Ed and then 911. Don't wait up for me," he says with raised eyebrows.

"I love you. Make sure you send Ryan down," she says and kisses his lips.

"I love you more," he says, and walks back to the attic staircase.

Chapter Thirty-Nine

Thursday, December 13, 2012

Alex sits propped up in bed next to Kate, while she reads one of Alex's vintage Stephen King novels. Emily is snuggled in between them. He's been watching Kate nod off for the past twenty minutes, nudging her a few times for the sheer sake of annoyance. He stares at her as the novel slips off her knees, through her hands, and slides down her red and green flannel pants to its final resting place on her maroon Boston College sweatshirt. Her hands are still by her knees. She doesn't stir when the book falls, and Alex knows she is officially done for the evening, though he could have made that call long before the book fell.

Alex puts his iPad on the night stand, and leans over to straighten Kate's legs. She stirs from the movement, and scoots herself down the bed so her head rests on the pillow. Alex turns off the light on his nightstand, and gently kisses her on the lips.

"I love you," he whisper, and she mumbles something back to him.

Alex pulls the comforter up to his neck and slowly drifts away, when his mind is suddenly jarred back into focus. He hears a muted sound, like a single, very distant clap of thunder, and sits up immediately. He grabs the night vision scope and USP pistol from the top drawer of his nightstand, and starts to walk toward the double window at the front of their bedroom.

His cell phone rings and he doubles back to get it. *Charlie.* He heads back to the front window, and glances down at Ryan, who is buried under a thick down comforter on the couch.

"Hey," he whispers.

"I heard it again. Closer this time, and it sounded like a shotgun," says Charlie.

"I heard it too. Very faint. Definitely gunfire. I'm checking it out right now. I'll get back to you."

"I'm headed upstairs with a scope," says Charlie, and the call is disconnected.

Alex raises the window shade a few inches, and puts the scope through the opening between the shade and the windowsill. The sky is mostly clear and Alex can see thousands of stars now that all of the area's lights are out.

He turns on the scope and starts scanning the neighborhood. The scope provides a clear green image of everything, despite a near complete lack of ambient light among the houses. He searches for any signs of activity. One by one, he moves the scope over the seemingly lifeless structures in his neighborhood. A few times, he spots light flickering from a house, which he figures to be candlelight or a fireplace. He sees nothing out of the ordinary in the immediate vicinity of his own home.

Alex shifts his focus to where Durham Road starts to curve and lead to the other side of the loop. He passes over the Carters' and McCarthys', and sees nothing unusual. He sees a faint wavering light inside the McCarthys' house. *Normal.* He's seen that before there. He passes the scope slowly over the Coopers' house and stops. *That's not right.*

He increases the magnification of the scope until he can only see the Coopers' house. Alex watches an erratic light show play out behind the Coopers' curtains. He sees the lights first in the room above the garage, which he assumes is their bedroom. From the shaky movement of the lights, he assumes they are flashlights. *Weird.*

The lights soon move to each of the other windows on the second floor, and Alex determines that someone is going room to room. One of the lights moves downstairs, and Alex catches a brilliant flash in the night vision scope, as one of the flashlights briefly shines out of a front door window toward Alex. Alex watches closely, as two more flashlights come down the stairs and fade deeper into the first floor of the house. *Three people?* Alex can tell they are moving around the first floor, but he can't pinpoint their location.

Alex watches the light show deep inside the house for a few more minutes, until the lights disappear. *OK, let's see what he have here.* He reduces the magnification of the scope, giving him a wider view. Staring through the scope, the Coopers' house sits in the middle of his view, and he can see both gaps on each side of the house. He watches the scene patiently. Behind him, he hears Kate breathing heavily. *Already deeply asleep. Amazing. There we go!*

Three dark figures emerge from behind the Coopers' house, and move swiftly across the gap toward the Hayes' house. Alex zooms in on the group. *Three of them. Way too far to make an ID.* Two of them carry some kind of a long gun. *Rifles, shotguns? Can't tell.* He also sees that they are each carrying large bags. *Duffel bags?* From this distance, he really can't tell.

Charlie's house completely blocks his view of the Hayes' house, and he loses them on their way across the gap. Alex walks out of the bedroom and calls Charlie.

"I saw them cross between the Hayes' and Murrays'. It's definitely the three scumbags crashed out at the Murrays," says Charlie, before Alex can utter a word.

"Are you one hundred percent sure it was them? I saw flashlights in the Coopers' house, upstairs and downstairs. Then I saw three figures moving between the houses too. I'm pretty sure one of them was wearing a ball cap, but my scope isn't powerful enough to get a close enough look."

"I couldn't see make out anything inside the Coopers', but I tracked them in the open, before they disappeared behind the Murrays' house. I'm one hundred and twenty percent sure it was them. No doubt. I'm using an 8X Trident night vision scope. Trust me, I got a good look," says Charlie.

"I lost them behind your house," says Alex.

"Alex. I have no doubt it was them. They were moving pretty slow with all of the loot they took from Paul and Nancy. Jesus. Do you think we should head over their right now?"

"No. Whatever happened there is over, I guarantee it. I'll head over in the morning," says Alex.

"I'll give you a hand."

"No, I'll need you to cover me. Plus, I can move unobserved around the back of the houses. I'll call you in the morning when I'm ready, and you can cover me with that nice sniper rifle of yours. Maybe you'll finally get a chance to put it to work," says Alex.

"I sure as shit hope so. You gonna call this one in?" he says.

"No. It took me over an hour to get through last night, and the best the dispatcher could do was promise a call from an officer. I'm still holding my breath," says Alex.

"Sounds like we're on our own," says Charlie.

"You were right Charlie. We should have done something about them earlier. I should have trusted my gut," says Alex.

"Hey, don't start second guessing yourself now. We'll check out the houses, and come up with a plan from there," says Charlie.

"Keep a good guard tonight Charlie. It's still early. I'll call you in the morning before I head over," he says.

"Sounds good. Talk to you then Alex," says Charlie, and the call is disconnected.

Alex sits down on the dark brown love seat next to the couch, and leans the shotgun against the outside of the cushioned armrest. He glances toward the bedroom door, and feels the urge to get up and check it. He knows the bedroom door is locked, and the house is rigged for the night, but his mind won't let it go. *Nancy and Paul are dead. Hayes too probably.* His eyes wander back to the bedroom door, and Alex takes a deep breath. The house is silent beyond the deep respiration of his sleeping family. Alex wishes he could fall asleep, but he's not optimistic about his chances.

Chapter Forty

Friday, December 14, 2012

Alex pulls a black turtle neck sweater over a gray crew neck t-shirt, and takes a pair of thick wool socks out of the walk-in closet. He walks over to Kate's side of the bed and sits down to put his socks on. A groggy voice addresses him.

"Any…uh, particular reason you're sitting there…and not lying in bed?" she says, focusing on the battery powered clock.

"I'd say I have a pretty good reason. While you were in dream land last night, I'm pretty sure I witnessed a break in and murder at the Coopers'," he whispers. *I could have broken that to her better.*

"What!"

"Sssshhhh…don't wake up the kids."

"What are you talking about?" she whispers forcefully.

He finishes putting on the socks and lies down next to her to whisper.

"Right as I was falling asleep last night, I heard a faint thumping sound. Gunfire. Charlie called a few seconds after it stopped. He heard the same thing. Said it was just like the night before."

"Jesus," she says.

"I grabbed the night vision scope and looked around the neighborhood. When I get to the Coopers' house, it looks like several people are going through the house, room by room, with flashlights. Then I see them leave, three of them, and walk toward the Hayes house. One of them looks just like that piece of shit that keeps coming to our door. Long hair and ball cap. Charlie's one hundred percent sure it was them. He watched them walk between the Hayes's and the Murrays', loaded down with stuff they took. I'd bet you anything they broke into the Coopers' and killed them. I'm gonna check it out and confirm what happened. Charlie's gonna cover me. We need to figure this out, and figure it out quick, so we can deal with these lunatics immediately," he says.

"Wait, so what are you doing again?" she says, rubbing her eyes and sitting up.

"I'm heading over to Paul and Nancy's. If I find them dead, then the neighborhood is going to have to deal with the Manson family fast.

Who knows where they're headed next. I might check the Hayes' while I'm at it. They're house is between the Manson's and the Coopers'."

"Do you have to do this right now? You just woke up," she says, lying back down and pulling the covers back up to her chin.

"Actually, I've been awake for an hour, and most of the night before that. No. I need to do this now. Then we'll have most of the day to come up with a plan for tonight," he says.

"No one's going anywhere tonight. We have a huge storm moving in," she says.

"Hopefully, this whole thing will be settled by the time the storm moves in. One way or the other," he says.

"Be careful, and bring me one of the radios. I'll hang out at the window and keep watch...just as soon as I can make some coffee. Can you wait a few minutes?" she says, and slides out of bed.

"I'll head down and get the coffee going. Then I'm starting my reconnaissance," he says.

"You know what worries me about you?" she says.

"I have no idea my love."

"Deep down inside, I think you enjoy this. Actually, it's not deep down inside. You can barely suppress your excitement."

"Trust me, I don't want to make this trip any more than you do. I hope I don't find anything," he says.

"Just be careful and stay out of sight. Leave a walkie on the island. I'll be down in a few minutes. How are you gonna keep in touch with Charlie?" she says and stops in front of the walk in closet.

"Cell phone," he says.

Alex steps into the closet and reaches up onto the highest shelf and pulls down a black, nylon holster rig. He takes two spare magazines from pouches attached to the holster rig. Staring at her, he tucks the magazines into his right front pocket.

"Don't worry about me," he says and checks the pistol already jammed into his jeans behind his back.

She leans over and kisses him.

"Hurry back, OK? And don't forget to switch your phone to vibrate. If numbnuts over there is your early warning system, you don't want him tipping off the entire neighborhood."

"I got it...thank you. We're professionals," he says and winks.

"Just hurry up and get back. Nothing fancy. I love you," she says and heads back to the master bathroom.

Alex pulls his cell phone out of his front left pocket and starts to walk toward the stairs.

"Where's the rifle?" she says.

"In the closet. I don't think it would be a good idea to sneak around the neighborhood with it. Someone might shoot me from one of the houses behind us," he says.

"Plus, I want to travel light on this one. In and out. Fast," he adds.

"Whatever. I think you should take it," she says.

"I'll be fine. Love you," he says.

"Love you more."

■

Alex approaches the corner of the Coopers' house cautiously and peers into the backyard. He sees that the entire area near the back of the house is full of footprints and dog tracks, including the deck. Several piles of dog feces poke out of the trampled snow near the back door to the garage, competing for Alex's attention with several yellow splotches in the same vicinity. None of this appears out of the ordinary to Alex, since he's seen Paul and Nancy play daily in the backyard with their dog Max. Alex walks toward the door, gingerly stepping around the frozen brown obstacles. He visually examines the door for signs of forced entry. *Nothing obvious.*

He leaves the door for the moment, and walks up onto the deck to peer through the sliding glass doors. His view inside the house is blocked by blinds extending the length of the glass door. Alex knocks on the glass, and backs up slightly. He contemplates his image in the reflection of the glass.

Jeans, blue winter jacket, black wool hat, sunglasses and gloves. Nothing out of the ordinary. He removes the glasses so that the Coopers might recognize him more easily. *Nothing.* He knocks more forcefully on the door and steps back again. He waits at least a full minute, glancing frequently in the direction of the Hayes' backyard. *Nothing, but they could easily be asleep. Maybe I did this too early.*

Alex walks to the far side of the deck and examines the back windows. *Blinds are drawn of course.* He notices tracks in the snow leading from the Coopers' yard to the Hayes' yard. *Going in both directions. That's not a good sign.* He sees that the tracks follow closely along the back of the Hayes' house.

Alex turns around and steps off the deck, returning to the garage door. He stares at the door knob. *I hate to do this if they're home.* Alex wonders if Max might attack him. *Highly unlikely. Where was Max when I knocked on the door?* Alex contemplates trying to sneak around to their mudroom to ring their doorbell. He debates the risk, then starts to laugh at the idea. *No electricity dummy.* Alex tests the doorknob. *Locked. Fuck it, let's get this over with.* Alex puts his shoulder up to the door and pushes. The door opens with no resistance, and flies inward, smashing into the shelves along the wall behind it. Alex stumbles into the garage and nearly falls onto several white plastic bags filled with trash. He regains his footing and returns to the door.

He glances around the garage and sees more white trash bags in front of the silver Volvo parked next to him. He also sees part of a wood pile between the two parked cars. Alex pushes his feet through the white bags, and moves halfway across the front of the Volvo. He leans over and sees that the Coopers' wood is thrown in a disorganized pile that extends from the front of the cars to the garage bay doors. He sees several small dents and scrapes on the doors of the black Toyota Highlander parked in the farthest bay. *Didn't waste any time getting the wood inside.*

Alex turns his attention back to the door. He examines the strike plate set into the back door's trim, and finds it completely loose. *I'm not the first person to put my shoulder up against this door.* Alex sees that the door is not fitted with a dead bolt and shakes his head. A few years ago, after a rash of burglaries in Scarborough, Kate insisted that they install deadbolts on all of their outer access door, including the door between the garage and mudroom. He takes the walkie out of his right jacket pocket and calls Kate.

"You there hon?"

"Yep, kids are still asleep up here. Where are you?" she says.

"I'm standing inside the Coopers' garage. Looks like someone muscled their way through the back door. I'm going to check out the rest of the house. I knocked on the back sliders several times. No answer," he says.

"They could be sleeping. Did they break through the deadbolt?" she asks.

"They don't have a deadlock back here," he says.

"What? Jesus, I hope they're alright," she says.

"Me too. I'm gonna check out the other door and head inside. I'll keep this on. Anything going on outside?" he says.

"Nothing so far. Keep me posted," she says.

"Yep, talk to you soon, out."

Alex puts the walkie back in his jacket and pulls out his handgun. He pulls the slide back and releases it, which chambers a round and leaves the hammer cocked. Since his version of the USP45 does not have a manual safety, he depresses the de-cocking lever, and the hammer springs shut. Now he would have to apply a considerably higher amount of pressure to fire the weapon. He holds the pistol in his right hand and pulls a flashlight out of his left jacket pocket. He walks around the trash bags, and slides alongside the silver Volvo sedan. He arrives at the mudroom door and directs the beam toward the door handle.

On first inspection, he sees damage to the trim. He leans against the door with his left shoulder and pushes lightly on the door. Like the garage door, the mudroom offers no resistance and swings half way open. On the brown tile in the mudroom, Alex sees splinters of wood. The door frame around the strike plate is splintered inward, indicating to Alex that this door was forced open. Alex turns off the flashlight and stuffs it in his pocket. He holds the pistol with both hands in front of him, his finger off the trigger. He crouches slightly and walks forward, aiming into the house, while further opening the door with his extended arms.

The mudroom appears to be in order. Alex yells out to the Coopers.

"Paul. Nancy. It's Alex Fletcher. Hello." *No response.*

Alex edges forward and looks into the kitchen from the mudroom. He sees several broken glass jars on the floor in front of their pantry and an electric can opener lying upside down in the glass. Empty Tupperware containers and silverware litter the kitchen floor beyond the pantry. Alex sees that the bathroom door off the mudroom is closed. He walks up to it and listens at the door. *Silence.* He opens it and finds nothing out of place inside.

Alex enters the kitchen and steps around the broken glass. The rest of the kitchen is in complete disarray. Every cabinet door or kitchen drawer is open. The contents of several cabinets lie smashed on the brown speckled granite counter top. He looks into the pantry next to him and sees that it is mostly empty. A few empty plastic containers sit against the back wall of one of the lower shelves. Two blenders, a stainless steel toaster, and several large mixing bowls sit unmoved on the top shelf. He turns and walks around the other side of the island, stepping on some of the glass. The sink is full of glass shards and half shattered wine glasses.

"Paul! Nancy! It's Alex Fletcher! Are you guys alright!" *Where's Max?*

He hears no response, and is now convinced that they are dead. He walks carefully around the other side of the kitchen island and approaches the stairs, aiming the pistol at the stairway. Keeping the gun pointed ahead of him, he walks to the top of the stairs and glances to the right. He sees that the door to the master bedroom is shut. He decides to check the two guest rooms first. Both doors are open, and Alex slowly enters the room facing the street. The dresser drawers are open and clothing litters the hardwood floor and neatly made bed. The closet door is also open and dozens of dresses are scattered at the bottom of the closet floor. The top shelf of the closet is empty except for one folded sweatshirt.

Alex backs out of the room and ducks into the second open door in the hallway. The room appears untouched, and contains an elliptical machine, recumbent bike, a full set of dumbbells. A small entertainment center with a flat screen TV and DVD player sits against the far wall, facing the exercise machines. Several exercise mats are folded up against the wall. Alex opens the closet and finds a large wall organizer filled with women's shoes and designer purses. *Wow, and I thought Kate had too many shoes.* Alex backs out of the room and stares at the closed door down the hall. *God I don't want to open that door.*

His radio crackles to life and Alex feels a surge of adrenaline shoot through his body.

"Honey, what's going on over there?"

"Jesus, you scared me. The house had been ransacked. I'm about to open the master bedroom door. I'll call you in a few minutes," he says.

"Be careful," she says.

Alex turns down the volume and tucks the radio back into his jacket. He walks up to the door and stands to the side of it, pressed up against the door trim. He listens intently for any signs of life on the other side of the door. He hears a low whine, which sounds like a dog. *Max?* Alex knocks on the door, keeping his body out of the doorway.

"Paul. Nancy. It's Alex Fletcher," he yells and waits.

Alex immediately hears a dog barking from further inside the room, but receives no response from Paul or Nancy. Alex grabs the door knob with his left hand and starts to turn it, keeping the pistol pointed at the door. The knob turns all of the way, and Alex pushes the door open firmly.

The smell hits his nose before the door strikes the wall. Alex thought he had forgotten the smell of death, but the distant memory of the putrid, unmistakable stench rushes back and seizes him. The sharp odor of gunpowder competes with the nauseating smell. Alex stands pressed against the wall, frozen. He doesn't want to see what's in this room. He doesn't need to. His assessment of the situation is complete. Paul and Nancy are dead. Max barks and jars him out of his thoughts.

"I have to get Max out of here," he says, and steps into the room, lowering the pistol.

He walks past the master bathroom to his left, and grimaces as the entire master suite comes into view. A transom window lining the back wall of the bedroom lets in enough direct morning sun for Alex to clearly see. A king sized dark pine sleigh bed sits under the transom windows, flanked by two dark wooden nightstands.

A massive crimson stain on the wall above the right nightstand catches his attention first, spreading across the far corner of the room onto the adjacent wall. The back board just above the pillows on the right side has been hit by a shotgun blast, leaving a basketball sized hole. Several smaller holes surround the massive gap in the back board. *Double odd buck. First blast was a miss?* He can't see behind the right side of the bed, but fears the worst.

Alex walks past the bed, and looks down on the floor behind it. As expected, he sees a body, face down, covered with drying blood. *Second shot scored a direct hit.* A three legged wrought iron lamp sits wedged between the nightstand and the adjacent wall. It's tan lamp shade is torn and splattered with blood.

The hardwood floor surrounding the body is covered in a dark, semi-reflective fluid. The pool of thickened blood extends all the way to the front of the bed and to the wall next to the body. He can't immediately tell if this is Paul or Nancy. Most of the head is missing. The body is dressed in a blood soaked gray sweatshirt and dark blue sweatpants. Alex sees a black athletic wristwatch. *Guy's watch.* What he sees next confirms that this is Paul's body.

On the left side of the bed, another body lies completely covered underneath a blood soaked light blue comforter. The blood stain radiates in a rough circular pattern, at least four feet in every direction, from a large, dark red hole in heavy blanket. Thick splotches cover the dark pine head board. Alex sees no blast marks on the wood above the second body. *No misses here.* Alex walks up to the bed for a closer look.

The intensity of the nauseating smell increases, causing Alex to gag. Voided excrement now overpowers the acrid smell of gunpowder. By looking at the shape under blanket, Alex concludes that the body is on its back. The shotgun blast lines up with the chest. Small blood speckled feathers lie diffusely scattered on the comforter and nightstand. Alex sees long, dark brown hair, matted with thick blood, falling down the side of a crimson stained pillow. He can't see the face, which is still covered by the blanket, but he doesn't need to pull the blanket back to see that this is Nancy. *Probably shot at point blank range, while hiding under the blankets.*

Alex checks the left side of the bed, and finds a small pool of blood on the floor just under the bed. *Jesus, the mattress must be drenched.* Alex realizes he is holding the pistol in a death grip and eases off the handle. He takes a few steps back and turns around.

He sees Max's cage tucked into one of the bump outs facing the street, pushed all the way back under the window. The cage is covered with a dark green comforter, leaving the front open, and Alex sees Max's black paws repeatedly scraping at the stainless steel grating. As Alex approaches the cage, Max starts to whine and bark frantically. *I don't know if this is a good idea.*

Alex looks around for a dog leash, or anything he could use to lead Max out of the room. He hopes Max is at least wearing a collar. Getting him out of the room could be very difficult without one. He remembers seeing several leashes and dog collars in the mudroom. *I'll need to grab some dog food too.* Alex tucks the pistol into his jeans, and kneels down by the front of the cage. Max starts to uncontrollably scratch at the cage door.

"Hey Max. Good boy. Oh yes you are a good boy. I'm going to open up your cage buddy, Good boy," he says in a childlike voice.

Alex takes the comforter off the cage, and sits attentively in the cage, looking up at him. He can't tell if Max's tail is wagging, but the dog seems calm.

"Good boy," he says again, and Max cocks his head. *Looks friendly enough.*

Alex slides open the latch and slowly opens the cage, afraid of Max's reaction.

"Come here boy," he says energetically.

Max bounds forward with his tail wagging, nuzzling Alex and licking his face. Max turns to Alex's left and starts to move toward the bed. Alex is relieved to see a dark purple nylon collar on Max, and grabs it. He stands up and starts to drag Max out of the bedroom. Max continues to tug in the opposite direction, with his tail wagging, but soon looks back at Alex and gives up.

"You want a treat boy?" Alex says, hoping to distract him.

Max's ears perk up and Alex leads him out of the bedroom and down the hallway to the stairs. Max frequently stops to smell the carpet and walls on the way down to the mudroom.

Once in the mudroom, Alex grabs one of the thick black nylon leashes and attaches it to Max's collar. He slips two large choke chains and another red collar into his left jacket pocket. He finds a box of dog treats and a thirty pound bag of dog food in the mudroom closet. He fishes out a treat for Max. With the treat box in his hand, Max follows him closely. Alex heaves the bag of dog food over his left shoulder, holding the leash and dog treat box in his right hand. He walks out of the mudroom into the garage and closes the door behind him. He sits the dog food and treats just inside the back door and steps outside with Max. Max urinates on the side of the house while Alex pulls the door shut. Steam rises from the large wet stain on the gray siding and Alex takes the walkie out of his pocket and.

"Hey honey, you there," he says.

"Yep. Nothing's moving out there. What did you find?" she says.

"You really don't want to know. We have a very big problem here on Durham Road. I'm headed over to the Hayes' to check out the situation there," he says, and starts to walk across the snow toward the Hayes' house.

"What happened to the Coopers?" she insists.

"Are the kids listening?" he asks.

"Hold on," she says.

A few seconds later she is back on the radio.

"OK, I'm in the bathroom. They're still crashed out," she says.

"They were killed in the bedroom. Looks like shotgun blasts. One took off the top of Paul's head, and the other…"

"That's enough…I get it. Why are you going to the Hayes'? It's too dangerous. I think we know what you'll find there," she says.

Alex considers her argument, which sounds reasonable, but doesn't satisfy him.

"I have to be sure. Charlie heard more shooting the other night. Someone might still be alive, though I seriously doubt it. I'll take a quick look and scoot back home. I have Max with me. He's fine," he says.

"Don't take him over there. Why don't you come home? Bring Max back, he must be scared out of his mind," she says.

"Don't worry, I'll be careful. Plus, I feel better having him with me. Nothing can sneak up on us. I'll be home in under ten minutes," he says.

"Can you find any food for Max at their house? I know you probably don't want to go back in there," she says.

"I'm one step ahead of you. I have a thirty pound bag waiting for the return trip. I'm almost at the house. Call you in a few," he says and puts the walkie away.

He reaches the corner of the Hayes' garage, and looks across the street at Charlie Thorntons' house.

"Fuck," he whispers to himself.

Alex crossed between the two houses, and can't remember if the Murrays' house came into view. He was talking to Kate and not paying attention. *Too late now.*

"Damn it. I can't believe I did that," he says aloud.

Alex decides to try the back door first. He moves along the back of the garage, staying as close to the wall as possible. He can't see the Murray house, but he doesn't want to take any unnecessary risks.

Alex reaches the door and notices brown cardboard on the inside of the door's window, which completely blocks his view into the garage. He pushes the door open with little effort, and Max pulls them both into the dark space. The smell of concentrated garbage overwhelms his senses as regains control of Max and scans the garage.

He sees firewood neatly stacked against the far wall, past a silver four door sedan. Alex closes the door behind him and the garage is plunged into complete darkness. He waits several seconds for his eyes to adjust, and starts to slowly walk forward. He stumbles through several plastic trash bags, as he slides along a mini-van to get to the mudroom door.

He effortlessly opens the door and sees that it was forced open just like the Coopers' mudroom door. He takes in the slack on Max's leash and steps in the house. He examines the mudroom. A very fine layer of white dust blankets the floor and a dark pine bench. Several jackets lie coated with dust on the bench. He doesn't see any footprints in the powder, or anything else out of order in the mudroom. *Strange.*

He takes a few steps into the house, and a feint, sickening odor confirms his worst suspicions. He closes the door behind him and walks forward through the mudroom. As he enters the kitchen, the smell intensifies, and he sees evidence of at least five shotgun blasts on the half wall between the eat-in kitchen area and the family room. Like the Coopers', the kitchen is ransacked.

Direct sunlight pours into the kitchen through the uncovered windows over the sink. This light fades beyond the kitchen and eat-in area, making it difficult to see into family room, where all of the shades are closed. Alex notices that the dust is thicker in the kitchen, and covers every horizontal surface. Max is quiet with his tail between his legs. Max looks up at him and yawns. *I'm nervous too buddy.* Alex edges forward, careful to navigate Max around any broken glass. He wants to get a closer look at the shotgun damage.

The half wall is capped with a glossy white trim shelf, and extends from the back of the house to a point two thirds of the way across the family room. A white, decorative pillar connects the top of the half wall with the ceiling. The shot gun blasts are concentrated on the corner near the opening to the family room, punching holes clear through the wall and shredding the wooden trim cap. Surprisingly, the pillar is mostly intact, with only superficial damage around the base. Alex is perplexed by the multiple blasts focused on the corner of the wall. The intensity of the gunfire is at odds with what he saw in the Coopers' bedroom, where each shot appeared to have its own deadly purpose.

Wait a minute, I know what happened. Alex stops at the end of the kitchen island and turns around. His suspicions are confirmed immediately. He sees a bullet hole in the white trim around the doorway leading into the mudroom. Three more holes are visible in the light blue mudroom wall just beyond the kitchen entrance.

Alex's eyes wander the kitchen to the left of the doorway. He sees another bullet hole in the refrigerator and one more in the cherry cabinet above the stove. *Small caliber. Probably the pistol shots Charlie heard before the shotgun blasts.* Alex shakes his head and turns back around to face the half wall. The shotgun blasts and bullet holes tell Alex everything he really needs to know about what happened to the Hayes. He creeps forward, mentally fortifying himself for the scene beyond the half wall.

The smell becomes excruciatingly as he approaches the family room, so Alex starts to breathe shallowly. A trick he learned in Iraq. He catches a quick glimpse of the carnage through one of the holes in the wall, but can't determine what he saw. He fights the urge to turn around. He knows what he'll find here. *Same as the Coopers'.* He presses forward, keeping Max on an extremely short lead. The entire family room comes into view and Alex stands frozen. An intense anger and hatred rises in him as he stares at the twisted sight in the family room.

The entire room is blanketed in the same dust found throughout the house, but it appears thicker. Alex assumes the fine dust came from the blasted drywall. He cut the drywall for his own attic conversion, and knows firsthand the mess it can leave behind.

A light blue slip cover couch sits against the half wall, a few feet down from the blasted corner, and a rectangular oak coffee table sits a few feet in front of the couch. Paper plates and cups litter the table along with chunks of drywall. Alex sees that one of the plates holds several pieces of thick tubular pasta, partially buried under white powder. Several small caliber shell casings lie covered with powder on the floor near the obliterated corner.

Without stepping into the room, Alex leans in the and sees that the back of the corner wall has been vaporized by the blasts, confirming his theory about the layer of drywall dust. Two oversized tan chairs sit up against the interior wall of the house, with a large oak table between them. He can't see any damage to the chairs, or the pictures of the Hayes' that adorn the walls behind the twin chairs.

A large flat screen TV sits on top of a three foot high black entertainment center in the corner of the room to the right of a fireplace. The TV appears undamaged. A small stack of wood sits in a black wrought iron wood carrier on the other side of the fireplace. A giant family portrait, taken at the one of the local beaches, dominates the wall above the fireplace mantel. Alex sees three rolled up sleeping bags stuffed behind the chair closest to the fireplace. *Now for the body.*

Kenneth Hayes is not right behind the wall where Alex expected to find him. A wide reddish brown stain, thick and pasty from the drywall powder, extends from the hardwood floor near the corner of the wall, to his body lying in front of the coffee table several feet away. A thicker pool of dried blood extends from his torso toward a black, window height bookcase underneath the rear picture window. Like everything else, the bookcase is sheathed in fine powder.

Kenneth lies on his stomach, with a gaping hole in the middle of his upper back, squarely hit by at least one blast at close range. *Shot in the back crawling away.* Alex glances again at the bloody trail in front of him, and assumes that Ken was also hit somewhere in the chest or stomach as he crouched to fire at his attackers.

Alright...that's one of them. What about the others? He's pretty sure Michelle Hayes isn't in the house. She was taken by Ken to a triage center a few weeks ago, along with the children. Alex heard that Ken returned with the kids, but not Michelle.

Alex's attention is drawn to the bookcase. The two tiered bookcase, filled with a mix of children's and adult books, extends the entire length of the back picture window. Several board games are stored on the bottom shelf closest to the couch.

This end of the bookcase almost reaches the corner of the coach, creating an open space in the corner of the room, where the half wall meets the back wall of the house. The space is big enough for an end table, but is unfilled. Alex sees something on the corner walls, and walks a few more feet into the room.

The smell of decomposition and feces starts to overwhelm Alex's shallow breathing trick. He raises his left arm to his nose, and breathes into his Gore-Tex jacket sleeve, which does little to help. Max is not having any problems with the horrifying odor, and is straining on the end of the leash. Alex is convinced that Max will try to lick the blood-paste mixture on the floor, so he keeps a constant tension on the leash and prevents Max's muzzle from reaching the floor. *That'll make us both puke.* Alex steps toward the fireplace to put a little more space between Max and the body.

As he moves toward the fireplace, he sees a small foot protruding from the small gap between the bookcase and the corner of the couch. Alex's chest tightens and he starts grinding his teeth. He immediately starts to fight back tears. *No, no, no...this...is not happening. This did not fucking happen. No.*

Holding Max tight, he edges forward with the knowledge that what he is about to see will stay with him forever. He stops, and stares at the wall behind the corner. He still can't see anything. *I don't need to do this to myself.* Alex tries to rationalize leaving, but finally concludes that he has to be sure.

He switches Max to his left hand, and takes a few more steps forward. He continues to edge forward until small quarter sized splotches start to materialize on the wall just below the arm of the couch. A few more steps and Alex pulls back when he thinks he sees the top of a head appear against the exterior wall of the house.

He backs up a few more feet and almost trips over Max. He stares again at the foot protruding from the small gap between the couch and bookcase. The foot rests in a separate pool of blood that extends from the bookcase, and reaches the coffee table, but stops short of joining the pool of blood spilled from Ken's body. *I'll kill every single one of them for this.*

Alex stops to process the scene. *I can't leave until I know what happened to all of them. What if one of the kids is hiding in the house?* Alex's shoulders slump and he swallows hard. He carefully steps back and ties Max to the leg of the oak table between the oversized chairs on the other side of the room, before he walks angrily past Ken's body toward the dark corner of the room.

Several minutes later, Alex stands with Max in the mudroom, ready to physically leave the grisly scene behind him. Mentally, he knows that what he saw in the corner of that room will never leave him.

He spits a few more small chucks of vomit onto the gray tile floor, and wipes the remaining tears from his eyes. The rest of the vomit is sprayed on the couch and coffee table in the family room. Some of it ended up on Ken's body. Strangely, Alex feels terrible about that.

"You ready buddy?" he says in a normal tone.

Max looks up at him and yawns again.

"I don't blame you Max. Well, let's get out of here. I know some people who can't wait to see you."

Alex opens the door and steps into the darkened garage. The smell of rotting garbage is a welcome relief to both Alex and Max. Max immediately starts pulling to get at the trash. Alex fights his way through the debris, pulling Max along the whole way. He gets to the door and opens it. He nearly trips on the dog as they simultaneously exit the garage door. *Dammit Max.*

Max starts barking and strains against the leash. *What is it now?*

"Oh shit," he mumbles, and quickly reaches for the pistol behind his back.

A man stands close to the border of the Murrays' property, still several yards on the Hayes' side. Alex's hand remains behind his back, gripping the pistol, and trembling slightly. *Jesus, if I had opened that door one minute earlier.*

The man's body is pointed toward the Murrays' yard, but his head is turned toward Alex. He wears faded jeans and a brown leather jacket. A black winter cap is stretched tightly over his head. Matted, shoulder length brown hair protrudes from the sides of the hat, splayed on the shoulders of the jacket. A goatee unmistakably identifies him as Daryll. He holds an oversized load of firewood in front of him and stares at Alex, clearly contemplateing his choices. *Keep walking or go for it.* A hunting shotgun is slung over his right shoulder.

Alex calculates the range between them to be about forty yards, which is too far for Alex to guarantee a hit with a pistol. Forty yards for a shotgun is also less than optimal. The shotgun blasts in the house indicated that these guys are using double odd buckshot, which could certainly reach Alex at forty yards, but would require a proficient shooter.

Alex hopes the man keeps walking. As much as Alex would like a chance to kill the man in his tracks, he knows that the gun battle's outcome can't be guaranteed, especially with Max in the middle of the fight.

He wonders if Charlie has a shot, but doubts it. He's pretty sure the man's position is still obscured from Charlie by the Hayes' blue colonial, plus Charlie never called to warn him, which leads Alex to believe that Charlie never saw him cross the gap in the first place. Still, Alex envisions Daryll's head exploding from a high caliber hollow point bullet.

Alex nods at the man, and moves his hand around the front of his jacket. He makes it clear to the man that this was not the chosen time or place for a shootout. *I have a better idea for you.* The man turns his head, and starts to hurriedly walk in the direction of the Murrays'.

Alex turns and starts running through the snow with Max, who sprints ahead of him in delight, oblivious to the human drama around him. He keeps checking behind him as Max strains at the end of the leash. Alex has a lot of distance to cover, and he is worried that one of the Manson's might try to snipe him with one of their hunting rifles. As Alex passes the Coopers' house, he thinks about the bag of dog food. *Sorry my friend. I'll get that for you later.* Alex barely hears Kate's voice on the radio as he lumbers through the snow. He reaches into his pocket and removes the walkie.

"Kate? Hey, I can't talk. I ran into one of them…I need to keep moving," he huffs into the walkie.

"What? Who did you run into? The Hayes? Honey, what's wrong?" she says frantically.

"No, not the Hayes. They're dead. I ran into one of the Manson's stealing wood. Hey hon, I can't talk and run here. I don't want them to take a shot at me. Open the back door," he yells.

"OK…OK, I'm headed down now. Where are you?" she says.

"Just past the Coopers' house. Gotta go!"

Alex stuffs the walkie in his jacket and pulls his pistol out of the back of his pants. *Don't want to lose this.* He tucks the pistol into the other jacket pocket, and makes sure the velcro catches on the pocket. Alex continuously glances over his shoulder and stays close to the houses, sprinting through the snow when he reaches a gap between homes.

Alex is physically wiped out when he reaches his own back garage door. He stops a few feet from the door and takes a knee, laboring to breathe. He feels slightly nauseous from the combination of sustained exertion and adrenaline. Max moves in and starts to lick his face. Alex pushes him away and continues to take deep breaths. The door opens and Kate appears, still dressed in her pink flannel pajamas. Max immediately runs over to Kate, who bends down to hug him. Alex looks up at her.

"Good thing I didn't need a rescue," he says.

She looks down at her outfit.

"What? I was on lookout duty," she says.

"Yeah you missed one. He was carrying a stack of wood back to their little headquarters at the Murrays'," he says, still panting.

"Why didn't you shoot him?" she says, seriously.

"Why didn't I shoot him? Trust me, I thought about it, but he was too far away and had a shotgun. I did the math, pistol against shotgun. No thanks. I have a plan to get them all at once," he says, and stands up.

Alex walks into the garage and kisses Kate. Kate opens the door to the mudroom and let's Max in. Alex can hear Max's claws repeatedly scrape the mudroom tile, as he tries to build up momentum for a run through the house. Alex locks the door behind him and engages the deadbolt. *Neither of them had a deadbolt. I wonder if it would have made a difference?*

They both step into the mudroom, which feels like the Caribbean compared to the air outside.

"I'm sorry I missed that guy…I went to get more coffee. Really, I'm sorry. I didn't know…"

"Don't worry about it honey. Charlie missed him too. I'm just a little disturbed that he got by both of you in broad daylight," he says, stroking her hair.

"What happened over there?" she says softly, searching his eyes. Alex avoids her glance.

"You really don't want to know," he says, still looking away.

"The kids?" she says and embraces him.

Alex stays silent.

"It's alright honey. I love you so much," she whispers in his ear.

"I know. I love you more," he says, and holds the embrace a few more seconds before he frees himself.

"We should definitely call the police," says Kate.

"What's the point? This'll all be over long before the police show up. They'll move against us pretty quickly. Probably tonight. I'm gonna use that to our advantage, and spring a little trap," he says, and walks toward the kitchen, leaving puddles of melted snow on the tile floor.

"We're getting slammed by another Nor'easter tonight. This might have to wait," she says.

"These guys aren't going to wait. They've killed two nights in a row…that we know of. I have no doubt they'll be paying us a visit tonight. Storm or no storm, we have to be ready for them," he says as he opens to basement door.

"What's your plan?" she says, leaning against the kitchen island.

"First, I'm going to talk to Charlie, and see if he's willing to help me take them down. I don't imagine that will be much of a problem, since he wanted to storm their house last night," he says, and drops his head in thought.

"I figure they'll leave the Murrays' after dark and make their way behind the houses to get here. I'm going to hit them along the way. Catch them in a crossfire. Catch them by surprise. The storm's timing couldn't be better actually. They'll never expect it," he says, and takes a few steps into the basement.

"You sound like you're enjoying this again," she says.

Alex leans his head back into the kitchen to face Kate.

"After what I just saw…you're probably right to some degree. I'd enjoy it even more if I could kill them up close. Slowly," he says, and vanishes into the basement.

Chapter Forty-One

Friday, December 14, 2012

Alex kisses Kate and holds her tightly. They stand several feet inside the darkened garage clutching each other, neither one ready to let go. A frigid wind blows through the back door of the garage, bathing them in arctic air and dusting them with fresh snowflakes. Kate shivers and Alex breaks up the embrace, still holding her hand.

"I'll be fine. Cold, but I'll be fine. You can talk to me all night," he says, staring into her teary blue eyes.

"I still don't understand why you can't take care of this from the house," she says, squeezing his hand harder.

"They'll be expecting some form of resistance at the house. We need to catch them off guard, and put an end to this on our terms, not theirs. I don't want them anywhere near our house. Who knows what kind of firepower they have. Don't worry, once it starts, it'll be over quick. Just keep the kids in Ryan's room tonight, that'll put the most house between you and whatever happens out there..."

"I'll be sitting in a chair, keeping watch on that house. If I see anything, I'll buzz you on the walkies," she says.

"I don't think you'll be able to see anything, but that's fine. Just make sure you don't have any lights on behind you, and when I tell you to get into Ryan's room, you have to promise me you'll do it. Promise me," he says.

"I promise," she says. *I don't believe her for a minute.*

"No matter what you hear outside, stay with the kids, and keep the Sig Sauer with you at all times. Remember, there's no safety on that gun. You just pull the trigger, and boom. Remind the kids of that again, especially Ryan. Alright, it's getting darker, and I want to be in position when the light is gone," he says, and gives her one more kiss.

"I love you," he says.

"I love you more. Be careful. Those people are..." she says, letting go of his hand.

"I know, and pretty soon, they'll be gone. I love you. Keep in touch, but remember, Charlie has one of the spares, so no juicy stuff. Once we start shooting, stay off unless there's an emergency at the house.

Charlie and I will need to talk. See you in a few hours," he says, and steps through the open back doorway, into the backyard.

He closes the door, and watches Kate through the window panes. He hears the lock click and waves goodbye to Kate. He glances up at the dingy, shapeless low ceiling of ashen gray clouds before starting to walk. As he trudges forward, he looks over his shoulder to the west, and can't determine the sun's azimuth or location on the horizon. The cloud cover is impenetrable.

Alex figures he has about ten or fifteen minutes of dusk left, before the darkness starts to envelope the neighborhood. In less than an hour, the block will be pitch black. He guesses that the Manson's will make their move soon after it turns dark. At least he hopes they do. He's not sure how long he can last out in the snowstorm

Alex pushes forward in the snow, and follows the same path he traveled during his outbound morning trek. His footprints are still visible in the snow near the back of his property, where the yard sinks into a shallow drainage area that runs along the entire property line, and connects all of the yards on Alex's side with a water retention area beyond the McCarthys' backyard. He plans to use it to ensure that he arrives at his preselected position undetected.

Alex steps into the ditch and starts to walk forward through the shallow gulley. The snow is slightly deeper here, and he slogs forward, watching the corner of his house. A few more steps, and he will briefly enter line of sight with the Murrays' house. After this morning's encounter, he figures the Manson's might be keeping watch on his house. He lowers his silhouette, and nudges forward until he is clear of the gap.

He continues walking forward, alert, but more interested in getting to his position than remaining stealthy. Charlie has been watching the Murrays' house for the past hour, looking for any signs of activity. If the Manson's leave the house from the front, he'll definitely see them, but Alex doubts they'll use any of the front doors. He's sure they'll sneak out the back like before, and Charlie will hopefully see them move between the houses. Charlie is perched at the window closest to the Murrays', watching with binoculars and an 8X wide angle, night vision spotting scope. Charlie's other night vision device, a 10X scope, is attached to a hunting rifle. The same rifle Charlie plans to use tonight.

Alex's AR-15 assault rifle is slung across his back. He attached an Aimpoint scope to the rifle early in the afternoon, while preparing the equipment needed for their night ambush. The scope provides an illuminated red dot for quickly engaging targets. Alex used a similar system in Iraq. His civilian version does not provide night vision capability, so he won't be looking at a convenient green image like Charlie.

He'll have to first pick out targets with his hand-held night vision scope, and then somehow find them with the Aimpoint scope. Not optimal, but Alex has done this under worse conditions. Despite the profound darkness, he figures that the Manson's should provide adequate silhouettes for a conventional rifle scope. Besides, the plan calls for Charlie to do most of the accurate shooting.

Alex works his way across the Thompsons' backyard. The Thompsons' house looks empty, but Alex knows it's occupied. A few days ago, he saw James wander across the backyard and head into the woods. He carried a shovel, and Alex concluded that he was looking for a burial site in the woods behind their property. James returned several minutes later, too quickly to have made any serious progress digging. At this point in December, Alex didn't think it was feasible to dig a proper grave without heavy equipment.

Alex pauses and looks into the woods to his right. The conservation woodland located at the eastern corner of the neighborhood contains a path that connects with Hewitt Park and hundreds of additional acres of protected forest and trails. Alex sees Jim's lone footsteps in the snow, approaching a trail head that disappears into a tangle of mature evergreens, oaks and birch. Alex turns back to the path he is following and is buffeted by a strong gust of wind. He notices an increase to the snowstorm's intensity. *This is going to be a long night.*

Aside from a small area of exposed skin below his ski goggles and above his mouth, Alex doesn't feel the effects of the bitter northerly wind. He wears two layers of full length thermal underwear, covered by two hundred dollar snowboarding pants, two layers of thick wool socks, a wool turtle neck sweater, and his favorite blue weatherproof winter jacket.

He ditched his combat boots for the best pair of storm boots sold by L.L. Bean, and his hands are covered by wool inserts and the warmest waterproof gloves he has ever owned. His head is covered by the jacket's oversized hood. Underneath the hood, his head is sheathed in a black balaclava under a standard black wool watch cap. Standing in the garage earlier, he felt his core temperature rising rapidly, and couldn't wait to get out into the cold.

Even now, his ensemble feels like overkill for the conditions, but he knows that as the storm picks up, and the sun departs, conditions outside will deteriorate rapidly. Lying prone in a static position will only make matters worse. The wind and cold has a way of penetrating even the best materials when you are motionless.

He continues across the Thompsons' yard, paying the same caution when crossing between the Thompsons' and Carters' property. Peeking above the top of the ditch, Alex sees that the Murrays' house is completely obscured by the Thorntons' house. He keeps moving. As he crosses the Carters' property, he hears his walkie-talkie crackle to life. The voice is muffled in his front jacket pocket. Alex stops and his heart starts to race as he fumbles to open the pocket zipper. He finds the slit and pulls the walkie-talkie out of the pocket. He pushes the talk button.

"This is Alex, say again, over."

"It's just me, Kate. I can't see you anymore. I just wanted to make sure you're OK," her voice crackles over the speaker. *Are you kidding me?*

"I'm fine. I'm almost past the Carters'. Let me get in position and we can chat a little. Alright?" he says.

"OK. How is it out there?" she persists.

"Fucking miserable. I'll probably end up pouring the hot tea over my head in a few minutes. Could you stoke up the wood burning stove really good. I'm going to be frozen when this is over. Talk to you later, out."

"Love you," she adds.

"Love you too, out," he says. *Out means out.*

Alex hooks the walkie onto the shoulder strap of his backpack and presses on. He can see his first choice of firing positions. The McCarthys' play set. He stays low and picks up the pace. Darkness is pouring into neighborhood and he checks his watch. 3:59. According to his handheld GPS back in the house, sunset is set for 4:04. The end of civil twilight, or the glow on the horizon, would be 4:37, but with the thick storm clouds, there will be no glow, and Alex expects complete darkness well before 4:30. *I need to move this along here.*

He picks up the pace, struggling through the snow, as he safely crosses between the Carters' and McCarthys' lots. The Murrays' house appears briefly between the two houses, almost completely shrouded by the snowstorm. Alex lowers himself to a crouch as he pushes through the ditch.

Once at the far corner of the McCarthys' property, Alex decides to leave the depression and approach the play set. The play set is located halfway between the McCarthys' house and the edge of the drainage area. The vast drainage area is significantly lower than the McCarthys' lot, and forms a steep slope along the entire back edge of the lot.

Alex considered a position along that ridge, but decided against it due to the distance. A position there would add another fifty yards to his firing range. Given the storm's increasing intensity, and the lack of lighting, he wanted to fire from a position closer to the Coopers' house. Alex reconsiders the ridge momentarily, looking at a spot closer to the Coopers' property, which might give him the same range. *No, if something goes wrong, I don't want to have to cross an open yard to re-engage targets.* More importantly, Alex reminds himself that he wants to stay between the Manson's and his own family. *These people are capable of anything.*

Alex arrives at the play set and slides his black backpack to the ground. He kneels down and removes a small foldable shovel from the back of the pack. Alex unfolds the shovel and ducks under the main tower of the play set, wading into a three foot snow drift under the tower. He rapidly moves snow out of the sandbox under the tower, digging all the way down to the frozen sand. The snow is easy to move, and within five minutes, he clears an area twice the width of his body. He digs a large hole into the front of his new snow fort, scraping the snow and ice off the thick wooden base of the sandbox. He lies down and looks through the hole, which gives him a complete view of the Coopers' yard, and the Hayes yard beyond it. He grabs his rifle and sets the barrel on the heavy log at the bottom of the hole. This will be Alex's firing position. Alex is convinced that the heavy wood frame of the sandbox will provide excellent protection from any return fire.

Alex steps up out of the fort, and retrieves his backpack. The wind slams him when he stands up out of the protective cover of the snow fort. The snow is coming down horizontally in thick waves. *Maybe it won't be so bad lying here. Better than out on that ridge.* He takes the walkie off the shoulder strap and puts it back into his winter coat pocket.

He lies back down in the fort and fully opens the backpack. He removes a gray and brown wool blanket and pushes it toward the front of the fort. He then pulls out several loaded magazines for his rifle, and stuffs them in the lower cargo pockets of his tan snowboarding pants. Alex leaves the pockets unzipped, hopeful that the backup Velcro tabs will keep the spare magazines from spilling out. He taps the black hip holster on his right leg, which holds his .45 H&K USP semiautomatic pistol and two spare magazines.

Finally, he removes the night vision scope and binoculars. He sets those down on top of a blue towel retrieved from another compartment of the backpack. He closes the backpack, sets it next to his body, and stands up to unfold the wool blanket. He folds it in half, laying it down on the frozen sand beneath him. Alex kneels down on the blanket, and pushes himself forward into the fort, lying prone and facing north into the ambush zone. Darkness envelopes the neighborhood and he strains with the naked eye to see past the Coopers' yard to the Hayes' house. He glances at his watch. 4:17. *Time to get in touch with Charlie.*

Alex digs into his coat pocket and pulls out the walkie. He removes the weatherproof glove on his right hand to make it easier to use the radio. His hand feels cold immediately.

"Charlie, this is Alex. Come in, over."

"Alex, this is Charlie. Read you loud and clear."

"Glad to hear your voice. I'm in position, with a clear view of the Coopers' house and yard. I can see over into the Hayes', but the snow is really picking up out here. How does it look from your position?" says Alex.

"Pretty good. It's getting pretty dark, and the snow is a problem, but I can see clearly between the houses. Night vision is working perfectly. Wish I had bought some kind of thermal imaging a while back. That'd be perfect for this kind of weather," he says.

Alex can't imagine why anyone, even a hunter, would need a thermal imaging device. Then again, most people would wonder why Alex would need a night vision scope.

"No kidding. These conditions are optimal for thermals. I haven't checked out night vision yet. I can still see without it. Not for long I imagine. It's going to be dark out here," says Alex.

"Yeah. No worries though. We'll pick'em up if they move your way," he says.

"Roger that. I have a good position and a great angle to hit them between the Hayes' and the Coopers'. Once we know they're coming, I'll need you to let me know when they are about half-way between those two houses. I don't have any way to judge that from here. I want the gap between the houses to be their most logical escape from my fire. That way, they'll be lined up perfectly for you. Remember, you shoot first, and I'll light up the rest. Got it?" says Alex.

"Got it."

"Keep your rifle ready to fire at all times, and be ready to shift firing positions. Once we see them, this'll go down quick," he says.

"Roger, I cut a huge section of the screen out earlier today. I'm ready for this Alex," he says. *I bet he's shitting his pants like me.*

"Alright, Check in with me every fifteen minutes or so, and stay sharp," says Alex.

"Be careful out there man. We got your back over here."

Alex sets the radio on the blue towel with the optic devices, and replaces the glove. He debates whether to check in with Kate, but decides to prep all of his gear first. He reaches down into his right thigh pocket and pulls out three rifle magazines. He places them on the blue towel, and scoots up to activate the Aimpoint scope on his rifle.

He looks through the scope at the far corner of the Coopers' house, where most of his shooting should take place, and dials down the intensity of the red dot. The scope will allow for quick precision shooting at ranges between twenty five to two hundred meters. Alex estimates he is fifty meters from the corner of the Coopers' house. *Possibly a little closer.*

He checks the safety on the weapon with his thumb, and can tell without looking that the safety is engaged. He closes the scope's covers, and lays the weapon down on the towel.

He picks up the binoculars and looks down the row of houses. There is just enough light for him to see all of the way to the end of the Hayes' house, though it's hard for him to pick out any details other than windows and doors. If the Manson crew appears now, he would definitely spot them with the binoculars. In about fifteen minutes, Alex is convinced that the night vision will be his only hope of spotting them early enough to spring their trap.

He sets the binoculars down and picks up the night vision scope. He activates the device and the previously dreary view is replaced by a sharp green image. Alex finds the corner of the Coopers' house, and then tracks along to the furthest back corner of the Hayes' house. Satisfied with the view, he turns off the scope to conserve batteries. Even though he packed plenty of replacement batteries for all of his electronic gadgets, the last thing he wanted to do was change batteries in the middle of trouble. *I really hope I don't have to be out here that long.*

Alex stares out into the murky darkness. He is still amazed by how dark the neighborhood becomes without streetlamps or house lights. He sits up enough to look over the snow drift at the McCarthys' house to his left. He's pretty sure that he can see some light through the blinds on their sliding glass door. *They're probably huddled near the fireplace.* Alex didn't have time to warn them of the possible firefight that might erupt in their backyard.

He lies back down and looks through the binoculars. *Useless.* He can still see into the Coopers' backyard, and most of the way to the Hayes' house with the binoculars, but it's not far enough. He switches over to night vision and decides to call Kate.

"Kate, this Alex. You there?" he whispers into the walkie.

"I'm here. It looks horrible out there," she says.

"I hadn't noticed, but thanks for the reminder. I hope this goes down soon, I'm not sure how long I can stay out here. How are the kids doing?" he says, and takes another look through the night vision scope.

"They're fine, staying warm by the stove with Max. I'll move them upstairs as soon as you guys spot them," she says.

"Thanks. I need to concentrate on the scope now. Love you honey. Are you still in your lookout post?" he says.

"No, I can't see a thing past the Thorntons'. I'm with the kids. Don't forget about the thermos of hot tea. I Love you, and don't do anything stupid," she says.

"Like sit outside in a snowstorm waiting to shoot someone? I Love you too. Out," he says.

Alex turns the volume on the handset to the highest setting, and checks the night vision scope again. *Nothing.* He checks his watch. 4:45. The walkie comes to life and Alex grabs the rifle.

"Alex, it's Charlie, just checking in. No movement over there. I can see some light in the house, but I can't tell anything by it," he says.

Alex relaxes his grip on the rifle.

"Thanks Charlie. Let's hope they're just as impatient as we are to get this going. I really don't know how long I can stay out here. The snow is piling up right on top of me," says Alex, shaking snow off his body.

"I don't think we'll have to wait long," he says

"I don't know. The Hayes' were killed in their kitchen, and the Coopers were shot in their bedroom. Could have been any time for the Hayes', but last night's shots happened around eight thirty. We could be doing this for hours," says Alex, doubting whether he could lie out here like this for more than another hour, let alone three or four.

"I don't think so. They know you saw their handiwork earlier today. I bet we'll see them within a half hour," says Charlie.

"I hope you're right. I really do. We'll chat later. Oh hey Charlie, make sure you get your family down in the basement when this starts. You guys are right in the middle of it," says Alex.

"Roger, first sign of these assholes, and they're heading down below. Talk to you in fifteen," he says, and Alex puts down the walkie.

Alex sticks his right hand into the backpack and digs around for the large green ceramic thermos. He finds the thermos at the bottom of the pack and sets it on the snow next to his rifle. He removes the lid and watches the steam escape from the mouth of the thermos. *Heat!* Alex turns onto his left side and takes a slow careful sip of the tea. The tea burns his mouth, but Alex doesn't care. The liquid streams into his stomach, warming him. *Green tea. I really need some coffee.* He checks his watch again. 4:50.

.

Alex shivers staring at the green image in the night vision scope. He changed batteries a few minutes earlier, after noticing a dimmer picture. The storm intensified over the past hour, and reduced visibility even further, however, he could still see as far as he needed to see into the Hayes' yard. Alex sips the last of the green tea and considers his options.

At this point, the cold has penetrated every layer of his outfit, and Alex does not expect the weather to improve. If anything, the storm will intensify, and the temperature will continue to plummet. About thirty minutes earlier, Alex stood up to shake all of the snow off and to stretch his arms and legs. When he kneeled back down, he unfolded the wool blanket so he could pull it over his body. He barely felt the difference.

Alex knows that staying here is not a permanent option tonight. He figures on a maximum of one more hour before he is rendered combat ineffective by the weather. He'll have to head home at that point, drawing the fight much closer to home than he had hoped. Alex could use his own house as a warming hut, and move quickly to a secondary ambush sight in his own backyard, or possibly the Thompsons', if Charlie sounds the warning.

If he relocated, Charlie might not be able help, and the fight would rest mostly on his own shoulders, which wasn't a problem. Just not ideal given the advantage Charlie's rifle could provide. Given the poor weather conditions, the current shooting gallery between the Coopers' and Hayes' is ranged perfectly for Charlie's rifle.

Alex's radio bursts to life.

"Alex, they crossed over to the Hayes'! I only saw the last one! Do you see anything?" Charlie says in a panicked voice.

A sudden wave of adrenaline washed through Alex's body, and the cold is a distant memory. He rips off both outer gloves and grabs the night vision scope, focusing on the back of the Hayes' house. *Son of a bitch, here they come!* Alex picks up the walkie.

"Got em Charlie, looks like three of them, moving slowly along the back of the Hayes' house. Reposition now. I say again. Reposition yourself now, and get ready. Let me know when they cross into the space between the houses. You fire first, then I'll pin them down. Remember to take the safety off your gun!" Alex whispers forcefully into the walkie.

"I'm on my way," he yells, and through the walkie, Alex hears Charlie yelling to his family.

Alex clips the walkie onto his jacket and grips the rifle. He lays the upper hand guard of the rifle on the wooden log in front of him, steadying the weapon. He then scoots up into the snow fort, nestling the rifle in his shoulder. Everything feels good. He opens the rifle scope's lens covers and peers through the scope.

He flips the safety off with his thumb and pulls the slide handle back again, ejecting an unfired round into the snow. He releases the handle, and recharges the rifle chamber, making sure that the cold has not locked up the weapon's action. He has done this once every half hour since he arrived at the play set. He grabs the night vision scope and locates the three targets at the closest edge of the Hayes' house. He can see that they are struggling with the storm, and that they are all clearly underdressed for the storm. *Fuck, this is moving too fast.*

He tosses the night vision aside, and searches frantically through the rifle scope. Beyond the red dot, he finds the corner of the Hayes' house. The image is dark and washed out by snow, but Alex quickly picks out his three targets contrasted from the surroundings. Alex shifts the red dot to what he perceives as the last in the line of targets. *They have to be moving across the gap.*

Alex hears an excited voice from his radio.

"Alex, they're almost half way across. Moving slow. I have the lead guy in my sights."

Fire Charlie, fire! We could get two right off. Come on Charlie. Kate must be out of her mind listening to this.

Alex watches the dark masses move slowly across the gap. For the first time, he notices that all three of them are armed with some type of long guns. *Goddamn it Charlie!*

Alex adds pressure to the trigger. *Can't wait. Here we go.*

He sees his target stop and turn, as the sharp echo of Charlie's first shot reaches Alex's ears. Alex sights in again, and squeezes the trigger twice, keeping the red dot on the target for each shot. The rifle kicks and settles in his shoulder.

Alex sights in again on what he thinks is the same dark shadow. He fires six rounds in rapid, but controlled succession. *I have no idea if I'm hitting anything. Fuck!* Alex sees a few flashes through the scope and hears something hit the play set. He sights in on the corner of the Coopers' house, where he sees another moving shadow, and fires another six rounds. He hears gunshots and sees some more flashes from the area between the two houses. *Alright, I have no idea what's going on!*

He picks up the night vision scope and checks out the scene. He clearly sees two men still in the fight. A man stands exposed to Alex at the corner of the Coopers' house, aiming a shotgun in the direction of Charlie's house. Another is on his knees at the corner of the Hayes' house, slumped against the siding. The figure is trying to reload his weapon while staying propped up against the house.

Through Alex's scope, he sees that the man is doing neither task well. *I'll take care of this one.* Just as Alex formulates that thought, he sees the man's head snap back violently against the side of the house. The figure slumps lifelessly to the ground, revealing a dark stain on the siding. *Jesus!*

He switches back to the rifle scope, and tries to sight in on the target near corner of the Coopers' house. The man disappears between the houses before Alex can pull the trigger. Alex swiftly switches rifle magazines, while keeping the sight of the scope on the corner of the house.

The walkie in his jacket buzzes.

"Alex, last one coming at my..."

Alex hears a sharp crack followed by several lower pitched explosions, all in rapid succession. *Shotgun.* Alex grabs the night vision scope, the spare rifle magazine, and his rifle. He stands up quickly, and starts to run, skimming the bottom of the play set tower with his head. The impact jolts Alex's head, causing him to drop the spare magazine. He feels a severe pain at the very top of his skull, but pushes through the snow drift and starts running toward the front corner of the Coopers' house.

He plans to run between the two houses and engage the last target. He hears another sharp crack, which he assumes is Charlie's rifle. *I hope you got him.* His hope is dashed when he hears at least a dozen rapid gunshots, which sound smaller than a shotgun. Alex stuffs the night vision scope in his left cargo pocket while running, and grabs the walkie from his jacket.

"Charlie, Charlie, I'm moving between the Coopers' and McCarthys'. What is your status?"

He hears another shot from Charlie's rifle.

"I can't hit him. He's at my front door. Where are you?" says Charlie in a panicked voice.

"Almost around the corner. Hang on Charlie," he says, and stuffs the walkie in his jacket.

Alex reaches the corner and slows down, raising the AR-15 to his shoulder. He cautiously takes the corner, keeping the weapon aimed toward Charlie's front door. Alex looks over the scope, not wanting to limit his field of vision, and sees a figure standing on the covered porch with a shotgun aimed toward Charlie's front door. The shotgun erupts three times, and Alex hears Charlie screaming through the walkie.

He puts the red dot on the figure, who is now kicking the front door, and fires two shots. He looks over the scope and sees the man stumble backwards, and fall down the porch steps. Alex starts to push through the snow toward Charlie's house, keeping the red dot on the fallen target. Out of his peripheral vision, he sees Charlie close the upper left window of the second floor.

Alex crosses the street, still sighted in on the heap at the bottom of Charlie's porch. *No movement.* As he reaches the short snow bank along the opposite side of the road, the front door to the Murrays' house swings opens, and someone steps outside onto the Murrays' stone porch. He can't make out any details, but sees a figure silhouetted against a dim light cast from inside the house. Alex throws himself against the snow bank and fires several hasty shots at the new threat, not bothering to use the scope. *Close enough.*

He scurries down the snow bank a few more feet, and pops up over the top of the bank, searching through the scope for a target. He doesn't see the figure anymore, but he can tell that the front door is still open. Another figure steps out onto the porch, and Alex adds pressure to the trigger, centering the red dot on the dark mass. A smaller figure appears, and Alex eases off the trigger. Both figures hop off the right side of the porch, and disappear into the bushes. Alex reaches into his cargo pocket to pull out the night vision scope. *Where's the scope?* He checks the other pocket. *Gone. God damn it.* He stays low and calls Charlie on the radio.

"Charlie, come in."

"Still here, did you get him? I assume you got him. That was you shooting right?" he says, less panicky.

"I hit the guy at your door. He's down. I haven't checked him yet. Someone popped out of the Murrays' house while I was crossing the road. I need you to scope out the front of the Murrays' house. Two people jumped off to the right of the porch into the bushes. I can't tell what's going on. Watch yourself up there," says Alex.

"Gotcha. I'm moving," says Charlie.

Alex looks over at the body near the bottom of the Thorntons' porch. He brings the rifle up over the snow bank and centers the red dot on the figure. Alex sees an arm claw at the snow. *Definitely still moving.*

"Alex, Alex," says Charlie through the walkie.

Alex presses the talk button, and realizes his hands are freezing. *Adrenaline is wearing off. I'll get the shakes soon.*

"Go ahead Charlie," he says, starting to shiver.

"I don't see any threat there anymore. I think we're fine," he says.

Alex shifts his glance out of the scope and looks over at the Murrays'. He can see three figures standing on or around the porch. The one standing in the doorway looks like a child. He can hear screams coming from the group.

"What exactly is happening over there? What are they doing in the bushes?" Alex demands. *I need a better SITREP than that.*

"Alex, I don't, uh…what about the guy down here? Is he dead?" says Charlie.

Alex looks into the scope and sees the same sight picture. The figure is trying to crawl toward the street. Alex pulls the trigger three times, centering the dot on the crawling mass, which stops moving altogether. He hears screaming from the Murray house.

"He's done," says Alex.

"What the fuck is going on at the house?"

"Alex, they're fine. I don't see any weapons. Trust me, we don't have to worry about them," says Charlie, and Alex senses once again that he's keeping something from him.

"Just tell me what you see. I'm not moving until you convince me it's safe," says Alex. *Actually, I don't plan to stay out in this shit weather another ten minutes.*

"Charlie, I'm fucking cold, and I'd like to go home. If you don't tell me what's going on over there, I'll fucking blast the entire front of the house away," he says.

"Well, it looks like you shot one of the kids…I'm sorry, I don't…they're picking the body up now. They're not armed as far as I can tell," he says.

"I saw an adult pop through that door. It wasn't a kid," says Alex. *It could have been a dog for all I know.*

Alex aims the rifle at the front door, and stares through the scope at the group. The image is grainy, but he can see three figures carrying a body up the stairs of the porch. The smaller figure in the doorway reaches up to grab the body. He hears more screams and then the front door is slammed shut. Alex grabs the walkie, which is sitting in the snow next to him.

"Let's grab all of their weapons and check the bodies. We don't want any surprises. Meet me on the street," he says, and puts the walkie in his jacket pocket.

He barely hears Charlie agree above the howling wind. He looks around at all of the houses, which appear as black shapes rising from an endless, flat dark-gray sea. Blankets of gray snow wash over the scene, providing the only movement his eyes can detect. He starts walking across the street, crunching the freshly fallen snow.

He reaches the snow bank on the other side, and leaps over it. He retraces his steps back toward the corner of the house and finds the night vision scope buried under a half an inch of snow. Ten more minutes and he might not have recovered the scope. He turns it on, and stares at the Murray house.

The door is closed now, and he sees faint lighting from within the Murrays' house. He turns off the night vision and drops the scope in his right cargo pocket. He feels the scope hit the spare magazines. The Thorntons' front door opens and Charlie walks out onto the covered porch, pointing some kind of a rifle at the crumpled body in the front yard. Alex yells out to him and walks over to join him.

Charlie is dressed in a dark green winter jacket, blue jeans and tan combat boots. A fur hat with a tail is pulled tightly over his ears. They meet in the middle of the street and shake gloved hands as the wind whips through them. Alex notices a black nylon holster like his own on Charlie's left thigh, sheltering a pistol.

"That thing's dead right?" says Alex, staring at the hat.

"Very funny. It's a Daniel Boone cap. My dad gave it to me in the sixth grade, and it's the warmest hat I've ever owned. It also happens to be a good luck charm. I've never missed a shot with this on my head," he says.

"Well, I think your record is still intact. Nice job," says Alex.

"I had the easy part. Warm house. Target rich environment," says Charlie.

"Nothing easy about killing someone. Even these guys. Trust me. Let's get this done, and get back inside," says Alex.

"I'll grab the two guns between the houses. You've done more than your share tonight," says Charlie.

"Actually, we should go together. Just in case. I don't mind a few more minutes out in this wonderful weather," he says, and they start walking toward the kill zone between the two houses on the other side of the street.

Waves of snow and wind pound him, as they approach the bodies. He slings the rifle over his shoulder and puts his right hand up to protect his eyes, wishing he had tucked the goggles into one of his pockets and not his backpack. He takes solace from the fact that the wind will be at his back for the trip home. He hears the walkie in his jacket and pulls it out.

"Hello. Hello!" he says.

"Alex?" says Kate, though he can barely her while walking into the storm.

"It's over honey. We got those fuckers. All of them. I'll see you in a few minutes. I love you!" he yells into the walkie.

"I love you too!" she says, and he hears it clearly.

He pushes forward with Charlie until they see the first body, slumped on the ground against the Hayes' house. A massive dark patch stains the siding a few feet off the ground. Alex doesn't care to look closely at the patch. He's sure he'll see chunks of brain and bone frozen to cedar planks. The shotgun lies a few feet in front of the body, partially buried in a drift, and quickly on its way to disappearing under fresh snowfall. Charlie pulls it out of the drift by the shoulder stock, and unloads the weapon, dropping the shotgun shells into the snow.

They both look around for the last body, but can't see it through the storm. Alex pulls out a flashlight, and starts to search the area right between the two houses.

"Where'd you drop the first guy?" he says.

"Got him maybe a third of the way across. He turned his body, like he was thinking of coming my way, and I hit him square in the upper chest. Went down like a bag of rocks," says Charlie.

Alex moves toward the Hayes' house, and starts to search the ground. He finds a bolt action hunting rifle and the start of a trail in the snow. He quickly brings his rifle around to a ready position and thumbs off the safety. Charlie draws his pistol and steps forward, even with Alex.

"Looks like he crawled a little. Definitely some major blood loss," says Alex, and they both edge forward.

They find Manson face down about twenty feet from where he was shot. Alex shines his light down on the prone figure, and sees a dark red pool of blood in the snow around Manson's upper body. The man's hands and arms are tossed in resignation, just forward of his head. The body is motionless.

"Sure he's dead?" says Charlie.

Alex takes a few more seconds to examine the body with his light, and doesn't detect any signs of respiration. Even if Manson was still faintly alive, the weather and blood loss would finish him off quickly. *Let him suffer.*

"He's done and I'm done. Let's grab the rifle and get out of here. I still have to grab all of my shit behind the McCarthys' house," says Alex, as he turns away from the relentless wind.

"Think we should take a closer look?" says Charlie.

"If he isn't dead, he'll be dead within the hour. Dead and buried under a foot of snow," Alex says, and starts to walk back to the street.

Chapter Forty-Two

Saturday, December 15, 2012

Alex hears a muted bark from across the bedroom. The bark settles into a low growl that lasts a few seconds and stops. Alex opens his eyes and reaches out to the nightstand for his watch. He moves the watch right in front of his face, and focuses on the time. Through foggy eyes he sees that it's well past nine in the morning, which doesn't surprise him. He expected the time to be later.

Last night, he emerged from the blizzard still wired and jittery from adrenaline. Thirty minutes later, he descended into a delirious exhaustion that even a strong cup of coffee couldn't shake. Less than an hour after that, he fell into a deep coma like sleep, holding Emily on the bedroom couch. He vaguely remembers watching TV on the couch with Emily, and he has no recollection of moving from the couch to their bed

THUNK. *Now what?*

Max barks once and pops his head up over the top of the couch. He gives a weak bark followed by a low growl that tapers off. Alex shifts in bed. BUNK. *Sounds like something hit the house.* Alex hears a voice emanating from the backyard, then clearly the sound of something hitting their house right behind their bed. *Son of a bitch!* He pops out of bed, and throws the comforter on top of Kate.

"What is it, what's wrong?" she whispers forcefully.

"Hold on." Alex says and moves quickly to the rear window of their bedroom.

He peeks out of the side of the window blind and stares for a few seconds. They both hear another cracking sound against the side of the bedroom and Alex pulls his head back. Max growls from his curled up position on the couch with Ryan, but makes no move to get up. Alex starts walking quickly, nearly jogging, toward the bedroom door.

"Honey, keep the kids away from the back windows, I don't want them seeing this."

He pauses, rethinking his choice of words.

"And I don't want them to get hurt standing near the windows. Todd is standing in our backyard in jeans and a fucking t-shirt, throwing rocks at the house."

"What? Why would he…"

"I don't know. I fucking thought I was done. Now captain caveman is having a mental breakdown in our back yard," he yells back into the bedroom.

Kate gets out of bed and starts to walks over to the closet. As Kate reaches the closet, Alex emerges holding the shotgun in one hand, and a box of shotgun shells in the other. He leans the shotgun against the wall, scraping the light blue paint, and removes four shot gun shells from the box. Kate stares intensely at the shells, and then looks up at Alex while almost imperceptibly shaking her head. Alex grabs the shotgun and rapidly slides each shell into the underside loading breech on the shotgun. *Four rounds should do it.*

"I really don't want to hurt him, but enough's enough,"

He starts walking down the hallway to the stairs. Kate follows closely behind, pleading.

"Hon, there's probably a reason why he's here. Don't just go out and shoot him. He hasn't bothered us in a while, and if he wanted to break a window, he could have done it by now. He's probably out of his mind. Maybe he lost another one of his kids. Imagine how you would feel?"

Alex starts down the stairs, stops halfway and replies.

"What am I supposed to do, just let him vent a little on us? Thanks for laying that guilt on me, but I am not going to sit around and be thankful that he hasn't hit a window yet. Maybe he'll take a shot at the solar panels. I am going out there to put an end to this. All of it."

Alex pauses, then continues, "I am going to do everything in my power not to use this. Just keep the kids away from the windows."

"Take it easy on him," she offers.

"I'm gonna to knock some fucking sense into him, and if that fails…clean up on aisle two," he says, and turns to continue down the stairs.

Downstairs, Alex grabs a bottle of water from the pantry, and takes a long drink. He puts the bottle on the kitchen island, and turns toward the mudroom. He skips the snow pants and slips right into his insulated boots. He stares at the snow shoes stacked in the small study adjacent to the mudroom. He's not sure how much snow last night's storm dropped, but he figures at least an additional foot. Given the effort it took to move across the yards last night, he seriously considers using them, but ultimately decided against it.

He'll need mobility when he reaches Todd, even if it means trudging through snow. He also decides against a winter jacket. A wool sweater should be fine for right now. He doesn't want to wear anything bulky that could get in his way. He still has no idea what he might have to do out there. *Worst case I'll have to drag a corpse off my property.*

He puts on a black wool watch cap, and pulls it tightly over his ears. He steps into the library and checks the old fashioned bulb thermometer just outside of the window. He catches a glimpse of Todd behind the garage and ducks. *Is he in a short sleeved shirt?*

The thermometer read thirteen degrees Fahrenheit, and he sees gusts of wind shake snow from the pine trees in the backyard. *He's gotta be freezing out there.* He thinks about the jacket again and shakes his head. Finally, he grabs one of the radios, but puts it back into the recharging cradle. *The last thing I need is for the voice of reason to chime in. This is going to be hard enough.*

Alex slings the shotgun over his shoulder and disassembles the planks and cans sitting on the stool in front of the door leading to the garage. Despite seeing all three of the Manson crew dead, he recommended that they keep the sound contraptions in place at night until they feel completely comfortable with the situation in the neighborhood and the greater Portland area. He steps into the garage, and can immediately see his breath. He looks at the back door to the garage, and catches another glimpse of Todd through the door's window.

He hears another rock hit the side of his house, and adrenaline starts pumping through his body. *I really don't want to go out there, but this shit ends today. All of it.* Alex steps toward the door, careful to keep out of Todd's line of sight, and peeks out to determine Todd's distance from the house. He estimates forty feet. *Far enough away that he can't effectively charge me.*

He reaches for the dead bolt, and turns it slowly until he hears the distinct release of the lock. He puts his right hand on the door handle, and starts to turn it slowly. The door knob is frozen to the touch, and Alex regrets not putting on gloves. *This is it, out we go.* He pulls the door open and steps outside, slamming it closed behind him.

A strong northerly wind makes the air feels much colder than thirteen degrees, and Alex is not pleased to be back outside. He looks up at the shapeless, uninterrupted ceiling of clouds, just as a strong gust of wind pelts his face. He returns his glares to Todd, who stands knee deep in snow, wearing faded blue jeans and an old Boston Red Socks T-Shirt. Alex can see that Todd has lost a considerable amount of weight. *I have a bad feeling about this. He's absolutely lost it.*

Alex glances around the yard at the young, snow laden young pine trees, and scans for signs of any other neighbors. *You never know.* He sees no other footprints in the snow, other than a line of prints ending where Todd stands. *Fair to assume he is alone.*

Todd seems oblivious to his presence, and picks up another solid object from a blue duffel bag at his feet. He cocks his arm back, and hurls it up the side of the house. THUNK! Alex starts walking toward him, but movement proves difficult in the snow bank behind the garage. A considerable drift developed overnight, and Alex fights his way toward Todd. Todd never looks at him as he closes half of the distance. Instead, he leans over, reaches into the duffel bag and pulls out a baseball. When he bends over to reach into the bag, Alex sees something tucked into his jeans, but the object disappears before he can figure out what it might be. He thinks it might have been the wooden handle of a revolver, but as far as Alex knew, Todd did not own a firearm.

Todd pulls his arm back, and aims at the house again. However, instead of throwing it at the house, he suddenly pivots his left foot, steps toward Alex, and whips the ball at Alex's head. At twenty feet, Alex doesn't have much time to react, and he barely moves as the ball sails by his head. It strikes the side of the garage with a much louder smack than anything else he's heard this morning, and Alex fights every instinct to point the shotgun at Todd. At that range, and speed, the ball could have killed him. *Lucky Todd's not much of an athlete.*

"Todd, what's going on here? I thought we had an understanding," says Alex.

Todd responds in a barely audible tone.

"They're all piled up inside the bulkhead door, frozen. The animals can't get to them there. Nowhere else to put them. All I have left is Jordan. I'm sorry about this Alex."

Alex strains to hear him over the wind. As Todd finishes, Alex takes in a deep breath of freezing air, and lets it out with a sigh. *What the hell can I possibly say to him.*

"Jesus Todd, I'm sorry, I don't...I don't know what to say."

Todd doesn't say anything, and just continues to stare at Alex. Bloodshot and glazed, his desperate brown eyes strain deep in their sockets. He sports a disturbed grin, which combined with months of unkempt facial growth, makes him look even more unstable. Todd barely resembles the man he was in early October. Several weeks of starvation, fear and perpetual tragedy has dragged him to the brink of existence. *This is it. He wants to die.* He continues to stare intently at Alex, then speaks.

"I didn't really have a choice Alex. I'm..." *What is he talking about?*

Todd's right hand slowly moves behind his right hip to the small of his back. Alex sees this, and swings the shotgun to face him. The motion is swift, and within a fraction of a second, Todd has a shotgun pointed at his head. The sudden movement surprises Todd, and he furtively moves his hand back around to the front of his thigh. His hand is empty.

Alex racks the slide mechanism on the shotgun, chambering a double-odd buck shell into the chamber. He thumbs the safety into the off position. He points the gun toward Todd's chest, and looks over the barrel to increase his field of vision.

"Time to go Todd, one way or the other."

"I'm not going anywhere," Todd says.

Todd reaches down to pick up another object out of the duffel bag. It looks like a large rock to Alex.

"Suit yourself," mumbles Alex. *God damn it.*

Alex stares into Todd's feeble eyes and tries not to picture the corpses stuffed below Todd's bulkhead door. An image of Todd's daughter, Jordan, flashes through his head, and his anger deflates. *Maybe I need to lighten up on him. Maybe I should help.* Todd's eyes flicker left, and Alex simultaneously catches movement in his peripheral vision.

His first instinct is to pull the trigger and kill Todd. He knows Todd set him up, and if the trap was set right, it might be his only chance of killing at least one of his attackers. Or he could swing the shotgun barrel to the left and try to engage what he assumes is the more pressing threat. He processes both options in a fraction of a second, and decides on neither. Alex charges Todd.

As soon as his body lurches forward, one of the pine trees on the edge of the Thompsons' yard explodes, shedding most of its snow. A distinct snap passes behind him. Todd reacts hastily, and whips the rock at Alex. The poorly aimed throw glances off Alex's right arm, and Todd turns to run, but Alex is already on top of him. He strikes a blow to the upper left side of Todd's head with the butt of the shotgun. The impact turns him off like a light switch, and he collapses into a pile.

Just as he starts to turn the shotgun toward the Thompsons' yard, the tree explodes again, and Alex feels a sledgehammer pound his upper left torso. The impact of several "double-ought" buckshot pellets spins him ninety degrees to the left and knocks him off his feet. He ends up on his left side, with half of his body ploughed into the snow, and his face jammed straight into the fresh drift. He lies there physically stunned, but not disoriented. He is painfully aware of his desperate situation, and acutely alarmed that he no longer holds the Mossberg shotgun.

Alex tries to slide his left elbow up and out from under his body, with the intention of using it to lift himself off his side. He gets no response at all from his arm. A sharp pain starts to fill the entire left side of his upper body. He shakes the wet snow from his face and glances down toward his shoulder. He sees bright crimson stains spattered on the snow. A dark red stain is starting to melt through the snow piled up around his left shoulder.

He strains to lift his head up a little further to look toward the source of the gunfire. He hopes that this involuntary prone position has given him some cover from the shooter. There is a small rise between the Thompsons' yard and his own, and it might be enough to keep him out of the shooter's sights long enough to get himself back into the fight. His hopes are immediately dashed by the sight of a brown camouflage patterned baseball cap emerging over the top of the snow.

Manson comes into view aiming a pump action shotgun at Alex's crumpled figure. He holds the shotgun in the crook of his right arm, with his left hand on the trigger. He appears unable to raise the shotgun to his shoulder, and Alex sees why. Manson's right arm is wrapped in a makeshift reddish brown stained sling. Alex starts to claw at the snow behind his back with his right hand. Manson casually closes the distance to Alex, keeping the shotgun trained on him the whole way.

Alex knows he doesn't have much time left. He's not sure how this man survived last night's ambush, and he doesn't want to waste any time or mental energy trying to figure it out. His body surges with adrenaline and he rolls over onto his back. He tries to move his left arm again, but only manages to shift it over his left leg. *Useless.* An incredible amount of pain surges through his left shoulder, radiating down his arm and into his chest. A quick glance down at his shoulder confirms the devastation. He sees a flash of bone in the carnage.

Alex looks back at Manson, who grins wickedly. He fumbles his right arm out further, digging randomly through the snow.

"You ain't anywhere close. Your little pop gun's by your feet. Nice one too. I think I'll add it to my collection," he says.

The man walks up to Alex's feet, and a wave of helplessness washes over Alex as the man towers over him. Alex focuses on his cold, blue eyes, which betray nothing about Alex's fate, though Alex has no delusions of being spared. He quickly scans the man. He can see that Manson took a hit to his shoulder, probably shattered his clavicle, or more likely, passed right through. *Had to have passed through. He wouldn't be here if it burrowed into his chest.*

"Wondering how I'm still around?" he says, and squats in front of Alex.

Alex nods once, his mental acuity fading as the pain in his shoulder spikes. He thinks about the garage door and is thankful that he forgot to unlock the door handle from the inside. *It'll slow him down a little. Kate can take care of the rest. I just need to buy her a little more time.* Alex tries to focus on the man aiming a shotgun at his head.

"Hurts like bitch. Don't it? Hurt like hell when I got hit last night, but I was a lucky son of a bitch. Bullet passed right through. In and out. Still dropped me like a fucking rock though. Once I got my senses, I crawled as far as I could into the Hayes' yard before I heard you coming back to finish me off.

You should've let your buddy put one in the back of my head. You were pretty much right though. I wasn't going anywhere lying face down in the snow, and I sure as shit couldn't have crawled back. But I got lucky again. My sister-in-law was hiding by the Hayes' deck with a shotgun. She came looking for us when the shooting started. Of course, she had no idea that her husband's brains were splattered on the side of that house just twenty feet away, or that you'd shot her son in cold blood. If she'd known that…who knows what might've happened? After you left, she dragged me all the way back to our house…"

"Not your house," grunts Alex.

"It's my house now," he says, and kicks Alex's leg.

"Anyway, my wife did a couple of years in the ER at Good Samaritan before the kids came along, and it came in real handy last night. It's almost like I got a guardian angel keeping watch over me," he says and sneers at Alex.

"Lucky me," says Alex, and Manson responds by viciously kicking his left thigh.

"Kept my little nephew alive too, though he'll probably never be able to use his hand again. Skimmed one off his head too. I knew you were all business, but I didn't think you had it in you to blast away at kids," he says.

Alex mumbles something indiscernible from the snow. *I should have gone over there and finished everyone off.*

"What was that? Nothing? Well, we're gonna need some serious medical supplies and plenty of food to recover," he says, and glances in the direction of Alex's house.

"Shouldn't be a problem now that we've found ourselves a new home."

Alex glances at the house and winces in pain. He tries to say something, but the words falter. Manson glances over at Todd's slack body.

"You did a good job on your friend Todd. I didn't expect that at all. For a second, I thought this might not go my way after all. But…here we are Alex. Ain't so chatty now are you? Don't fade out on me!" he says, and kicks one of Alex's feet.

Alex struggles to talk. He's cold and starting to feel light headed. The pain in his shoulder is slowly subsiding, and he knows that neither of these developments is a good sign.

"Everyone knows. It's only a matter of time before they come for you," says Alex.

"Before what? The cops show up? Haven't seen much of them lately have you? Besides, you think they'll put up much of a fight against that assault rifle you got locked up in there? Shit, by the time they show up for real, we'll be long gone. Fact is, there's a new sheriff on the block, and nobody's gonna fuck with him," he says.

Todd stirs again. Without warning, Manson points the shotgun at Todd and fires. Alex hears the sickening wet sound of the shotgun pellets ripping into Todd, and is jarred out of his haze. *Jesus Christ.* Manson pumps the shotgun, chambering another shell. An empty red shotgun casing flies out of the ejection port, and Alex hears it sizzle when it hits the snow.

"No need for him anymore," he says and grins.

Manson keeps the shotgun in his left hand, pointed at the ground.

"I'm not seeing much need for you either, although I might need a little leverage to keep that wife of yours from blasting away at me," he says.

"Fuck you. Either way she'll take your head off," says Alex.

"Don't bet on it," he says and a flashes a sickly pleasant smile at the house.

"Up on your feet soldier. We have some work to do," he says.

"Marine," corrects Alex.

"Whatever. Now get off the ground," he says.

"No."

"Get off the ground, or I'll kill every last one of them. Or worse," he says with a scowl.

"You'll just have to take your chances against an assault rifle and my wife. Good luck. She wanted to kill all of you days ago," says Alex dryly.

"Sounds like my kinda woman. Maybe we'll spend some quality time together," he whispers, and then screams, "Now get the fuck up!"

Alex stares at him.

"I'll leave them all alone if you walk into that house with me. I don't have a problem with them," he says in a calmer voice. *He's really worried about going in there alone.*

"Just like you didn't have a problem with the Hayes' kids," Alex says, and Manson takes another step toward him.

Manson flashes a wicked smile and relaxes his stance.

"You and me ain't that different…Alex. We're both just doing whatever it takes to keep our people safe. I'll kill every person on this block before I let my family suffer," he says.

"Looks like you're off to a good start," mutters Alex.

"What, you think you're different? The only difference between you and me, is that I don't have the choice to sit around. I gotta hunt for my family. I'm a predator Alex," he says.

"You should get your own Animal Planet show," Alex says, and quietly laughs at his joke.

"Think about this smart ass. How many people around here have you killed by doing nothing? You're like those fucking Germans that lived around the gas camps. Just ignored what was happening," says Manson.

Alex shakes his head in mock confusion.

"Time to get up. You tell them everything'll work out just fine," says Manson.

"Can I get another one of your history lessons instead?" says Alex.

"Look here bitch, one way or the other the house is mine. We can do this the easy way, or the very, very hard way. I promise I'll make it horrible for them," he says.

"Go fuck yourself," says Alex.

"Fine," the man says.

Manson braces the shotgun in the crook of his right arm and swings it toward Alex. Alex turns his head slightly to the left and looks up at the nearest bedroom window. *Please don't let them see this.* Mercifully, all he sees in the window is the muted reflection of a dull gray sky.

Just as he starts to turn his head to face his executioner, the bottom right pane of the window shatters, and the snow around Alex's feet explodes. Supersonic cracks fill the air between the two men, and Alex feels a warm spray on his face, as the deafening sound of rapid gunshots catches up with the bullets flying past them.

Manson plummets to his left knee, just as a red mist explodes into the air behind him his right shoulder. Several more bullets strike the snow between the two men, and Alex sees a massive red hole in the back of Manson's left thigh.

Manson twists on his knee toward the house and fires the shotgun at the house, obliterating the top window pane. The ear shattering drum of the assault rifle ceases, and Manson fires the shotgun again, scoring a direct hit on the bottom half of the window.

Alex tries to get up in the snow, desperate to reach his shotgun, which lies just a few feet away. Alex manages to struggle to his knees by the time Manson turns the shotgun back on him. *Almost did it.* Alex closes his eyes, and hears the distinct snap of a single bullet passing within a few feet of his head. He opens his eyes and sees that Manson's attention is drawn somewhere up and behind Alex. Manson fires the shotgun toward Ed's house, and struggles to chamber another shotgun shell. While fumbling with the shotgun, a small red hole appears between the man's eyes, and snaps his head back, ejecting the camouflage hat and blood onto the snow behind him.

Manson grunts as the sound of a single gunshot echoes through the backyard, and drops face first into the edge of a snow drift.

"I don't know how to eject the magazine!" he hears his son yell from the upstairs window.

"He's dead. It's over," he yells weakly up at the window.

Alex feels lightheaded on his knees, so he gently lowers himself back down onto his back. He looks up at the window and sees both Ryan and Kate slowly peer down.

"Oh shit!" she yells down and disappears.

"Yeah. I'm…I'm going to need some help," he mumbles to himself, and rests his head all the way back onto the snow.

Alex hears snow crunching behind his head, from the direction of the Walkers' yard. He twists his body to the right, and writhes in the snow toward his shotgun.

"Alex! Alex! Take it easy. It's me. Charlie," he hears, and the crunching gets closer.

Alex relaxes and twists his head back. Charlie bears down on him holding an assault rifle similar to Alex's. He kneels by Alex's head.

Alex hears someone else approaching from the direction of Ed's house, and starts to contort his body to get a better view.

"It's just Ed. You need to lie still until we figure out what to do. You took a hit to your left shoulder," Charlie says, and slings the rifle over his shoulder.

A few seconds later, Ed arrives and stands over Charlie, staring Manson's body, and then Todd's. He holds a .22 caliber bold action rifle in his right hand.

"Did I hit him?" Ed says in a daze.

"Right between the eyes. He was dead before I got around the corner. God I wanted to kill that mother fucker myself. Nice shooting," says Charlie.

"Jesus Christ. I actually hit him. I haven't fired this thing in forever," says Ed.

"Punched one right through his skull," says Charlie.

"I used to shoot this with my dad every weekend," Ed says, still in a daze staring at the bodies.

"If I hadn't put these goddamn gloves on, I would've been there to blast his head clearly off his shoulders," says Charlie.

"I should've let you finish him off last night," whispers Alex.

Ed snaps out of it, and kneels next to Charlie to take a close look at Alex's wounds.

"We need to get you some help buddy. I'm gonna load you up on a sled and we'll pull you over to the surgeon staying at the Carters'. You just hang in there. You've lost a little blood," he says, and digs his hands under Alex's back.

He prop's Alex's torso up, and applies direct pressure to the mangled shoulder. Alex winces and cries out. Charlie walks over to examine Todd's body.

"Sorry man. You're bleeding, but not too badly. Nothing spurting. I just need to slow this down a little."

"Make sure he's dead," whispers Alex.

"Which one?" says Ed.

"This guy's definitely dead, but Todd's still breathing. Barely. Want me to finish him off?" says Charlie.

"I don't care," says Ed.

"No, leave him alone. We can't orphan Jordan," says Alex.

"What's he rambling about," says Charlie, still pointing the gun at Todd's head.

The garage door opens and Kate spills out, followed by Ryan. Both are still dressed in their pajamas. Ryan moves forward, and points the AR-15 at Manson's body and then shifts it to Todd's. Kate runs up and grabs Alex. Ryan follows closely, edging forward. He stands vigilant guard with an empty rifle. Alex can see that he is disturbed by the grisly, blood splattered mosaic in the snow. He starts to drift slowly back to the garage door.

"Careful! Careful! Where's Emmy?" says Alex.

"She's hiding in the closet with Max. She's fine. We need to get you to a hospital immediately. I'll start up the car," says Kate.

"I have a better idea," says Ed. "Let's get him over to the Carters'. The young couple there...the guy's a surgical fellow, or something like that. Grab as much medical stuff as you can, and meet me over there. I'll drag him over on one of your sleds."

"I don't know. I think we need to get him to an ER."

"The hospitals are slammed with the flu. He needs attention now. This guy can do what needs to be done right now. Sew him up fast, and pump him up with meds. We can take him later if we need to."

"Alright. We have a makeshift surgical kit that might work. I'll grab everything and meet you there. The sleds are on the wall in the garage," she says.

"Charlie. Get the medical kit from Kate, and run it over to the Carters' house. Let the surgeon kid know what happened, and that we'll be there with Alex in ten or twenty minutes," says Ed.

"Got it," say Charlie.

"You might want to leave that behind," says Ed, glancing at Charlie's rifle.

"Not while any of those fuckers over there are still alive," he says.

"How are you feeling hon?" Kate says, caressing his face.

"Like I've been shot. Are you sure Emmy's OK?" he says.

"She's scared," Kate says and stands up.

"Kate. Have her dress up in her snow gear and head over to our house. Sam and the kids can take care of her while we're dealing with this," says Ed.

"Alright. I'll get her over there with Max," she says and sprints back to the house.

Charlie and Ed follow her, and Ryan starts to turn toward the house.

"Ryan!" he says.

Ryan turns slowly, and walks over to kneel next to him, still clutching the rifle. He looks pale and nauseous. He avoids looking at Alex's shoulder, and can barely look at Alex's blood spattered face.

"I love you dad. You'll get fixed up quick," he says.

"Damn right I will. Whose idea was it to use the rifle?" he says.

"Mom's, but she didn't know how to work it. Sorry I barely hit him. I just kept pulling the trigger. I didn't want him to kill you daddy," he says, and breaks down crying, leaning into Alex.

Alex grabs him with his right arm, and grimaces through the pain.

"You did great buddy. Two hits was all it took," he says and squeezes his son.

"I didn't know how to reload it dad," he says, sniffling into Alex's good shoulder.

"You didn't have to," he says.

Ryan hugs him harder.

"Alright. Alright already. You're starting to dig into the shoulder," he grunts.

"Sorry dad."

Ryan stands up, and grabs the rifle.

"Let me see that for a second," he says to Ryan.

Pain shoots through his entire left side, as Ryan holds the rifle out. Alex slowly moves his right arm and points to a button on the right side of the weapon, just forward of the trigger well.

"Press this and the magazine slides out. Put another one in, and pull back..."

"On the handle," Ryan says, and places his right hand on the charging handle.

"Right," Alex whispers as a wave of nausea passes over him.

"I saw that in Modern Warfare. Just never saw the magazine release button," Ryan says and manages a smile.

"I don't think your mom's gonna bitch about that game anymore. Go help her out. I love you buddy," says Alex.

"Love you too dad," Ryan says, and disappears into the garage.

Just as Ryan vanishes, Ed emerges from the doorway with a green sled.

"This is the biggest one you have in there," says Ed, as he approaches Alex.

"Can you fit on this?" Ed says, and knees down next to Alex.

"You calling me fat?"

"Oddly enough, you're probably the fattest fuck on the block right now," says Ed as he carefully lifts Alex and tries to slide him onto the sled.

"Aghhhh. Jesus. Careful man," says Alex, struggling not to laugh.

"Sorry. This might hurt a little," he says.

"Thanks for the warning. What about Todd?" says Alex.

"You're my only priority right now. He can wait," says Ed, staring angrily at Todd's motionless figure.

"He won't make it if we don't help him. Jordan's home by herself. She's gonna be really freaked out," he says, mumbling the last sentence.

"We'll take care of her. Just stay with me buddy," Ed says, and lifts him again.

A wave of heaviness drops over Alex, and he tries to lift his head. *Nope.* His vision narrows and darkens, and Alex vaguely remembers being lifted onto the green foam sled. He regains full consciousness a little later when Ed tugs hard on sled's tow line.

They break through a deep drift, and Alex lifts his head to see where they are. They emerge from between Alex's house and the Thompsons'. Alex watches Ed struggles to pull Alex's dead weight forward through the deep snow. Alex's gaze settles on the back of Ed's dark green jacket as he fades into another world.

Chapter Forty-Three

March 2003
Euphrates River bridge on the outskirts of An' Nasiriyah, Iraq

"Here they come!" Corporal Reyes announces over the internal communications circuit.

All of the gun turrets in Captain Fletcher's Amphibious Assault Vehicle (AAV) company start firing at once, sending a continuous maelstrom of heavy caliber bullets and high explosive grenades across the river. A few seconds later, assault rifle fire erupts from the Marines along the Euphrates river bank, joined by bursts of light machine gun fire.

Captain Fletcher turns his attention to the other side of the Euphrates canal. Two hundred meters back from the opposite side, he sees droves of disorganized enemy fighters rushing forward through the palm groves and dilapidated shacks. Hundreds of tracer rounds reach the onrush, as rifles, machine guns and grenades pulverize the oncoming enemy troops.

"All Zombie tracks, continue to your new positions. I say again, move to your new positions," Captain Fletcher reinforces. *They have to move.*

A salvo of several high explosive artillery shells lands fifty meters closer than the last barrage, launching columns of rocks and dirt skyward, and spraying shrapnel at anything exposed nearby. This encompasses most of the AAV's and over half of Charlie Company's Marines. The shockwave from each successive blast rocks the AAV's and pulses through the prone Marines. The last artillery shell in the barrage lands two meters behind one of the AAV's near the bridge, and blasts through the thin armor, shredding the rest of the vehicle with shrapnel. The AAV immediately ignites from the heat of the explosion.

One of the explosions throws Alex sideways, and the right side of his helmet strikes the lip of the hatch opening. Dazed, he regains his balance and spins around to scan the impact area. He can barely see the damaged AAV through the descending dirt and debris. *Shit.* He sees the gunner jump down from the turret onto the front of the vehicle, and help the vehicle commander get out of his hatch.

"Zombie Three Eight, this is Zombie Three actual, over." *Come on guys. Someone answer.*

Captain Fletcher scans the vehicle again, and assesses the damage as a mission kill to the AAV. He doesn't think anyone in the rear compartment could have survived the blast. Several infantry Marines rush from a nearby position to the burning AAV, and a corpsman from the nearby aid station joins them. Within seconds, they start to carry the vehicle commander to the aid station. From his stretcher, the vehicle commander frantically points to the back at the AAV, yelling something to the other Marines near the vehicle. Two Marines enter the damaged rear hatch of the burning AAV, which is consumed with flames, and pull a limp human form back through the hatch. As the group moves to the aid station, several mortar rounds fall into Charlie Company's perimeter, spraying dirt and creating havoc, but mercifully failing to injure any Marines.

The Zombie Three Eight burns fiercely, along with the Zombie Three Nine, the first AAV destroyed, sending columns of thick black smoke into the air. *Maybe someone will see this and figure out we're all fucked over here.* With two of his ten vehicles destroyed, and no radio contact with battalion, Captain Fletcher feels an impending sense of doom.

"Gents, I really hope our counter-battery folks take out that artillery," he says into the vehicle comms. *Not likely.*

The volume of fire from the Marines picks up after a temporary lull caused by the last series of impacts, and Charlie Company's mortars fire furiously in response to the enemy mortars. He sees a group of Marines carrying disassembled 60mm mortars, and moving in the open toward the AAV's. *Sanchez is spreading out the mortars. Smart.*

They make it halfway to the AAV's, when another round of enemy artillery shells lands directly to the north of Captain Fletcher's AAV, right on top of the Marines and the mortar position they just departed. Blast waves from successive explosions jar the AAV, slamming rock and shrapnel into the sides of the AAV. Alex hears a quick buzz near his right ear, and ducks into the AAV more out of instinct than logic. Whatever snapped by his head was long gone by the time he reacted.

"Banshee Six, this is Zombie actual, those rounds landed on our mortar position."

"Roger, sending help."

"Hillock, Manny, we have Marines down just north of the track. Let's get them out of that kill zone."

Alex disconnects his helmet comms cable and steps up on the seat to pull his body out of the hatch. His driver, Lance Corporal Manuel Rodriguez, hits the ground seconds before Alex, and they both see that Sergeant Hillock is already half way toward the downed mortar team.

Alex and Manny merge with several Marines sprinting over from positions near the canal, and Captain Fletcher tells at least half of them Marines to help out the mortar position, which is about twenty meters further along, just past a small rise of ground. Two of the corpsman sprint across the area recently hit by artillery, and arrive at the mortar position to assess casualties. They split up and one heads toward Alex.

Alex and the other Marines stagger at the sight of the destroyed mortar team. Immediately, Alex can see that at least four of the Marines are dead, and the rest are wounded. *Obliterated.* 1st Lieutenant Dave Pardell, weapons platoon commander, is the only apparently uninjured member of the team. He stumbles onto his feet, face blackened with dirt, and starts to run toward the bridge. He is missing his helmet and rifle.

"Grab him," Alex shouts to one of the Marines closest to the lieutenant.

Mortar rounds start to hit the area south of the Marines, and straddle the AAV's next to the canal. All of the Marines hit the ground, except for Pardell. A sergeant pulls him to the ground by his left arm, and Pardell screams. Alex now sees that his left forearm is bent at a right angle. *Jesus.*

"That might'a fucking hit some of 1st platoon," says one of the Marines, still hugging the ground.

Alex looks past his debris sprayed vehicle to the canal. He sees one of the 1st Platoon radiomen give a "thumbs up" to the group.

"2nd squad just checked in. They got dusted good, but no injuries," says a Marine crouched down with a radio.

Alex considers their position in the open. This is not where he wants to be when the next round of artillery crashes in. He waves to Zombie Three Three. The vehicle's commander must have anticipated his next move, because the vehicle immediately springs to life and heads toward them. *Three Three is now the official medevac vehicle.*

"Load all of the dead and wounded in that track, and get them back to the aid station!" says Captain Fletcher.

Captain Fletcher turns to Gunnery Sergeant Fitzgerald, a hulking black Marine feared by every Marine in Charlie Company, and Alex himself.

"Fitz, get'em moving."

"You heard the Captain, load'em up and get the fuck back to your positions! Let's go people!" Gunny Fitzgerald says and slaps one of the Marine's helmets.

Alex meets the AAV as it approaches, and heads over to the right side of the vehicle. He bangs on armor, and yells up at the vehicle commander, who leans down over the side to hear him. Bullets ping off the vehicles near Alex and crack overhead. He doesn't flinch anymore.

"You're the medevac track. Load them up, and get back over to the aid station."

The vehicle commander nods, and Alex looks back at the Marine's helping their ruined comrades. He sees a lone rocket propelled grenade fly several feet above the Marines and trail off north, heading toward nothing. He stares at the trail of white smoke, waiting for it to explode in the distance. Out of the corner of his eye, he catches another flash of smoke. He never really sees the rocket propelled grenade that strikes short of the AAV, and detonates against the hard ground several feet in front of him.

Chunks of rock and steel slam into Captain Fletcher and hammer him against the side of the vehicle. For a few seconds, he feels like he's been submerged underwater. Then nothing.

Chapter Forty-Four

Saturday, December 15, 2012

Captain Fletcher rises slowly and suddenly breaks through the heavy surface sheet of unconsciousness. He kicks his legs and strains against a weight on his chest. His eyes struggle to focus, but all he can see is a shaky, blinding light above him.

"Hold his legs down," someone yells.

He feels something heavy envelope his legs.

"So much for that plan," the same voice yells.

"Alex? Alex? It's Ed," he hears.

Alex is confused.

"I need a… corpsman?" he says, suddenly aware that his request doesn't make sense given his surroundings.

"What are you doing?" Alex says, looking up at a vaguely familiar man with a medical mask over his face.

"Alex, I'm Dr. Glassman, and I'm trying to remove the shotgun lead from your wounds, then I'm going to clean the wound and stitch it back up."

"Without anesthesia? Fuck me," says Alex lucidly.

"He sounds like he's back," says Kate.

Alex looks around him. He sees Kate holding his legs down, with a strained smile. Ed looms above him again, pinning his right arm and chest down on a hard surface. A thin soft towel or shirt rests under his head. Alex can tell he's in someone's formal dining room, but not his own, or Ed's. A young dark haired woman stands next to Ed holding a bright flashlight.

"Alex, I can give you some Percocet for the pain, but it won't kick in for a little while. I need to get you stitched up pretty quick. You've lost a little more blood than I would have hoped," he says.

"How much would you have hoped for?" Alex says, and realizes that he is fading again.

"Ah….I don't know what…"

"He's fucking with you Ben," says Kate.

"Alright. OK. He's got a strange sense of humor," whispers Dr. Glassman.

"OK, so we'll give him the Percocet, and then I'll start. Alex, this is going to hurt…I wish I had some anesthetic to give you, but obviously I don't. I have to dig the pellets out and then close you up. Ten to fifteen minutes tops," he says.

"Sounds great," says Alex.

He stares straight up at the chandelier with hazy vision. *With any luck, I'll be out for this.* He feels a warm hand take his right hand and squeeze gently. He tilts his head and sees Kate standing next to the doctor's wife. She smiles and mouths the words 'I love you.' He manages a smile and does the same. He then leans his head back down on the table and closes his eyes.

"Alex, I'm going to start by digging around. If I can get it all out that way, then I won't have to cut…"

"You're not going to announce every move like that, are you?" says Alex.

Hannah Glassman starts to laugh.

"Thanks honey," Dr. Glassman says.

"You do like to talk everything through," she says, and starts to laugh again.

"You don't want me to tell you what's coming?" he says impatiently.

"Not really," says Alex.

"OK," he says, and the next thing Alex feels is an intense burning pain in his upper chest. He keeps the screams inside as his face contorts. The pain jumps to the next level, and Alex mercifully passes out.

Chapter Forty-Five

Sunday, March 31, 2012

Alex lounges on the couch in the great room and inhales the warm breeze gently blowing in from the open windows. The air smells damp and slightly aromatic, and Alex closes his eyes to savor the pleasant gust. The breeze carries a sound he hasn't heard since last November. The sound of children playing. Alex sits up and looks over the back of the couch to see outside.

He hears feet pounding the stairs and knows what's coming his way. The sharp sound of Max's nails follows the kids on their way down. Alex knows they are about to drop the highly anticipated bomb on them. Both kids round the corner and run into the room.

"Mom. Dad. Can we ride our bikes? All the Walker kids are out, a bunch of other kids. Everyone's out playing," they patch together.

Kate awakens quickly from what must have been a shallow sleep, something she had never experienced before Alex was nearly killed in their backyard. She took over as the first line of defense and security in the Fletcher household, and met the challenge well. Fortunately for all of them, Durham Road fell deathly quiet after the shootings. The overall situation outside of Durham Road stabilized in January, and gradually improved as the spring drew closer.

"What's going on out there?" she says as the kids round the couch.

"Everyone's outside playing, even Chloe and Abigail," says Emily.

"Daniel's out too dad. They're all out front riding bikes. Can you get the bikes out of the basement?" says Ryan.

"Hold on a minute," says Alex.

He puts his left hand on the back of the couch and pushes forward to sit up. His shoulder radiates a dull painful ache that causes him to grunt. He stands up and tries for the thousandth time to stretch his left arm up and around in a circular motion. He can barely lift it ten degrees above a parallel plane with the floor. He shakes his head imperceptibly.

Ben Glassman did the best job he could with the limited resources on hand. The surgery wasn't pretty, and Alex has three nasty scars to prove it, but thanks to Dr. Glassman, there was never any doubt that Alex would survive the damage done by the shotgun blast.

"Can we go outside right now daddy? Please! Please!" begs Emily.

Kate answers without hesitation.

"CDC says it take two weeks to build up a full immunity to the flu. For children it may be longer. We only have five more days…"

"I think they'll be alright," Alex says, and winds his other arm in a full circle.

He purposely ignores her glare.

"I don't know. We've gone this far, this long. Another couple days won't kill them," she says authoritatively.

"Aw come on mom! Dad says its fine," says Ryan with a slightly rude tone.

"Take it easy Ryan. Your mom's right, plus a lot more than just the flu happened on this block. Things won't be the same, and we need to be cautious," says Alex.

"Everything's pretty much back to normal. The stores are open, cable works, the flu is pretty much gone…"

"That's not what I'm talking about. Why don't you guys head back upstairs and let your mother and I discuss it," says Alex.

"What is there to discuss?" counters Ryan.

"There won't be anything to discuss if you keep up your tone. Get upstairs. We'll call you down when we're done," he says on the verge of yelling.

"Can we play in the backyard with the Walkers while you guys talk?" says Ryan.

"How is that going to work if everyone else is out playing? Kids can walk right up into the yard?" says Alex.

"I don't think anyone's ever going to walk right into our yard dad," says Ryan solemnly.

"Give us a couple minutes."

"We promise we won't go out front," says Ryan.

"Just give your mom and me a few minutes to talk about it. Alright?" he says, and glares at his son.

"Let's go," says Emily, tugging at Ryan's arm.

"Five minutes and we're coming back down," Ryan says and starts to walk away.

"You'll come down when summoned," says Alex in an outrageous Monty Python like British accent, hoping to cut some of the tension.

"Oh god, alright, alright. No more. We'll go," says Ryan with a smile.

Both kids leave the room and Alex can hear them stomping up the stairs.

"They're going crazy," he says, and starts to walk over to the front windows.

"I know. Do you really think it's alright for them to be out in the neighborhood?" she says as Alex leans toward one of the windows.

"Damn, the Walker kids are out in front. Getting ready for a bike ride too," he adds.

He doesn't see Ed or Sam.

"Are you still worried about the flu?" he says.

"No, not really. Not at this point. I'm way more nervous about the neighborhood. I don't think a few months are long enough to heal this neighborhood," she says and gets up to join him.

"I don't think it'll ever be the same, or anywhere even close to the way it was before. We all turned on each other in some way," he says.

"Don't start up on that guilt trip again honey. It doesn't do either of us any good. We did what we did, and kept our family intact. Helped plenty of others along the way. Any different, and who knows."

"I know," he whispers.

Alex looks across the street and sees Derek and Ellen Sheppard playing in their backyard with their three boys. They're all kicking a soccer ball back and forth. Derek lightly kicks the ball to their five year old son, Gavin, who reaches his foot out to tap the ball, but misses. He doesn't chase after the ball, but instead stands slightly slumped, fixed to the ground.

From this distance Alex can't see the portable oxygen tank and nose tube that he'll be forced to wear for the rest of his shortened lifespan. The flu devastated his pulmonary alveoli, and his lungs' capacity to transfer oxygen efficiently to his bloodstream. Derek mentioned that he can't live with the tank forever, and Alex didn't ask any more questions.

"Is that Gavin out with them?" she says.

"Yeah," says Alex.

She puts her hand on his shoulder.

"They're lucky they get to spend this extra time with him. That's how they look at it, and I think they're right," she says.

"I know. It still makes me feel bad. I don't know what to say when I see them," he says.

"You don't have to say anything. They don't expect it. Hey look, Jamie's girls are heading across to the Walkers. I guess I feel alright about them being out front on our side of the street. I don't want them riding out of sight. The bikes can wait," she says.

"Sounds like a reasonable compromise. Want to call down the troops?" he says.

He hears the kids suddenly descend the stairs.

"We can get the bikes later!" yells Ryan.

"Wait up Ryan!" says Emily.

Ryan hits the landing, and heads toward the front door.

"Hold on!" says Alex.

"You understand the restrictions right?"

"No bike riding. No going on the other side of the block," says Ryan.

Emily eagerly joins Ryan on the landing nodding her head in agreement.

"No going out of our sight," adds Kate.

"Alright. No going out of sight of the house," says Ryan.

"Negative! You stay in our sight at all times. That's where we start. Got it?" says Alex.

"Got it. We promise. Let's go," Ryan says, and flies out the storm door onto the front granite stoop.

The door flies back and almost knocks over Emily, who chases after him yelling. They both watch out of the window, and listen to the excited babble of several kids gathered on the Walkers' driveway.

"Beer?" says Alex.

"Sure."

Alex heads to the refrigerator and retrieves two pale ales. He twists open the caps and walks to the front door.

"I'm gonna relax on the front stoop," he says.

"And spy on the kids?" she says, taking one of the beers.

"Of course," he replies.

Alex and Kate sit down on the cool granite, and from the porch, he sees signs of life everywhere. Alex looks up at the clear sky, and sees one contrail heading south. Two months ago, the skies were empty. Kate catches his eye.

"It'd be a lot easier on your parents if they would just fly over with your brother's kids," she says.

"My dad hates flying. He only flies to warmer weather, plus, the seats were like three grand a pop. They needed the SUV to fit all of the kids' stuff anyway," he says.

"We could've sent them the money and shipped all their stuff. It's a long drive out," she says.

"I offered. They'll be fine. They're leaving tomorrow. Probably take them five or six days tops. It's perfectly safe," he says.

"I know. It's just a long trip for the kids," she says and pauses.

"It'll be nice having them here," she says.

"It's going to be a major adjustment," he says.

"It won't be that bad. The kids really get along," she says.

"They did as cousins, but as brothers and sisters, all bets are off," he says.

"True," she says.

Daniel and Karla never identified godparents for their children Ethan and Kevin, so custody fell upon his parents after Daniel died from a massive secondary pulmonary infection. Alex and Kate offered to adopt the kids, and a plan was hatched to deliver them once the pandemic situation cooled. His parents also hinted that they would use the trip to scope out the real estate situation in Maine. He wondered if they would ever drive back to Colorado.

Alex looks up the street toward the Walkers' and sees Ed near the edge of garage. He waves at Ed, who raises a dark colored bottle of beer above his head.

"Look. Great minds think alike," he says, and they raise their beers to acknowledge Ed.

"I could get used to this," Kate says and sighs, "I can't believe I agreed to head into work tomorrow."

"You should hit them up for a raise," says Alex.

"I'm coming back as an equity partner, which will be a huge raise…if we can get the firm back on solid footing."

"As long as there's money, there'll always be a need for accountants. Your firm will be up and running in no time. Statistically speaking, the firm only lost about twenty percent of its clients. The real problem is that most of your clients have probably lost all of their money. On paper at least," says Alex.

"I don't even want to think about it," says Kate.

"The money?" says Alex.

"No. The twenty percent," Kate says and takes a long drink from her bottle.

"Hey, look at the bright side," he says, baiting her.

"I can't wait to hear your interpretation of the bright side," she says.

"You'll have a much more difficult time counting all of our money this year," he says.

"I still can't believe it," she says.

Kate refers to Alex's early November reallocation of the entire non-retirement portion of their Fidelity Account to gold backed mutual funds. Their decision was based on an economic study sponsored by the ISPAC, which painted a devastatingly bleak picture of a modern post pandemic economy. A complete collapse of the international credit system, sparked by the default of nearly every major institutional and national loan, would change everything, and force an international rewrite of economic rules, or worse.

ISPAC economists recommended a fifty percent reallocation to precious metal funds in the face of a serious pandemic threat, but Kate and Alex could only stomach thirty percent, even after Dr. Wright's ominous midnight phone call. The non-401K portion of their portfolio was an easy target, since it equaled roughly one third of their total assets.

"What was the last price?" says Alex.

"Nearly twelve thousand dollars an ounce, and rising," she says.

"Unbelievable. The only successful investment decision I ever made," he says.

"Well, if you had agreed to fifty percent, I wouldn't have to go back to work," she says.

"Neither of us really has to go back to work," Alex says, and finishes his beer.

"Biosphere is hiring. I saw four open positions in the paper," she says.

"In Portland?"

"Southern Maine," she comments.

"I'd rather work for Al Qaeda," he says and stands up to stretch.

"I don't think Al Qaeda pays well."

"Probably not, but the work environment might be a little friendlier. Take a look at that," he says, and nods toward the top of the street.

A large dark blue Ford F-150 pickup truck rounds the corner at the top of the loop and passes Todd and Jordan. Standing in their driveway, Todd pulls his daughter in close as the truck continues past the Andersons' and Walkers'. It slows down in front of the Fletchers', and the truck's powerful engine hums as it passes. Alex sees two men in the front.

"I thought they got'em all," whispers Kate.

"No, Jim didn't want them disturbed. Gave the town hell about it," he says.

By the end of the second week in December, an unsettling reality descended on most of New England. The sheer number of deaths caused by the flu solidly overtook local efforts to handle the dead bodies, and the coroner's office no longer responded to civilian requests. Temporary morgues located in any and all available refrigerated spaces, including refrigerated trailers, filled up within days, leaving most households with no real option for removing a dead body.

It didn't take long for outdoor morgues to materialize, usually within a securely fenced industrial facility, or a local baseball park, and early everyone with deceased family members was directed to one of these sites by early December. The outdoor morgues became loosely monitored dumping grounds, quickly descending into disorder and plagued by nasty rumors. Many households opted to keep their own dead safe in a shed, or just inside their basement bulkhead doors, where they would remain refrigerated or frozen until spring.

James dragged the bodies of his wife and seven month old child into the conservation woods in late March and buried them in graves that took him nearly a week to dig in the solid ground.

All of the kids in front of the Walkers' house fall silent and watch as the pickup truck pulls into Thompsons' driveway. Ed says something to the kids, and they all start walking toward Ed's house. James Thompson appears at the top of the driveway to meet the truck. The men from the truck hop out and James shakes hands with them. The driver, a man dressed in faded jeans and a flannel shirt, pats him on the shoulder when they shake hands. The second man displays a badge and tucks it back into his back pocket. James nods to them and walks back into his garage.

The two men go to the back of the pickup truck and lower the gate. The driver pulls two shovels out of the bed, and the deputy removes what Alex knows will be two dark green, military issue body bags. They both meet James, who carries a shovel over his shoulder, at the top of the driveway, and James leads them around garage.

"I think we should go inside. Last thing he needs is for the whole neighborhood to watch as they load his wife and baby on the truck." says Alex.

"Should we tell the kids to come in?" she says and reaches a hand up to Alex.

Alex pulls her to her feet.

"No, they're fine with Ed," he says, and looks over at Ed who nods toward them, and turns to go about the business of moving the gaggle of kids over to the opposite side of his house.

"I don't like them out of sight," says Kate.

"They'll be fine for a couple minutes," he says, and they both step inside.

Alex and Kate walk back into the kitchen. Alex places his empty bottle down on the island and opens the refrigerator to get another beer. *I could use something stronger than a beer.*

"Someone called while we were out front," Kate announces and picks up the phone.

"Probably Ed or Charlie," Alex says, and fishes around the refrigerator for a beer buried near the back.

"Actually, it was the police," she says suddenly.

Alex lifts his head above the refrigerator.

"Really?"

"Yep," she says.

Alex quickly pulls a beer from the back of the refrigerator and almost knocks a yellow ceramic bowl filled with salad onto the floor. He catches the bowl between his left forearm and thigh, burying his elbow in the salad. Kate comes around to help him.

"Nice catch, huh?" he says.

"Yeah, I love the taste of elbow in my greens. I'm tempted to stand back and see how you'll figure this one out, but I'm afraid to see what might go into the salad next," she says, and after a slight pause, grabs the salad bowl.

"Thank you my love," he says and steps out of the way of the refrigerator.

"I thought the cops were done with us," she says.

Kate places the bowl back on the bottom shelf and closes the door.

"I have a feeling we'll be hearing a lot more from them. Frankly, I was surprised they didn't spend more time around here…once they finally got around to checking it out," he says.

During the third week of January, state police officers arrived to conduct a preliminary investigation into the reported murders and shootings. They walked a half mile in snow shoes, from High Rise Road, which was the nearest passable road in the area. Escorted by Charlie and Ed, they took a look at the Hayes' and Coopers' houses. Their response was underwhelming, but expected. They said that the bodies couldn't be removed any time soon, and that nobody should disturb either crime scene.

Charlie and Ed also led them to the retention pond, to show the officers where they had dumped the three neighborhood shootout casualties. The troopers took a few notes, and asked even fewer questions. Apparently, the shootout on Durham Road didn't qualify as unusual to either of them. They took a cursory look through the Murrays' house, which was once again empty, and took a few more notes before leaving the neighborhood. Alex twists off the top of his beer and takes a long swig.

"Well, let's see what they want. I'll be up the office," he says.

"I'm gonna head over to Sam and Ed's. Head over when you're done," she says.

"Love you," he says.

"Love you more."

Alex heads upstairs and sits down in his office chair. He stares out at the neighborhood and sees Derek with his family, still playing in their backyard. He stands up and opens the windows. A warm breeze rolls gently in, lazily displacing a few sheets of loose paper on the desk. Alex spots Jamie heading across the street toward Ed's. *Probably saw Kate heading over.* He sits back down and stares at the phone, not in the least bit interested in talking to the police about what transpired in December. Just then, the orange LED screen lights up. "Murray, Gregory." Alex picks up the phone, hopeful that their friends are finally on their way home.

The End

The author welcomes any comments, feedback or questions.
skpandemic@gmail.com

Made in the USA
Charleston, SC
27 November 2010